Beyond the
Bridge of Time

Beyond the Bridge of Time

LEILA RAE SOMMERFELD

Pleasant Word
A Division of WINEPRESS PUBLISHING

Pleasant Word (a division of WinePress Publishing, PO Box 428, Enumclaw, WA 98022) functions only as book publisher. As such, the ultimate design, content, editorial accuracy, and views expressed or implied in this work are those of the author.

Unless otherwise noted, all Scriptures are taken from the Holy Bible, New International Version, Copyright © 1973, 1978, 1984 by the International Bible Society. Used by permission of Zondervan Publishing House. The "NIV" and "New International Version" trademarks are registered in the United States Patent and Trademark Office by International Bible Society.

Scripture references marked KJV are taken from the King James Version of the Bible.

Scripture references marked NASB are taken from the New American Standard Bible, © 1960, 1963, 1968, 1971, 1972, 1973, 1975, 1977 by The Lockman Foundation. Used by permission.

ISBN 13: 978-1-4141-0902-2
ISBN 10: 1-4141-0902-4
Library of Congress Catalog Card Number: 2006910449

Dedicated to:
All my wonderful children, grandchildren, my
great-granddaughter, and those to come.
A little fantasy does wonders for us all....

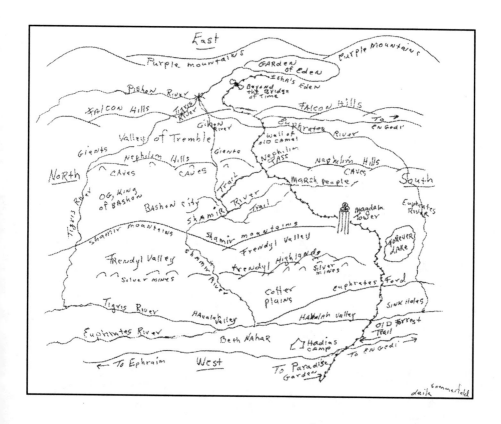

Oh bright stallion
Israfel
Take me away on
Phantom journeys
Over green fields and
Swollen streams
Beyond my hopes, beyond
My dreams

Oh bright stallion
Israfel
Let's drink the wind
Together
Fly beyond moonbeams
To magic places where
Others cannot find us

—Hadia

Israfel

Table of Contents

CHAPTER ONE

Genesis

"Once upon an age...."

In the days before The Flood—

"Hadia, I will not live to see the sun rise. Your father is unable to raise two babies. Wrap some gold wire around the wrist of the baby girl," my mother said, pointing to a little purple bag on the ground. "Take her to the wayside and leave her."

A lump grew in my throat. "Mother! I can't throw the baby away!"

"Hadia, we are not throwing her away. We are giving her back to God. He will send His chosen one to rescue her and raise her. You will reunite on your journey to the Land of In-Between."

I grimaced as I gazed at the tiny, pink baby boy and girl squirming in their basket. Hair like flames of fire crowned their heads. My mother's request seemed cruel. Being only eight ages old, I didn't understand.

"Hadia," my mother said, "you are not to tell anyone about the baby girl. Now hurry—take her to the wayside."

I wrapped gold wire around the baby girl's wrist, tucked her in a blanket, and clutched her to my heart. My mother's eyes rolled backward as she pressed her sides and groaned. "Hurry, Hadia. Hurry!"

I ran outside, stumbling in the driving wind. A coyote howled mournfully in the distance. Salty tears stung my face. My heart anguished. *God, why is Mother dying? Why do I have to give away my baby sister?* I did as I was told and carefully laid the baby girl in the dirt and sobbed. *Oh, God, send someone soon, before a wild animal tears her apart!* I turned and hurried home.

When I entered the tent, deafening quiet hung in the air. The glow from the oil lamp cast strange shadows about the room. I peeked at the baby boy. Searching for his mother's milk, he tried his fist.

I turned to Mother's bed; she lay silent. My heart picked up speed; my mouth went dry. I grabbed her shoulders and shook her as hard as I could.

"Mother! Mother!"

She didn't move or speak. Her eyes held a look, one I had seen before in death: staring, but not seeing. "Mother!" I fell across her lifeless body and cried until I could cry no more.

My body heaved. My eyes swelled. Then, I thought, *The baby…maybe she's still where I left her.* Racing out of the tent, I ran back to the wayside.

"She's gone—she's gone! Oh, God, I want my baby sister back! I want my mother back!" My wail rose to a high-pitched scream. I crumbled onto the ground, crying and shaking. *Won't someone come and share my grief?* The space in my heart, once filled with Mother, was empty. *Who will fill it now?*

No one came.

Ten ages later—

"Hadia, run! Don't wait for me!" my father shouted, leaning on his walking stick.

With terrifying certainty, I knew the approaching dust clouds concealed thieves. The chance of being followed was always a possibility, and now my worse fear was about to come to pass. The sales from goods and animals in En Gedi proved lucrative. Town robbers were always quick to notice. The adversaries advanced boldly on camels, swinging clubs and shouting foul curses.

Horribly afraid, I faced a cruel choice: either run for safety or remain with my Father. I grabbed his hand. "I can't leave you. Hurry! There are caves in the ravine."

Stumbling, we slid down the hillside, with the marauders brandishing clubs and stones close behind. We shrank back and covered our heads with trembling hands.

"Please, have mercy, take our booty, but spare our lives," my father pleaded.

"We spare no one. We are not mercenaries—we are Destroyers. Give us your silver!" a voice cracked. Clubs slammed against our heads.

The heat of the sun awaking me was full in my face. I don't know how long I lay in darkness. I only know when I awoke I wished to sink into weightless unconsciousness again. Drawing a deep breath, I struggled to rise. I winced. The salty taste of blood was in my mouth. My vision blurred, and my head pounded as the land spun around me. Gradually, the land stood still; my eyes focused on my father. "No!" I gasped.

I hobbled over to his crumpled body that lay face up. His eyes held an empty gaze, like Mother's, when she died. Flies buzzed around his bloody nose, mouth and ears. Kneeling, I pressed my hand to his chest. There was no life.

I choked back rising bile, and then collapsed over his body and cried. My wail slowly turned to a whimper. I then drew aside and slumped onto my back. My nerves screamed, my muscles ached, and my bones felt cracked. A stirring breeze did not soothe my throbbing being. I lay silent, hearing nothing.

Grim reapers arrived—vultures. They swooped up and down, around and around, circling death. Tree leaves trembled. Cooing doves clung to the branches. Whirlwinds hurried by on their way to where, I did not know. The day was beautiful—the day was ugly.

Rising, I removed my shawl and laid it over my father's body. I had to get him home before nightfall. Every minute delayed was another minute without light. I needed to find help. I was surprised to see Raz, my donkey. "Raz, thank heaven you're still here." I wrapped my arms around my faithful donkey and sobbed.

My ride back to En Gedi was painful—to body, mind, and soul. "God," I said, "the world is full of violence and evil. Why did You let Father die? Where's life's joy? Eden, where are you? God, where are You?" No answer came.

Another empty space in my heart.

I knew En Gedi was chaotic on market day, but today held more pandemonium than usual—it was the New Moon Festival. It was a tent city for a time, filled with boisterous foreign voices and pleasant odors.

A motley multitude of peddlers trod the dusty lanes, bringing strange tools and creations such as I had never seen. Storytellers gathered on street corners. Vendors' booths were piled high with clothing, jewelry, trinkets, and luscious food—melons, herbs, and sweet breads. I heard their bark: "Come and buy! I have spices from far away islands and perfumes from exotic places."

I heard a lady ask, "What hast thou, young man?" He answered, "Leeks, tubers, and caravan bread." A withered, one-eyed hag offered to tell my fortune. Ironic that she should offer that now.

Young boys laden with baskets, eggs, and birds hawked their wares, screaming, pushing, and chattering. Women hung filthy-looking black skins filled with goat's milk around their waists. Old men squatted against the village walls like shabby old statues.

Young dancing girls in gaudy garments of fern green, blazing red, and sun yellow shook and quivered their bodies in exaggerated gyrations, hoping for silver thrown their way.

Ladies in drab blue tunics and coarse black veils, walking stately, balanced huge crowns of water-jars upon their heads. Wrinkled old women thrust bouquets of live fowl in my face. The chickens squawked; the vendors yelled; the buyers haggled loudly.

Dismounting, I pushed my way through the surging, elbowing crowd, tugging on Raz. I squinted between the slits of my swollen eyelids, searching for someone to help me.

Pain shot through my body. Stooping, I reached for my swollen foot and collided with a scraggly young man. We tumbled to the ground, landing side by side. The crowd continued flocking through the square, destined to plough us under its feet.

The lad stared at me with friendly astonishment. "Eee! I'm sorry!" He struggled to stand.

I pulled my tunic down. Blushing, I said, "It's all right. It's my fault. I shouldn't have stopped to look at my wound."

Staring at the broken skin on my foot, he gasped, "How did you come about your hurt?"

I sat up, rubbed my elbow, and eyed him warily. "I was injured when my father and I were beaten by robbers on our way home from market. They stole our silver and murdered my father," I replied through broken sobs.

Compassion filled his eyes. He took my hand, his face pensive as he helped me rise. "God's curse on them!" he said through his teeth. The tall young man was dressed in a worn and rent length of blue cloth draped upon broad shoulders. Thick brown hair poked out from beneath a soiled white head cloth secured by a black cord.

I reached for Raz's rope and said, "I came back to town for help. I need someone to lift my father onto my donkey."

"I'll help you. I'm Tobias."

I cleared my throat. Hesitating, I wondered if I could trust this person. "Thank you. My name is Hadia. I am of the Yousif clan of the Karka Tribe. I live in Beth Nahar," I said, squeezing my eyes hard. Despair pooled deep within my soul. *How was I going to live without Father?*

"I'm sorry 'bout your father...so sorry." Tobias brushed himself off. "We best be going. I'll help you onto your donkey."

My frightful state of excitement probably gave reason for Tobias to quickly accomplish his mission—I doubt rescuing a wailing woman was an everyday occurrence. We turned and headed toward

Beth Nahar. Tobias took the liberty to tell me all about himself—it didn't matter if I wanted to hear or not.

"I'm a tent maker from the Bebe Tribe," he said with a look of pride. "I'm twenty ages old. I have seven older brothers and one older sister. They're all married with children. My mother and father died during the great northern plague."

"My mother died in childbirth. My father would probably still be alive if my half-good, fanatical Uncle Zor hadn't swindled him out of his inheritance, reducing him to peddling wares at the market." I sighed.

"So, you are an orphan too."

"My brother Levi, my sister Phares, and my grandfather Josef are home."

I concluded we had only one thing in common—our parents. Both were deceased. In the midst of apprehension, I found some relief in his happy company. I was to learn later that he was a lad of sober courage.

The sun slowly lowered itself over our forlorn march, making ready to slide beneath the horizon. A watch-post man searched the plains from a stone watchtower, looking for wolves and jackals, enemies of his flock. Hawks wheeled in the desert sky.

"There he is!" I called.

Maybe Father isn't dead, I thought. *Maybe I just couldn't feel his heartbeat. Maybe he's alive. Oh, please God, make him alive!*

We rushed to where Father lay. His body felt like clay—cold and firm—like that of yesteryear's Master Creation. *He really is dead.* I collapsed over my father. Blackness closed in.

"Miss—miss, are you all right? Wake up—wake up!"

My shoulders jerked back and forth. I tried to make out a voice from far away.

"Quit shaking me—it hurts," I mumbled.

"I'm sorry. I didn't mean to hurt you. I was afraid you'd died. I'm glad you're alive."

Tobias' concern touched me. "Thank you, Tobias," I said in a hollow voice. "I'm all right now."

"Are you sure? You don't look all right to me."

"Yes—yes, I'm fine." Trembling, I reached for his hand. My legs wobbled. "I'm fine—I'm fine."

Tobias' eyes revealed doubt about my well being. He turned and gazed at Father. "I hope I can lift him," he said, bending over the crumpled corpse.

"I'll help you."

"Eee! Your beating has left you too frail to hoist a dead body!"

"I know, but it will take both of us to lift him."

Tobias stood mute, weighing his decision. "Well...I could use your help. All right." Together, we struggled and finally boosted Father onto Raz.

"Hadia, you're in no condition to travel alone. The sun will be setting soon. Let me see you safely home."

I hesitated a moment, looking heavily upon the lad. *Nothing could be worse than what I have just gone through. What could mortal man do? If he kills me, I will be absent from my body and be with God—and Father.* I welcomed a companion, even if he was a stranger. "Thank you, Tobias."

Day faded into blackness. Stars winked; a full moon cast a good amount of light enabling our way. Jackals called their mates as Raz plodded carefully with his precious cargo.

Tobias took a whistle stick from his pocket and placed it to his mouth. Lyrical notes rose into the still night air. I thought the music captivating, like it had arrived from a faraway land. I had never before heard such lovely strains. It comforted my soul.

Watch fires appeared, flickering up and down in the empty hour. Spirals of musky smoke drifted in the night air as we neared home. I heard donkeys braying and dogs barking, signaling villagers of our arrival. My grandfather and my little brother Levi stepped outside.

"Hadia, you're late," Grandfather said, moving closer to Raz.

Torment twisted my face as I collapsed into my grandfather's arms. "Destroyers killed Father!" I shook and sobbed uncontrollably.

21

"No! Zamir! My son! My son! Zamir!" Grandfather wailed, looking over my shoulder at Father. "How can this be?" He let go of me and wrapped his arms around his firstborn. "Zamir! Zamir!"

Levi screamed, "Father! Father!" He threw himself on the cold body and wept.

"Grandfather, we tried to get away, but Father's legs wouldn't let him run fast enough. We begged for mercy. The villains had the brawn of butchers. We were no match for them."

Grandfather pulled his hair. "Zamir! Zamir!"

Tobias and I stood aside, helpless to comfort them. *Oh, God, I don't know how to help them!*

Though reluctant to intrude on Grandfather's grief, I touched his arm and spoke gently. "Grandfather, this is Tobias. He escorted me home."

Levi and Grandfather finally took notice of the stranger. Overwhelmed with shock, my grandfather cradled me in his arms. "Thank you for seeing Hadia safely home," he said in a hollow voice. "Let's put Zamir in the goat shed. We'll bury him in the morn."

We led Raz to the shed and carefully laid Father on a blanket. Tobias and Levi walked back to the house. I stayed awhile. My grandfather leaned his tall, sturdy body against a post. His silver beard glowed in the moonlight as he gazed sorrowfully at his son. He then lay down beside him to wait for the morning light. I returned to the house and sent Levi to notify the villagers of the impending rites. Father was to be buried beside Mother at Potter's Field, a place for the impoverished.

The stark, cheerless morning dawned. I began gathering the food friends were bringing: breads, stews, wine, and fruit, when my younger sister arrived from visiting Aunt Reza. I dreaded bringing her tidings of the disaster.

"Hadia, Grandfather, I'm home," Phares called cheerfully.

I stood mute, my throat constricted. I could feel my face contort. Phares looked at me and could see worry upon my face.

"Hadia, what is it? What has happened? Tell me."

I broke into sobs. "Phares, Father and I were attacked by Destroyers on the way home from market. They killed Father!"

Phares' face blanched; her hands flew to her mouth. "Where is he?"

"In the goat shed."

Tears streamed down Phares' face as she wheeled around and raced to the shed. I quickly followed. Throwing herself upon Father, she cried, "Father! Father! Come back!"

I gazed painfully at Phares, helpless to soothe her anguish. *Our family is shrinking. First Mother, now Father. Who will be next?*

Sobbing, Phares looked sorrowfully at me. "Did Father suffer?"

"No, I don't think so. I believe he died instantly from the first blow to his head. He begged for mercy. Offended at his plea, the Destroyers cursed him with foul gestures and continued beating him."

Phares wiped her eyes with the sleeve of her tunic. "Father was a good man. He didn't deserve to die at the hands of evil. It's not fair!"

As Phares' crying subsided, we prepared Father for burial. Layer by layer, we removed his dirty, bloody clothing. We covered his nakedness with a blanket and proceeded to wash and anoint him with balms and oils, and then dressed him in layers of clean white linen. I would ask Tobias to help lift him onto a blanket. Friends would carry him to the burial field.

I stepped outside and handed the pile of soiled clothing to Tobias. "Tobias, would you please take these to the house?"

"Yes, of course. What's this?" he asked, holding up a length of leather. "Looks like a map of sorts."

"Oh, Tobias," I said, grabbing the leather girdle, "it's nothing—nothing."

"Well, if it's nothing, you're sure in a hurry to take it from me."

I was annoyed with Tobias. Until yesterday he was a stranger; as far as I was concerned, he still was. Who was he to admonish me for taking my own property? I ignored his remark, hoping he wouldn't press me any further.

A gathering crowd of friends arrived at Potter's Field as the sun raised its golden brow. Their countenance showed grave and devout attention. Some threw handfuls of dirt upon their heads. A few cried horribly; some gestured frightfully; others prayed silently. All were sad.

A small, feeble man—poorly clad—swayed to and fro. His wrinkled face looked ghostly under its layer of dust. He began to wail loudly like a broken-hearted dog. Friends waxed eloquently, the high chief gave last rites, and all sprinkled dirt over Father's body. Then, the earth closed coldly around him.

That evening we gathered around the table for supper. We were a depressed, sullen group. We ate in silence, picking at our food. We spoke little, nodding occasionally. The evening fire crackled. Oil lamps smoked, giving little light. Strange shadows danced across the walls. Outside, a brisk wind whipped around the corners of the house.

Tobias brought out his whistle stick and began to play. It was lovely music—haunting, sweet, consoling. After a bit he stopped, removed his head cloth, and ran his fingers through his hair. Clearing his throat, he said, "I must be 'bout my business. I will leave in the early morn."

"Yes," I said, "I suppose you do need to leave. We have kept you long enough."

"Thank you for your hospitality."

"It was fitting to offer you hospitality," I answered. "I can never thank you enough for your help. May God lengthen your life." Silence prevailed, and then I said, "Perhaps we'll see you again someday?"

"Perhaps. I should like to come back and visit."

"Well, the night is most gone and morn will arrive soon enough. Let's get some rest," my grandfather said.

No one protested. I was exhausted and mentally worn down. I welcomed sleep. Perhaps it would erase the sordid memory of the vanished day.

CHAPTER TWO

The Folly

"The fire in my heart won't cease until I avenge Father's death."

Reflecting water sparkled as it lapped the bank of the Tigris River, snaking its way through the Assur Valley, locking arms with the Euphrates River. They called it the Land of Three Rivers. I don't know why, I never knew where the third river was.

The lingering day drew down. Shepherds' watch fires dotted the plain. The sky was a brilliant kaleidoscope of crimson colors, making a perfect backdrop for the silhouette of rolling hills.

I waved my ox goad, and called my dog, O-No, to help guide the sheep to the safety of the bottomland. He eagerly circled the sheep, gently snapping at their heels, sternly barking orders. He glanced at me with his dog-smile, looking for approval. "He's far too tall and elegant to herd," the villagers said, when I told them I was training him to herd.

Raven, our pet bird, perched on Raz's back cawing, *"My name is Raven. Fly with me up high. There's joy in the sky."* I never had to tie Raz, which was good and bad. Good, because I could always count on him being close by; bad, because he was always in the way, looking for attention.

The sweet, dry air was perfume to my senses. Wild doves flew up with a great rattling of wings. Close by, a crow scolded me with his *kra-kra*. A few locusts were flying and lighting. A pair of wild fowl with whitish and gold-speckled feathers fluttered nearby in a languid green palm with a rusty crown.

I love the outdoors. I'm grateful Father taught me to hunt and be self-reliant. I know the villagers were scornful of him teaching me manly skills. They said women belonged at home doing handwork, taking care of babies, and preparing meals.

My heart warmed at the sight of my sister drawing near. I could hear her whistling. Her short angular frame gave her the appearance of a boy. She was born one age after me. We often called each other, "Sister."

I waved. "How are things at home?"

Phares drew near and pushed back her long, chestnut hair. "Pretty good, except for Levi. He sure tries my patience these days." Her mossy-brown eyes flashed.

"Now what's he up to?" I grinned.

"Ever since Father died he doesn't want to obey. Grandfather can soothe the beast in him sometimes, but other times he's dreadful."

I laughed. "Let's gather firewood."

The day faded as the sun kissed the horizon. We set our meal on wool blankets before a blazing fire. We ate quietly, munching on soft, chewy bread and lovely figs. We washed it all down with a jug of cool, smooth goat's milk. I wiped my mouth with the back of my hand.

"Phares, what do you dream about?"

Phares raised her brows and paused. "I dream of getting married and having as many sons as possible."

"Sons?" I said sharply. "Why sons? Why not daughters?"

"Well…because sons bring honor to their fathers."

My voice hardened. "Sons! Sons! Why do we have to bear sons? One would think females a burden rather than a joy. Do daughters mean nothing to fathers?"

Phares twisted her hair. "Of course daughters mean something to fathers."

"Without daughters," I said, "there would be no sons. Just let men see if they can produce sons without wives!"

Phares' brows contracted, giving me a puzzled look. "Hadia, why are you so angry? It grieves me to hear you speak like this."

I stood and glared at Phares. "I'm not angry—well, maybe I am. I don't know why women are treated like flocks of dumb sheep. Are we less than men? When baby girls are not wanted, they are thrown by the wayside."

"Mother and Father didn't throw *us* away."

"Mother made me—" With a small quick pulse, I strangled the words in my throat and took a deep breath.

"Mother made you what?"

Phares fastened her eyes upon mine. My words faltered. "Nothing...never mind." *I can't tell her now.*

Phares' voice lowered. "Not all men are unkind."

Sighing deeply, I sat back down. "Show me one."

Phares gave a thin smile. "I'll show you two: Father and Grandfather."

O-No rubbed his head against my leg, as though he was trying to console me. There was a strained silence between us, and then Phares said, "Hadia, what do *you* dream about?"

I hesitated a moment, gazing at the sky. "I dream about having a horse. I could ride the wind on a horse, fly over the land and escape to far away places."

"A horse? Horses are wild. Nobody rides horses."

"I've heard there are some who do," I answered.

"I've never seen anyone on a horse. That's quite a fancy. What else do you dream?"

"I dream about falling in love with someone special. I don't want an arranged marriage. How could I trust a stranger? And, I'm tired of being a shepherdess. I long to leave Beth Nahar."

"Hadia, you can't leave Beth Nahar. Besides, there's no guarantee you'll find a trustworthy husband or happiness somewhere else. Why are you never satisfied?"

I stood and kicked the dirt. My voice rose. "I'm not satisfied because that's all I've ever known. I want to experience life outside Beth Nahar—take a journey." I took a deep breath. "Remember when Father would tell us about the Garden of Eden?"

"Yes."

"Wouldn't it be exciting to search for it?"

"Surely you jest. Women don't do those things."

"I'm not making mirth. I've thought about it a long time. Ever since Father and Mother died, it's all I think about."

"Grandfather would never allow us to go."

"He needn't find out until after we have left. We could leave a note telling him about the journey. By the time he receives it, we would be well on our way. We could take Raven. He could bring messages to Grandfather, letting him know we're safe. We can take O-No and Raz. Besides, we know how to take care of ourselves." I rolled out my blankets, punched a small one into a pillow and continued to present a basketful of arguments to my sister.

"Grandfather and Levi would be devastated, not to mention worried sick. Why do you want to do this?" Phares asked.

"Don't you remember Grandfather and Father talking about carrying on the tradition?"

"The tradition?"

"The eldest son of each generation is commissioned to keeping the Garden of Eden's memories alive by returning there—so we won't forget."

"Forget what?"

"To never forget what Eden was like: perfect and beautiful before Adam and Eve ate the forbidden fruit from the Tree of Good and Evil. Father was to make the journey before he was murdered. If we don't go, the trail may be lost forever, even with a map. I have this unshakable longing to fulfill Father's covenant—it's our duty."

"Isn't that Levi's responsibility?"

"Yes, but he's too young. He can make the journey when he's older." My voice lowered. "Maybe we'll find the men who murdered Father. I would like to drive a stake into their black hearts."

"Hadia, don't talk that way!"

"Why not?" I answered with mocking scorn. "The fire in my heart won't cease until I avenge Father's death!"

Casting bitter eyes upon me, she answered, "It's shameful to speak that way. Besides, it's not for you to take revenge. God will take care of that."

"Ha! God didn't prevent Father's death; how can I trust Him to take revenge?"

"You have always trusted God, but Father's death has shaken that trust. Your soul is heavy. Someday, you won't be angry, and you'll find peace."

"Maybe—maybe not," I retorted.

The moon rose ruddy. I tossed a tree limb into the fire. Sparks crackled and flew into the still night air. Phares crawled under her bedding. "I'll think about the journey. Good night, Sister," she said, turning her back.

I lay down on the fern-covered ground to pass the starlit night. Drawing my blanket close to my head, thoughts of going where the Parents of Humanity were created consumed me.

I know we'll have to cross the Shamir Mountains and the Falcon Hills. They have caves occupied with ghosts, lions, and bears. People never venture beyond the Falcon Hills. Giants roam that land. I wonder if we'll see Leuce, the white raven. She carries jewels in her mouth, often dropping them. Many men have died seeking her. My eyelids grew heavy. I could think no more. I drifted into the pleasant sweetness of sleep.

The eye of the sun had risen. Distant barking rang in the morning air. O-No perked up his ears, listening for one of his kind. Raz swished at a pesky fly as Raven bounced across his back. The sheep milled restlessly, anxious to return deeper into the hills and graze upon sweet grass.

Phares peeked from beneath her blankets and took notice of me fussing around the watch fire, singing a languid tune. I stopped when I saw she was awake and waved my arm. "Come on, let's eat."

"All right," she said, wiping sleep from her eyes.

We folded blankets. I placed one near the fire to sit upon and wrapped another around my shoulders.

I set out chewy bread, nuggets of cheese, soft figs, and the remainder of yesterday's milk. I popped a fig into my mouth and threw one to O-No. I then leaned close to Phares and looked deep into her eyes. "Phares, what have you decided about the journey?"

Phares squirmed; her lips tightened. "You never give up, do you? Why must you go?"

"Because I'm middle-aged, and I'm tired of being a mother."

"Middle-aged? What has that got to do with your flight-of-fancy idea, and what do you mean by middle-aged and being a mother?"

I sighed with exaggerated impatience. "Our tribe is cursed. Women rarely live beyond forty ages. I'm eighteen ages—almost middle-aged."

My sister shook her head. "I still don't understand."

"Look what happened to Mother. She died in childbirth—she was barely twenty-seven ages. Most of our aunts lived only a few ages longer than Mother. Think about it—how many women in our clan are old?"

Phares paused. "You're right. We have none."

"I have taken care of you and Levi from the day Mother died. Ten ages! It's not that I don't love you two, I just don't want to *mother* anymore. Do you only want to plod through life? Who knows, we may never marry. We could be kidnapped and thrown into slavery, or worse yet, become a concubine. I don't want to reach the end of my life and discover I hadn't lived."

"You're a dreamer, Hadia. Falling in love with someone special, leaving Beth Nahar, flying away on a horse…you seek a kingdom that doesn't exist. I don't even believe Eden exists."

"You're wrong. Eden *does* exist." A tight smile pulled at my mouth. "Come with me, and I'll prove it." My voice lowered. "I'll go alone if you won't come with me."

Phares' shoulders stiffened; her face flushed. "I'm not as brave as you. It sounds frightening. Besides, I think you're a little selfish and self-centered to consider putting us at risk for a folly."

"It's not a folly, it's a tradition. And since when did keeping Eden's memories alive become selfish and self-centered?"

"When two blithe maidens journey without a man. Women just don't do that sort of thing. It's insane."

"It's not insane if God blesses it," I answered curtly.

Phares shook her head and smiled rudely. "So, now you know the mind of God?"

My voice rose like a howling wolf. "No! I just know Father would want us to go, to keep Eden's history alive. Phares, when Father was murdered, I determined in my heart to fulfill his commission. I must do it—with or without you."

Phares stood and gave me a brittle look. "Well, you don't need to yell."

"I didn't mean to yell, Phares. I'm sorry."

Phares let out a deep sigh and turned her head away. We were silent a moment, and then I continued to champion my cause.

"Phares, I know what I'm doing. I can take care of myself and so can you."

"You know what you're doing—what's that supposed to mean?"

"It means I'm not dumb enough to start something I can't finish."

"You may be clever, but you're not always wise. Even some animals are wiser than humans," Phares answered.

"Are you comparing me to an animal?"

"No—it's just…I'm not sure…."

"You're not sure about what?"

"I don't know, Hadia. Could we really journey safely to Eden? My confidence is frail. I'm afraid my fear might hold you back."

"Phares, the Book of Wisdom says when you rely upon God, you will not rely upon yourself. He can guide you and turn darkness into light and make rough places smooth. Replace fear with faith," I said, though my inner self was saying, *I'm a fine one to talk.*

31

Phares twisted her hair. "But my faith is weak, like a falling leaf in high wind. I know you sacrificed your childhood to care for Levi and me. I do want you to fulfill your dreams and Father's Commission. But, how will Grandfather react to our absurdity?"

I took a deep breath and gave a thin smile. "No, your fear won't hold me back, and yes, I believe we can accomplish a journey to Eden. I know it seems impossible, but it isn't. You'll see if you go with me."

Phares gathered supplies to take home. "All right, I'll go with you on this crazy quest. But what's in this for me?"

"You'll fulfill Father's Commission for him! That's what's in it for you. Oh, Phares, we'll have a grand time. You won't regret it. I promise."

"How can you promise? You don't know the future."

"Oh, ye of little faith, we'll be fine."

Phares paced around the firepit. "Hadia, we must tell Grandfather. We need him to bless the journey. Besides, I won't feel safe leaving without it."

"No! He'll stop us!"

"Well then, I guess I'll have to stay home."

I sat silent. *If Grandfather doesn't bless us, everything will be ruined. I shall be dashed. Maybe I shouldn't have shared my dream. Maybe I should have gone by myself. Well, it's too late now. I shall have to wait and see what happens.*

I shrugged my shoulders. "All right, we'll ask him."

"Good. When shall we ask?"

"After we return home on the morrow."

O-No curled up on the bedstraw mat beside Levi as the evening fire blazed.

Grandfather sat on the floor against the wall, staring into space. Phares and I sat next to each other, opposite Grandfather, waiting for the perfect moment to ask for "the blessing."

I squirmed and rubbed my fingers together. "Grandfather, there's something I want to ask you."

"Oh?"

I glanced at Levi. "Levi, why don't you go visit Izmir? He hasn't seen you in a bit."

Levi stamped his feet. "You just want to get rid of me. You have secrets."

"Maybe. Now be a good lad and leave." Levi scowled and left the house.

"Grandfather, we know about the tradition of going to the Garden of Eden. Father isn't here to fulfill it, and Levi is too young. Phares and I want to make the journey. Please, Grandfather, give us your blessing. Let us go," I pleaded.

Grandfather's eyes widened. "I never expected this to happen. I always assumed your father would make the journey. I don't know. It is too dangerous. You're women, and young women at that. I can't let you do it."

"Grandfather, if a man escorted us, would you let us go?" I asked.

"Nobody outside of our clan is to go. If the word got out, it would be a disaster. Everybody would be racing to Eden. It would become a spectacle. God would not be pleased. He has entrusted this tradition to our clan and our clan alone."

"I could ask Tobias to go with us. He could protect us. Please, Grandfather," I pleaded.

"I can't believe you're asking to do this. My only son is dead. Am I to send my granddaughters into the wilderness to die too? No! It's out of the question. I will not discuss it any longer." Shaking his head, my grandfather stood, turned on his heel and went outside.

I rested my hands on my hips. My brows tugged together. "See what you've done, Phares. We'll never get to go now."

"It's not my fault. I just wanted to do the right thing. Let's pray about it. Maybe God will change Grandfather's mind."

Her words failed. I couldn't hide my anger. "I can't believe I gave in to your whim. Now you want to pray about it? We should have prayed before asking him."

Phares' chin quivered. "I'm sorry. Maybe I should have stayed out of your plans."

Except for O-No's snoring and the crackling fire, the room fell quiet. We sat in silence for a long time as I pondered my outburst. *What have I done? I have attacked my sister, and over what—my frivolity?* "Phares, I'm sorry. Forgive me."

"It's all right. I know you mean well."

I turned and went outside. I knew it would take a miracle to change Grandfather's mind. He was so stubborn. Perhaps a day or two would accommodate his mind to the idea of allowing us to go to Eden. I raised my eyes to the sky.

"Heavenly Father, incline Your ear to my cry. Let my prayer come before You. Create a miracle. Change Grandfather's mind," I pleaded. "Oh, and give me courage to tell Phares about the baby girl. So let it be," I whispered.

The prospect of starting my cherished journey hung on a slender thread—Grandfather's blessing.

CHAPTER THREE

The Blessing

"I had to unravel the arguments in my head."

I slumped heavily to the ground under a myrtle tree. *Grandfather hasn't changed his mind*, I thought. *Only the lack of his blessing stands in the way of leaving for Eden. What good does it do to be obedient? It brings only disappointment. Men—they can be so....*

Men are warmongers, leaving little peace in the land. They keep women in bondage. Men killed Father. Uncle Zor cheated Mother and Father out of their inheritance. Imagine! He convinced Father his prized camel died so he could steal it and sell it for a tidy sum. I burned with anger. Resentment welcomed unforgiveness as it climbed into my heart.

The sweet aroma of the myrtle tree was pleasant. It was a scent like no other; I thought it came from paradise. I wondered if this was the tree God said Adam could take with him when he was banished from Eden. They say the myrtle tree brings good fortune and happiness to the house where it's planted. This myrtle seemed to have found small favor with our household.

The hills and valleys were green; young flowers blossomed. Beth Nahar was a lovely little village tucked between the cities of En Gedi and Ephraim. The fertile valley and plains held great herds of cattle owned by King Jehu. He had many farms, vineyards, and wells. The village was fortified by elite troops of the king's army—an army with the best weapons available: shields, spears, and bows and arrows. The King even made slings to shoot stones from the towers of bulwarks. Everyone paid tribute to him, for he was powerful.

People felt safe, until recently. Word of war filtered down from outlying towns. Several villages of the lowland had been invaded by King Amoz from the land of Zora. Many people had been captured and made slaves.

Even if we left for Eden today, it would be risky, I thought. *Skirting King Amoz's troops would not be easy. I wonder how close the war is to En Gedi. If Tobias were here, he would know. I do wish he would return.*

I decided to visit Granna, the village centurion storyteller, and ask her what she knew about Eden.

Breezing past towers of ovens, delicious aromas rose from baking caravan bread, crunchy hard cakes, and sweet fig buns. Passing through the east middle gate, I turned into the area of the cotter's cottages. There it was: a shabby little hut, an insult of a shelter. I knocked softly on the door.

The door swung open. "Hadia, come in!" Granna said, waving her long spindly arms. "What brings thee hither?"

I stepped inside the musty, cramped room. Granna reminded me of a little hen: small, colorful and feisty. Standing barefoot, she was dressed in a white tunic, with a purple and gold shawl wrapped around the shoulders of her diminutive frame. Her long white hair fanned out across her shoulders like a huge broom. Canyons of wrinkles set off pools of blue eyes—the bluest eyes I had ever seen. Some people thought Granna a bit daft, others found her charming. I found her to be both.

"Granna, I need to talk to you. Is this a good time?"

"Oh, child, I gets restless and need to talk too. Yes, let's talk, but first let me tell you how lovely you look! Your skin glows like golden dates. Are you in love?"

"No," I said, blushing. "I want to find the Garden of Eden. Grandfather won't give me his blessing. I'm so angry, I could spit."

"Not in my house, you won't," Granna replied with a wily smile.

I rubbed my fingers together and sat down with a thud. "Oh, Granna, you know I won't spit. I'm just frustrated."

"Me dear, why do you seek the Garden of Eden?"

I can't tell her the reason. It will give away our family secret. "I only know I feel drawn to this quest," I answered.

"Even if you find it, you can't enter in. The cherubim are guarding the entrance with fiery torches. Will just finding it satisfy you?"

"Yes!"

"Well, me innocent, if you're determined to go, I might as well tell you—"

"Tell me what? What do you know about Eden?"

"When I was grow'n up, my mother and father told me 'bout a family in Beth Nahar finding the Garden of Eden. S'pect it's just an old wives' tale. But then, there was your great-grandfather, Damoor. I knew him when I was a young'n. Such a handsome man, I had eyes for him awhile." Granna's eyes twinkled as a sly grin curled her lips.

"Anyway, I believe he went to the Garden of Eden. Never told me so, but he talked a lot about it, and seemed to know more than he should. Now, child, you come and tell me you want to search for it. Lordy, Lordy, mebe the tale is true." Granna's fragile body teetered. "If you insist on finding it, I must warn you of possible dangers. First of all, you won't get very far if you fall into the hands of the Nephilim giants."

"I've heard of the Nephilim giants. What do you know about them?" I asked curiously.

"They are an aggressive tribe of giants, strange of speech and feared far and wide. They are many heads tall and of great strength. Women are no match for them. They roam the Nephilim Land in the Valley of Tremble and rarely leave except for an occasional

hunt in the Shamir Mountains. They expect outsiders to stay out."
Granna turned her back. "Excuse me, dear." She hung a little copper kettle filled with water over the fire, and then reached into a
small cupboard and took out some hard cakes.

"Now, where was I? Oh yes, their tale is an odd one. Ages ago,
fallen angels looked upon the beautiful women of humankind and
sought them for wives. Their offspring grew into giants. The town
folks called it an evil thing for angels to marry women of humankind, and they were shunned for it. So, the Nephilims wandered far
away to seek a land of their own. As the ages passed, their hearts
hardened and they became hostile toward strangers.

"Your knees will give way as your body trembles at the sight of
them. They stride the earth with huge steps. You have to marshal
all your strength to run from them. Even then, it could be useless.
They play with the Shayba bird and run with the behemoth. They
are empowered people capable of atrocious assaults on trespassers.
There are deep shadows in the Land of Tremble. If you're captured,
there is no return."

I closed my gaping mouth.

"There's more," Granna said.

"I don't think I want to hear more. Your hints and warnings are
terrifying. I may think twice about going."

Granna chuckled, "I knew you might think that, but you need
to know what you're up against. It will be dangerous. You durst
not venture forth without a warrior to escort you."

"I told Grandfather we would take an escort, but he refuses to
let us go. We can't depart without his blessing."

"Well, child, you'll just have to pray and ask God to change
his mind."

"It's going to take more than prayer; it's going to take a
miracle!"

"You have made God too small in your eyes. He who made the
heavens can bring about miracles."

"Maybe," I muttered. Granna's meal left me full and sleepy.
The day was young; the stories could wait. "Granna, I'm going to
take a short nap."

"Child, take as long as you like. I have little company and I welcome them—awake or asleep."

Curling up on the floor, Granna placed a pillow under my head and a soft shawl around my shoulders. It wasn't long before dream images gathered in the secret chambers of my mind, creating mysterious characters: tinkers, goliath beetles, a white raven, and a man wearing an alabaster amulet. The tinkers danced, the beetles jumped, and the man kept reaching for the white raven. Soon my slumber came to an end as the ephemeral dream slipped away with only snatches of memory remaining.

I'm sure the dream is important, I thought. *But what does it mean? Who's the man with the alabaster amulet? He seems familiar. Maybe he was from a past dream. I won't reveal the dream to Granna. I'll try to interpret it myself.*

"Ah, my sleeping lovely has come back from her dream world. Are you refreshed, me dear and ready to hear more?"

"Yes, I'm ready."

"Let's see, what else should I warn you? Well of course, there are plenty of wild animals. Don't relax too much, you'll be caught off guard. Also, you'll have to cover your tracks; make sure no one is following you, like Destroyers and raiders. They hold life cheap. The shedding of blood and robbing are normal activities for the likes of them. It's their spice of life."

"Tell me about the Destroyers," I said.

"Oh child, they are the devil's angels! They kill, but cannot be killed, unless of course, they fall into bottomless pits. They live everywhere, like nomads. They are the human wolves of the desert—always ready to prey upon the skirts of journeying caravans.

"They swallow the wind on swift camels. Some ride horses of flaming coals. Fierce, black dogs race alongside. Even the air about them reeks of evil. They smell like moldy blankets."

"They ride horses? Then the tale is true. Some people do ride horses."

"Destroyers have been seen on horses," Granna answered.

"Destroyers! Destroyers killed Father. I'll never forgive them!"

"Well, me dear, I don't blame you. But remember, unforgiveness hardens the heart and sours the soul. Do not take revenge. Leave room for God's wrath. He will repay."

"It's not for you to take revenge. God will take care of that." I ignored Granna's warning. "Are there others to watch for?"

"There is a Vilda, a wild mountain man. He acts crazy and his speech is gibberish, but he's harmless. Believe his name is Bidinko. Oh, and pay heed to caves—full of snakes and scorpions; Shadows guard some."

"Shadows—what are they?"

"I'm told they are ghosts of the Nephilim giants who guard hidden wealth. It too could be an old wives' tale. Another thing: watch for djinns—evil spirits. There is only one way to render them dead. One fell blow will kill them. Two blows will bring two back to life."

I sat silent a moment, stunned by the possibility of facing such danger.

"Granna, your warnings may save our lives. Thank you."

Granna smiled, went to a small limestone box and opened it. Her bony fingers shuffled about inside, and she pulled out a small piece of jewelry.

"Here, take this for a safe destiny. It has been in our clan for generations. You may return it when you have returned from your journey, should you go."

The old woman extended her gnarly hand and held out a small, gold pendant. The face of a woman was etched into one side of the round medallion, and foreign words etched on the other side. It appeared to be very old.

"Granna, what is this and what does 'Na Amasla' mean?"

"It's a family talisman. The ancient language says *'go safely.'* It will protect you. I know you probably don't believe such things, but it doesn't hurt to consider it." Smiling sweetly, she closed my fingers over her family heirloom.

"Another thing, Hadia, seek wisdom. It's more precious than gold. It's one of God's greatest gifts to mankind."

Slipping the pendant into my pocket, I gave a lame smile. Hoary hair tickled my cheeks as I hugged the vintage woman. "Thank you, Granna. I must leave now."

It was middle-afternoon. A soft breeze danced about swirling dust at my feet. The smell of sweet breads baking in the ovens infused the air. Shopkeepers in the colonnade yelled from their booths, "Buy here—buy here!" Children herded bleating goats into holding pens. Phenias Frairhair, the town storyteller, was reciting poems and stories. His crisp-ringed hair and grave countenance gave heed for me to stop. I loved writing poems; I couldn't resist listening.

"Hark," he said, "where would stories be if the mouth had not blabbed? When one is tired and hungry, turn him not away. Make him a bed and give him something to eat."

An old lady dressed in green, with a white scarf around her neck and a black shawl on her head, shoved chickens at me. "Here, best chickens 'bout. You buy?"

The black and white speckled chickens, with their sun-orange necks and blood-red combs, squawked and flapped their wings in my face.

"No thank you," I said, brushing past her.

An impish boy in a tattered shirt and white skullcap shrilled loudly, waving a stick of dangling bone combs, bead bracelets and silver nose-rings.

I shuffled on when my eye caught sight of an anthill. The ants were lined up in a row, running like an army going into battle. *I have a battle too—Grandfather. How am I to change his mind?*

The land smelled of fresh plowed earth and tender green grass. Grandfather was outside with Nanny, our goat, when I arrived home.

"Grandfather, I called upon Granna today. She told me many tales. I love visiting her."

"Yes, I like visiting her, too. We have exchanged many stories. Hadia, I want to share some good news with you and Phares."

"What is it Grandfather?"

"You'll have to wait until this eve. Be patient, it will arrive soon enough."

Grandfather's dark, piercing eyes glowed in the dim light as shadows deepened. "I had to unravel the arguments in my head." His lean, brown face was grave as he continued in a sighing voice. "I have made up my mind. I will bless your journey to Eden."

"Grandfather, this is a miracle!" A feeling of gratitude washed over me.

"It was your father's wish. He told me many times he had planned to take you and Phares with him to Eden, and he even wrote about it."

My grandfather reached for the body scroll with the map carved into it and a thin, tattered book containing nothing more than a few pieces of papyrus paper bound together with worn pieces of leather. I took the map and little book and clutched them to my heart. He looked deep into my eyes and said, "What is written must come to pass."

Now, I know I must make the journey. "Grandfather, we can ask Tobias to escort us. What do you think?"

"We don't know anything about him. Bringing you home safely from En Gedi is one matter, taking you to Eden is another. Is his character honorable?"

"We don't know. We'll have to trust God."

"A cup of wisdom wouldn't hurt either," Phares said.

"Grandfather, let me go. They don't need Tobias. I'll protect them," Levi cut in.

"You're still a child, Levi," I said. "You must stay home. You'll get to go another time. Besides, Grandfather needs your help. Be a good lad; you durst not disobey. All right?"

Levi raised his fist and pounded the table. A shock of flame-red hair fell across his flashing, brown eyes. "It's not fair. I never get to do anything. I always get left out!"

"Levi!" Grandfather said sharply, "I will not tolerate any display of angry fits. For that, you will stay home all day on the morrow."

Ignoring Levi's protests I said, "Phares, we must go to En Gedi in the morn and find Tobias."

Phares twisted her hair. "Yes, I suppose so."

A journey I took, back to
Beyond where it all began
Behind the Garden wall
I could not enter in
Nor could I see, or hear, or
Taste what was before The Fall
I'll wait for the Master's call
To invite me back inside to
Paradise behind the Garden Wall

Hadia

CHAPTER FOUR

Seeking Tobias

"You must swear by your father's beard you'll keep it a secret."

I watched an eagle overhead as it eyed the creatures below. They say the eagle lives a thousand years. It reminded me that God alone created all things and stretched out the heavens. He measured the water in the hollow of His hand, weighed the mountains on a scale and the hills in a balance.

The land teemed with life. Geese dallied among the cattails, reeds and rushes along the Haj Creek. Mist swirled through the boggy water, rising and disappearing like a fading light. Footpaths and wildflowers laced the fields.

I felt Granna's talisman in my pocket. *I'm not superstitious, but maybe it will bring good luck, like finding Tobias. But, what if he can't be found? We can't go to Eden without him.*

Phares walked steadily in concert with me, whistling and kicking stones. Soon, her whistling ceased. She twisted her hair and said, "Hadia, I'm such a coward. If I don't go with you to Eden, will I always wonder what I missed?"

I scowled. "Yes, you would always wonder what you missed. Why are you questioning your decision now?"

"I'm frightened. We've never been away from our family. What do we know about taking a journey to who-knows-where?"

I felt my face tighten. "We're not going to who-knows-where, we're going to Eden. We don't need to know anymore than that. God will guide us."

"I thought you didn't trust God anymore."

I rolled my eyes. "I trust Him. I'm just not sure He will avenge Father's murderers. That doesn't mean *you* can't ask Him for courage."

Phares pushed a strand of hair out of her eyes and gave me a thin smile. Kicking another stone, she said with an air of melancholy resignation, "I've asked for courage; it's just hard to exercise it."

Dust veiled our feet. The miles wore on, but our vision waned not. At length, we spoke again.

"Oh no!" Phares wailed.

"What's wrong?" I asked.

"It's Raven. He followed us."

"It's all right. Who knows, we might need him."

"*My name is Raven. Fly with me up high. There's joy in the sky,*" he cawed.

"I hope he doesn't start talking in town; someone might try to steal him."

I laughed. "They'll have to catch him first. Oh look, the cross-road! We're not far from En Gedi now."

"Hadia, what's that noise?"

"I don't hear any…oh, someone's coming!"

A jolting wagon stormed the road with donkeys charging full speed. Wheels clattered, cracking whips stung the air. Swords and spears flashed. Thick dust clouds swirled about. Suddenly, the wagon stopped. Sweat lathered and dripped from the donkeys. Foam drooled from their mouths. Prancing nervously, their eyes opened wide.

"Hail! I am Khan, the army commander from southern En Gedi," the soldier said with stern military speech. "We are of King Jehu's army. King Amoz's army is advancing. You maidens should not be wandering around. There be slave traders, spies, and ne' er-do-wells about." The militiamen lifted their shoulders to high-light their medals, proving their credentials.

"It isn't safe for women. These are hazardous times and places," shouted another soldier through broken teeth.

I found my tongue. "Thank you, sirs. We are beholden for your warning."

The soldiers drove manfully on. Phares and I stared at each other in dismay. My shoulders drooped. "War? It can't be!" After a stunned moment, I straightened my back.

"We'll just have to keep going. Remember, nothing is going to stop us."

Slipping stealthily into the sleepy town, we heard drumbeats, soft music, and sweet singing in tents. In other tents, some were chanting devotions. The town was deserted, save for a few travelers. Some lay stretched like dogs by the side of the dusty road. A little lad threw knucklebones on the ground, taking his turn at Hounds and Jackals as a tattered mutt looked on. Soft, glowing oil lamps were a welcome sight. Booming laughter rang from the Talon's Claw Inn.

"Phares, I know the Talon's Claw Inn is dreadful, but I think we should seek food and lodging there. If anyone knows where Tobias lives, someone there might."

"Hadia, this place is horrid. Do we have to?"

"Yes. We'll be fine."

Phares shook her head. "Oh dear."

Exhausted and hungry, I paid little heed to Phares' protest. I pushed opened the Talon's Claw door. It was stale, dank, and thick with smoke from pipes and guttering lamps. A squalid old man sat nearby. The pungent smell of wine overtook us. Some men were arguing about what I did not know. A lad played raucous music on his sistrum.

The innkeeper, a sour-faced man with three chins that moved in chorus, looked up and nodded. His beady eyes squinted as he stared at us.

"Sir, we need lodging and food. Be that possible?" I asked.

"Yes; what do you have to barter?"

I dug into my pocket and pulled out a piece of silver. "Will this do?" I asked.

"Yes, that's enough for a room and bread and soup." He grabbed the silver, mopped his brow and retreated behind a counter.

"Thank you." Weary, I pulled a chair from a rickety table and sat down.

"Hadia, I hope we won't regret staying in this miserable place. It doesn't feel safe."

"Yes, it is wretched, but it's only for one night. Besides, where else can we stay?"

I glanced around the room. Two boisterous men sat close by, pounding the table, laughing. The squalid old man was halfway out of his chair, sliding toward the floor. The musical lad had stopped clanging his sistrum. Three old men sat square-legged on the floor, throwing knucklebones. My gaze stopped at the startling figure of a witch-like woman with dark visage coiled like an adder in a shadowy corner. Long dark hair fell like a cape around her clay-like face onto her shoulders. Milky white eyes like the white heat of lamps glared as she drew a cup of ale to her mouth. I shuddered. *She looks demonic.*

A servant set two bowls of hot, steaming soup and a huge loaf of bread before us. We eagerly tore open the steaming bread, using it to stir the hot broth. Washing chunks of soft bread down with the smooth, spicy soup left us full and sleepy. I approached the rotund innkeeper. "Sir, do you know a man named Tobias?"

"Eh! He lives just down the road, first cottage past the stable."

"Thank you. Now, where's our room?"

"Upstairs," he said, waving his arm toward a dark hallway.

We entered a black narrow chasm leading to a staircase. I heard heavy footfalls and turned to see the woman from the corner following us. Stopping short, she turned away, leaving a putrid smell like rotting flesh behind.

Feeling our way, we climbed the stairs to a tiny room. A slender beam of moonlight shone through a yawning window. Raven perched on the sill. Our forms cast shadowy images on the walls as we adjusted our eyes to the darkness. There were no beds; a nest of straw lay on the floor. Rats scampered across my toes. Devoid of any comfort, it would have to do. Phares was right; it was wretched.

I heard drumming outside and looked to see a torchlight procession in dance. Lights flitted and leaped as if alive. The dancers circled and bobbed at each other, whirling their torches in the air. I turned back to Phares.

"Phares, did you notice that strange looking woman who followed us to the stairs?"

"Not only did I notice her, I could smell her. What a foul odor."

"She seemed quite interested in us. I wonder why? I have never seen her before."

Phares piled straw to lie on and unfolded her blanket. "Hmm... she did behave curious. Maybe she's that way with everyone."

"I doubt it. There was something about her that gave me the chills."

Phares wrinkled her nose at me. "Maybe she's a witch."

At the new day's light, I heard crowing roosters, and Raven pecking on the window sill. I rubbed my back. We had sorry night quarters. "Oooh! My back is killing me."

"Mine too. Those dreadful rats wouldn't leave me alone last night. Let's get out of here." Phares kicked straw aside. "Do you suppose there's a place to bathe? Between dusty roads and dirty rats, I feel about as clean as a pig."

"We can ask while looking for Tobias. Let's pray first." I bowed my head.

"Heavenly Father may this day be fortunate. May we find Tobias. Give us safety that we see not evil. So let it be."

We hurried down the narrow staircase and stepped outside into the early morning crowd. Merchants, beggars, laborers, villagers, and travelers in a variety of dress and complexion color crowded the narrow lanes.

Dodging ill-tempered camels ladened with heavy cargo—snorting, snarling, craning their scrawny necks above us—we made our way past vendors dangling red and yellow sandals and shawls in shades of mulberry, olive, and melon at the end of long poles. Others tempted us with trays piled high with "sweet lumps of delight."

Wine vendors held out brass pitchers of wine with one hand, and copper cups in another. Cooks' shops exhaled a savory perfume of lentil soup.

"Phares, let's buy some bread and fruit. I'm starved," I said.

"All right. Wait! There's the stable. Let's find Tobias first."

We scurried past the stable and stopped at the first cottage. It was plain, without a stoop. I knocked firmly on the door and waited...and waited.

"He can't be gone! Tobias, please answer the door," I pleaded.

"Maybe he's sleeping. We can buy bread and come back," Phares said, turning around. "Let's go."

Suddenly, the rickety door opened slightly. "Hello, who goes there?" a sleepy voice rang out.

"Tobias, we thought you were gone," I said. "Are we glad to see you."

Tobias swung the door open wide. "Hadia! Phares! What brings thee hither?"

"We need to talk to you. It's important. Where can we buy bread?" I asked. "We'll bring some back and eat while we tell you why we've come."

"The baker is 'bout ten cottages down the lane—can't miss it."

"Good! We'll be right back. Don't leave."

Bounding down the lane, we dodged stray dogs seeking food scraps. Market vendors continued their boisterous barking. Then, there it was—the bakery, a simple brick oven outside an old man's cottage. The copper-colored baker looked up as he slid a warm loaf of bread into a covered basket. We were his first customers of the day.

His comely wooden face was sober. He seemed to be a man of inept humor. His long, saffron-dyed beard was startling against his worn mantle. He did not seem very happy in his wits.

I smiled. "Good morn. Two loaves of bread, please."

"Good morn. What have you to trade?" he answered solemnly.

I handed him a small piece of silver. He knitted his shoulders and turned up his palms to receive the nugget. He looked at it carefully, and then satisfied, he nodded and handed each of us a warm loaf. We tucked the bread under our arms and hurried back to Tobias.

Ceremonial worship was taking place in a nearby temple; divine images and idols dwelled within the costly shrine. Chanting hymns of worship to the gods rang out. Holy vessels, treasured perfumes, and burning incense enveloped the massive walls with mystery.

Tobias was waiting outside upon our return. His face was broad with a smile as he waved us inside. Breathlessly, we laid the bread on the table, tore it open, and handed some to him. "Tobias, we're going to take a journey and need protection. We want you to escort us," I said.

"What kind of journey?"

"We can't tell you unless you swear by your father's beard you'll keep it a secret. This will be the journey of your lifetime. We must be confident of your honor. If you give your word, how can we know you'll keep it?"

"I only own one thing of value, a gold ring that belonged to my mother. I treasure it. I will give it to you for safekeeping. If I don't keep my word, you'll have the ring." He turned and opened a small wooden chest, reached in, and pulled out a slender gold ring.

"Here, see?"

I took the ring and examined it closely. It was lovely; it looked valuable. *Tobias, I'm desperate for your honor—you're our passage to Eden. If this ring belonged to my mother, I certainly wouldn't sacrifice it for a farce. Perhaps I can trust you.*

"All right Tobias, we'll accept the ring as a pledge. You may have it back when we return," I said, slipping it on my finger. We smacked our hands together, sealing the agreement.

Moving closer, I whispered, "It's about Eden. It has been our ancestral custom since the time of Adam for the eldest son of each generation to return to the Garden of Eden. Grandfather has been there. Father was to go before he was murdered. Now it's up to Phares and me to keep the tradition alive."

"By founds, this will be the journey of a lifetime!" Tobias said, wide-eyed. "When do we leave?"

"We must be gone at once. There's no time to waste. Our journey must be completed before the sheep give lamb. Where might we bathe? We'll wash up while you prepare to leave," I said.

"The bathhouse is just past the baker, on the right."

"Good. We'll take leave and be back soon." We closed the door and hurried down the lane.

Bang! Bang! Bang! The cottage door rattled. Tobias stuck his head out the door.

"Eee! That was quick. Are you clean already?"

"We are clean and ready to leave," I said.

"All right! Let's go!" Tobias grabbed his sack of goods, and we left the tiny cottage.

We hadn't gone far when I said, "Tobias, we heard ungenerous stories about you this morn."

Little drops of perspiration popped out on Tobias' forehead. "What's that?" he asked, wringing his hands.

"When we mentioned your name in the bathhouse, some women were taken aback. They said you were the town's liar. They said you were slimy and that you would rather scheme than earn. Is that true? Let not you deceive us, Tobias."

Tobias' large brown eyes grew wide. He removed his head cloth and ran his fingers through his hair. "Yes, I have been known to lie, but I don't know 'bout that slimy, schemy bit."

"Oh, thank heaven!" I said.

"That I'm a liar?"

"No, for being truthful. Now we know your word is sacred."

"Bye the bye, why did you tell the truth now?" Phares asked.

"If I lied, you probably would find out and not let me go with you."

I studied Tobias. *Do I only believe him so I can continue the journey? I guess time will tell. By then, it may be too late.*

The sun lowered itself, ready to leave the broken fellowship of the day. Tobias pulled out his whistle stick. Smiling broadly, he shouted, "By founds!" He then proceeded to play cheerful music.

A pair of white oryx ambled by, their long black horns bent backwards, pointing from whence they came. Huge white hares jumped across the horizon seeking burrows for the night. Tent people cooked their evening meal over smoky fires, perfuming the air with musky soot. Trudging along, our strides shortened as the plains crawled by.

"I'm hungry," Phares said. "Let's eat."

"All right. We can eat by the creek and be home by dark," I said.

We sat down. Tobias passed bread, olives, and dates. Gnats quickly gathered as a symphony of crickets started their evensong.

"Hadia, did you know I taught myself to read and write?"

"You taught yourself the mystery of letters? You must be clever."

"Well, I never considered myself clever—determined, maybe—but not clever."

"Grandfather taught us grandchildren to write and read," I said. "Tobias, what do you know about the war? Will it advance to Beth Nahar?"

"I don't know. Sometimes I see a few men from the King's army pass through our village. They set a garrison above En Gedi, you know."

"Yes, I know. I just hope we don't encounter any skirmishes on our journey."

"Don't be worrying 'bout such things. We can avoid them. We'll be safe."

We sipped water from the creek and then took leave. Phares whistled. Tobias played his whistle stick. Raven cawed, *"Home! Home!"*

Night closed dark around us as we entered Beth Nahar. Neighborhood dogs first gave notice of our approach. O-No was first to greet us. "Grandfather! Levi!" I called.

Stepping outside, my grandfather said, "Welcome back. Come and rest. You must be tired."

Phares and I kissed Grandfather. Then we went inside and plopped on a bed pushed against the wall. Grandfather patted Tobias' back. "I'm glad to see they found you, Tobias."

Tobias smiled. "Well, sir, I really wasn't lost. I'm excited 'bout the journey."

"Tobias, no one outside of our clan has ever gone to Eden. This is a sacred privilege. You must never divulge it. To do so could cause disaster and displease God. I trust you won't disappoint us."

"You can trust me, Sir. It will be bound to eternal secrecy."

"Good. Now, is anyone hungry?"

"Thank you, Grandfather, but we've already eaten," I said. "Our only want is a full night's sleep so we'll be refreshed to leave on the morrow."

Grandfather reached for three little cups. "Very well, then sleep it will be. But first you must have a cup of hot herb tea. It will help you to sleep soundly."

Sooty oil lamps cast strange shadows across our faces. Steam rose from the boiling copper kettle. Soon, our tea finished, Grandfather blew out the oil lamps. Everyone crawled under their blankets. I was tired and ready for sleep. It came without delay.

CHAPTER FIVE

The Body Scroll

"It seems there is a book of lost secrets."

Oh no!" I cried, standing in the doorway. The dark sky frowned as wind slashed against the cottage. It blew through the wadi, uprooting trees, gathering debris. I clasped the ends of my shawl and pulled it tight around my shoulders. *Maybe the raging wind is a sign from God, warning us not to go.*

"Hadia," Phares said, holding out the body scroll, "let's look at the map. We can make ready to leave as soon as the wind dies down."

Sighing, I took my sister's arm. "All right, we need to study it anyway."

The leather scroll was tattered. Bits and pieces of the map had worn away. A long, crooked trail zigzagged from the bottom of the map to the top. The trail ran east and west, starting just outside Beth Nahar, beginning at the Old Forest Trail. It curved gently past the Shepherd's Camp, crossed rivers, and passed through plains and valleys. It crossed the Shamir Mountains, passed Shadow Caves, and crossed the Valley of Tremble and the Falcon Hills, ending at the Purple Mountains, supposedly the gateway to the Garden of Eden.

"Hadia," Phares said, "do you believe we can find Eden?"

"Of course. Our ancestors did. Why shouldn't we?" I answered adamantly.

"I don't know; it looks so far away."

"There you go Phares, worrying about a bee's nest before you ever see one," I chided.

Tobias waved his hand. "Girls, let's not start striving before we even begin our journey. There'll be plenty of time for that later."

"Tobias, how long do you think the journey will take?" I asked.

"Hard tell'n; I know it can be anywhere from four to five days to Magdala Tower."

"It will also depend on what kind of trouble we run into," Phares said, in an apprehensive tone.

"Let's make ready our supplies," Tobias said. "We'll need more knives, bows and arrows, nets and sling missiles. Oh, and papyrus paper and writing sticks, and lamp oil. Do you have these?"

"We have all of them. Each of us will carry a food sack, so we can take as much as possible. Help me gather everything, Phares," I said, grabbing a blanket. Grandfather set out caravan bread, dates, nuts, olives, figs, flour, olive oil, and pressed raisin cakes.

Excitement rose as we laid in a good store of portable preparations for the journey. I noticed even Phares seemed enthused as she bustled about, whistling.

With our provisions completed and our writing material duly laid in, we were prepared to leave. However, the relentless wind continued, making departure impossible.

The day slipped by slowly. Tobias and I paced the room. Phares twisted her hair. Grandfather tried entertaining Levi with storytelling.

The driving wind soon gave way to a gentle breeze. Brilliant pink and gold clouds drifted across patches of blue sky. The morrow looked promising.

I lay awake that night, thinking about Eden and what might be going through everyone's mind. *I want to see Eden in all its splendor. Grandfather is probably concerned for our safety, and Levi is probably trying to devise a way to go. Tobias, he's probably dreaming of wealth. And dear Phares, she's afraid of her shadow. She's probably trying to figure a way out of going.*

Gauzy darkness gave way to the eye of the sun showing its golden brow. No one could sleep any longer. Oil lamps were lit, casting shadows on the walls as everyone stirred about.

Breakfast was a flurry of eating like starved animals. I gulped bread, cheese, and dates and washed it all down with a bowl of goat's milk, carelessly wiping my dribbles.

"Hadia, I would be pleased to help you pack Raz," Tobias said.

"I'm not helpless!" I said, surprised at my sharpness.

"I know you're not helpless. I just want to do my part."

"Thank you, Tobias. I shouldn't be so touchy. Guess I'm just a little nervous about our journey."

Tobias nodded, and then gathered bundles and carried them outside. I followed him as he threw the first bundle on Raz's back. It landed with a thud, nearly knocking the wind out of the little gray donkey. Raz grunted, bloated his belly and did his usual side-step dance.

"Hold still!" Tobias bellowed. "Behave, old boy and we'll get along fine. I have to carry a load too, you know." Raz placed his hoof squarely on Tobias' foot. "Ow! Raz, get off!"

I laughed and thought Raz looked at Tobias as if to say, "I'm not old and I'm not a boy." Tobias piled on all the bundles and securely fastened them to Raz's harness.

"Hadia, it's time to leave. Or…you can change your mind and stay," Tobias said, teasing.

"I'm not staying, and nothing can stop me from going. I know I'm to make this journey. How about you? Do you still want to go?"

"Are you making mirth? This will be the journey of a lifetime. There's no stopping me either!"

We hastened back to the house. I stepped inside and stopped short. "Granna, what are you doing here?"

"Well me dear, I had a feeling you were leaving and wanted to give you me blessing. I have some honey bundles for you too."

Granna stretched out her frail arm and handed me a small package. "I hope you enjoy them," she said in a croaking voice, tottering backwards.

"What are honey bundles?" I asked.

"Stuffed dates. You put an almond into a date, dip it in honey, and then roll it in crushed nuts. There you have it, bundles from heaven, honey bundles."

I laughed. "Oh, you mean 'sweet lumps of delight'!" I held the sack to my nose. The aroma of sweet dates and honey made my mouth water. "Thank you, Granna."

"Here, Hadia, don't forget the map," Grandfather said, handing the body scroll to me. "Guard it well, wear it safely."

I reached for the stiff leather girdle and briefly studied the map. I opened my mantle and tied it snugly around my middle. "Thank you, Grandfather. I'll guard it with my life."

A momentary frown marred Grandfather's face. "No, don't guard it with your life; you're more valuable than the scroll. You are a pearl beyond price."

I'm a pearl beyond price? I wondered.

"Hadia, there's a legend I have never shared before. It seems there is a lost book of secrets. It hasn't been seen for generations. Perhaps you will have the good fortune to find it on your journey."

My brows knit into a frown. "A book of secrets? What's in the book of secrets?"

"No one seems to know," Grandfather answered.

Levi poked my shoulder and laughed. "It's a secret! Get it? Book of secrets."

Tobias drew in a sharp breath. "Maybe it tells of hidden treasure."

"One other thing," Grandfather said, "you must take these. You'll need them." He held out silver daggers.

"Grandfather, it's not custom for women to carry weapons," I protested, shrinking backward.

"Yes, I know, but I'm not sending you into the wilderness defenseless."

I stared cautiously at the threatening knives, and then reached for one. "Thank you, Grandfather." Carefully tucking the dagger inside my sash, I hoped I would never have to use it offensively. "Grandfather, you've never mentioned what dangers we may face. Why?"

"There's more to the journey than the destination. Facing the unexpected will cause you to call upon all of your integrity, all of your courage, and all of your sensibilities in time of danger and decisions. You'll be the better for it. You'll come home a different person; one you didn't know existed."

There's more to the journey than the destination?

"Now, let me give everyone my blessing. 'God, give them a hedge of protection, and let no peril touch them. Let them neither stay nor turn back before finishing the quest. Let undaunted courage diminish their doubt. So let it be.' "

I gave Grandfather a weak smile, opened the door, and stepped outside. A soft gray dove landed at my feet, cooed sweetly, and left as quickly as it had arrived. *I love doves.*

We set forward. Walking away, I heard Grandfather's voice.

"Hadia, bring back some branches from the Weeping Tree. Remember my prayer and trust God."

Trust God? Can I? I want to, but—

Trust Me—

I nodded and waved good-bye.

CHAPTER SIX

Sinkstreams

"Maybe I am putting others at risk."

I adjusted the bow and quiver of arrows on my back, taking notice of the silver sword swinging from Tobias' hip. We left town through the eastern, middle gate. O-No ran ahead barking. Raven glided gracefully above. The morning came bright.

We wound our way through Shepherd's Camp, past the lower road to En Gedi, and set out on the Old Forest Trail, edging our way towards the Euphrates River. A ferry would take us across the river and deliver us to the Cotter Plains. From there, we would have to ford the Lower Euphrates River without help. We crossed slender streams on the valley floor. Yellow and purple wild flowers snuggled deep in the grass. Occasional palm trees dotted the plains, waving like green umbrellas. A few ground squirrels surfaced from their dens, scolding the uninvited visitors.

The Euphrates River came into view. It flowed swiftly, leaping merrily down to embrace the Tigris River. Reeds and bushes along the bank murmured in conversation. A faint mist rose and curled above the gleaming water. Then I saw the ferry. It looked much too small to carry all of us. Two crossings would be needed. O-No barked furiously; Raz planted his hooves firmly in the dirt.

Tobias stroked Raz's neck. "I know what you're thinking Raz. It's not going to work. You're going across with us. You'll be fine. Trust me."

I laughed and thought the look on Raz's face seemed to say, "I don't know Tobias. How does he know I will be just fine? I will not go!"

A young lad with his scruffy, brown dog shouted, "Come aboard!" The hem of his white tunic was wet and dirty as well as his turban. His hands were red and raw from pulling on the rope. He was captain of his ship, if one could call a ferry a ship. Smiling broadly through broken teeth, he waved us on. I boarded the wobbly craft with Phares and O-No and waited for Tobias and Raz. Raz wouldn't budge.

"Boy," Tobias shouted, "take the ladies and the dog across, and then come back for me."

Nodding, the lad pulled the rope attached to an overhead rope, forcing the rickety ferry away from the bank. There wasn't much to hold on to, just a wobbly wooden railing. O-No slipped, slid across the wet, slimy deck, and crashed into Phares. She teetered back and forth. I screamed and grabbed her. "O-No, you almost knocked Phares into the river! Well, I suppose it wasn't your fault *this* time. The deck is slippery." Phares clung white knuckled to the railing.

I let go of Phares and decided to enjoy the crossing. I threw my head back and let the wind billow my hair like a lovely sail.

"What's wrong with you, Hadia? Don't you know the ferry could sink? We could all drown."

"Nonsense, Phares. We'll be fine."

Our little voyage was soon over. The ferry bumped into the bank and off we hopped. The brown, scruffy dog jumped off too. He scampered over to O-No, wagging his tail, hoping to play. O-No gave a brief sniff and trotted away. Looking indignant, the little brown dog turned back and leaped on the ferry. The lad pulled the rope again and drew it to the other side. I looked across the river and noticed Tobias in serious conversation with Raz.

Tobias pulled on Raz's rope. Raz wouldn't move. "Boy," Tobias shouted, "give me a hand with my donkey."

The lad jumped off the ferry and went behind Raz. He pushed while Tobias pulled. Raz wouldn't move. Finally, the lad picked up a slim reed.

Raz spotted the reed with a look that seemed to say, "I don't know what would be worse, a whipping or crossing the river." He put one hoof at a time on the ferry, swaying in rhythm with the churning water.

"I knew he could do it!" Tobias shouted.

The ferry pushed off, rolling and pitching. Raz spread all four legs to steady himself and brayed loudly. Soon, it bumped hard against the bank, lurching back and forth. Raz leaped high off the ferry and slid on the slippery bank, dragging Tobias.

"Whoa, slow down. It's all right, old boy." Turning to us he said, "I think he'll be fine now."

"Welcome to Cotter Plains," the lad announced.

"Boy, is one piece of silver enough for the crossing?" I asked.

"Eh, that be enough."

I handed the silver to the lad. "What can you tell us about Cotter Plains and the Frendyl Highlands?"

"There's not much to tell. A few tent people live on the Plains. The Frendyl Highlands are full of caves. King Og of Bashon mines silver, copper, and turquoise. Sometimes Shadows—the ghosts of giants—move in and guard them for their own. One never knows if a mine belongs to King Og or Shadows. It would not be wise to get close and find out. One might not return. Oh, sometimes there are lions and bears in the caves and water lizards in the rivers."

Phares' eyes opened wide. "I hope there's not more!"

"There could be. I hear tell there are man-eating plants, but I don't know if that be true. Be careful of sinkholes and sink-streams. Plains are full of them. Oh, and the Shayba bird—tall as a camel!"

"Eee!" Tobias croaked, "I thought you said there wasn't much to tell!"

"Oh dear," Phares moaned, biting her lower lip.

"Look, you two, we're on a mission and can't worry about the future. Let's carry on," I said cheerfully. I was grateful for the scattered crumbs of information warning us of possible danger.

"Now, what tidings do you bring from your land? What 'news' is there?" the lad asked.

I hastily told him who we were, where we were from, and about the disaster of impending war.

"Ah! That be grievous news. I pray they durst not come my way," he said.

"I hope they don't either," I replied. I turned and searched the sun-drenched plains. The land was silent except for a whispering breeze and a few cries of unseen birds. "We must take leave now."

The plains rose gently, advancing to the feet of the distant Frendyl Highlands. A circle of steamy fog floated above the peaks. Broom and locust trees dotted the plains. The sun continued mounting in the tender blue sky. *We could be at the Lower Euphrates River by late middle-day if we don't dawdle.* "Let's rest and eat before we go on."

"I'm ready," Phares answered.

O-No flopped on the cool grass. Raven glided effortlessly to the ground to glean crumbs. We ate dates and raisin cakes until full and content. Stretching out on my back, I squinted at fat, floating clouds.

Flocks of birds flew in sprays across the sky as hawks circled, surveying the strange creatures below. A huge land tortoise crawled by. Its neck craned high out of its helmet house, rising like a snake in the air. I thought it could observe snail trails and cat tracks from its view. Raven hopped on its back to hitch a ride.

"Yum, turtle soup," Tobias whooped.

"We don't have time to make soup. We need to leave," I said, standing up.

Refreshed and energized, we gathered our supplies and marched on. O-No ran eagerly ahead with his nose to the ground. Raven cawed, *"My name is Raven. Fly with me up high. There's joy in the sky."*

"Hadia," Tobias said, "your grandfather asked you to bring back branches from the Weeping Tree. What's the Weeping Tree?"

"It's a tree that grows at the entrance to the Garden of Eden," I answered.

"Why is it called the Weeping Tree?"

"When Eden was created, the branches grew upward. When Adam and Eve were banished from Eden, the tree wept, causing its limbs to droop to the ground. They have never raised their limbs since. Their leaves smell delicious."

"By founds, never heard of such a tree!"

"Listen," I said, abruptly. "Horses. Wild horses!"

The rumble of pounding horse hooves shook the ground. Dust clouds billowed; wild beauties of power, strength, and grace stampeded past us. In a flash of a moment, the horses were gone, leaving lonely, barren space. The land stilled once more.

"Someday, I'll have a horse and ride the world over," I announced, awestruck.

Tobias laughed. "Sure Hadia, like someday I'll fly."

"You'll see, Tobias—you'll see."

Limestone dust worked its way through the grass, giving way to a stretch of dry ground and then a sinkhole. Black-laced brine circled the round, rusty-orange crater. Steep sides thrust downward. I stepped in front of Phares and Tobias and stretched out my arms.

"Stay back—don't get too close! We don't know what danger lies in this hole."

"Eee!" Tobias cried, "I've never seen such a sight!"

Once again, Raz planted his hooves firmly on the ground. O-No stood at the edge, wildly spinning his tail in a circle, barking furiously. His bark echoed in the hole, which sounded like a barking enemy.

Phares laughed and handed Raz's lead rope to me. "There's not a dog down there O-No. That's you barking. Hadia, lead Raz awhile."

"Well, we can't stand here all day, we must keep moving," I said, taking hold of Raz's rope. I turned away from the menacing sinkhole, guiding the others carefully around it, and continued east. We hadn't traveled far when I felt water seeping into my sandals. The ground had become wet and spongy. The plains gave no indication of its treacherous devouring tombs—sinkstreams!

"Oh dear!" I cried, "my clothes are getting wet." Reaching down, I gathered my garments and pulled them above my knees. Flushing, Tobias turned his eyes away from my naked legs.

"Help! Help!" Phares called, waving her arms in the air. Water rushed and whirled around her, pulling her under. "Help me!"

"Sinkstream! Hadia, Get a rope, quick!" Tobias ordered.

I grabbed a rope from Raz's pack and rushed it to Tobias. "Tie the rope around Raz's neck. Hurry!" He threw the rope to Phares. It didn't begin to land near her.

"Help! God, help me!" Phares cried with terror in her voice.

Tobias drew the rope back, lifted it high, and threw it with all his might. It splashed close to her. She reached for it, but rushing water pushed it away. Her long dark hair swirled around her head as she barely bobbed above the water.

"Help me! Help me!"

Tobias threw the rope again. Phares grabbed it before the water snatched it away. "Hadia, lead Raz away. Hurry!" Tobias yelled, tugging on the rope.

"Raz, let's go!" I demanded.

Phares moved at a snail's pace through the churning water. Soon, she stumbled onto solid ground, falling in a soggy heap, coughing raggedly. Trembling, I ran to her and cradled her slippery body in my arms. "Phares, you're all right now—you're safe."

Phares answered in a hollow voice, "I shall always be in your way."

"You're not in my way. I love you and there's nothing you could do or say that would make me regret asking you to come. Besides, you couldn't help getting caught in a sinkstream. Let's get these wet clothes off before you get sick. Tobias, take a walk."

Phares changed into dry clothes. I threw the wet ones over Raz's back.

Maybe Phares is right, I thought. *Maybe I am putting others at risk just to satisfy my own selfish desires. Phares could have died. But what about Father's commission? Should we continue?*

"Hadia, I'm ready to leave," Phares said.

I searched the plains, and then turned and gazed from whence we came. I heard my voice waver. "I'm not sure we'll be going any farther. I'm afraid I have led us into perilous danger. I can't continue to put everyone at risk."

"Hadia, no. You vowed never to let anything or anyone stop you from finishing your mission. Remember Grandfather's prayer: *'Let them not turn back before finishing the quest.'* You must fulfill Father's Commission. It was his vision…now, it's your vision."

My grandfather's prayer was a fading memory and a distant promise. *Are faded memories to be trusted?* I hung my head and closed my eyes.

"*Let undaunted courage diminish their doubt. Let them not turn back before finishing the quest.*"

I opened my eyes and gazed across the land.

"We'll continue," I said.

CHAPTER SEVEN

O-No in the Hole

"Don't ever frighten us again. You may not be so fortunate next time."

We're almost there. I smell the water," I said, tilting my nose in the air.

"I hope this river isn't like the other river. I want no more ferry rides," Phares said.

"There you go again, Phares, always thinking the worst. Think good thoughts. It will help you overcome fear," I said, patting her back.

"I'll try." Her arms fell heavily to her sides.

"There's the river," Tobias called.

The Lower Euphrates River appeared more like a stream, probably not more than knee deep. It moved slowly, playfully, without deliberation. The river's bank revealed a rich mixture of palm trees, reeds, rushes, willows, and grasses. Quail and little brown birds fluttered about. It was a water source for the plains animals. Wild black and white donkeys and a strange, large beast punctured the mud, taking drink. The odd beast was rust in color with narrow yellow stripes. His boat paddle ears stuck out from his head below two horns that curved out and then in, somewhat like an oxen yoke.

Dark, low tents were pitched downstream. The silhouette of camels burned through the haze of the bright middle-day sun; some lying down, some milling around. Heavily cloaked men in tall, black turbans walked aimlessly about. Two men with two huge, black dogs broke rank and strode toward us.

"Uh-oh. Company," Tobias muttered. "I hope they're not trouble."

The massive dogs leaped out with hideous affray. They looked savage, powerful, and threatening. Pouches hung from wide, thick collars studded with silver spikes and turquoise stones. They did not dog-smile. O-No hid behind me. I fixed my eyes on the pouches. *What's in those pouches?*

The strangers approached slowly, palm staffs in hand, and stopped in front of Tobias. "Welcome to Cotter Plains. My name is Dathan, and this is my brother, Korah. We are nomads from the land of Nod. We are of the Canaanite Tribe. Who do you say you are?" They eyed us uncertainly, but it didn't make them any less threatening.

Piercing eyes squinted from sun-blackened faces as fierce as butcher birds. Frown lines carved deep into their leather-like skin. Black mustaches shadowed pursing, purple lips. Beak shaped noses and sharp beards thrust out like daggers. I wondered if the swarthy louts were trying to figure out where we were *really* going. I prayed Tobias wasn't going to speak amiss.

Tobias wiggled his foot in the sand and said with a thin-lipped smile, "I'm Tobias of the Bebe Tribe. This is Hadia and Phares of the Karka Tribe. We're going to deliver supplies to a friend."

I studied the menacing-looking men. There lingered some uneasy remembrance. *Are they the Destroyers who killed Father?*

"The sun is high; we must take leave," I said, in dread for ourselves.

"Yes, we must go," Tobias replied.

"Wait. Join us for nourishment and share 'the news.' Surely you don't want to go farther without food," Dathan said. The brutes looked more interested in breaking our necks than breaking bread.

"You are most gracious," I said, not swallowing their false courtesy. "We took eat a short time ago. We must continue."

Dathan's face tightened. "Very well."

"Farewell, friends. Blessed journey." Korah waved and walked away.

Tobias' eyes narrowed. "Hmm, blessed journey indeed. God's curse be upon them! They're up to no good. They are Destroyers or raiders. We'll have to cover our tracks. We won't be safe until well out of their sight."

"I didn't like the way they looked at us," I said warily. "Their eyes betray their hearts."

"I didn't like the way they smelled—like moldy blankets," Phares said.

A low growl rumbled from O-No. His tail stood straight out and the hair on his back bristled. He was not dog-smiling.

"See, even O-No is suspicious," Tobias said.

"Well, hems high," I said, lifting my tunic. I laughed and plunged my feet into the icy water and pushed across the river.

"Why does Hadia always laugh when it comes to crossing rivers?" I heard Phares ask Tobias. "I don't find it fun. Being cold, having wet clothes, and not knowing what might grab my feet does not leave me happy."

O-No barked loudly and leaped into the water. He didn't seem to mind getting wet. He acted like he enjoyed it.

The great and terrible wilderness stretched out before us in gloomy grandeur. Massive, rugged mountains composed of tiers of red, gray, and black granite cut deep gorges to the north and south. A spine of forested sandstone and shale hills flanked the limestone plains, honeycombed with caves and more sinkholes. Sunshine and shadows fell over the land. Silence surrounded us as we marched on.

I turned to Tobias and grinned. "Well, Tobias, that was quite a story you told the nomads."

"By founds, I couldn't let on what we're doing. Those ne'er-do-wells would follow us if they knew where we were going. I wasn't 'bout to let that happen. I hope you aren't mad I sorta lied."

"What do you mean 'sorta' lied?"

"We aren't bringing supplies. That's my lie. Had to tell something. Hope you won't hold it against me."

I shook my head and laughed. "Of course not. I thought you were clever to come up with such a believable story on short notice."

"I don't want to lie anymore. It will be hard, but paths have been straightened before and so will mine. What I learned not in my youth, I will learn in my old age. Now is a good time to start."

"Tobias, I'm proud of you. When did you decide to do this?"

"While in En Gedi, you asked if I was the town liar. I said, 'yes.' You were pleased I told the truth. You accepted my word as sacred. Never before have I been told my word was sacred. It was then I made up my mind to change my lying ways. I don't want to disgrace you, Phares, or myself anymore."

I giggled. "By founds!"

Tobias laughed. "Eee! Now you sound like me!"

The Old Forest Trail was fading, but visible. Small shrubs and thorny acacia trees sprang up. Quails whirled in the air, startling everyone. In the distance, jackals tearing at a carcass fought over middle-day food, breaking the silence.

Smudges of grays, greens, and brown colored the Frendyl Highland as it rose gently before us. Little streams twisted back and forth across the Old Forest Trail, sometimes swerving around pockets of marsh. At times the trail felt spongy. We were still in the land of sinkholes and sinkstreams. Occasionally Raz balked, nose to the ground, testing it with pawing hooves. I trusted Raz's intuition. He was stubborn, but he wasn't dumb.

"Look out, there's another sinkhole!" Tobias warned, stopping short.

The cavernous hole was much larger than the first one. The sides sloped gently outward, narrowing as it plunged deep into the ground. It was black, slimy and looked bottomless.

"O-No, stay back. You're getting too close!" I shouted.

Paying little heed, he peered closer, barking. Scrambling to catch himself, he slid on loose gravel. He yelped a terrifying cry as the edge gave way. Tobias rushed once again for the rope. He fashioned a noose and swung it toward O-No's head.

"No—missed!" Tobias cried. He swung again, barely looping it around O-No's neck. "Help me pull the rope!"

Phares and I grabbed the rope and pulled. I prayed we wouldn't strangle him. Soon it was over; O-No finally lay safely at my feet. His deep, gentle eyes bulged and his tongue gaped from his mouth as he lay quivering on the ground. Black dirt ground into his short, creamy coat. He was quite a sight!

"You're safe now, O-No. You'll be all right," Tobias said, hugging the shaken dog.

"O-No, don't ever frighten us again! You may not be so fortunate next time you get into trouble," I said sternly. "Just do your job. Warn us of danger and we'll make a great team."

O-No stood, shook his body vigorously and gave a big dog-smile. It was impossible to stay angry with my loveable, clumsy dog. Wagging his long, slim tail, his soft brown eyes pleaded forgiveness. I threw my arms around his neck and hugged him. "Yes, I still love you. All right everyone, up we go."

I am no more
But gone before
I'll meet you
There
By the
Garden Gate
I am no more
But gone before
Bring the key and
Don't be late

Phares

CHAPTER EIGHT

Uninvited Visitor

"I felt eyes watching me, though I saw no one."

The blazing sun advanced slowly across a cloudless sky as we moved closer to the Frendyl Highland. Earlier smudges of color now became gray boulders, brown shrubs, and green trees. Mists of pink and white blossoming flowers drifted among foliage.

Quork! Quork! Omens of good and ill flew overhead. Spiraling up on a thermal, they polished the wind with corkscrew dives and backward loops. Hurtling earthward, they rode the wind with outspread wings. The bearers of truth were the mischiefs of the skies.

"Look! Ravens!" I shouted. "What do you think our Raven makes of them?"

Raven rode on my shoulder, staring at his kind, and then flew into the sky, racing after the winged tumblers. They flew together, making it hard to tell Raven from the other birds. He pulled away, landed back on my shoulder and cawed, *"Tinkers!" Quork! Quork!*

"Oh, Raven, thank heaven you didn't leave us. All right, everyone, we're making good time. We can still cover a goodly distance before dark."

"Yes, if we don't meet any more encounters of the awful kind," Phares replied, glancing over her shoulder.

"Phares, you can be so doubtful, I do declare!" I snapped.

"What do you mean 'doubtful'? I almost drowned and O-No almost died. I don't think that's being doubtful. That's frightful!"

"I know, but look—you came through it safely and O-No was saved. That should leave you feeling hopeful. Try, Phares. I know you can."

Phares took a deep breath and sighed. "I just need more courage."

"To have courage, you have to do something courageous," Tobias said.

"What do you mean, Tobias?" Phares asked.

"Once you've done something courageous, you'll be filled with courage. You'll be lionhearted, stalwart, unflinching. Never again will you be a coward. You'll see."

"How can I hope to do something courageous?"

"You must have faith. You have been brave by taking this journey. That's an act of courage, and of love."

"Stalwart...lionhearted...eh, sure," Phares murmured.

We stopped and removed our packs for a rest. O-No flopped in the shade of a wild olive tree and stretched out. Sighing deeply, his eyelids fluttered. He was soon asleep. We portioned our food, being careful not to eat too much in one sitting. Raven pecked at the ground, looking for leftovers.

"Tobias, have you heard of a white raven called Leuce?" I asked. "I've been told it's pure white."

"Yes, I've heard of such a raven. They say it flies above the Falcon Hills. Sometimes it carries jewels, often dropping them."

"That's the story I have heard. I wonder if we'll see it. To follow it might lead to the treasure."

"To keep up with it would be impossible, but Raven could. He could lead us to the treasure. By founds, wouldn't that be something!" Tobias said, grinning.

"Dream on, Tobias. I doubt that would ever happen," Phares said dryly.

"Phares, there you go again. Your memory is as short as a bee's stinger. I thought you promised to start exercising faith."

"Well, I did, but—all right, if I see Leuce, I'll believe there's a treasure to be found."

"Ha! That remains to be seen," Tobias cackled.

"Come on you two, up we go," I commanded.

O-No leaped to his feet at the words "up we go." Everyone followed single file through light and shadows. A sweet-smelling breeze stirred the air. The only sound heard was feet crunching leaves on the forest floor.

A raucous chorus of birds fluttered in the bushes, scampering for wild berries. Trees and shrubs multiplied into dense thickets. The Old Forest Trail narrowed, curving, taking on a new look. Tree limbs reached out, scratching arms and poking eyes. Miniature rabbits darted about startling everyone.

Something caught my attention. I stopped walking and stood riveted to the ground. "Phares, Tobias, I believe someone is following us."

"What makes you think so?" Phares wanted to know.

"Every once in a while, I hear a noise. When we stop walking, the noise stops."

"Maybe it's an echo. Maybe it's us," Tobias said.

"No, I don't think so. Somebody is following us. Look, O-No's hair is standing up and Raven is chattering more than usual. We're in danger."

"Oh, Hadia, it's probably just your imagina—"

"See? You hear it too."

"Eee, how do we find out who's following us?" Tobias whispered, looking around.

"You two go ahead. Keep walking as though we're not suspicious. Keep O-No with you. I'll stay behind and see who the culprit is," I replied.

"Oh, no! What if it's the Destroyers?" Phares asked, biting her lower lip.

"Phares, quit worrying, Tobias is with you. Hurry, we must not appear watchful."

Phares scowled at me, and then moved slowly ahead, placing each foot quietly in front of the next, following Tobias.

I crouched low and waited for the unknown. *Who could be following? Maybe it's Destroyers. Maybe the two from Cotter Plains. What could they possibly want? We don't have anything of value—or do we? The map. Maybe they want the map! But, how do they know of the map?*

Gazing upward, my eyes followed busy ants scurrying over knotty fists thrust out of a scaly tree trunk. Silence broke the air as a muster of crows scolded each other. Dappled light winked at the forest floor.

What will I do if someone is following us? How am I going to get to Phares and Tobias without being seen? Breaking branches cracked the air. Crouching low, I watched. Seconds passed, more seconds, more crackling.

"Oh, I can't believe it. It's only a wild pig!"

A grunting pink pig waddled into view, wiggling its curly tail. Its pudgy snout rooted the forest floor. Stopping a moment, it stared at me with cold green eyes. I felt an evil presence and smelled a putrid odor. I wanted to flee. I turned around and ran as fast as I could to the others.

"Tobias, Phares—stop!"

"Hadia, did you see anyone?" Tobias asked, turning around.

"No, not someone, but something. It was a wild pig and it looked evil."

"Pig! They have knowledge of past lives. It could tell us plenty."

"Oh, for heaven sake, Tobias, you're foolish to believe such nonsense," I retorted.

"Well, at least it wasn't someone. Now, we're safe," Phares said, sighing.

"Not entirely. We must be on guard all the time. I still think we're being followed. And, that pig! There was something about it that chilled my bones."

"Oh dear, all of this scares me."

"Look at it this way, Phares. Here's your chance to practice faith in action," Tobias said. "Remember, your strength for courage is within. If you pray, why worry? If you worry, why pray?"

"OK, you two, the day is almost gone," I said, moving ahead. "Let's keep going." I looked over my shoulder to make sure we weren't being followed.

A huge, horny-skinned lizard with a razor-ridge back scurried across my path. Its long, broad tail dragged on the ground. Fat legs with large, widespread, clawed feet were ready to grasp anything that moved. The sun hung low, ready to kiss the edge of the earth.

The Frendyl Highland is so close; I can almost touch it, I thought. *Maybe on the morrow we'll see the infamous silver, copper, and turquoise mines riddling the slopes. Perhaps we'll put an end to Shadow's ghost stories—or confirm them.*

I turned and looked back once more. I shuddered. The horny-skinned lizard glared at me in stony silence. I listened. I heard nothing. I felt eyes watching me, though I saw no one.

I strode the Forest Trail on a bright
And sunny day
I laughed and played and sang
And danced—hey, hey, hey!
I strode the Forest Trail on a dark
And cloudy day
I laughed and played and sang
And danced—hey, hey, hey!

Tobias

CHAPTER NINE

Dragon Bird and Shadow Ghosts

"This is our cave. Leave now, while you're still alive."

Morning came, pale. Piteous doves cooed gently, awaking me. My hand twitched sending dust flying into my nostrils. I sneezed ferociously and grabbed my side. *Oooo, that hurt.*

O-No had been curled up tight against me until my sneeze sent him scurrying. I lay still, opening my eyes only enough to squint into the thicket. Tiny birds hopped around, scratching and pecking, fluttering deeper into the bushes. A large cobweb sparkled, deceiving its prey. I rolled over.

"Heavenly Father, here I am. Hadia. Forgive my sins. May this day be fortunate, that we not see evil. Help me to trust You so that I might find strength and courage to complete this journey. So let it be," I whispered.

I sat up and yelled, "Wake up, everyone! Wake up!"

"All right, all right," Phares grumbled.

"By founds, I'll be ready to leave soon. I can't wait to get going," Tobias said, folding his blankets.

"Oh Tobias, don't sound so happy. Your cheeriness so early in the morn clangs like a bell in my ears," Phares complained.

"Look who's talking. Your constant worrying clangs in my ears too."

"I don't worry all the time."

"There you two go again. We don't need to start the day arguing. Now both of you apologize or we aren't leaving," I snapped.

Tobias grumbled. "I didn't start it."

"I don't care who started it. Apologize, or we aren't going."

"All right, I'm sorry. I take back my words."

Phares shot a sideways glance, looked down, and muttered, "I'm sorry."

"Good. Now I'll give my face a wake-up call," I said, walking toward the stream.

"Wake-up call?" Tobias questioned.

"She's going to splash her face with water," Phares replied, wrinkling her nose.

I leaned over a small pool of water at the side of the stream. Looking intensely at my reflection, my eyes locked eyes with the ones staring back. *Yes, it's still me. But who am I?* Gathering the icy water in the hollow of my hands, I drank deeply.

The water escaped between my fingers and dribbled down my chin. I splashed my face with water, and then I rose, wiping the dripping water with the sleeve of my tunic. I kneeled down again and peered into the water. *Strange, where's my reflection?* Sighing, I stood and turned to return to the others.

"Hadia, come back, and I'll tell you who you are."

I jerked to a halt. *Did I hear someone?* I looked all around. I saw no stranger.

"Come back, and I'll tell you who you are."

Who's calling me?

Slowly, I returned to the water. "Come closer," a voice echoed.

I kneeled down and peered into the water. The face of a woman came forth. She was lovely. Piercing blue eyes looked intently at me. Long golden hair floated in gentle waves around her face. Her skin was ivory white, her mouth delicate. She spoke sweetly, like a child. I stared long and hard at her.

"Who are you?" I asked in awe.

Her mouth curled into a smile. "I am Ara-Belle. I am God's messenger. You are Hadia, a woman of great courage, but you are not at peace. Bitter roots of revenge and unforgiveness choke you. Take inventory—examine your heart. You will not change until you surrender. In time, you will reap sweet fruit; your reward will be great. Seek God—ask Him to give you a heart of flesh. Turn not a deaf ear to this message, but let it be your passion at hand. Then you will not ask yourself, 'who am I?' "

I wiped my chin and closed my mouth. *Take inventory?* Truth pierced my heart. The water lady's face bobbed up and down in the current. Her hair swirled around her face. She searched my eyes.

"I...I...I'll remember your message," I said lamely.

She laughed lightly. "Good. I'll remind you along the way."

You'll remind me? I started to ask her how that can be when she disappeared.

"Ara-Belle, Ara-Belle. Where are you? Come back!"

Faint laughter drifted away.

I grabbed my shawl as a gust of wind caught it. The wind swirled through the camp. It grew fierce. A long, piercing scream pounded my ears. It was coming nearer and nearer.

"Run!" I screamed. Grabbing Raz and O-No, we ran deep into the thicket, crouched low, and craned our heads upward, searching the sky.

"Raz, lie down," I demanded, tapping his legs. O-No bared his teeth and growled. "O-No, stop! We must be quiet."

A giant Dragon Bird flew overhead, screaming and scanning the forest floor. Its brilliant orange body shone like a massive fireball. Wings as wide as the length of a horse flapped vigorously, creating sucking whirlwinds as its lizard-like tail navigated it. Its long neck swayed back and forth, carrying a huge head with an enormous mouth filled with jaw-crushing teeth. It exhaled a fiery breath of stinking smoke. Long ostrich-like legs with V-shaped feet dangled. Its long talons clawed the air.

Scarcely daring to breathe, my eyes went wide. Droplets of sweat beaded my forehead. A wave of cold fear swept over me. *We could all be gathered in one swallow if seen or heard. We mustn't move.*

The fiery creature hovered above our heads, whipping hot wind onto the forest floor with its massive wings. It quickly swooped down and screamed. I felt the blood drain from my face. I froze, praying we hadn't been discovered. Slowly, it edged toward us, exhaling its smelly smoke.

I don't know how long I can keep quiet. The smoke is suffocating me. Unable to hold back, I coughed. The Dragon Bird stopped short, cocked its head, and with piercing eyes, fixed them on our little huddle. He readied to pounce upon us.

Without warning, a black haze streaked in front of the monster's head, diverting him. It flew back and forth, back and forth. We ran, seeking safety in a nearby cave. Reaching the mouth of the cave, I turned to see Raven.

"Oh no! Raven! Come quick—into the cave!" I cried.

Raven turned to escape when the demon's claw clipped a bit of his wing, hurling him to the ground.

"We must help him!" Phares shouted.

Raz ran out braying. O-No barked. We yelled and waved our arms frantically, trying to distract the Dragon Bird. O-No dashed around some bushes and crawled low to the ground, edging his way toward Raven.

"God, please, don't let them get caught," I pleaded.

A blast of hot wind blew up in the face of the Dragon Bird, blinding him just long enough for O-No to grab Raven. Turning tail, O-No ran with Raven and streaked into the cave. Everyone followed. The narrow passageway prevented the Dragon Bird's entry.

Shaking and exhausted, we fell down to catch our breath. Raz shook like a lone leaf in high wind. I could feel O-No's heart racing as I embraced him.

"We're safe now," Tobias said. "Let's take a look at your hurt, Raven."

Tobias looked him over carefully and said, "It's only a slight scratch. I'll find some cobwebs to cover your wound. Your injury will heal in no time. In the meanwhile, you should ride on someone's shoulder."

Quork! Quork!

"Look," I said, "we'll have to stay here awhile. We must make sure the Dragon Bird has gone for good. We can't take any chances." *But, are we safe in here,* I wondered.

Cold air eddied out from deep within the cinder black cave. Sticky cobwebs dangled from the ceiling and the wet, craggy walls. Dampness draped like a morning mist, leaving everyone shivering. The light outside the cave enticed us to leave, but it wasn't safe yet. We would have to wait.

"I wonder where this cave leads," Tobias said, with a twinkle in his eye.

"I don't know and I don't want to go looking to find out," Phares answered.

"I knew you wouldn't be interested. Too scary for you," Tobias teased.

I ignored their cutting remarks as I listened to a dreadful sound. "Shhh…listen."

Raz's ears twitched back and forth, and he snorted. O-No stood still, cocked his head, and perked up his ears. His hair stood straight up and he did not dog-smile. No one moved. Discordant cries broke the silence—pitiful cries. Our hiding place was safe no more.

A thick and dreadful fog closed around us. Terrifying noises grew loud as grim-faced phantoms flew towards us, wielding weapons. A choking stench caught my breath short. Shadows—ghosts!

Raz reared, knocking Tobias down. O-No growled furiously, snapping at the Shadows. I was frantic. *Where can we escape? If we go outside, the Dragon Bird could be lying in wait. If we stay, who knows what will happen? How do we defend ourselves from something seemingly transparent and yet, armed? It's like trying to fight the wind.*

"This is our cave," a guttural tongue voiced. "Leave now, while you're still alive, or stay and die!" Ghosts swirled around and around, waving their weapons.

"Are you Shadows, ghosts of the Nephilim Giants?" I asked in a cracked, shaky voice.

"Yes, we are Shadows, guardians of the mine."

"We can't leave yet. We are hiding from a Dragon Bird. It may still be outside. We come in peace. Please, let us stay a short while. We won't take or bother anything—we promise."

The monstrous ghosts, echoing their eerie songs and swinging their weapons, burst into boisterous guffaws. "Do you really think we believe you? Humans lie and steal."

"Not all humans. We don't lie or steal!" Phares cried, stamping her feet.

"Prove it."

"Oh dear, what can I tell it?" Phares muttered. "Well, instead of taking something of yours, we'll add a treasure to your cave."

"What do you have to offer?" the Shadow asked in an unearthly voice.

I stared at Phares. *How is she going to keep that vow?*

"Well, let's see. Uh...I...Oh, yes. I have it! We'll either leave Tobias' gold ring or the gold talisman Granna gave Hadia. Yes, that's it."

"Wait a minute! I get my gold ring back after the journey. That was our agreement," Tobias protested, stepping forward.

"Phares, Granna gave us the talisman for protection. We are to return it when we get home," I cried. The choking stench scorched my throat. The Shadows whirled their weapons in the air.

"Hiss...sss...sss," gravelly voices echoed. "Make up your minds. We will accept your offer, but you must be quick."

"If we leave a treasure, may we have it back on our way home?" Phares asked.

"No! That's not part of the bargain," hissed a Shadow.

"Tobias, Hadia, what shall we do? If we don't give them something, we'll have to leave now."

"We'll leave now," I replied resolutely.

"What about the Dragon Bird? What if it's still out there? We can't outrun it."

"Let's take a vote. We go and take our chance, or we stay and give a gold piece to the Shadows. What do you say?" I asked.

"There are treasures that give you no profit, and there are treasures that repay you double. The only profit you receive by giving the gold piece, is safety—maybe. Leaving and taking our gold pieces repays us double. We have the gold pieces *and* our freedom. God will protect us," Tobias said. "Hands up if you agree!"

After a tense moment, I warily raised my hand; Phares did the same.

"Have it your way. Leave, while you can!" hissed a Shadow, swinging its weapon.

Ghoulish sounds echoed against the chamber walls. Stench burned my nose and throat. Peering cautiously outside, we emerged into the refreshing air and light of day, anxious to escape the Shadows, lest they change their minds and kill us.

CHAPTER TEN

The Hitchhiker

"I told you we're being followed. I feel it in my bones."

S quirrels foretell warnings," Tobias said as a few scurried by. "Maybe they're warning us of danger."

I scowled. "Tobias, you're so superstitious. Whoever taught you that silliness?" I asked.

"'Tisn't superstition—'tis true; you'll see."

"I hope we won't. I can't stand any more awful encounters."

We hurried towards the Old Forest Trail, cautiously looking around. Still on edge, I expected to see the Dragon Bird, but it was nowhere in sight.

"Let's sing the Forest Trail Song," Tobias said cheerfully.

"I don't know that song. How goes it?" I asked.

"I'll play the music first on my whistle stick." Putting the whistle to his mouth, he played a sweet melody. "Now, here are the words: 'I strode the Forest Trail on a bright and sunny day. I laughed and played and sang and danced, hey, hey, hey. I strode the Forest Trail on a dark and cloudy day. I laughed and played and sang and danced, hey, hey, hey.' Let's all sing and dance."

Phares complained. "Maybe we shouldn't. It would alert the Dragon Bird."

"Phares, you can't live in fear all the time. Sometimes we must take risks."

And so we danced down the trail, singing sweetly off key, ringing in concert, "Hey, hey, hey...."

The Old Forest Trail widened and straightened out a bit. Soon, we came to a dilapidated, mossy footbridge crossing a wide creek. Splashes of water showered thickets clustered with wild sweet berries. Musky herbs and mushrooms grew around the base of resin-scented trees. The air was intoxicating. O-No and Raz rushed to the water and drank deeply.

"Let's pick berries and mushrooms," I said, "then we can eat and take rest."

It wasn't long before we had more than enough food. "I'm ready to stop picking. I have enough berries for an army," I said, holding up my mantle of fruit.

"I think I have enough herbs and mushrooms for everyone," Tobias hollered from across the creek. We gathered together on a grassy bank and sat down to eat.

"Yum," Phares said, "these berries are wonderful." Shoving more of them into her mouth than it could hold, brilliant blue juice escaped, dripping and staining her lips.

I giggled. "I do declare, Phares, you look silly. Your teeth are as blue as the sky."

"The mushrooms are delicious too," Tobias said.

We passed around raisin cakes and stretched out to rest. I was just about asleep when Raz brayed fiercely. O-No growled. His ears and hair stood straight up.

"Now, what's going on?" Phares asked, looking over her shoulder.

"I told you we're being followed. I feel it in my bones," I whispered. "Let's cross the creek and hide in the thicket. Quick!"

We all ran except O-No. He stood gazing on point, back from whence we came. All at once he bounded back down the trail, barking.

"No! O-No, come back!" I called. "Tobias, go after him!"

"Am I thy foot-runner? What if there's danger? Do I give my life for a dog?" Sighing deeply, Tobias hastened to follow O-No.

"See, Phares? That's courage," I said.

"That's foolish!" Phares replied.

I felt a shudder of doom and held tightly to Raz's rope. I didn't want him to get away. Time passed slowly. I was beginning to wonder if we would ever see Tobias and O-No again.

"Where's Tobias?" Phares' question hung in the air.

Only twittering birds answered. Time dragged, and then I heard a faint sound, like voices. I strained my ears for clues. Then, there they were: Tobias, O-No, *and* Levi!

"By founds, I was right," Tobias said, as he came into view. "The squirrels did warn us of something." "I told you so" was written all over his face.

"What in the world? Levi, it's you who's been following us! You've really gone and done it this time," I scolded. "You could have gotten lost or kidnapped. And what about Grandfather? Does he know where you are?"

"I told Granna what I was doing and asked her to let Grandfather know where I was. She tried to stop me. Don't be mad at her."

"Oh dear, this complicates the journey. Levi, I'm disappointed. You have disobeyed Grandfather, not to mention that he'll be worried sick. We'll have to have Raven take him a message letting him know of your safe arrival."

I found my writing stick and paper and scribbled a message. I then attached it to Raven's leg. "Raven, home! Levi, has anyone seen you?" I asked.

"Yes, a couple of nomads down by the Lower Euphrates River."

"Eee!" Tobias groaned.

"Did they ask any questions?"

"They asked who I was and where I was going. I told them my name and said I was catching up with my family."

"Did they ask anything else?"

"They asked if we were delivering supplies to a friend. I told them no."

"Uh-oh. That's worrying news," Tobias muttered.

"Why, what did I do wrong?"

"You didn't do anything wrong, but those men are not to be trusted. We believe they could be Destroyers out to do us harm. After talking to you, they probably suspect we're hiding something. From now on, we're going to have to be more careful than ever," I warned.

Levi's lower lip trembled. "I'm sorry. I didn't mean to get you into trouble. I only wanted to be with you and have fun. I'm sorry, I'm sorry." Burying his face in shaking hands, a mass of bright red hair tumbled forward.

"Well, you're here now. We'll just make the best of it. Please follow orders so everyone will be safe, all right?"

Levi looked up. Tears streamed from his watery brown eyes. Scattered brown spots dotted his flush cheeks. "I will, I promise. I won't cause any trouble."

"I do declare," I said, "it looks like we've grown into quite a troop! From now on, we shall call ourselves the Troop. We're running behind. We must make haste. I suggest we depart from the Forest Trail for a while so the Destroyers will lose our tracks. It might be rough going, but we'll manage. Let's go!"

And so we went—all four of us.

CHAPTER ELEVEN

People-eating Plants

"You below, watch where you go. You below, watch where you step."

The warm blue dome of the Frendyl Highland receded behind a helmet of clouds. A mass of trees grew out of the trunk of an ancient, mammoth tree. Thick pads of moss embraced its limbs. Scrubland of berries, ferns, and wild ginger clung to the cleft of the forest trees. I gazed at slugs inching along the moist forest floor. *They should be grateful Raven isn't around.*

We veered off the trail and descended deep into the hushed green tangle. Tobias and Levi led the way, swinging staffs, swords and stomping the ground to clear the path. O-No forged ahead, his long nose sniffing the air, his keen eyes searching for critters. He was always game to chase a rabbit or two. Phares and I brought up the rear leading Raz, peering over our shoulders from time to time, making sure no one was following.

I turned my attention to Levi when I heard him say to Tobias, "I can't believe I'm traveling this long-awaited journey. Of course it would have been better if I had had permission from the beginning. No matter, I'm here, and facing Grandfather is another world away."

My heart skipped a beat. I stopped abruptly and listened hard. Tobias' and Levi's voices droned as Phares whistled. Then, out of the corner of my eye, I caught a fleeting glimpse of two men. A chill ran through me. *I need to warn the Troop.* Rushing to Phares, I grabbed her arm. "Phares, I saw two men. Hurry, we must hide," I whispered.

Brushing aside Raz, I crowded between Tobias and Levi. "We're being followed. Over here—quick—behind the bushes." Crouching low, we sat motionless, holding our breath.

"Shh, O-No, don't growl," I said sternly. "It's all right, I know someone's out there."

Two shadowy figures passed, stopping once to turn around and gaze. They were like jackals, sniffing the air for prey. Then they vanished soundlessly, leaving me visibly shaken. *Why didn't their dogs detect us?*

"By founds, I will put a curse on them!" Tobias muttered, throwing his head cloth on the ground.

Phares snorted. "Oh no, there you go again with your superstitions. Your curse won't work."

Tobias picked up his head cloth and pulled a tent peg from his tunic. "I'll drive a stake into their footprints. It will cause them to be lame," he said, walking away.

"I did it," Tobias said. "I pounded the peg in the ground where they walked. In a little while, their legs will be full of sharp pains. Walking will be a curse."

"Dear Tobias, I know you mean well. But superstitious acts work about as well as carrying water in a sieve. Neither holds substance," I scolded, shaking my head.

"We'll see," Tobias smirked.

The sighting of the Destroyers flattened my joy in our search for Eden. Since we had grown to four, we were more conspicuous, making travel challenging.

"Maybe we can return to the trail since the Destroyers are ahead of us," Levi said.

"Not yet. It's too soon. We'll stay off the trail a little longer," I replied.

I gazed at Levi's blood-red cape draped over his shoulders. His white tunic dragged the ground. A bow and quiver of arrows hung from his shoulder. A long silver sword— an important symbol of manhood—dangled from his waist. It had belonged to Father. A shofar hung around his neck. He looked prepared to do battle if necessary. It mattered not to him he was only ten ages old. I knew his desire for adventure dampened any fear of danger.

I heard Levi asking Tobias dozens of questions, Tobias embellishing his answers.

"Rabbits," Tobias said. "Did you know if you eat rabbit you'll gain speed, and if you eat gazelle you'll gain strength?"

Levi looked amazed. "Really? Then we had better eat both of them, because we need all the speed and strength we can get to make this journey."

I thought Levi had finally met his match. His riddles were as silly as Tobias' mirth and superstitions.

The day lingered as the sun shone bright, curving ever so slowly downward.

Rustling tree branches sounded like whispering voices as a breeze swayed through the forest. For a moment I thought I understood them: "You below watch where you go. You below watch where you step."

Wonder what that means? I thought. *Now not only do I have to look where I go, but now I have to look where I step. Is the ground going to turn into sinking sand and suck us in? What are the trees warning?*

"Phares, wait a minute. I heard the trees whispering. They said, 'You below, watch where you go. You below, watch where you step.' I think the trees are warning us of danger. Tobias, Levi, stop." I gulped deep breaths as I repeated my information.

"By founds, if it isn't one thing, it's another!" Tobias thundered.

Levi's eyes flashed as he raised his sword in the air. "I'm not afraid."

"Look, your mightiness, we don't have to be afraid, but we do need to be alert. From now on, everything is suspect," I replied.

We warily pressed forward, eager to return to the trail. Ducking under low-lying limbs, our eyes searched the ground, looking for anything suspicious.

O-No ran ahead, nose to the ground, sniffing for critters to chase. He loved a good race. He excelled at speed. He could bring down a gazelle as quickly as a lightening bolt. He wandered over to an odd plant.

Green stems arched waist high, balancing yellow, hollow horns filled with water. The plants looked like cobras rising out of the ground. Stiff bristles pointed ominously toward the sweet water. Curiosity took hold. O-No stuck his nose in one and started to lap the sticky water.

Snap! In a blink of an eye, the leaves swept together, interlocking tightly. O-No yelped frantically and tried to pull out his nose.

"Everyone, open the leaves," Tobias shouted.

We grabbed the leaves and pulled and tugged to no avail. Tightly and more tightly the leaves squeezed with an unrelenting grip.

"Pull hard!" I screamed. "He won't be able to breathe much longer."

Raz walked over, chewed the stem in half and looked at everyone as if to say, "Why didn't you do that?"

Immediately, the leaves relaxed enough to force them open. O-No flew back on his haunches and shook his head.

"O-No, are you all right?" I asked, shaken. O-No sat still for a few seconds. Then he leaped up and gave everyone a wide dog-smile.

"O-No, thank heaven you're all right. There you go again getting into trouble. Will you ever learn?" Phares scolded.

"That's why he was named O-No. When he was young, he was forever getting into mischief. We were always saying, 'Oh no!'" Levi said, grinning.

"Well, he better be changing his ways, or he's going to get *us* all in a lot of trouble," Tobias complained.

"All right everyone, let's keep moving," I said.

Eyeing the snake plants cautiously, O-No skirted far around them, trotting ahead through the dewy undergrowth.

The ground glistened with hundreds of tiny jewel-like flowers. Ruby-tipped tentacles waved in the middle, with droplets glistening temptingly on the leaves. Innocent looking, they belied their hazard.

"Oooh, look at these beautiful shiny flowers!" Phares said, reaching down to touch them. "Oh! Help!" she cried.

Forceps-strength leaves closed like a spring-trap, imprisoning her hand inside the man-eating plant. Gluey threads stuck and wrapped tightly around her fingers.

"Help me, help me!"

I ran toward her, but the sparkling beauties snatched my feet. "Help, Tobias, I'm stuck!"

"Stay still," Tobias said.

"Stay still?" I answered. "Just where do you think I'm going?"

"Stay back, O-No or you'll get stuck too." Tobias quickly looked around and spied the tent cloth on Raz's back, but Raz was between the plants and him. "Raz, come close, but don't step on the plants."

I knew Raz was only a donkey, but prayed God would help him understand. Raz stood and stared. Then he moved forward ever so slightly.

"Good boy. Now just stay there." Tobias thrust his staff out as far as he could, trying to grasp the tent cloth. "Move just a little, watch the plants—don't step on them." Raz did as commanded. Tobias tried again, this time touching the cloth.

"How am I going to get the cloth off with a rope holding it down?"

"Tobias, what are we going to do? We're going to die here, I just know it!" Phares complained.

"Phares, this is not the time to give up. Pray hard. Exercise that seed of faith—for all of us."

Exasperated, Tobias poked and pushed the tent cloth to no avail. "I don't know how I'm going to get that cloth off Raz."

Quork! Quork!

"Raven, you're back! Keep off the shiny plants, they'll devour you," Tobias warned. "Untie the rope on Raz. Hurry!"

Quork! Quork!

I struggled to pull my feet from the gluey plant; they wouldn't budge.

"Don't worry. God will get us out of this somehow," Levi said in a reassuring voice.

"Well, He'd better hurry. I don't think I can last much longer in this twisted position," I replied.

Raven poked and pulled on the rope. Finally, it loosened a bit. Tobias pushed the tent cloth with his staff, moving it slightly. He pushed the cloth a little more. He then hooked a corner and pulled it to him.

"Raven, if we get out of here alive, I'll dig you a huge batch of worms," Tobias promised. Gathering all the muster he could, he swung the tent cloth hard. It floated down, landing wide over the plants with a soft thud.

"Phares, I'll help you first."

"Hurry Tobias, I'm faint with dizziness!"

Stepping gingerly on the squishy tent cloth, Tobias bent over and hacked the leaves with his dagger. *Pop! Pop!* "There you go, Phares. You're free."

"Oh, Tobias—thank you!" Phares said, with a sigh of relief.

"OK, it's your turn, Hadia." Tobias then went to Levi. Levi was laughing.

"Why are you laughing? This isn't funny. We could have all died a slow death," Tobias said crossly.

"Well, we might as well laugh. We're not dead. We cheated death."

Everyone looked at each other and soon grins spread across our faces.

"Raz, you've been a good old boy," Tobias said, patting the donkey's fuzzy neck. I thought Raz looked at Tobias as if to say, "I'm not a boy! You're driving me crazy with that good-old-boy talk."

We had lost a lot of time. I wanted to continue as soon as possible. "Let's get back on the trail."

"Good riddance you little man-eaters," Tobias said, sneering at the deceptive plants.

CHAPTER TWELVE

The Vilda Man

"I saw someone in the brush with a little black and white dog."

The green tangle thinned a bit as the Forest Trail straightened slightly. The sun spread dappled light all about. Beads of perspiration dotted my forehead as thoughts swirled in my mind.

Things have certainly been challenging, I thought. *I do hope I won't find myself among ruined hopes before this quest is over. I started bravely for this noble cause, but now…I don't know.*

What am I going to do after returning home? I can't shepherd again, nor can I tend Grandfather's house. I love horses and writing poems, but who can spare food for poems?

Perhaps the time has come to leave Beth Nahar. Maybe love and labor can be found in another land…with horses.

My thoughts were interrupted when I heard Levi ask Tobias about Witch Rasha.

"Tobias, what do you know about Witch Rasha? I heard she lives somewhere around your village," he said.

"Eh! That sorcerer! She lives in a dirty, smelly place called Vulture's Hollow. When she was young, there was only one man she wanted to marry. Her father didn't like him or his tribe. By the time her father died, the man had died too. Her heart hardened after that; she didn't want to marry anyone else.

"She became friendly with the Witch of Endor. The witch taught her how to cast spells, consult the dead, and interpret omens. After that, she became a medium—a witch. She's an evil doer. Been told she sometimes goes to caves in the mountains to chant and talk to the dead."

"If she's not married, how does she take care of herself?"

"Oh, she does just fine. She's a strong woman; can hold a camel by its tail. She has sheep, goats, chickens, and donkeys. She sells eggs, dates, olives, and livestock for her keep. She'll cast you a spell too.

"She raises herbs and roots to brew for medicines. Has one for 'bout any ailment: colds, bee stings, backaches, boils and risings, or stomach aches."

"Is she ever seen away from her home?"

"Eh, she sure has. She brings her animals, food, and potions to barter in the village. I don't know who trades with her—I wouldn't. I don't want to be near her. I want nothing to do with her."

"I hope I don't ever run into her!" Levi said.

I shuddered. *Me too!*

Phares was humming a melodious little song. It floated like notes on a cool happy spring. The words she sang were sweet and faint. "I am no more, but gone before, I'll meet you there by the Garden Gate. I am no more, but gone before, bring the key and don't be late."

Where did she learn that song? I wondered. *I'll have to ask her.*

Tobias retrieved his whistle stick and tried to put music to her words. After a bit of trial and error, they orchestrated a lovely duet.

Hello, who's that? "Stop, I see someone," I called. Everyone stopped and waited for me. "I saw someone in the brush with a little black and white dog. I wonder if it's the Vilda, the crazy man."

"I hope so," Levi said gleefully. "I have never met a crazy man."

"Oh, Levi, you never show one ounce of caution," Phares said. "In that case, if it's the crazy man, you can greet him."

"Gladly," he replied, grinning.

A lonely cumulus cloud topped the ridge of the Frendyl Highlands. We stopped to splash our faces in a trickling stream and let the animals drink. Without warning, O-No whirled around, growled, and stared into the brush. Raz brayed, Raven squawked. The bushes moved slightly. A little black and white dog appeared. He wagged his tail vigorously and pranced to O-No. O-No leaped forward, swinging his tail wildly, giving a big dog-smile.

"Heee!" a gray-haired man, bent with age, screamed. He ran at us, swinging a white stick. "Heee! Heee! Heee!"

It's the Vilda, I thought.

O-No and the little black and white dog barked sharply. Everyone started to run. Then Levi stopped and turned around. "I'm not afraid of you. You're just a feeble old man." He laughed.

The Vilda stopped screaming and stared at Levi. The dogs stopped barking. "Levi," I said, "mind your manners—keep still."

The Vilda lowered his stick and stood mute.

"Is your name Bidinko?" I asked.

He nodded.

"Did two men with black dogs pass here recently?"

He nodded again.

"We had better slow down," I said. "I think Destroyers are close by. We should draw back and give them a chance to advance. I hope they don't slow down too. If they do, we'll run into each other."

To my surprise, the wizened old man greeted us with tranquil dignity. He touched Tobias' hand and then his own forehead, bowing slightly. His worn, creased face opened with a toothless smile. "I am Bidinko, the Vilda man. Peace be upon you. I'm not crazy. I chose to speak because I fear for your safety. What brings thee hither? Where be thee bound and who be thee?"

He was a lazy-eyed man with a soft voice. A red silk scarf tucked rakishly into a yellow turban that wrapped around his skull. He was a comely person of good stature.

"I'm Tobias from En Gedi, of the Bebe Tribe. And unto you be peace. This is Hadia, Phares, and Levi. They are sisters and brother from Beth Nahar, of Karka Tribe. We're going to Magdala Tower to see our friend, Shade."

"I too know Shade. A friend of his is a friend of mine. I'm proud to meet you."

"What can you tell us about the trail from here to Magdala Tower?" I asked.

"The trail goes uphill at a steady pace and gets steep. You're not far from Forever Lake. It's a good place to set up camp—lots of herbs, berries, and a fresh water creek. You'll know the cut-off from the trail by a broken snag, a large tree trunk. The trunk is quite jagged, and there are ferns and fronds growing out of the top. Looks rather like a silly hat," he said with a crooked smile.

"Is it dangerous there?" Phares asked.

"There are water lizards and a large coiling serpent that treads the lake. It blows mighty sprays of air. At night it swims close to shore. Don't get close to the water's edge; it can suck you into the lake. There are also bears, leopards, and vultures in these mountains."

"What's a water lizard?" I asked.

"It's an ugly beast with greenish, scaly skin as rough as a tree trunk. It's as long as an olive tree and has a huge mouth full of jaw-crushing teeth. It moves faster than you can run, and it can devour you as quickly as blinking your eye."

"Eee!" Tobias croaked.

"Oh well, what's another challenge? We have mastered others; we will master these as well," Phares said.

"Phares, I can't believe you said that. Awhile back you would have trembled hearing such news," I said, teasing.

"I didn't say I wasn't afraid. I only said we would master the challenge. Maybe I'm gathering courage," she replied with a faint grin.

"Look, I can journey as far as the Nephilim Hills. Perhaps I can be of help. My dog Scratch would love a little 'dog company.' I can escort you to Magdala Tower. What do you say?" Bidinko asked, with a gleam in his eyes.

"I thought you didn't like strangers or company," Tobias said cooly.

"Usually I don't, but you're a curious lot, one I think I want to know better. May I join you?"

At length, I shrugged my shoulders and nodded. "Yes, please join us."

And so we continued on to Magdala Tower—all five of us.

CHAPTER THIRTEEN

Monster of the Lake

"You'll hear many strange sounds walking the Old Forest Trail."

I heard Levi shoot questions at Bidinko like speeding arrows: "How old are you? Where do you come from? Do you have family? Do you know God?" Bidinko said he was seventy-five ages old, he was from Og, had no living relatives, and definitely knew God. Levi loved to ask riddles. "Bidinko, I have a riddle for you: 'I kiss the flowers, I spin the gold, my tail is sharp, so I am told.' Do you know the answer?"

"Hmm…I don't know the answer yet, lad. Give me some time. My mind has to think about it first."

Forever Lake lay just ahead. The winding trail gave vista to a cloak of green, somber and foreboding, savagely graceful, clothed in dense evergreen thickets. In the muffled quiet, prickly shrubs caught our mantles, causing an "Ow!" that broke the silence.

Ancient trees thrust sinuous branches out of knotty trunks. Giant hawks rose, wheeled in formation, poised upon the air, and then vanished into the distant highlands.

The sun floated downward, ready to hide for the day. Light and shadows played hide and seek, the shadows ever seeking to smother the light. Tobias pulled out his whistle stick and played the Forest Trail song. Phares whistled along with him.

Raven flew to my shoulder. *"My name is Raven. Fly with me up high. There's joy in the sky."* Quork! Quork!

"Look, there's the snag!" Levi yelled. "Now I'll get to explore."

"What do you mean, explore?" I asked.

Levi laughed. "You know, I'll do what boys do, poke around and see what kind of trouble I can get into."

"Oh no, you won't. We don't need you to go out of your way to find trouble. Trouble finds us easily enough. You just behave yourself. Remember, you promised."

"I know, I'm just making fun," he said, grinning.

"I hope so. I can't stand another unwelcome surprise."

We hastened our steps, anxious to set up camp and eat.

"There's the lake!" Levi whooped. Running to the water's edge, he slipped off his sandals and gingerly stuck his toe in the frigid water. "Oooo, it's cold. Don't think I'll go for a swim."

"I don't think you'll go for a swim at all. Is your memory so short that you have forgotten about the lake monster and water lizards?" Bidinko warned.

"Oh, those old things; I'm not afraid of them."

"Look, little man, it isn't a matter of being afraid. It's a matter of using your head and not tempting Yahweh with your foolishness," Bidinko retorted.

We removed our packs and relieved Raz of his. The dogs raced up and down the shore. Levi, Tobias, and Bidinko gathered firewood while Phares and I spread blankets and set out food.

Twilight was so short that night closed suddenly upon us. Soon a cheery fire blazed and we settled in for the eve.

Shoo! Ahhh! Shoo! Ahhh!

"What's that?" Levi whispered, jerking his head toward the lake.

Shoo! Ahhh! Shoo! Ahhh!

"The lake monster!" Bidinko cried. "Run! It can suck you into the water!"

Struck with terror, we ran into the forest. Tobias' feet tangled, sprawling him on his face. "Eee! Here I go again!"

O-No and Scratch lagged behind, edging close to the water. "O-No, Scratch, no! Come here!" I commanded. The dogs glanced at me, hesitated, and then started to retreat.

Scratch yelped a pitiful cry.

Against his will, he was being pulled into the water. Tobias ran for the rope. Swinging high, the rope flew through the air and settled around the terrified dog's neck.

"Pull hard, everyone! Pull! Pull! Pull!" Tobias chanted.

Finally, Scratch was rescued. Looking hopelessly drowned, he shivered at our feet. He was a wet ball of fur, looking quite frightful.

"Scratch, see what happens when you don't obey?" Bidinko said sighing. "You'll be all right now. Let me dry you."

"Let's start a fire a respectable distance from the shore. I don't wish to awake in the belly of the lake monster," Tobias said, with a grin.

"Bidinko, why is the lake called Forever Lake?" I heard Levi ask.

"At one time, the lake seemed to go on forever. No one knew where it started or where it ended. Because of that, it was named Forever Lake. One day there was a dreadful earthquake. The ground shook violently and caused the lake to split, flooding the Frendyl Valley. What you see now is the remains of the lake."

"That must have been some earthquake."

"Yes, it was over sixty-five ages ago. I was just a lad."

"Bidinko, have you seen any sign of war?" I asked.

He rubbed his forehead. "Not around here, Missy. However, I have seen soldiers on the King's Highway. I don't know why they are this far east."

"What's the war all about?" Levi inquired.

"I'm not sure, other than that neither side made a truce after the last war. It just became a cold war. The Book of Wars says King Amoz of Zora drew himself up against King Jehu of Beth Nahar about twenty-five ages ago. The sound of battle was everywhere. They killed and plundered the land. The hearts of Beth Nahar were faint with fear. Yahweh told them to march against King Amoz's army and not to be afraid. Fear seized King Amoz's army and it fled. The victorious warriors escaped the swords. Now, it seems King Amoz has attacked again."

"Oh my, I hope we can get past the King's Highway safely," Phares said, twisting her hair.

"I know the area well. We'll find a way to stay clear of the armies."

"We'll leave at first light on the morrow," I said. "Let's turn in and get a good night's rest."

The morning came, raw. Mist rose from the lake like vapor from a witch's brew. Rushes, sedges, water lilies, and cattails crowded the water's edge—a perfect place for wild fowl, turtle eggs, and water parsley to hide. An adjoining marsh held the rank smell of rotting vegetation. Giant green pincushions—balsam bog plants—filled the air with resinous odor. A few plants amidst damp earth bloomed elegantly among spiny bushes, supplying perfume to the pungent air. A burbling creek flowed hastily into the lake. Mystery pervaded as gauzy suspense draped itself over us.

Music sang from the glistening white bodies of lake geese. Low, hollow, hooting whistles filled the air. *Wowwww! Whoow! Whoo!* Huge webbed feet paddled frantically, scooting their bodies airborne, pumping rhythmic wings in waves. Sooty ravens punctuated the dawn sky veiled with splashes of vivid color.

Everyone was up. Tobias packed Raz while Levi fed the dogs. Phares and I prepared breakfast. Bidinko helped gather supplies. We dove eagerly into our breakfast of herb tea, figs, raisin cakes, and caravan bread.

"Let's give thanks to Yahweh for our safe night and today's journey," Bidinko suggested.

We gathered, and each in our own words gave thanks. Levi sneezed loudly, ending prayer abruptly.

"Eee! Sneezing during prayer is a sign from God that something special will happen," Tobias said.

"Tobias, there you go again with your superstitions," I said, shaking my head. "Let's go."

Slippery stones cluttered the muddy Forest Trail causing one to lose footing. Trekking was difficult. Raz picked his way carefully, while O-No and Scratch ran ahead.

I chuckled as I listened to Levi tease Bidinko.

"Well, Bidinko, have you figured out my riddle?" Levi asked, cocking his head.

"I thought overnight about your riddle, and here's my answer. It's a bee."

Levi raised his eyebrows. "How did you know? No one ever figures out my riddles that fast."

Bidinko laughed. "That's my riddle for you: how did I figure it out?"

Levi scowled thoughfully and chewed his lower lip. "That's not a riddle, that's a question."

"That's all right, lad. I'm sure you'll have a riddle I won't be able to figure out, and then we'll be even. At least we can laugh about this. Did you know that when you laugh, all the meanness drains out of your body?"

"What if I don't have any meanness in me?"

"Everyone has a little meanness in them. When we talk behind someone's back, that's mean; when we take more than our share, that's mean; when we don't tell the truth, that's mean. Yes, we all have a little meanness in us."

"Hmm…hadn't thought of 'mean' that way," Levi said sheepishly.

I frowned. *I never thought of 'mean' that way, either.*

"Oh, a snake!" Phares cried.

"Where?" I said, looking around. "I don't see a snake."

"Oh, Hadia, it's not a snake, it's a branch…just my imagination. Why am I so fearful?"

"Maybe you find comfort in fear. Maybe you depend on it."

"What kind of a person would want to depend on fear?"

"A person who hides behind it," I said dryly.

"Why would I want to hide behind fear?"

My brow furrowed from a headache. "For heaven sake, Phares, I have no idea why you would want to hide behind fear. If God is all you say He is, then you shouldn't be so afraid."

Phares opened her mouth to speak, but no words came. Squinting, I raised my face to the sun. I wanted to be at Magdala Tower by middle-day.

"All right, everyone. Keep going."

The morning sun warmed the ascending trail. Tongues hung limp from the dogs' mouths like red warning flags. Bidinko slowed his pace, lagging behind Tobias. Silence imposed itself in remoteness. Not a breeze stirred. Peaceful mystery breathed heavy as a parliament of owls seemed to question our invasion.

"Stop!" Tobias commanded. "The Destroyers are close by."

"How do you know?" Bidinko asked.

"Look," he said, pointing to the ground, "there's fresh evidence of dogs."

"Our Troop has grown, making us conspicuous. Maybe we should split up," I said anxiously.

Bidinko paused and looked around. "No Missy, 'tis better to stay together. There's safety in numbers."

"I suppose you're right, but how can we avoid being seen?"

"We can't. We'll just keep moving. We're not far from Magdala Tower. We'll be safe there."

The trail continued to rise, as well as the sun. Our calm was shattered with high, quavering screams. They were much like a human cry of distress. The screams seemed to come from different directions.

"Bidinko, what is it?" I cried.

"Don't worry, Missy, just hawks."

"They sound so human."

"You'll hear many strange sounds walking the Old Forest Trail. Most are harmless. Only a few are dangerous."

"How will we know the difference? We have never walked the trail before."

Bidinko smiled. "You'll know the difference; your spirit will tell you."

We moved through deep shade and tall trees. Fear and anxiety ceased for the moment. Our voices turned to lively chatter. O-No and Scratch scurried far up the trail.

Nature proudly displayed herself without apology. Wrinkly vines wound through the forest like climbing snakes, looping through the treetops. Ants marched in precision, each carrying a green morsel as tiny toads splashed in murky puddles. Streams cascaded down mountain sides, spilling past mosses and enormous ferns.

Layers of spider webs draped in the undergrowth, where creatures real and unreal made their abode. Disquieting sounds of unseen birds, falling branches, and other unidentified forest noises echoed as invisible animals padded softly about. Swirling mist wafted through the enchanted woodland like a gossamer legion unfolding. I marveled at how it was so utterly different from Beth Nahar.

I continued to eavesdrop.

"Bidinko, why do you act like you're crazy if you don't want to be with people? Why don't you just hide?" Levi asked, frowning.

"Hiding becomes tiresome, always having to be on the lookout. It's easier to be found and scare folks."

"That's not nice. You could just wave, and then be on your way."

Bidinko sighed and said, "I suppose so. I've been proud to be with you, Levi. Maybe I should try harder to be with others."

"Yes, you should. You could be helpful to travelers."

"I'll give it some thought."

"Good. Now I have another riddle for you: 'My feet are leather, my eyelids three. I go extra miles for thee.' "

Bikinko grinned. "Oh, I know that one, it's a camel."

"That's not fair! You didn't even guess."

Bidinko chuckled. "Remember, I'll tell you a riddle and you can out-guess me."

I laughed. *It's good for Levi to lose once in a while. It will keep him from being so big-headed.*

I walked with a deliberate pace, preserving both energy and balance on the precarious trail. Fatigue was forgotten as Magdala Tower beckoned me. Mist faded, leaving a canopy of forest, breaking enough to reveal a blue-gray sky and pale sun.

"Bidinko, should we worry about the wild animals you spoke of?" Phares asked.

"You need not worry, but be alert. They're out there. The vulture is a mean one. He can swoop down and pick you up—just like that!" Bidinko answered, snapping his fingers.

"Eee!" Tobias muttered.

"Oh dear, it's not enough we're being followed by Destroyers; now there are four-legged enemies to watch for too," Phares moaned.

"Phares, you'll never *find* courage if you don't *need* courage. Life doesn't matter a bit-of-wit if everything is easy," Tobias said sternly.

A low growl rumbled, piercing the air like far away thunder. Everyone froze.

Raz pawed the ground, flicking his ears back and forth. The rumble became louder and closer.

"What is it?" Levi whispered hoarsely.

"Sounds like a bear. You can't outrun a bear, and climbing a tree won't help either," Bidinko warned. "They're good at scaling trees."

"What shall we do?" I asked, looking over my shoulder.

"Make ready your bows. We'll have to slay him if need be."

We fitted our arrows to our bows, ready to send them flying. Crashing sounds echoed as a rotund black bear lumbered toward us. O-No and Scratch ran toward the bear.

"No! Stay back!" I yelled.

Slinging his paws, the bear caught Scratch by the neck and threw him in the air. With a loud yelp, Scratch landed with a *thud* and lay silent. Then surprisingly, the bear stopped. Appearing mountains high, it stood on its hind legs. Everyone took aim. Arrows twanged, hitting their target, digging deep into thick fur.

Growling with a wide-open mouth, the huge bear leaped forward. It thrashed, stumbled, and swayed like a toppling tree struggling to stay upright. More arrows flew, striking their mark. The bear collapsed, groaning and flinging his paws. He tried to rise. Then his head dropped backward. The battle was over.

Scratch lay motionless, eyes closed.

"Scratch, Scratch," Bidinko yelled. "He's breathing; he's alive. We'll have to carry him the rest of the way. Hurry, help me make a sling."

O-No hovered over Scratch, softly licking his eyes, urging him to wake up.

Bidinko and Tobias knotted four corners of a blanket and ran long sturdy limbs between the knots on each side of it, making a stretcher. We carefully placed Scratch in the middle of the makeshift litter.

"We must make haste. We need to get to Magdala Tower as soon as possible," Bidinko commanded. We gazed solemnly at Scratch for a moment, and then promptly headed for our destination.

Bidinko and Tobias trotted briskly; Scratch swayed back and forth in his sling. Levi walked beside him, stroking his scruffy coat, murmuring words of endearment. O-No wouldn't leave his side, occasionally licking his face.

The white sun shone high without a trace of mist. Soon, we saw the tower—Magdala Tower—crowning Shamir's summit, reaching for the heavens. It stood proudly against the brilliant sky. The round, white goddess displayed a turret at the top, like a stunning hat. She was indeed lovely.

"Shade, Shade! Peace be upon you," Tobias shrieked. Handing the hammock branch to Levi, he ran fiercely ahead.

"Tobias, Tobias! Upon you be peace."

Tobias' feet tangled, causing him to tumble end-over-end.

"You haven't changed a bit," Shade said, laughing.

They grinned affectionately at each other then collapsed into a bear hug.

CHAPTER FOURTEEN

Night Stalkers

"That was close. What do they want from us?"

Magdala Tower was dark and damp inside, sending a shiver through me. A small chair and a table draped with a dull gray shawl sat inside near the door. An oil lamp, water pitcher and a couple of clay tablets lay on the table. Thick sandstone walls with small windows let in thin streams of light. A steep, spiral staircase wound toward the top of the turret. More light filtered softly through large windows near the ceiling. The staircase ended at a wooden platform. It held another small table with an oil lamp and water clock. A makeshift bed of straw and blankets lay in disarray on the floor.

The men carried Scratch inside the tower and laid him on the table.

"Shade, Scratch was attacked by a bear. He's alive, but doesn't respond. Can you help?" I pleaded.

"Let me look." Shade lifted an eyelid, exposing a rolled-back eye. "Hmm…he's knocked out good. He's in a deep sleep, but I'm sure he'll come out of it. Let's keep him warm." He reached for the shawl. "Massage his eyes. Keep stroking him. He needs to feel loved. That will help him want to wake up."

Levi stroked Scratch's scruffy body as Phares massaged him. Bidinko prayed and spoke words of affirmation. Suddenly, Tobias caught sight of Scratch's tail wagging. "Ay, he's moving!" Scratch's eyelids fluttered. He lifted his head and squeaked a weak bark.

"Oh, Scratch, I thought for sure we lost you," Bidinko murmured, burying his head in Scratch's neck. "Thank heaven you're all right. From now on, please stay away from danger. I can't take any more of your near death experiences."

Scratch planted a sloppy kiss on Bidinko's cheek.

"Well, we can relax now that Scratch is going to be all right," Tobias said.

"Eh, ye can relax. However, he durst not be running around," Shade warned. "He should be kept quiet a few days."

"I guess my travels with the Troop end here. I shan't endanger my dog. Maybe we'll meet again when you return home, heh?"

"We would love to have you travel with us, but you're right, Scratch needs time to heal. We'll meet again, I'm sure," I said.

"Yes," Bidinko murmured wistfully.

"Let's celebrate. Friends are here and Scratch is going to get well. We shall eat and share 'the news.'" Waving everyone outside, Shade ordered us to follow him to a flat, grassy spot, and then left to prepare food.

Shade was a gaunt young man with pale eyes and the stubble of a beard. His long black locks and sly grin made him look more foe than friend. Old acquaintances rarely paid a visit, and when they did, merrymaking was in order. He hadn't been gone long when he hollered, "Come and eat! Eat! Ye are hungry!"

We sat down, for it was shameful to stand while eating. Reclining on our elbows, we celebrated in a proper and sociable manner, feasting on figs, olives, cheese, nuts, and unleavened wheat bread slathered in honey. We polished off the meal with smooth goat's milk. It was a lovely feast. Everyone stretched out on the sweet smelling grass and groaned contentedly. It wasn't long before my senses were soon lulled to repose.

"Tobias, what is 'the news'? Why have you come this way?" Shade asked. "You didn't come to visit me."

Tobias stammered. "Well...uh...well...we're on an adventure. We have never traveled this trail and wanted to see the land. We'll go as far as the Nephilim Hills and then decide if we'll travel further."

"Why, for heaven sake, would ye want to go further? Ye take your lives in ye hands crossing the Valley of Tremble. No one ever comes back. They simply disappear. Ye best reconsider that crazy notion."

"We'll think 'bout it."

I stirred and sat up. "Shade, have you seen any Destroyers? I think we're being followed."

"Eh, a few passed by just before your arrival. I was up in the tower and I hid. They came inside and looked around. They looked fiendish. I was relieved when they left."

"Eee!" Tobias said, looking over his shoulder.

"I'm not afraid of those men. They better not start a fight with me," Levi said, shaking his fist.

"Look, your mightiness, you had *better* be afraid. Fear can be a gift when it may save your life," I snapped.

The men grinned. Levi rolled his eyes. Phares and I shook our heads.

"Shade, have you seen any armies on the King's Highway?" Tobias asked.

"I occasionally hear rumbling and see them from the top of the tower. But, I really don't know what's going on. I stay close to the tower, which doesn't allow me to venture far. It's all a mystery to me."

"We don't want to get caught in the middle of fighting, or worse, captured," I said frowning.

"Eh, I don't blame ye. Perhaps ye should leave Raz with me. It would be easier to hide from the armies, and—if ye insist—cross the Valley of Tremble without being seen," Shade replied.

The suggestion seemed to find small favor with Raz. He looked at me as if to say, "Don't leave me behind."

"What about our supplies?" I questioned.

"Divide and carry them. Ye are young, strong, and resolute. Ye can do it."

"Oh, my aching back. I feel it already," Phares grumbled.

"Bidinko, are there any people living between here and the Shamir River?" I asked.

"There are the Marsh people. They live in huts on little islands in the Shamir River. They will receive you with friendliness."

"Eh, I have met them myself," Shade said. "Sometimes I have seen them on the King's Highway going to Bashon to barter. They'll probably help ye cross the river."

"Oh, good—nice, helpful people," Phares said.

We exchanged "news." Shade had little to tell. I told him the events of the days past. Time passed quickly, and soon everyone readied for bed. I removed the scratchy scroll and placed it beneath my blanket. It made a better pillow than a girdle. Exhausted, sleep came without delay.

A sudden sound brought me to my feet. My heart picked up speed. I heard padding footsteps. A distinct odor hung in the air—one I recognized: moldy blankets! We sprang to our feet. O-No flew up barking. Scratch chimed in. I reached under my bedding and pushed the body scroll deep into the blankets.

Tobias yelled, "Who's there? We know you're out there!"

Black-turbaned forms leaped into our circle, pushing and shoving everyone and everything. They overturned supplies, kicked blankets aside, and tried to grab Phares and me. Shade, Tobias, and Bidinko quickly pounced upon them, swinging pans and anything they could get their hands on.

"Curse your fathers," shouted ferocious voices.

O-No wasted no time attacking the insurgents. He growled, sinking his teeth into their tunics, pulling hard. The interlopers broke loose and left as hastily as they came, but certainly not as quietly.

I fumbled through the mess that had been strewn about, searching for the body scroll. My fingers soon felt something firm and scratchy—the map. *Thank you, God.*

"Eee! That was close. God's curse be upon them! From now on we'll have to take turns keeping watch," Tobias said breathlessly.

"What do they want from us?" Levi asked in an awestruck whisper. "We don't have anything of value."

"Oh, but we do," I replied, raising my brow. "You may not think we carry valuables, but to them, we do. There's the gold ring and the talisman. Our supplies and animals probably look good to them, also. And, don't forget, there's the map."

"But they don't know about the map."

"How do we know they don't know?" Phares replied.

A strained silence fell. Then Bidinko announced he would keep watch the first half of the night.

"I'll keep watch after Bidinko, until light," Levi said.

"Good," I replied, "the dogs will alert us if the Destroyers return. Now, let's make good use of what's left of the night and try to sleep. I know it will be fitful, but we must not let this invasion steer us from our goal. The strength of our determination can only be demonstrated by our perseverance. The Destroyers are like earthquakes. They try to shake our confidence, but my determination is strong. I hope yours is too." Everyone nodded solemnly at me, and then we retreated to our beds.

I lay shaken, staring at the stars, thinking Phares wasn't the only one gripped with fear. *I'm not going to let this encounter shake me. I'm afraid, but it's not going to stop me. I could, however, use a little more courage and faith.*

I fell quiet, listening to silence. And then, a tiny, far-away voice sang, "Forward faith triumphs." *Hmm...forward faith triumphs.*

The tiny voice rang out again, "You know—like the stars. You see them now. It doesn't require faith to see stars when you see them at night. But in the daylight, the stars are invisible. It takes faith to believe they are there, beyond the day. That's *forward faith.* To visualize your journey a success is faith that moves forward—

forward faith triumphs." *Having faith means trusting God,* I thought. *But can I?* I closed my eyes.

Trust Me—

"Everyone up," I commanded loudly, banging a pan. I marched around like a soldier, stepping high, striking the pan to the rhythm of my footsteps. *Clang! Clang! Clang!*

"Eee! I hear you. You can quit any time," Tobias said, covering his ears.

Everyone groaned and crawled out from under their covers. The aroma of flatbread baking floated in the crisp morning air. Soon, morning became a beehive of activity. Shade had been up for some time preparing breakfast. The dogs searched the underbrush for critters. Raven glided overhead. *"Hungry! Hungry!"*

"Breakfast!" Shade bellowed.

"Yum, smells delicious," Phares said, wrinkling her nose.

"Eat! Eat! Ye are hungry. Help yeselves. There's plenty."

We eagerly dove into our meal, stopping only to shovel more into our mouths.

Shade's smile broadened. "Ye do me a kindness by enjoying my cooking. That's what life is all about, breaking bread with friends. Bidinko, have you ever heard of the Land of In-Between?"

"Eh, I have heard tales of that place. Supposedly, it's the Garden of Eden," Bidinko replied.

"Yes, I too, have heard such a tale. Occasionally, travelers tell me they're searching for it. I laugh and tell them they're searching in vain," Shade answered with a thin smile.

The Land of In-Between; where have I heard that before? I strained hard to remember, but no memory came to mind.

"Shade, we'll take Raz with us. I'm sure he won't be a problem. We'll turn him loose to find his way back to you if he poses a danger to us. Bidinko, let's keep in touch. We'll look for you and Scratch on our way home," I said.

"Wait," Bidinko said. "I promised to steer you away from the army. I'll leave Scratch here and go with you as far as the King's Highway."

"If you insist."

"Oh, Hadia," Shade said, "I meant to tell ye of a man who may help ye cross the Valley of Tremble, should ye decide to pursue that crazy notion. His name is Jude. He is of middle-age, slight of build, with dark eyes and hair as black as night. He rides a red stallion. No one seems to know where he abides."

I drew in a sharp breath. "He rides a red stallion? I know of no one who rides horses!"

"Well, he rides one," Shade answered.

A horse! He rides a horse. Maybe I'll get to ride it!

"We'll keep a lookout for him. We can use all the help we can get. All right, Troop, up we go!"

CHAPTER FIFTEEN

The Way of the Earth

"Shut up, old man. If you have a god, say your prayers."

The descending trail lay smooth with plenty of room for walking double. The King's Highway was a short distance from Magdala Tower. I dreaded crossing it for fear of capture, yet eager to cross it and be on our way. I would soon know our fate. Hearing a duet of joyful talk, I listened to Levi and Tobias chatter.

"Tobias, do you believe you can do anything you desire?"

"Why do you ask, lad?"

"Well, like this journey. We want to find Eden, but will we really find it?"

"Levi, God blesses those who practice His laws."

"What are His laws?"

"The Book of Commandments says we are to act justly, love, show mercy, and have faith."

"That seems like a lot."

"Not really. If you don't act puffed up, and if you stand by the weak, you show justice and mercy. Hope follows faith."

"What *is* faith, Tobias? I don't know if I have any."

"Faith is believing in things hoped for, like this journey. Even though we haven't seen Eden, we believe we will find it. To trust

God with your request, great faith must face great trials in order for your roots to go deep. It's the *trying* of your faith that determines how much you have. Faith is not faith until it's tested."

"Hmm…" Levi pondered. "Tobias, I have another riddle for you. Here it is: 'I'm senseless, without knowledge, can't speak or walk, but master over all who squawk.' What do you think? Know the answer?"

"I'll have to think 'bout it awhile."

"Good, maybe I'll befuddle you. I'll race you to the King's Highway!"

"I'll beat you!" Tobias answered. Their burst of speed left a wake of dust in our faces. We joined in the race.

"Beat you," Levi bragged.

"Eee! You cheated with your pushing and shoving."

"I did not." Levi plopped on the ground.

I sat down beside Levi. "I ache all over."

"Me too. Maybe it was our middle-night fight with the Destroyers," Phares replied.

Levi laughed. "What a couple of weaklings. I'm ready for another race."

"Levi, you are such a braggart. Didn't your mother teach you any manners?" Tobias said, scowling.

Levi swung his sling in the air. "I never had a mother."

"Oh, that's right. Well, remember, bragging is not acting humble."

Levi rolled his eyes and shrugged his shoulders.

"Listen! Someone is coming. We must hide," I ordered.

We turned off the trail and crouched in dense brush. "Oh, Raz, please don't bray," I begged. "O-No, don't bark."

Soon, a charging cavalry stormed the road. The soldiers were clad in scarlet, bearing red shields, glittering swords and silver spears. They were ready to shed blood. King Amoz's army was not only seeking to conquer Beth Nahar, but Bashon too. Ashen-faced, we readied to marshal ourselves against the enemy.

Who are we fooling? I thought. *We can't defend ourselves against them—there are too many. We must not be discovered.*

The soldiers passed by quickly, vanishing in huge clouds of dust.

Tobias wiped his brow and whispered, "Close call."

Trembling, I looked in all directions. "We can cross the highway now, but no talking. There may be more. Hurry, let's go."

The words no sooner came out of my mouth when I heard thundering camels' hooves and the cries of menacing voices. "Run, everyone! Run!"

"My foot is caught!" Bidinko shouted.

Levi turned around. "I'll help him."

"No, you'll get killed!" I grabbed his arm. "We must hide."

Running into the brush, we crouched breathless and watched in horror as death on camelback charged with spears in hand.

"Spare me, good men!" Bidinko pleaded.

"Shut up, old man. We take no captives. We're not good, and you're not worth sparing. If you have a god, say your prayers. Maybe it can save you," yelled a soldier viciously.

They had clearly determined in their iniquitous hearts to do evil. Raising their spears high, they thrust them into Bidinko's body, killing him instantly. They jerked out their spears, laughed wickedly, and spurred their camels on. Death hung in the air *again*.

"Why did Bikinko have to die? He was a good man. He didn't do anything wrong. *Why? Why?*" Levi sobbed. "God, take away their breath!"

"I don't know, I don't know." I cradled Levi in my arms.

We huddled together in shock, staring at Bidinko's lifeless body. "We must take him back to Shade and bury him," Tobias said.

Tobias and Levi carefully draped Bidinko over Raz's back. Then we turned toward Magdala Tower.

A burning anguish kindled deep within my heart. The dark recesses of my brain filed away another iniquity committed against mankind. I squeezed my eyes hard. *Bidinko's death wasn't supposed to happen. Where were You, God? Can one have faith and bargain with You? Can faith overcome evil? It doesn't seem so today.*

Despair, doubt, and discouragement consumed me. I was beginning to have dismal forebodings about our journey.

I saw Shade looking out the tower window. "No!" he wailed. Rushing frantically down the tower, he ran to meet us. "What happened? Tell me!"

I leaned despairingly on Bidinko's walking stick. "King Amoz's soldiers attacked us. We ran for cover. Bidinko fell. He begged for his life. The warriors took no pity; they killed him."

Shade covered his face with trembling hands and cried loudly until only muffled sobs were heard. "We must bury him. Come, we shall find a resting place for him," he said.

We followed Shade to a quiet glen, and the wizened old man went the way of the earth. Scratch hung his head over the newly covered grave. His sad eyes seemed to ask, "Why?" No one had an answer.

"Well Scratch, looks like I'll be taking care of you from now on," Shade murmured.

Scratch looked deep into Shade's eyes and licked his face.

Tobias cleared his throat. "If we leave now, we can reach the Shamir River before sundown and take rest. Then we can continue to the Nephilim Hills and spend the night. We can cross the Valley of Tremble on the morrow."

"Tobias, how can can we cross the valley without being captured by the Nephilim giants?" Phares asked sharply.

"I don't know. That's where our faith will have to come in. We must believe that God will provide a safe passage," he said, glancing sideways at me.

"My faith is pretty shaken right now. If Bikinko's death is a *trying* of our faith, I don't like it. What's next? More fatal disasters?" Phares asked. By now, her face and composure had crumbled.

"Your faith is shaken, but not lost. You'll see, Phares," I said.

My slippery tongue left me feeling fraudulent. My faith too is all but gone. Is our journey the cause of Bikinko's death? He wouldn't have died had he not met us. Must the sword devour forever? Should we continue?

I clenched Bidinko's walking stick. "*Don't let Bidinko's death be for nothing,*" a voice whispered. "*Be for nothing, be for nothing, be for nothing....*"

"All right, Bidinko, I'll continue—just for you," I whispered. "Well, what's everyone waiting for? March on!"

And so we went, the four of us.

CHAPTER SIXTEEN

The Marsh Man

"I've heard of a far-away place called the Land of In-Between."

So, what do you think?" I heard Levi ask.

"What do you mean, what do I think?" Tobias answered.

"You know, the answer to my riddle: 'I'm senseless, without knowledge, can't speak or walk, but master over all who squawk.' "

"I think you have me. Can't for the life of me figure it out."

"Gotcha!"

"Well, what's the answer?" Tobias asked sorely.

"It's a scarecrow, of course."

"By founds, you sure fooled me!"

Grinning from ear to ear, Levi pushed a bushel of red hair from his face, wiped his forehead, and proceeded to dance around Tobias singing, "I fooled you! I fooled you!"

"There you go again, bragging. Remember what we talked 'bout, or is your memory so short you don't remember what a braggart is? You need to learn how to be a humble winner."

"What's wrong with being happy about winning?" Levi asked.

"Nothing, but you don't have to be puffed up about it."

"All right, but I'm happy about outwitting you."

Tobias shook his head and cackled, "Eee!"

I waved Bidinko's stick at them. "Hey you two, quiet. We might be heard. We can talk further down the trail." Tobias and Levi covered their mouths with their hands and took off running with O-No in the lead. I grinned. *Those two! What clowns!*

The winding trail opened to vistas of sheltered glens. Sun streamed through rolling clouds, outlining treetops with rays of golden light. Birds chattered, hopping from tree to tree, scolding the invading Troop. A network of smaller trails branched away. Some criss-crossed back and forth to the King's Highway near the Shamir River. Others led to mysterious lakes and dead-ends. A whiff of intoxicating fragrance tantalized me. The scent of flowers, cedar, cypress, and damp earth left an invigorating perfume in the air.

We lengthened our stride, anxious to reach the Shamir River. Tobias and Levi bantered in rowdy conversation. Phares and I walked silently.

"Hello! The river—the Shamir River!" Tobias yelled.

"Wonderful! We'll reach the Nephilim Hills by sundown," I said.

Bounding down the trail, we halted at the river's edge. It flowed gently in front of us. It was full of small islands dotted with grass huts.

"Marsh people," I murmured.

We stared in awe at the maze of huts. Dwellings and barns made of clay, reeds, and water buffalo dung straddled the waters on little islands. Secluded villages were tucked in among marshes along the river. The wetlands gave refuge to rich fisheries. We saw little children and livestock everywhere. Soon a slender boat made of reeds and blown goatskins floated toward us.

"I hope Bidinko was right. I hope they're friendly," Phares whispered.

"Hail," called a man laden with age and gentle in manner.

"Sir, peace be unto you. We need to cross the river. Can you help?" I asked.

"Unto you be peace. Yes, I'll take you across, but please stay and share 'the news.' We'll break bread." His smile signaled acceptance.

"Thank you. We would be honored to sup with you."

"I'll take you to my island. We'll need to make two crossings. Who goes first?"

"I'll go with them," I said, pointing to Phares, Raz and O-No.

"Your donkey will have to swim the river. He's too large for my boat."

"We'll have to remove Raz's supplies. We can't get them wet," Tobias said, undoing the ropes.

The lapping water tickled the riverbank, bobbing the boat up and down. I thought Raz looked at the river as if to say, "Now's a fine time to find out if I can swim."

"All right, we're ready," I called out.

Phares, O-No, and I jumped on the rocking boat. Phares held tightly to Raz's lead rope and gently tugged, urging him into the water. Raz balked a moment, and then plunged in.

"Here we go," the Marsh man said, pushing his oars through the water.

Raz paddled his legs furiously. Holding his head high above the water, I thought his face seemed to say, "I wish you had left me behind!"

Swaying and bobbing, the little boat found its way to the Marsh man's island, setting everyone ashore. Then the man returned for Tobias, Levi, and the supplies.

"I am Trevez, sandal maker from the Ma'adan Tribe. What 'news' do you bring? To whom do you belong? From whence do you come and to whither you go?"

I looked at him, inquiring but cautious. I was sure we were safe with this kindly man, but I remained guarded.

"I'm Hadia, and this is my sister Phares and brother Levi. We are of the Karka Tribe from Beth Nahar. This is Tobias from En Gedi, of the Bebe Tribe. We're traveling to the Nephilim Hills."

"Only hunters go to the Nephilim Hills. What's there for you?"

"Well…um…we just want to see the land. We've never been this far east," I stuttered.

"Isn't it risky for young people to be out and about without elder supervision?"

"Perhaps, but we have met our challenges successfully and expect to continue to do so."

Trevez's tolerant eyes took measure of us. "You are my guests. Come in, let's eat." As he walked ahead, his voice could be heard echoing, "Come in, come in."

He was a mere cinder of a man—frail and shriveled, with a full beard and watchful eyes. His smile was broad, exposing a single tooth protruding over his lower lip. His eyebrows crawled up his forehead to the ample folds of his white turban, like caterpillars on a mission. His body jerked from side to side as he ushered us in.

His hut was clean and spacious with reed mats and wool rugs covering the floor. A small cooking hearth and a table and bench sat to the side. He set food before us and implored us to eat. We did—without restraint. We devoured fluffy white rice, golden dates, and pink melon. I was amazed at his graciousness. It was as if we had been old acquaintances. Leaning close to me, he asked, "What 'news' do you bring?"

"There is a war raging above En Gedi. King Amoz of Zora has drawn his sword against Bashon and is advancing toward Beth Nahar. I don't know what will be left of our beloved village when we return. Our friend Bikinko was killed by the murderous army while crossing the King's Highway," I answered.

"God, give Bashon and Beth Nahar victory!" crackled Trevez. His voice lowered. "I'm sorry about your friend."

"Thank you. Have you ever heard of a man called Jude?" I asked.

"Yes. It's rare to see him around here. However, he has been seen many times in the Nephilim Hills. I've been told he travels the Valley of Tremble. He is the only one I know to travel that nefarious valley and return alive. Why he goes there is a mystery to me. He rides a brilliant red stallion. They drink the wind with ease."

A red stallion! "How far is it to the Nephilim Hills?" I asked.

"It is about four days from here. The trail is not too rough. As far as I know, you shouldn't encounter any problems. As I said before, hunters stalk game up there. You will probably have a bit of company."

"Thank you. Your information is helpful. We must be on our way. Could you ferry us to the other side of the river now?" I asked.

"Yes, but first I leave you with words for your heart: Be kind to everyone. Practice it as if your future depends on it. Your friend could one day become your enemy; your enemy could one day become your friend."

"Thank you, Trevez."

"I'll take you across now," he said.

We went afloat upon the water and reached the shore without mishap. Raz climbed the muddy bank and shook himself, spraying water over all of us.

"Raz, you're getting me wet. Hold still so I can pack you," Tobias said, waving Levi over to help him.

"Thank you, Trevez, for your help and hospitality. We are grateful." I pressed a nugget of silver into his hand.

Trevez smiled, nodded and tucked it into his pocket. "I wish I could go with you. I have always wanted to travel and feel solid ground beneath my feet for long stretches at a time. I have heard of a far-away place called the Land of In-Between. Some say it's the Garden of Eden. I should like to find it. Have you heard of such a place?"

There it is again—the Land of In-Between. Where have I heard that before?

"Of course, everyone has heard about the Garden of Eden, but I can't tell you how to find it."

Disappointment traced Trevez's face, and then he smiled. "Here, take these with you," he said, handing me a bundle of leather sandal latches. "They may come in useful."

I reached for the sandal latches. "Thank you, new friend. Farewell. May God lengthen your life." Trevez lingered on the riverbank, waving. I looked back once. He remained only a speck in my eye.

Dragon Bird
Shadow Ghosts
Sinkholes deep
They could not keep
Us
Bear attack
Man-eating plants
Coiling serpents
Did not defeat
Us

Hadia

CHAPTER SEVENTEEN

Solitary Rider

"The day I forgive them will be the day I give my father's sword away."

Tobias, that's a lovely song. What's it called?" I asked.

"It's called 'The Shepherd's Song.' Let me sing it again: 'Under starry skies, my sheep bed down. I whisper words of love. Sleep safe and sound, my little ones, morn will sweetly come.'" He pulled out his whistle stick and began to play. It was a sweet little melody, a singsong rhythm urging one to skip.

Leaving the river behind, we forged ahead. Whispering breezes floated through the forest trees; little rustling noises broke the silence. Squirrels scurried about, running here and there. The forest made itself known by its sounds: falling branches, unseen birds, skittering small creatures, and other mysterious noises. The awesome beauty enveloped me.

"Tobias, I have another riddle for you," I heard Levi say.

"All right lad, what's the riddle?"

"Here it is: 'Two ears I have but cannot hear. Two eyes I have but cannot see. I cannot walk, nor can I talk, and yet you fall down at my knees.'"

"That's a tough one. It may take a bit for me to figure that one out."

Levi chuckled. "That's all right. I can wait."

"Levi, did you know a boiled egg in the morning is hard to beat?"

"Oh, Tobias, that's silly."

Tobias laughed. "I know. That's why I said it."

"Tobias, why are people evil?"

"While the heart is the wellspring of life, it is deceitful above all things. When we follow the way of the world, wickedness can take root, drawing us to the ruler of the kingdom of the air—Satan."

"Those murderers, I hate them!" Levi spat, and his voice hardened. "They killed Father and Bidinko. I hate them! I'll never forgive them!"

"Levi, God will repay those who deserve it. You can't let hate live in your heart forever or it will eat you alive. Someday, I pray you'll let the hate go and forgive."

"The day I forgive them will be the day I give my father's sword away!"

I sighed. Tobias' words cut deep into my heart: *"You can't let hate live in your heart forever. Someday, I pray you'll let it go."*

The day lengthened as our stride shortened. O-No slowed his pace. His tongue hung from his mouth like a limp rag. Raven flew to my shoulder. *"My name is Raven. Fly with me up high. There's joy in the sky."*

The forest was thinning. Trees grew farther apart. Shrubs grew sparse. It was beginning to look more like a lost forest. Scrubby trees split down the middle by lightening dotted the land. The wild, remote call of jackals rang from distant hills.

We stopped to eat and rest near Dead Lake. A few jumbled hills, holding little life, bordered one side. As soon as we had eaten, we pushed forward.

Hello? What's that? Squinting my eyes, I tried to focus on a moving object in the distance. It was moving at great speed at the base of the Nephilim Hills. *It's a horse and rider!* "Tobias, Phares, I see a solitary rider—look!"

"Maybe it's Jude," Tobias said in a hopeful voice.

"Oh, Hadia, do you suppose it is he?" Phares asked.

127

"I hope so, but we'll never know unless we keep moving."

The possibility of meeting Jude sparked a surge of vigor in me. Gathering speed, I pressed on.

Shadows lengthened across the high valley as we reached the base of the Nephilim Hills. A soft breeze caused treetops to bend and sigh. A fire was in order. We gathered gnarled branches and twigs and piled them in a heap. Soon, cheery flames leaped in the dusk of eventide. A wave of fatigue overtook me. I looked forward to a good night's sleep.

"We mustn't be lax in keeping watch. I believe the Destroyers are still seeking us. They're just hiding, waiting for the perfect moment to strike," I said.

"I'll take first watch," Tobias answered.

"Oh dear," Phares said, twisting her hair, "I assumed we were safe since we haven't seen them."

"Never assume anything, Phares. Assumptions are useless thoughts that can get you into trouble," I retorted. "Let's turn in. Morn will arrive soon enough."

We piled more twigs on the fire, spread blankets, and drew close. Soon, we slumbered, except O-No and Tobias.

O-No's ears twitched. He cocked his head back and forth. Jackals howled.

"Trouble," Tobias whispered. "Troop, wake up."

Phares sat up. "Wake up? I just got to sleep! What's the matter?"

"I hear a camel and something else. Someone's nearby. Levi, stay with the girls and keep O-No here. I'm going to go see who's out there."

"Wait," I said, "I'm going with you."

Tobias paused, opened his mouth to speak, and then turned and slipped into the dark.

Treading softly, I followed Tobias and listened. My eyes adjusted to the dark and focused on forms and shadows. I heard a camel and the sound of voices. I slid my hand onto the smooth handle of my weapon. The voices came nearer. Soon, a flicker of a fire glowed in the dark, casting shadows on three squatting men.

They were clothed in white tunics. A thick white turban covered the head of one. They were deep in conversation. Then their talk ceased abruptly. One man put a finger to his mouth; his other hand reached out to one of the men.

No one moved. Not Tobias, not me, nor the three men. My heart jumped as the three men leaped to their feet.

"Who's out there? We know you're there. Shew yourself or you'll be sorry," called one of them. "We'll come after you."

Stepping into the light of the fire, we raised our hands. "Hello! Peace be unto you. We're friends," Tobias said. I looked grimly upon the men, sensing a coolness in the atmosphere.

"Who do you say you are?" cracked a growling voice.

"I'm Tobias, tent maker from En Gedi, and this is Hadia from Beth Nahar. Who do you say you are?"

"Hold your tongue. We're asking the questions here," a chilly voice responded. Their quick, restless eyes moved from Tobias to me.

"Sir, I did not mean to displease you," Tobias said.

"How do we know you're telling the truth?"

"Lying is easy," another accused. The men glared at us.

"Hear me, and I shall make it known to you." Tobias reached deep into his tunic. He pulled out a tent peg with his name and En Gedi carved into it.

"Here sirs, one of my tent pegs."

"Hmm…" one man muttered as he fingered the peg. He handed it to the other two. They examined it closely. Glancing at each other, they nodded in mute agreement.

"Well, perhaps you are telling the truth. Come sit down and have some of me brew," one said.

"Thank you, sir. We can stay only a bit. My friends will come looking for us if we don't return soon."

"Perhaps you should return to your camp. It's late. We can meet in the morn. We'll share 'the news,' and have rice and tea."

"Sir, I will return in the morn with my friends. God preserve you!"

Tobias and I left quickly and made our way back to camp. O-No barked as we stepped into the light of the fire.

Phares sprang to her feet. "Tobias, did you find anything?"

"Yes, three men. We don't know anything about them. They asked us to return in the morn; all of us. They want to serve us rice and tea. They seem harmless. We can go back to sleep."

Phares yawned. "Good. Now, maybe I can finally get some rest."

The morning dawned, bright and clear as we arrived at the mystery men's camp. Tobias waved. "Peace be unto you." The three men stood. "Sirs, this is Phares and Levi of the Karka Tribe from Beth Nahar."

"Welcome guests," each said, bowing low. "And unto you be peace."

We entered humbly, consenting to join their encampment.

"Sirs, now please tell us who you are," Tobias said.

"I am Faikon and these are my brothers, Joel and Javan. We are of the Tutuka Tribe. We're here to hunt the Hills. Please sit. We will share 'the news' and eat."

Faikon was a swarthy man of elder years, proving later to be stiff in opinions. Joel and Javan appeared much younger. Long, matted locks hung from their heads. It gave them a wild appearance. Their clothing was tattered and odorous. Our visit was made quite pleasant by their clement nature. We sipped tea, ate rice, and exchanged "the news."

Faikon's most prized possession wandered to him; her tinkling anklets rang cheerfully. She moaned and lovingly planted a kiss on his forehead. Reaching up, he scratched her neck. "Blessed morn-sweet beast. Akka—her name is Akka." A crooked smile waved across his face.

"Yuck." Levi made a face. "I don't want camels kissing *me*."

Faikon laughed. "We love our camels. They are daughters of joy. We will fight their battles with our last breath. It's hard to survive without them. They give us food, milk, leather, wool, and dung for our fires. They are Yahweh's greatest gift to mankind. You should have camels too."

"We are poor. We're blessed to have Raz, our donkey," Levi said.

Raz looked at Akka and raised his lips, showing slimy, yellow teeth.

"Maybe God will give us a camel someday," Phares said.

"Maybe Yahweh will give you several, perhaps even the Red Camel."

"Red Camel. Is there such a beast?" I asked.

"Old village men tell stories of seeing it. They say it would bring good fortune to anyone owning it, but it belongs to no one."

Faikon's suggestion is out of the question, I thought. *We have no means to purchase camels thanks to Uncle Zor stealing our family wealth. And finding the Red Camel is as likely as catching a falling star—impossible!*

"Faikon, we must be on our way, but I have a question. Do you know of a man called Jude?" I asked.

"Yes, I know of him. He rides a beautiful red stallion. We saw him yesterday racing at great speed. He travels the Valley of Tremble where the Nephilim giants reside. He always returns unharmed."

"We need to find him. How can that come about?"

"It would have to be a divine encounter arranged by the gods. You best pray about it, for I know of no other way to find him."

"Yes, we'll do that," I replied wistfully. "Thank you for your hospitality."

"Please take one of our camel-hair blankets." Joel held out the gift. "Your sleep will be sweet. Now, go safely."

I took the blanket. "Thank you, Joel." We then bowed and continued east with full hearts and high spirits.

Trees and shrubs thickened as the ascending trail narrowed demanding single file walking. Little waterfalls cascaded down hillsides, creating tumbling streams. Every hill and every dell was ever changing, always mysterious, always fascinating. The Nephilim Hills held a lush variety of landscape. Pines, larches, silvery birches, and unnamed trees nudged in between. Sometimes gauzy mists of moss carpeted the forest floor. Looking back, Dead Lake disappeared.

A slender bridge crossed a turquoise-blue stream. It was quite shallow, exposing glittering sand and pebbles on the bottom.

"Look," I said, "do you suppose that's gold in the strea—"

Snap!

"Ow! My foot!"

Throbbing pain shot through my leg as I tumbled forward onto my knee. I thrust out my hands to catch my fall.

"I'll get you out!" Tobias yelled.

I struggled to raise my foot from the splintered boards. "Oh Tobias, now look what I've done."

"Hadia, that wasn't your fault. Give me your hand." Tobias steadied me while I pushed myself up. With help, I hobbled to the far side of the stream and found a clearing in which to sit. I removed my sandal and examined my injury.

"Looks like you've torn your ankle badly," Tobias said, bumping my leg.

"Ow!"

"I'm sorry. I didn't mean to hurt you. I'll mash some figs with olive oil for your wound. We'll unpack Raz. You can ride him."

"What about the supplies?"

"We can carry them a few days. We'll manage."

Phares gave me a hug. "Hadia, I know how much this quest means to you. We're committed to complete it no matter what. We want your ankle to heal. We'll be fine."

"We're strong, Hadia, don't worry about us," Levi said, flexing his muscles.

"All right. I'm sorry to be a bother."

"Hadia, I've heard those words before. Remember when I said I was a bother? You said I wasn't. You said you loved me. Well, the same goes for us. You aren't a bother. We love you too."

Shivering, I gave a thin smile.

"Here, let me clean your wound." Phares tore a piece of cloth from her tunic. She applied the fig mash on the gash and bound it with the strip of cloth. Tobias and Levi unpacked Raz and hoisted me up. We then continued down the trail.

My mind filled with accusing thoughts. *Why didn't I notice the splintered boards? We need to be home before the sheep lamb. Now I'm going to slow us down.*

Heavenly Father, please heal my ankle. Oh, and help us find Jude. So let it be.

CHAPTER EIGHTEEN

The Secret

"She told me to put her at the wayside and not tell anyone."

"Phares, there's something I need to tell you," I said, "something I should have told you a long time ago."

"Hadia, what is it? You sound so serious."

"It is serious. I mean…well, you'll understand after I tell you."

"Tell me what? What is it?"

"It's about the twins."

"What twins? Whose twins?"

"M-Mother's twins," I stammered.

"What? Mother never had twins."

"Yes, she did. Mother had twins. One boy—Levi, and one girl." I paused and took a deep breath. "Remember, you were with Father at the market in En Gedi when she gave birth to Levi."

"Two babies! Mother had two babies? What happened to the baby girl?"

"Mother was dying. She was afraid Father's infirmity would not permit him to raise two babies. She told me to put the baby girl at the wayside and to not tell anyone about her. The secret has been a heavy burden to carry. I've always wondered what happened to that beautiful baby girl."

Phares took a deep breath and swallowed a lump in her throat. "Hadia, don't be sorry. You were just doing what Mother asked you to do. Now I know why you brood so much."

"Yes, I am consumed with thoughts of Mother and Father's deaths, and the baby girl."

"Since you told me, maybe your mind won't be held captive anymore. A secret shared cuts the burden in half."

"I hope so. Oh, Phares, the baby girl had beautiful red hair, just like Levi! I wrapped gold strands of wire around her tiny wrist. After Mother died, I ran back to the roadside to get her, but she was gone. I cried for weeks."

Phares gazed gently at me. "I'm so sorry. Gold wire? Where did the gold wire come from?"

"A man on a red horse rode into town one day and asked Mother to trade food for gold wire. He had a large amount wrapped around his wrist. She agreed to the exchange. She didn't know his name, where he was from, or where he was going."

Phares sighed and stared into space. "Red hair...we must find the baby girl. I don't know how we'll do it, but we must."

"She's not a baby any longer, Phares. Trying to find that little girl might turn out to be a wild camel chase, like this journey."

"I thought you were the determined one. You do believe we'll find Eden, don't you?"

"I'm not so sure."

"We will, Hadia, and maybe we'll find our little sister. Imagine! Levi has a twin."

The thought of finding our sister helped me take my mind off my throbbing ankle.

"Let's take rest," Tobias called. "Hadia, let me help you down."

I slid effortlessly off, but squealed when my injured foot touched the ground. "Ouch! It doesn't feel much better."

"It will probably feel worse before it feels better. You'll have to give it time."

"I know," I answered, feeling lightheaded.

Swish! Swish!

"Raven," Levi hollered, "come here!"

Raven hopped on Levi's shoulder. *"Hello! Hello!"*

Levi retrieved the note and read it aloud:

"Dear Hadia, Phares, Tobias, and Levi: I am fine, but have bad news. Moushere has died. He was well one day, and then dead the next. Nobody knows what he died of, poor man; such a fine person. Take care. Love, Grandfather."

"Moushere! No, not my friend, Moushere!" Tobias wailed. "It's not fair! He was a good man."

I took a shaky breath. "Tobias, our days are numbered. God knows when it's time to be with Him. Moushere has been promoted to glory." *At least I'm not responsible for Moushere's death!*

Tobias removed his head cloth and ran his fingers through his hair. His eyes watered; tears slid down his cheeks. Sighing deeply, he shook his head. He muttered something under his breath, and then sat heavily on the ground.

I touched Tobias' shoulder. "I'm sorry, Tobias. I'm so sorry."

"I'll miss him; never had a better friend than Moushere," his voice trailed off.

We sat silent a moment. "I guess we should take time to eat," I said.

Raisin cakes, dates, and nuts were passed around. Tobias ignored the food. The rest of us ate. Soon, we were ready to leave. Tobias helped me mount Raz.

The hills climbed rapidly, leaving everyone out of breath. "It's getting steep," Tobias said.

"We must reach the summit by nightfall," I said, ignoring his protest.

"Did you figure out my riddle?" I heard Levi ask Tobias. "You know: 'Two ears I have but cannot hear. Two eyes I have but cannot see. I cannot walk, nor can I talk, and yet you fall down at my knees.' "

"That's a hard one Levi. I don't know the answer. What is it?"

Levi laughed. "A stone idol."

"Eee! I would never have guessed that. You fooled me this time."
Levi picked up a pebble, threw it, and continued to laugh.

"You still don't know how to be a gracious winner, Levi. I guess
it's 'cuz you're young."

Hello, I see something. "Stop, everyone," I called.

"What is it, Hadia?" Phares asked.

"I think I saw someone."

We stood quietly, straining our eyes to catch sight of anyone.
Then he appeared from a grove of cedars—a man on a magnificent
red stallion with a coat that shone like sparkling red wine. Prancing
and tossing its head, the stallion nickered. "Hail, my name is Jude.
Peace be upon you. This is my horse, Israfel."

"And peace be upon you. From whence come you?" I asked.

"I tell you the truth. I am from nowhere, I am from everywhere.
I have been before and will be after."

Levi scratched his head. "That doesn't tell us much."

"Son of man, it tells you enough."

I was awestruck. The very man we were searching for stood
right before me.

*Why didn't I think he would be found? After all, we prayed we
would find him. Why is answered prayer always such a surprise?*

CHAPTER NINETEEN

Jude

"Destroyers are the devil's angels. They are weavers of lies."

I'm Hadia, and this is my sister Phares and my brother Levi. We are children of Zamir Yousif, of the Karka Tribe from Beth Nahar. This is Tobias of the Bebe Tribe from En Gedi," I stammered.

Jude dismounted and surveyed us with intense brown eyes. His ebony hair glistened in the sun. A dagger and a whip poked out from under a gold sash. A silver sword with a whalebone handle straddled his shoulder. Coils of gold wire wound around his wrist. A bow and arrows with peacock feathers hung from a rope draped around Israfel's neck.

"Jude, we've been told you travel the sands, the Valley of Tremble. Is the tale true?" I asked.

"Yes, it's true. Why do you ask?"

"We need someone to escort us safely across the Valley of Tremble. Can you take us?"

"You know not me, I'm a stranger. How do you know I am worthy of such a deed?"

"We don't know, but we trust God," Phares answered. "We knew the only way to find you would be to pray—and here you are!"

"I see," Jude said, with raised brows. "Very well, I will escort you. We shall leave at first light in the morn."

"Thank you." I bowed low. "All right, everyone, let's set up camp."

A few weak thunderheads moved in blotting out the host of evening stars. Pink flashes of distant lightening lit the sky like ribbons gone berserk. Peals of thunder grumbled.

"Thunder is Yahweh's voice; lightening is His weapon. He rides thunderheads," Jude murmured to no one in particular.

A balmy breeze fingered our clothing. O-No growled, answering the distant thunder. I nudged Phares and whispered, "Did you notice Jude hasn't asked about 'the news.' What do you make of that?"

"Maybe he doesn't need to hear any 'news.' Maybe he already knows."

The thunder rumbled away. Stars winked above the treetops. Moonbeams shone among tree trunks, casting creepy shadows that seemed to move. A nearby owl ruffled her feathers and screeched, *Hoo...Hoo...Hoo.* Forest sounds came to a hush.

"Jude, do you know Destroyers when you see them, and have you seen any around here?" I asked, folding my bedding.

"Yes, I tell you the truth, they are the devil's angels. They are weavers of lies. They kill, but cannot be killed, unless they fall into an abyss. Why do you ask?"

"We believe they may be following us. We were attacked at Magdala Tower."

"I see. We'll keep a close watch for them. Hadia, I noticed your wound. Let me take a look."

I sat on a rock and lifted my injured foot. Jude's touch felt warm and soothing.

"It doesn't look severe. A few days off it should help it heal quickly. Repack your donkey and save your backs. You may ride with me on Israfel."

Ride Israfel? Maybe getting injured isn't so bad after all, I thought.

Tobias and Levi packed Raz while Phares prepared food. We finished off the raisin cakes leaving flour, olive oil, dates, nuts, cheese, and caravan bread.

"If everyone has eaten, we need to fill the waterskins. It will take ten days to cross the Valley of Tremble," Jude announced.

"Everyone has eaten. Let's give thanks and pray for safety," Phares said.

We bowed our heads and prayed silently. Our prayers were cut short by the interruption of a field cricket wailing, *Treeee! Treeee!*

"Eee! Crickets! They bring good luck."

"There you go again Tobias, you and your useless superstitions," Levi teased.

"Well, we found Jude. That was good luck."

"That wasn't good luck. That was an answer to prayer."

"Maybe so."

"Follow me; I'll shew you the way," Jude said, mounting Israfel.

Phares helped me mount. I looked down to find a place to hang on. I grasped onto a roll of blanket behind Jude, hoping my grip wouldn't give way. I couldn't wrap my arms around a stranger, and a man at that!

Levi led Raz alongside Tobias. Phares lagged behind. O-No raced ahead of everyone, loping in a long-legged gait, bobbing his head up and down. He sniffed the ground and then the air, waving his tail back and forth like a flag. Stopping on point, he spotted a little grey field mouse grooming his whiskers. He leaped to catch the mouse, but it skittered away.

The trail was alive with activity. Crouching motionless, a jumping spider looked ready to pounce upon unsuspecting victims for his morning meal. A covey of quail burst from a thicket, scattering every which way, chattering peevishly. A small gray fox appeared at the edge of the trail and stared at us. He then turned, glanced over his shoulder, and padded away. A mother deer and her fawns snorted and hurried deeper into the thicket upon seeing the fox.

Gradually, the forest became dry and sparse as we descended the trail. Dry needles layered the ground. Rocky formations jutted out of brushy slopes leading to dry gullies and riverbeds of eroded rocks.

Israfel stopped abruptly, causing Jude and me to collide. He held his head high and twitched his ears back and forth, and then froze them in place.

"Israfel hears something. We're not alone," Jude warned.

"It may be Destroyers. I don't think they give up easily," I replied.

"There are few places to hide on the valley floor. It's desolate down there." Jude turned Israfel around and faced the others.

"We must be on guard. We're not alone. Destroyers may be close. They may attack on the valley floor where there is little cover."

"I'm ready for them!" Tobias yelled, raising his fists.

Levi raised his sword. "I'm ready."

"Look, your mightiness, put your sword away. Don't go out of your way for trouble," I scolded.

"Come! We've no time to waste," Jude ordered.

We became silent, full of suspicion. Any unseen sound seemed threatening and unfriendly. O-No stopped from time to time, cocking his ears, listening to what we could not hear. Raz and Israfel twitched their ears back and forth to decipher unheard sounds.

Dust devils whirled in the haze of heat. Sun scorched leaves lay in disarray beneath withered bushes. Scorching air rose from the baked soil as we drew closer to the valley floor. Faint sounds echoed and died. The echoes grew louder—more sounds—they did not die. Breaking twigs and crumbling rocks cracked the air. Then they appeared—fierce centurions, the principals of ruin.

Two sun-blackened men on black horses charged like angry wasps, waving silver spears high above their heads. Savage black dogs loped alongside. They were human wolves—the Destroyers. The battle was on!

Jude instantly whirled Israfel around and faced the enemy. "Hadia, hold tight!"

He took his sword from his shoulder and charged at the advancing steeds. Swinging the sword, it sliced one rider's rein. He pursued the other Destroyer and cut one of his reins. A single rein made it difficult for the Destroyers to guide their mounts; however, they were still able to throw their weapons. Spears flew through the air. The Destroyers' effort to close in on us was to no avail.

The cruel black dogs leaped at O-No with open throats. One caught him by the neck; the other caught his hind leg. O-No howled a loud, piercing cry and struggled to free himself. The evil dogs growled, tearing eagerly at his body.

"Jude—stop! We must rescue O-No!" I cried.

"No, I must hide you first. Hurry, everyone. Follow me. I'll return for O-No."

The Troop quickly followed, stumbling down a narrow gully. Crumbling slopes gave way to a cracked riverbed of dry bones. Strewn about were zebra and wildebeest carcasses, jaws open, frozen in time. A sprinkling of tunnels, dark caves, and rock crevices lined the slanting slopes.

I clung to the blanket roll, lurching and bouncing as Israfel sprang ahead. My heart leaped to my throat with each pounding hoofbeat. The body scroll cut deep into my ribs as I flew up and down. I was losing my grip. Frantically, I wrapped my arms around Jude, shuddering to think of Grandfather's disapproval.

"Hurry, get in the cave!" Jude shouted, dismounting. He reached to help me down.

"Jude, I must go with you. O-No needs me."

"There is nothing you can do to help. You'll just be in the way."

"Please, Jude—"

Jude hesitated. "Oh, all right." He then mounted and we tore away in a cloud of dust.

I heard O-No's cries as we drew near. Soon, three dogs appeared, tangled into a mass—rolling, snarling, and biting. The Destroyers stood by helpless, unable to untangle them.

Jude untied his rope and swung it at the fighting dogs, looping one dog's head. He wrapped the end of his rope around his waist, and spurred Israfel ahead. The evil dog yelped as he was yanked away. Jude then took the remaining rope from his waist and swung it, dropping it over the other dog's head, pulling it away.

Jude shouted, "Stay back! I'll tie your dogs to a bush and they will live. Come near and I'll drag them away. They may not survive."

The adversaries started forward, and then stopped, giving a slight bow of agreement.

"Tie up the dogs," cracked a voice.

"That's a wise decision. Now, I suggest you go back where you came from. You may not be so fortunate the next time you attack us."

Jude tied the dogs to a bush, and then went to O-No. He tore a large swath of cloth from the bottom of his tunic. Panting hard, O-No lay exhausted. Blood gushed from torn flesh. Jude wrapped the cloth around the wounds. "You're going to be all right, O-No. 'O Ancient of Days,' don't let O-No die. Yahweh, heal him, please!"

O-No's dark eyes showed gratitude as he tried to plant a kiss on Jude's face. He was too weak. He couldn't even give a dog-smile. Jude lifted O-No into his arms.

"Hadia, help me get O-No onto Israfel. You pull him while I push."

Jude pushed—I pulled. Together, we met with success.

Jude led Israfel back down the trail. An owl flew past us landing on the branch of a lone scrub pine. It shook its feathers and preened its wings, gawking at the strange travelers. A stiff breeze blew down the gully, grabbing dust, tossing it in the air as a small ground squirrel popped out from his burrow to see what was going on.

"Jude, is O-No going to be all right? He's been with me since he was born. I couldn't stand to be without him."

"Time will tell. Pray and don't worry."

Pray and don't worry?

"Here's the cave, Hadia."

Cool air ebbed down through the underground chamber. Blackness closed in as we adjusted our eyes to the dimming light. Only the sound of Israfel's hooves clipping against rocks was heard.

"We're back," Jude called.

Tobias and Levi stepped forward. "Jude, is O-No all right?" Phares asked.

"He's in bad shape, but I think he'll survive. We'll stay awhile in the cave. Perhaps the Destroyers will return to their camp. If they insist on following us, they may be in for a nasty surprise. The giants don't like outsiders, especially Destroyers. They will go to great lengths to slay them."

Stroking O-No, Jude leaned over him and spoke words of affection. O-No's eyes were closed, but his eyebrows twitched when Jude whispered to him. "O-No probably won't be able to walk without pain for a while. He can ride Raz a few days, and then we'll see how he does."

O-No's legs twitched and jerked. His tail rose occasionally as he drifted asleep.

Phares stroked him. "I'll carry as much as I can. He must get well."

"Let's make good use of this time. A short nap is in order." Jude sat down against the damp wall, rested his head in his hands on propped knees, and prepared to doze.

Tobias and Levi lay on the musty ground and closed their eyes. They could not sleep.

Phares and I didn't want to lie on the ground or sit against a wall. We didn't want scorpions and snakes for company. Fatigue won out. We sat down, leaned our backs against each other and closed our eyes, but did not sleep.

Dull, dark time passed. Israfel moved in circles, pawing the ground and snorting. Raz tried to inch his way toward the cave opening.

"Jude, need we stay longer? I'm ready to leave," I said.

"Yes, we can leave. Tobias, help me put O-No upon Raz. Careful, he's probably in pain."

So we left the lair—the five of us.

Singing sand beneath my feet, you sound so nice
You sound so sweet
Where do you live, melodious melody, that
Captivates my soul?
Beneath the sand, beneath the shrine, or will
Your secret ne'er be told?

Hadia

CHAPTER TWENTY

Valley of Tremble

"I am the spirit of the dead. You can't have him—he's mine!"

The weary wilderness appeared dead and empty, without voice to any living creature. It stretched out endlessly north and south, ending eastwardly at the base of the Falcon Hills. The sun hovered above us like a crown of hostile flames. Spreading skirts of sand glowed like a hearth beneath our feet. Rays of sun filtered through the desert haze, landing on mirages.

"Buhaer An Nar," Jude said.

"What do you mean 'Buhaer An Nar?' " I asked.

"Mirages. In my land, they call mirages 'Buhaer An Nar,' Lakes of Satan. Like Satan, a mirage lies to you. Blurry images belie water on a bed of sand. Many have died trying to reach the ghostly water. One cannot always believe what he sees."

"How can one tell the difference, Jude?"

"You can't at first. What appears right to man can, in the end lead to the shelter of the grave. You must seek wisdom. Ask Yahweh. He'll never fail you."

"Another thing, Hadia, seek wisdom. It's more precious than gold."

The wind swelled my shawl as I pulled it over my head, shielding my eyes from the burning white light. The inhospitable desert of naked rocks and parched sand shouted, "keep out," echoing in the enormous empty silence. Faces flushed and throats grew tight as we faced a new enemy—torrid heat. It was as dry and crisp as a baked cracker.

Jude turned his face toward mine. "A desert ship would conquer this sea of sand better than Israfel, but we'll make do."

"What's a desert ship?"

"A camel—the beast of burden created by Yahweh to help man rule the desert. It moves effortlessly over the waves of sand like a merchant ship conquering the waves of the sea. It will keep moving when other beasts tire and faint."

"Have you ever seen a *red* camel? They say it brings good fortune to those who own it."

"Where did you hear about the Red Camel?"

"A traveler told us. I thought it just a fable."

"It's not a fable. I've seen the Red Camel. It's held captive by no one."

"How can it bring good fortune?" I asked.

Jude laughed. "Questions—you never tire of them, do you? Well, daughter of man, the Red Camel is huge. Its strength is beyond measure, its stamina, boundless. It can transport more cargo, travel faster and go farther than any camel on earth. That brings good fortune."

"I would love to own a camel."

"Someday, you will."

I will?

"Jude, why did God make the desert so hostile?"

Jude turned, gave an impish grin. "Questions! The desert is Yahweh's garden. He emptied it of excess humans and animals so you can draw near to Him. Quiet strength can be found in solitude."

I furrowed my brows. "Well, I can think of nicer gardens to be in."

"Yes, but you would have many distractions."

"Perhaps."

"I must stop and protect Israfel and Raz from this inferno. You can stretch a bit while I cover them." He bade me dismount.

Phares' eyes squinted, scanning the barren desert. Nothing moved on the pathless sands. "Hadia, crossing this desert looks dangerous. What if we can't find water? We could die like rabid hounds in this barren land. What a horrid way to meet my Maker."

I sighed and tried to feel compassion. *Sometimes my sister is just too contrary for my patience.* Baked by the sun and choked by the dust, I said, "Phares, you can be fearful, but don't let fear have you."

"Ay, everyone," Levi yelled, "it's time for another riddle. Here it is: 'I have no voice and yet I sing. I have no arms, and yet I touch. I have no legs, and yet I race across the land to another place.' "

"That's a good one. Where do you come up with these riddles?" Tobias asked.

"Oh, that's my secret—for you to wonder and for me to know." His voice lowered. "Do you suppose Jude would laugh at our riddles?"

Tobias rubbed his chin. "Why not—he's human, or is he? He does seem different from anyone I've ever met."

Raven swooped down and landed upon Levi's shoulder. *"Hot! Hot!"*

"I know, Raven, but there's nothing I can do about it, so please don't scream in my ear."

Raven continued cawing, *"Hot! Hot!"*

"Well, does anyone know the answer to my riddle?" Levi asked.

"Let me guess—it's the wind," Tobias said.

"By my father's beard! You're right again!"

I smiled. *At least they don't seem bound by fear. Not yet.*

The velocity of the wind picked up, lifting grains of sand and tossing them in the air, stinging our faces.

"Ruh," Jude muttered as he helped me mount Israfel.

"Ruh? What is Ruh?" I asked.

"It's the wind—the desert wind. We may be in for a sandstorm. There's a small rock shelter just ahead. We must get there quickly. Follow me!" he shouted to the others.

The wind grew fierce. It lifted billows of sand in the air, enveloping us in yellow fog. We covered our faces and trusted Jude to be our eyes. Stumbling, the Troop ran as fast as it could. Other things were running too—giant beetles.

Mammoth beetles, an army of them the sizes of a man's fist, crawled through the sandy wash. Bronze colored faces, legs, and tails anchored apple-green helmet backs. Large black eyes bored into us as long wavy tentacles reached out to grab sandals, tunic hems, and animal legs.

Phares swung her arms wildly. She jumped and kicked at the beetles, knocking the hitchhikers to the ground. "Ugh! Get away!"

Everyone joined in the battle. There was great commotion as we fled to the safety of the rock shelter. I struggled for breathing room. It was tight inside, squishing me against the others.

"We made it," Tobias said.

Grateful to be rid of the beetles and out of the blinding sand, I relaxed a moment, but soon felt panic; someone was missing.

"Where's Levi?" I cried. "He's not here! Levi, where are you? Levi! Levi!"

The wind howled eerily, like a *djinn*—a spirit of the dead. The yellow fog thickened, making vision nearly impossible.

"Jude, Levi's not here. We must find him. Please help us!" I felt alarm growing in my voice.

"Levi! Levi!" Raven cawed.

Pulling a kerchief from his tunic, Jude stepped outside and placed it over Israfel's head. "I'll go find him."

I followed Jude. "Wait, I'm going with you."

Jude scowled, probably knowing full well it was useless to argue with me. He helped me mount. Plodding steadily, Israfel pushed his head low into the driving wind, twitching his ears back and forth.

"Levi!" Jude called, "Levi!"

"Levi!" I called, "Levi!"

"Levi! Levi!" a djinn mocked. "I am the spirit of the dead. You can't have Levi—he's mine." A chilling laughter rang in chorus with the wind.

"You can't have Levi. I am the one who came before you. I have all authority over you! Leave! Now!" Jude demanded.

The mocking laughter whimpered, and then slowly died.

"Levi! Levi!" I called. Israfel stopped abruptly. His ears twitched rapidly back and forth.

"Help, Jude! Over here!" Levi wailed in a frail, muffled voice.

"Israfel, find Levi. I know you can do it," Jude said, dropping the reins.

The red stallion turned to his left, digging his hooves into the deep sand. "Levi, keep calling!"

Israfel stopped, and then turned slightly as the yellow fog played hide and seek. Levi's call came clear and closer. Israfel nickered. Jude dismounted and stretched his hand through the sandy curtain. Another clasped it firmly.

"Levi, you're safe now. Why didn't you blow the shofar?" Jude asked.

"I did, but the wind must have drowned the sound."

"We'll get you to the shelter. The storm won't last long, and then we'll leave."

Levi wiped sand from his eyes. "We can't leave soon enough."

Relieved to find my brother safe and sound, I wondered if I caused him to be added to the list of near death experiences. I never dreamed our quest would require so much risk and hardship.

The storm roared away, fierce and steady, leaving drifts of sand in its wake. Little clouds of sand choked us as it sifted through our clothing and camp supplies. We left our rock shelter and rode on through the heat.

Erosion gullies cut into the trail, which made trekking uneven. Small, irregular scarp lines stretched across the broken terrain to the east, flattening out north and south. Jumbled hills like loaves of bread poked up here and there.

The sun glared without respite, extracting moisture from us like a sponge. My skin felt scorched to the quick. My temples throbbed and my lips withered. Not a blade of grass or a drop of water existed. Our goat-skin bags held precious water to be rationed in tiny sips.

"There's an oasis close by. We'll stop and take food and rest," Jude said.

"Jude, I hear music. Where's it coming from?" I asked.

Delicate notes sounded with each step Israfel took in the sinking sand. A gentle chirping rose in the air like notes of music. The singing rang *woo, woo, woo* in a slow beat.

"It's singing sand. It rings of many musical instruments. Sometimes there are bells, at other times, drums. Some say the bells ring from an old buried temple. Camels are frightened by the underground music."

"I've never heard such music. It's nice."

We joined Israfel, producing a strange concert as we trod across the sand. I sang a little melody: "Singing sand beneath my feet, you sound so nice; you sound so sweet. Where do you live, melodious melody that captivates my soul? Beneath the sand, beneath the shrine, or will your secret ne'er be told?"

I sang the melody over and over, and then tiring of it, I let it drift away.

"We're almost there. The oasis is just ahead," Jude called out.

CHAPTER TWENTY-ONE

The Shayba Bird

"Don't move. We must wait until it's a good distance away."

A fringe of feathery date palms swayed around a small spring-fed pond. A fine lawn of wild grasses cloaked the bank, drifting among the trees. It was the ultimate welcoming committee: life itself—sweet water! The palms gave gifts of life too: food for the stomach, thatch for the hovel, wood for the water-wheel, ropes, mats, cups and bowls.

"Water!" Tobias shouted as he ran to the pond. His feet tangled. He sailed into the air, and landed against the ground, banging his crown. "Oops!" he laughed.

O-No leaped off Raz, raced three-legged to the water and lapped vigorously. Israfel and Raz hurried to the spring and thrust their heads deep into the wellspring of life. Raven jumped in for a bath. We relieved our parched throats with the cool, sweet water.

"I have never felt so dry and dirty," I said. "I need a bath."

"Me too," Phares and Tobias echoed.

"Let's put up the tent. Phares and I will wait inside. We'll prepare something to eat while you men bathe, and then you eat inside while we bathe," I said.

Phares arched her brows and rested her hands on her hips. "Wait a minute. How do I know you men won't peek while we're bathing?"

Tobias laughed. "Would we do a naughty thing like that? Don't you trust us?"

"Well, maybe. But remember, God is watching you."

"Yes, and God is watching you, too. How do I know you won't peek at us?" Tobias laughed again.

"Ha! Women aren't interested in a man's naked body," Phares retorted.

"Oh?" I teased.

We worked together assembling the tent. Soon we had bathed and were ready to eat.

"I forgot about the 'sweet lumps of delight' Granna gave us," I said, opening the sack. "She told me much about the giants."

Phares scowled. "Oh, for heaven sake, what does that old yenta know of the Nephilims? She hasn't been any farther than her front door."

"You're wrong. Granna has done and seen more than one would suspect."

"Hmm," purred Phares, twisting her hair. "What's that supposed to mean?"

"She often told me of her late husband's escapades with the Nephilims. Village hunters and the Nephilim giants would stumble upon each other while hunting. Her husband saw them many times. She described them vividly."

Phares wrinkled her nose. "I thought they never left the Valley of Tremble."

"Apparently, they do. If we see them, you owe me an apology," I said.

"How *did* Granna describe them?"

"She said they were a tribe of ne'er-do-wells. The pariahs are huge and fierce—many heads taller than us. She said they ride elephants on vapors of boiling copper and carry tree-size spears of bronze. They worship themselves, believing they are gods. She warned me of two noisome ones—Beguiler and Wrath. What tempers! She said it doesn't take a bit-of-wit to set them off. You want to stay away from those two."

"Curse their father's mustache!" Tobias said, raising his fist in the air.

Levi grinned. "Tobias, what happens when you curse a mustache?"

"I'll tell you what happens. Their mustache falls out—right onto the ground."

"Maybe they don't have mustaches."

Tobias laughed. "Then, I'll curse their mother's mustache."

"Jude, what do you know about the Nephilim giants? Are the stories about them true?" Phares asked.

"The stories are true, especially about Beguiler and Wrath. They do indeed exist. They stir up trouble and spread evil."

"How can we tell them apart from other giants?" Levi asked.

"Wrath is always mad. He is easily angered. His fists are doubled—ready to fight. His left ear is missing a piece of earlobe. Beguiler is cunning. He will coax you with flattery, and then deceive you. He has a scar above his right eye."

"I hope I don't run into them," Levi answered, wide-eyed.

"To them you may look like a grasshopper, but grasshoppers can do much damage. What's in your head is more important than your size. Wisdom is mightier than muscles. A strong person is of little use if he doesn't have the intelligence to go with his strength," Jude said.

"He's right, Levi. You have to outwit them, not try to outrun them," I added.

Winged shadows flew through the dark as night settled in. Palms nodded; birds dozed; stars came on stage for their dazzling night show, blinking and twinkling. A clear white moon poured shimmering tides of light over the desert. Phares and I took shelter in the tent, glad at the falling, empty daylight. We collapsed onto our blankets and soon fell asleep.

Morning came, holding no dew. The sun-baked air was wonderfully still. Slanting sunlight passed through the trees and cracks in the tent. A slender sun ray found its target—my eyes. "Phares, get up. We need to make haste. I hear the men making ready to leave," I said.

Phares struggled to sit up. "All right, I feel like I have been run over by a herd of camels."

I watched the sun rise above the brow of the desert. Shelves of red sand glinted green and gold at the horizon. Occasional sandhills of paler colors stood out. It was the land of images—always changing—always challenging.

We took breakfast by the pond. Tea, 'sweet lumps of delight,' cheese, and caravan bread were passed around. Soon, the men dismantled the tent. Phares and I gathered supplies and filled waterskins. Levi and Tobias climbed the palms and picked rich clusters of blood-red and amber dates from their tufted crowns. We offered morning prayers.

"There's an oasis ahead in a stretch of land that holds the shelters of the giants," Jude said. "The water is brackish, but will do. It is about half a day away. We'll travel around their village. Hopefully, we won't be seen."

"I want to see where they live. I can't wait!" Levi answered.

"I can wait," Phares said. "I don't wish to become a part of their harem."

Tobias laughed. "Why not, Phares? Your offspring would be little giants."

Phares wrinkled her nose. "Tobias, that's not funny."

The torment of the naked sun was upon us. We advanced in follow-the-leader formation. O-No was left to walk three-legged for a short time. He would later be lifted upon Raz for a rest. Levi and Tobias fell into step.

"Tobias, do you ever have bad thoughts?" I heard Levi say.

Levi's question intrigued me.

"Sometimes. Why do you ask?"

"Sometimes I have bad thoughts too. I don't know where they come from. Like thinking I don't like someone before I even get to know him."

"Me too. But, there's a big difference between thinking something and acting upon it. Bad thoughts can be banished. Bad acts are not so easily done away. You must master your mind before you regret your actions."

"I suppose."

"Levi, what do you have that you can always count on?"

"I don't know, Tobias, what is it?"

"Your fingers!"

"Tobias, I don't know where you come up with all your silliness. Maybe you should change your trade from tentmaker to storyteller. You should get to know Phenias Friarhair, the storyteller in Beth Nahar. He would love to leave his stories to someone like you. His tales need to be carried on, you know."

"Hmm…hadn't thought 'bout that. Not a bad idea," Tobias said, stroking his chin. "Maybe story telling would be a good trade for me. After all, I come by it naturally. Imagine, getting paid to tell stories—true or not."

Jude helped me mount Israfel. We rode on without slacking. Israfel's nostrils flared, sniffing odors familiar to him. He was in great form, stepping high, drinking deep the morning air.

"Jude, I know that, being a woman, I'm expected to do womanly things. But I want to travel and fall in love with the man of my choice. Am I wrong to want these dreams?"

"Oh daughter of man, it's not wrong. Your spirit aches to soar. But you must want these dreams for right reasons. Dreams sought with heartbreak are not golden even when accomplished."

"What do you mean?"

"Your passions are at war within yourself. You desire what you don't have. You covet what you cannot obtain. I tell you the truth, what you really seek is peace. Your greatest desire should be to know God—not know *about* Him, but *know* Him. When you do, He will turn your heart of stone into a heart of flesh."

A tear slid down my cheek. I felt a churning in my spirit. "I'm angry and bitter about the senseless ending of Father and Mother's lives. They were young. They had much to live for."

Jude perceived that I was grieved. "Love has strength when it's greater than anger. Anger and bitterness harden the heart. I pray someday you'll let it go."

"I pray someday you'll let it go." I thought I heard laughter far away.

"Ara-Belle?" I whispered.

Drying sand cracked and formed deep fissures making homes for scorpions and other nasty creatures. A few boulders were strewn about, shelters for snakes and desert rats. Then it appeared—the Shayba bird, as tall as a camel! The formidable bird glared at us, ready to charge.

"Stop! Don't move. We must out-wait it. If we move, it will attack. It will leave if we are patient," Jude warned.

I had never seen such an enormous bird. A short beak and beady eyes peered from a tiny head perched high upon its ladder-long neck. Legs like tree trunks held up its elephant shaped body. With no wings, it was flightless, but it was powerful. I didn't want to find out just how powerful. We waited and waited and waited.

"Why doesn't it leave?" Levi whispered.

"It's probably as intrigued with us as we are with it," Jude answered, shielding his eyes from the sun. "However, unlike us, it's in no hurry."

Something in the distance caught the bird's attention, and it turned to follow its curiosity. Slowly, it strode off.

"Don't move. We must wait until it is farther away. Your patience will save our lives," Jude said quietly.

Finally, we could see only its swinging head behind a pile of boulders. We moved forward, eager to put distance between us and the ancient-looking bird. The bird's head was only a speck in our eyes when it turned around and stared. With alarming speed, it raced toward us.

"It's coming back!" Tobias shouted.

The massive bird ran, unwieldy, swaying and jerking as each foot thudded in the sand. Its high-pierced scream punctured the desert air, sending a chill through my veins.

"Over here—quick!" Jude pointed to a pile of boulders. "Make ready your bow and arrows. We'll have to attack it."

We ran behind the boulders and readied our weapons. The Shayba bird was almost upon us when we fired our arrows, striking our target. Stunned, it stopped, shook its head and screeched. More arrows found their way into the raging bird. Staggering, it struggled to flee its enemies. The mammoth bird stumbled and fell, unable to move. We stood silent, waiting to see if it would get up. It didn't.

"Whew!" Tobias said. "That was a close call. If I never see another bird like that, it will be too soon."

I gazed across the enormous desert and sighed. *We've been pursued by many evil people and creatures. I've put the Troop in harm's way. God, should we turn back?*

My attention was arrested by the flapping of wings. Raising my hand to the sun, I shielded my eyes and focused them on a soft, gray dove gliding to the ground. It landed softly at my feet and cooed. "You're a long way from home, little dove," I murmured. I didn't know why, but the gentle dove comforted me. It reminded me of Grandfather's prayer: "Neither stay nor turn back before finishing the quest. Let undaunted courage diminish your doubt." Brave thoughts winged on Grandfather's prayer gained mastery over my doubt. *Heavenly Father, magnify my courage. Diminish my doubt.*

Ghosts of mammals past lay cradled beneath thousands of layers of desert earth.

Fossilized remnants of a long ago time: horned gophers, giant sloths, pygmy elephants, leaf-nosed bats, warthog-like ungulates, and saber-tooth cats. We marched on, skirting around broom shrubs, scattered rocks, and drifts of sand. The trail rose for a short time and then flattened out.

"By founds, who comes riding yonder?" Tobias cried.

I shadowed my eyes with my hands and focused on what looked like moving boulders. "What's that?" I asked, amazed.

"It's a Nephilim giant caravan," Jude replied.

I was transfixed by the sight of huge elephants striding the Valley of Tremble. The sun beamed on glinted bronze and gold body shields of the giants riding in wooden towers on leather-armored elephants. The towers swayed back and forth as the elephants' clumsy feet ploughed the deep sand.

"Are we safe, Jude?" I asked.

"I hope so. One never knows for sure. We'll stay out of sight and let them pass, and then we can move on."

The Nephilim caravan stopped and stood at a standstill. Suddenly, a bull elephant laden with warriors charged across the desert. The battle-trained elephant lumbered toward us.

CHAPTER TWENTY-TWO

To Slay a Giant

"Little man, you can't outrun me. Don't even try."

Hadia, ride with Phares! Levi, ride Raz. Carry O-No!" Jude leaped off Israfel. "Tobias and I will stay behind and set a trap. It's our only way of escape. Quick, run until we're out of sight. Hurry!" Following his command, Phares and Levi fled. I stayed.

Jude glared at me; there was little time to argue. Instead, he turned to Tobias and told him to take one end of the rope, string it across the trail, and secure it under a boulder. The boulder would hold the rope and trip the elephant.

"We'll have to stand still long enough to fool them. When they get close, we'll run," Jude shouted.

Tossing one end of the rope to Tobias, they stretched it across the trail and waited. The enormous elephant continued charging, screaming. The warriors waved their weapons and yelled, "Slay them! Slay them!"

"I have never been in such a dreadful dilemma in all my life. Oh, to be back home in En Gedi!" Tobias wailed, terror stricken.

"Run Hadia, Tobias! Hurry!" Jude shouted.

Jude, Tobias, and I turned and dug our heels into the sand. We sprinted away at arrow speed.

The screams of the elephant rang so loud in my ears, I was sure its trunk was going to grab me. Then it happened. The beast tripped, flew forward, and crashed hard like a shooting star hurtling to earth. The ground shook like an earthquake. Two giants sailed through the air. They bounced across the ground and rolled to a stop. One stretched lifeless, the other lay quiet for a moment, and then pushed himself into a sitting position.

Trembling, the stunned elephant rose. The sun-scorched land became oddly quiet. The desert held few places in which to hide. We crab-crawled to a small boulder to see what was left of our enemies.

"Good—only one. We'll see if he comes this way. If he does, we may have to slay him; we have no other choice," Jude said firmly.

The giant grunted and stood, rocking back and forth on his feet. Holding his head with one hand, he turned around and drew his dagger with the other. Gathering his balance, he stumbled toward his companion; his companion was dead.

"Arrgg!" the brutish giant roared and raised his fists. His face flushed; blood dripped from his nose. Thick cords of neck muscles bulged; veins swelled purple. Clearly wroth at the death of his companion, he howled, "I'll hack you into morsels!"

Another enemy was about to appear upon the scene; a slimy, slithery one with no voice. Tobias' eyes reflected in the eyes of a viper—a cobra. He was a whisker's hair from the snake. Moving not a muscle, he whispered shakily, "Jude...."

Jude turned to answer and saw the evil reptile. He drew his sword. "When I get its attention, move away." He then threw a pebble, distracting the snake.

Tobias crawled backwards into a prickly plant. "Ow!"

"Run, Tobias," Jude commanded. "You too, Hadia."

Tobias ran; I did not. I had to help Jude. He was caught between a snake and the giant. As the snake coiled to strike, Jude swung his sword, slicing it in half. Now there were two snakes, each threshing and whirling frantically. The ominous coils rose and fell, rose and fell, until they lay limp at Jude's feet. He turned and faced the giant. Looming high above him, the giant spoke in a thick, strange voice.

"Little man, you can't outrun me. Don't even try!" The giant's threat thundered and echoed through the nefarious valley. " 'Tis a pity you did not die earlier. Now, I'll make piecemeal of you!"

"You vile orge, your bitter prophecy rings dull in my ears. I have no intention of outrunning you—I don't need to."

The giant beetled his brows and narrowed his eyes. "What do you mean, you don't need to run?" he asked in mock disbelief. "Everyone runs from giants."

"Vain-glorious boasts," Jude replied, pulling his whip from his sash. He lashed it around the giant's ankles, crumbling him to the ground with an oomph and a cry of "arrrgg!"

The burly giant grabbed Jude's legs and jerked them out from under him. He slammed his fist into Jude's stomach and face. Jude's sword bounced away from him, and from me. I could not help as he tried to reach it.

"I must get the sword," he yelled, in labored breathing.

I knew O-No could dodge the giant and push the sword to Jude. Frantic, I screamed. "O-No, come! O-No, come!"

Soon, O-No hobbled three-legged into view. "O-No! Thank heaven! Push the sword to Jude." O-No looked at the sword for a moment, and then at Jude.

"Push the sword. The sword! Please O-No, push it to me!" Jude gasped between smashing blows.

O-No placed his nose behind the sword and pushed it. Jude clasped the sword and lifted it high, trying to avoid the giant's blows. He thrust the sword into the giant's neck. Blood flowed like a waterfall. The giant grabbed his neck and keeled over motion-less. Jude pulled himself away and lay back, struggling to catch his breath. "O-No, you knew I was in trouble."

O-No gave a dog-smile and licked Jude's face. He looked as if he were trying to say, "Of course I knew you were in trouble. Dogs have perfect hearing."

"Of course, dogs have perfect hearing," Jude said with a wan smile, wiping blood from his face. "Tobias, it's safe. You can return."

Tobias ran to Jude. "I've never been so afraid in all my life. Are you all right?"

"I'm fine, just a few cuts and bruises; how about you?"

"I'm all right, except for my backside. Could you please pull out those nasty thorns?"

Chuckling, Jude said, "Of course, bend over."

We trudged in silence toward Phares and Levi. Soon we heard Israfel nicker.

Tobias waved. "There they are."

Phares ran to us. "Are you two all right?"

"We're fine, we're fine," Jude replied. "Come, we must be on our way. The caravan has moved on. We'll be safe."

Levi and Tobias lifted O-No onto Raz. Jude and I mounted Israfel and fell into follow-the-leader formation, recovering our right line of march.

The burning desert sun rose above a shallow ravine. The narrow bed of red sand, crumbling rocks, and scrub broom made walking a challenge. We picked our way up the ravine to flat ground. Passing wild frankincense trees gave Tobias reason to share another superstition. "Good wives burn frankincense in their tents at sunset. It keeps evil spirits away."

We shook our heads and rolled our eyes.

"Look! I see something," Levi yelled. "What is it?"

In the middle of the valley, strange-looking abodes lined up in a row. Each had two doors and flat roofs. The roofs held a canopy of trees and shrubs, looking like roof-top forests. In front of the abodes were large, round structures with mounded sod roofs. The village clung to the valley floor, repulsing any wave of invaders.

"What strange shelters. What are they?" Levi asked.

"The Nephilim giants live there. It's their village. The large round abodes are for their elephants and supplies. They grow vetches on top of the roofs. They have spring-fed ponds, and they forage the Falcon Hills for game. They are quite comfortable there," Jude said.

Levi frowned. "I would like to see the inside of those shelters."

"Look, your mightiness," I warned. "You may get your wish the hard way. If you're not careful, you'll get captured and either be made a slave or killed. Don't let curiosity be your demise."

"I may be curious, but I haven't lost my mind. I'll be careful."

"Good. We've seen enough trouble. We don't need any more," I said sternly. "Jude, how long will it take to go around the village?"

"Not very long. There's another oasis near here, but well out of sight. We can take rest there. The water is as sweet as honey."

The sun continued its downward curve toward earth. We turned south, skirting the Nephilims' village. It was late afternoon when we arrived at the "sweet water" oasis. The sight of water was bliss to my eyes.

O-No jumped off Raz and ran three-legged to the pond. We threw ourselves down to gulp the liquid gold. Palm branches drooped, heavy with luscious dates. Ashab grass grew abundantly on the pond banks. Deep crimson glowed from the hem of the sky. Night was ready to trade place with the sun.

We ate our evening meal and prepared for bed. We said our prayers and "good nights." Tent flaps were left open, inviting the evening breeze to join us. O-No curled up with me while Raven found a palm branch to roost. Quiet hovered around us like invisible fog.

Black shadows passed between the trees, alerting the animals. Israfel nickered and pawed the ground. O-No's low growl stirred Phares and me.

"Someone's out there," I whispered.

I shoved the body scroll deep into my blankets and grabbed my dagger. The others woke to the sound of Israfel's nicker.

"Quiet," Jude whispered. "Make ready your weapons. We'll wait for them to shew themselves and then we'll attack."

I picked up sounds of slow, heavy footsteps. Two monstrous shadows moved toward the tent, looming high above the top.

"Now!" Jude shouted.

Boisterous laughter filled the air, echoing like rumbling wagons. "You little people don't stand a chance," a loud voice boomed.

Two fierce looking, ill-clad giants reached down and grabbed Phares and me. We tried to stab them. The giants twisted our arms, forcing the daggers out of our hands.

"I wouldn't come any closer if I were you," ordered one giant in a flat, chilly voice. "These women would make perfect concubines or slaves." Sinister smiles drew across the swarthy faces of the giants. Their guffaws echoed across the desert.

"You spineless brutes! If you were real men, you wouldn't pick on women," Tobias yelled, hurling his head cloth to the ground.

Brows bent and eyes flashing, another giant said through glittering teeth, "We intend to keep the women and kill the rest of you."

"Never!" Levi ran at them with sword in hand.

They laughed. "A grasshopper! We step on grasshoppers!"

"Stop, Levi. We work as a team," Jude commanded.

I remembered Jude's words: *"You can't outrun them. You must outwit them. Size without intelligence is useless."* But, how can we outsmart them? It will take a miracle.

"It may interest you to know of my secret treasure," Jude said.

"Secret treasure? What is it?" the giant with a scar above his eye asked.

"I have something that can bring you riches—it's of great value."

"Where is this treasure?"

"It's for us to know and for you to wonder," Tobias snickered.

"Aaagg!" growled the tight-fisted giant. "Don't play games with us. We'll smash you like a bug."

"Hear me and I'll make it known to you. Exchange the women for the treasure," Jude offered.

"The women for the treasure?" the scowling giant said, lowering me to the ground.

"Keep talking," the smooth-talking giant ordered.

"Let the women go. You leave. Come back in the morning at first light. You will find the treasure by the palm trees nearest the pond."

The tight-fisted giant laughed without humor. "Surely, you makest mirth of me. You're so entertaining."

I stared incredulously at Jude. *How is he going to get us out of this mess? He'll have to perform a miracle!*

"Do you know our names?" Jude asked.

"We have seen you from a distance many times, fast rider; you are Jude. We do not know their names," one ugly giant replied, waving his hands toward us.

"I know your names. You, smooth-talker, are Beguiler; you, tight-fisted one, are Wrath," Jude said.

Flabbergasted, the giants' jaws dropped. "How can you know our names? I have never known one possessing such knowledge. You must have magic. The treasure must hold magic. I want it!" Beguiler shouted.

"Will the treasure give us magic to know great knowledge like you?" asked Wrath.

"If you use the treasure given, you will grow in knowledge and power."

"Power. I like the sound of that. I don't know. What guarantee do we have the treasure will be there when we return?" Beguiler asked, stroking his chin.

"You have my word. It's true. It never returns void."

Wrath and Beguiler stared at Jude in disbelief. "We have no proof your word is good," Wrath said, raising his brows.

"Yes, but you neither have proof my word is naught. Look, risk-takers take chances. You can always kidnap women; you cannot always reap riches."

Wrath and Beguiler talked together in a little knot, and then nodded. "All right, we'll take you at your word. For your sake, it had better be good." Beguiler let go of me.

"Good. I'll leave the treasure for you by the pond."

The giants turned and left camp. They stopped once and looked over their shoulders.

"Jude, what will you leave them?" I asked anxiously.

CHAPTER TWENTY-THREE

The Merchant Caravan

"Is it foolish to cross dangerous land out of curiosity?"

I left them the Book of Wisdom," Jude said. "Wisdom knows the past and forecasts the future. Wisdom does, indeed, bring knowledge, power, and riches. I tell you the truth, wisdom is truly a treasure."

"Eee! Are they going to be mad! I don't think that's what they expected."

"We never recognize treasure when we see it. We have to discover it. It's usually right at our feet. It may not be what they expect, but it is a treasure," Jude replied.

"They probably won't read it, much less follow its instructions," I said dryly.

"We must keep moving. There's an oasis not far from here. We should be there by middle-night," Jude said.

"Middle-night! Oh dear, I hope I can make it," Phares complained.

"You'll make it Phares," I said. "The sooner we finish our journey, the sooner we can look for our little sister. You'll be riding, so how can you be tired?"

"I'm not tired, I'm sleepy."

"There'll be plenty left of the night when we arrive at the oasis. You can catch up on your sleep there. Until then, think about Little Sister."

"Little Sister," Phares murmured, "I wonder where she is."

"Do you think the Destroyers are still following us?" I asked.

"If they're not dead, they probably are," Tobias answered.

"Being hated by the giants would be reason enough not to follow. On the other hand, greediness can override fear," Jude said. "They have drawn off for now, but they will attack again if they think we have something of value."

I chuckled. "Maybe the Destroyers will run into the giants and they'll kill each other."

"Ha!" Tobias cackled, "wishful thinking, Hadia."

We broke camp and left. Phares and I rode Israfel. O-No rode Raz; Jude walked with Tobias and Levi. We fell silent, listening intently for any unfriendly sound. It wasn't enough that we were being pursued by Destroyers; now giants were added to our list of enemies.

The moon jumped up and touched a lone cloud. The desert appeared empty in the feeble moonlight.

"Look! Flying stars!" Levi cried. "I wonder where they come from and where they're going. Jude, do you know?"

"The Ancient One—Yahweh—made them and knows where they land. He hangs the moon and stars for lamps, creating light for the night. They are under the canopy of heaven."

"Where does He live?"

"Heaven is His throne and Earth is His footstool. Sometimes He rides clouds pulled by the wings of the wind, and glides the morning skies."

Levi grinned. "I've never seen winged wind pull clouds."

"What do you think He does when He rides His clouds?" Tobias asked.

"He scatters jewels of love, mercy, and forgiveness."

"Speaking of jewels, Jude, have you seen a white raven called Leuce? I've been told when she flies, she carries jewels in her mouth," Tobias said.

"Yes, I've seen the white raven. Sometimes, she does carry jewels. But I tell you the truth, wisdom outweighs folly. It is a detestable practice to chase hidden treasure when honest work will provide ample riches. Wisdom is worth more than jewels."

I considered Jude's view of folly and wondered if we should continue to seek the white raven. "Jude, is it foolish to cross dangerous land out of curiosity?"

"It is the motive of the heart that determines foolishness. Only you can answer that question."

"Despite Destroyers and giants, can we reach our destination?" Phares asked.

"Time and chance happens to everyone; success is uncertain. You cannot always control the events in your lives. The Book of Wisdom says it doesn't take speed to win the race, and it doesn't take strength to win the battle. Faith and perseverance lead to success. Have no regrets if you have done your best. It's better to do something and fail than to do nothing and succeed."

I wonder if Jude's answers are yes, or no, I thought. *Only the future will tell.*

Time passed quickly. The aroma of sweet grass and water signaled our arrival at the ancient oasis. We drew rein. "We will rest here tonight and mount again when we see the morning light," Jude announced.

We kindled a watch fire on a hollow bank and lay down on the pleasant sand to sleep. A stirring breeze soon lulled me to dreamland.

The new day lightened. It was as hot and dry as the day before. Raven cawed, *"Wake up! Wake up!"*

Phares covered her ears. "Raven, those are not pleasant words."

"Hurry up, everyone. We must be on our way," Jude said. "We're only a short distance ahead of the giants. They may be angered with the treasure I left and pursue us. There's an oasis between here and the Falcon Hills where we can refill our waterskins and take rest. We can take food there."

The white sun continued to rise as the day wore on. Thankfully, no harsh wind blew, just a soft breeze. No voice of birds broke the air. Silent boulders refused to tell their stories. Horned vipers burrowed deep in the sand, along with scorpions. Huge, hairy spiders with reddish legs scuttled about. The unforgiving desert stretched away. Scarred by broad tracts of stones and sand, the loneliness of the desert was frightfully oppressive. Above the brow of the desert, the Falcon Hills appeared close at hand.

I reached down and petted Israfel. "Oh, Israfel, I do love you. I feel so safe on you. I wish you were mine. Maybe someday I'll have a horse just like you. Maybe I'll meet a handsome man who loves horses, one who wants to share his life with me. Oh, Israfel, is it possible?"

Israfel shook his head up and down and nickered softly. At that moment, I felt a special connection to the wonderful stallion.

"Look, prints in the sand!" Levi called. "Someone has traveled before us. Who could they be, Jude?"

Jude drew rein and dismounted. Kneeling, he crumbled dried dung between his fingers, and then studied the faint imprints. "These are camel tracks and droppings. Six camels made these tracks. Three pregnant camels are carrying six Awamirs, and three bull camels are carrying supplies. Smooth prints tell me they have come from far away, the gravel plains. They passed here about ten days ago. They were fortunate not to have met the giants—or maybe they did."

"How do you know all of that?" Tobias asked in awe.

"I have traveled the desert and shared the tents of hair with nomads much of my life. The desert knows the inevitability of events. Its sands are like an open book. All can read what living creatures leave behind. Birds, beasts, and insects leave clues in the sand. The clues are there until the wind blots them out."

I tried to read the book of sand. I saw no clues of birds, beasts, or insects.

"The Well of the Old Camel is not far, about halfway to the Falcon Hills. It will refresh us until we arrive at the oasis. Phares, you ride with Hadia. I can walk awhile."

The overhead sun was fierce. It drained our energy at an alarming rate. The Well of the Old Camel came into view. It didn't come any too soon. We drew water from deep within. It was brackish, but one takes what one finds in the desert or one goes without.

The grainy water stuck in my throat. *I hope we find a 'sweet water' well soon.*

"We mustn't linger. Let's take leave," Jude said.

Eagles flew overhead, signaling an encampment nearby. The relentless heat showed no mercy, swallowing us like a bread oven. We were ready for the oasis, but didn't know we would be sharing it with strangers. As we moved closer, I saw tents, people, camels, and zebras.

"Who are they?" Levi asked, wide-eyed.

"It looks like a merchant caravan," Jude answered.

"What's a merchant caravan?"

"They are merchants with their guards and drivers. They bring goods from around the world, shipped in by sea to the inland people—goods such as rice, tea, mandu beans, pepper and spices. They also bring silks, gold, silver, and gems. They bring things we can't grow, mine, or make."

"Are they dangerous?" Phares asked.

"I've never known them to be dangerous. Dishonest? Sometimes."

"Well, merchants or no merchants, I'm going for a swim," Levi said.

Jude drew near to the strangers, picked up a handful of sand, and threw it into the air. "Peace! Peace be upon you!" he shouted.

Guarding themselves, the merchantmen grabbed their weapons.

"Jude, why are you throwing sand into the air?" I asked.

"It's a custom of the desert—a sign one gives to signal peace."

"Oh," I said, amazed at yet another strange tradition of this foreign land.

"We will introduce ourselves and share 'the news.' Those living in the wilderness are always greedy to hear tidings."

The merchants took notice of our peaceful demeanor and put their weapons away. They returned the sign of peace, and then approached us.

"Sirs, from whence come you, and who do you say you are?" Jude asked.

One foreigner with a face as withered as dried figs smiled and said, "And unto you be peace. My name is Asmakiah, and this is Shaul, Dan, and Zophar. We have come from the Ramic Sea and have sailed many days and many nights, from isle to isle, sea to sea, and shore to shore. We have been from Aisre to Shira and from the foot of the Akmal Uplands to the base of the Malik Mountains. We have bought, sold, and bartered everywhere we went. Please, come into our house of hair for nourishment. We treat you as guests of Yahweh."

"Thank you. We can stay only a short while," Jude replied.

Asmakiah bowed low. "Ah, verily! A little while is enough time to make new friends. We are honored."

Asmakiah was a well-clad, sturdy graybeard. He wore a fine, yellow linen tunic. A purple silk mantle draped around his broad shoulders. It was fastened with a gold cord. A silver sword studded with turquoise hung at his waist. A silken turban of many colors girded his head. He smelled faintly of flower water. I could see he was a man of elegant leisure in the desert life.

Dan, Shaul, and Zophar seemed a little broken-headed, bumping into each other and knocking things over. Their attire was simpler: dull gray tunics and mantles. White turbans crowned their pointed heads.

Moving with regal deliberation, Asmakiah waved us ahead. It was plain to see that he was pleased to have visitors. For that

I was glad. I was starved and felt a measure of gratitude for the middle-day feast.

Soon, desert hospitality began. Dan jumped up to milk one of the camels. In an elaborate balancing act, he sat on a small stool, braced his right foot against his left knee, and cradled a milk bowl in his lap under the camel. The milk started to stream as he stroked her udder.

Rice boiled as the fire was lit for mandu. Shaul roasted mandu beans in a long-handled skillet and then proceeded to pulverize them in a heavy bronze mortar, along with cardamom seeds and ginger. The rhythmic sound of fresh-roasted beans being pounded sounded like the clapper of a bell, summoning us to eat. Shaul poured the powder into a long-beaked, copper brewing urn along with boiling water, setting it back on the fire to boil up again.

We went into the tent. Asmakiah took Jude by the hand and said kindly, "Be seated! Be seated!" He then turned to the rest of us. "Sit we down!"

We sat cross-legged on fine wool carpets. Goodwill broke forth as rice and dates were passed around, along with small cups of camel's milk. Frothy foam floated on top of the milk; white mustaches graced everyone's lips. The merchants wadded the rice into a ball with their hands and popped it into their mouths.

I nudged Phares. "I've never thought of eating rice that way. I'm going to try it." Phares watched me pop rice balls into my mouth, and then she followed suit.

Shaul balanced a stack of tiny clay cups in one hand, and a pot of rich, thick mandu in his other. He moved around the group, filling each cup about one-quarter full, and offered one to each person. Later, he circled again to pour refills until each drinker wiggled his little finger to indicate he had had enough.

"The land you passed through—is it bare and empty? What 'news' do you bring?" Asmakiah asked.

"The desert we passed through is dry and empty," I said. "Beyond the desert from whence we came are hills and valleys green with tender grass. The trees share their limbs with falcons, hawks and numerous other kinds of birds. We are from Beth Nahar and En Gedi. They are lovely towns."

The merchants fixed their eyes upon me, lending doting ears to my "news."

I felt my face cloud. "There is war in my land."

"War!" Asmakiah's mouth tightened. "That is worrisome news. I'm sorry."

"Yes, I'm sorry too. I hope we have villages to return to." Everyone was silent a moment.

Then Jude spoke. "Asmakiah, did you travel from En Gedi on the upper road?"

"Yes, we did."

"Have you traveled this route before?"

"Never."

"This desert is known as the Valley of Tremble. The Nephilim giants roam the sands. They slay more often than not. There are also Destroyers, an evil nomad tribe. Sir, I suggest you go back to the village Ivor and take the road to En Gedi. Then, take the King's Highway, which will lead to Beth Nahar and other villages. But remember, there's war in that area." Jude frowned. "None of the routes look promising."

The merchants sat mute a moment, and then Asmakiah spoke. "Sir, thank you for the warning. We will not take leave until the morrow. It will give us time to pray and seek Yahweh's guidance."

Zophar unwound his headdress and reached for a studded bronze burner.

"It's custom to rid our tents of unsavory odors with incense of sandalwood," he said. Closing his eyes, he inhaled deeply and fanned the perfume over his hair and beard in strange rapture. "It comforts the soul and soothes the brain. Now, pass it to the others."

Each of us took a bracing whiff. I fanned the fumes *away* from my face hoping no one took notice. *It's going to take more than a puff of incense to make me smell clean.*

A dish of perfumed sweet reeks was passed around. "Snuff one, and then put it under your mantle. Your clothes will be well-smelling," Zophar said. "Snuff the sweet reek! Snuff the sweet reek!"

Phares and I rolled our eyes at each other and obeyed Zophar. *Didn't it ever occur to them to bathe and wash their clothes?* I wondered.

"When I chew zat, I am able to speak an unknown language. If you relax and chew zat, success will come to you," Asmakiah said, offering some to Jude.

"Sir, we don't mean to offend, but we do not chew zat. Thank you anyway," Jude replied with a thin smile. The merchants looked at each other, as though amazed we didn't "chew."

"Since you were kind enough to warn us of danger, I will also warn you of danger," Asmakiah said. "It's a Great Spirit Snake about three camels long, one dog wide, with enormous gems in its eye sockets. It can overcome you with evil if it looks at you. It lives in a cavern where the desert and the Falcon Hills meet. We did not see it, only the cavern. An old man on the road warned us of the danger. He says the Great Spirit Snake only comes out of the cavern once a day, when the sun is rising. You must avoid the cavern at that time of day."

"Yes," Jude said, "I have seen the Great Spirit Snake."

Levi laughed. "I hope I get to see it. I'm not afraid of snakes. I'll use Tobias' whistle stick to charm it."

"Oh dear," Phares murmured, twisting her hair, "snakes terrify me!"

"Look how far you have come, Phares. You have met every challenge with victory," Tobias said. "Besides, we may not see it."

"The day is half spent. The possibility of sighting the Great Spirit Snake is unlikely," Jude said.

"You'll have warning; it leaves wide tracks in the sand," Dan remarked.

Raven flew in circles cawing, *"Snake! Snake!"*

Asmakiah questioned Jude. "I have circled the world, and have heard many tales about the Garden of Eden. They say it's in your land, after crossing a bridge called The Bridge Beyond Time. Do you know of such a bridge? Could the legend be true?"

"I know of no one who has seen such a bridge. If Yahweh had wanted us to know where Eden was, He would have left us a map."

"Yes, I suppose so," Asmakiah replied in a hushed voice.

"Asmakiah, have you passed other travelers?" I asked.

"Yes, we saw two men on brown horses and a little girl on a white horse. We were startled to see them on horses. They also had a large red dog, and one man had a hawk. They were on the upper road to En Gedi. Hunters, I suppose. I don't know why the little girl was with them. Girls should not be away from home. 'Tisn't safe." Asmakiah scowled at Phares and me.

Phares and I looked at each other. "I wonder if the little girl had red hair," I whispered. Then I said, "Asmakiah, thank you for your hospitality. We must take leave. We need to be at the Falcon Hills before dark."

"Of course, of course. But, please I pray, take some of our food. The chance of birth and fortune has made me a wealthy man. I have more than enough to share."

"Thank you. You're most generous."

"There is one more matter—gifts. Please, take these," he said, pointing out two peacock-colored silk shawls, rice, roasted mandu beans, and a bag of spices.

"Oh!" I gasped. "The shawls are beautiful. Thank you." I bowed low.

Asmakiah fixed his eyes intently upon mine. "Here is my blessing for you: 'May your mount glide on heavenly streams; may you sleep like a baby; may your eyes flame like lamps at night so your enemies cannot hide in the dark.' "

"Thank you, Asmakiah. I'll treasure your blessing."

We bowed, and then bade farewell.

I wonder where you are
Oh little one, born so long ago
The one I never held
Nor stroked your little cheek
I wonder where you are
Oh little one, the one we didn't keep
Don't weep, we'll find you, dear
And when we do, we'll always
Keep you near

Phares

CHAPTER TWENTY-FOUR

A Peculiar Cavalcade

"We were unaware of the Great Spirit Snake as it slithered down the tree."

The fierce, glaring sun hung over us like a fiery furnace. The wind whispered a low, mournful wail over the sweeping, immeasurable land. Dust swirled and drifted, coating everyone like a floured breadboard. I stared at the cracked desert floor. If it ever held messages, the sand had erased them.

"This was once the land of caravans and conquest, before the giants seized it," Jude said. "At one time a fanatical warrior called Azrikam ruled this vast sweep of desert. He acted with nobility, yet was treacherous, killing all enemies of his faith. He lived for absolute power—the power of conquest. His great tribe was known throughout the land for its brute fighting courage, equally savage. War, famine, and disease eventually eradicated the religious warmonger and his tribe."

My eyes searched the barren desert, grateful the evil warrior wasn't still around.

"What do you plan on doing after you arrive at the Falcon Hills, Tobias?" I heard Jude ask.

Tobias' face flushed. "We…um…we'll explore the hills, and then maybe go home."

"There is a town near Ivor called Dowlatabad. It sits at the base of the Falcon Hills. The old upper road to En Gedi begins there. It would be a good place to rest before you return home."

"I did not know 'bout that village. I-it isn't on our m-map," Tobias stuttered.

"Map? You have never mentioned a map before."

Tobias' face flushed as he wiped his forehead. "Well...uh... uh...well, Hadia's grandfather had a map of this area—of a sort. We examined it, but it was hard to read. Some of the writing had worn off." Jude studied Tobias. "I see."

"Jude, who comes riding yonder?" Levi asked, straining his eyes toward the horizon.

A cavalcade advanced toward us, dust drawing before it in clouds. A long single column of strange objects—huge, monstrous shapes—moved closer and closer. As we drew near, we saw large, horned bulls, almost hidden under enormous frameworks holding numerous items. The makings of a household of a nomad chieftain and his wives were piled and hung on the beasts—rugs, pillows, cooking equipment, tents, and personal belongings. Ostrich plumes jutted out everywhere, waving in the breeze. Beaded bands and leather tassels hung across the foreheads of the bulls.

A gollywog of women sat on top of each peculiar animal. They wore loose, graceful robes of brilliant colors. Ornaments of silver and gold dangled everywhere: brilliantly colored beads, silver anklets, bracelets, necklaces and earrings. Strings of golden coins swung from noses to ears. Women attendants swathed in petticoat veils and tent-like tunics walked like formless ghosts beside the overloaded bulls, balancing the whole unwieldy burden. A titter of excited murmurs arose.

An old, flat-faced, fish-eyed man—bent and knotted up—sat with dignity on a huge black bull. He was clad in a white tunic and beat a pair of drums in steady rhythm. The sound of the marching column was strange. It was a curious scene to behold.

The tribe's chief led the odd procession on a scrawny little camel. Shining metal studded the camel's trappings. Bells tinkled from reins and anklets. Cross-bands of silver fastened the chief's robe that hung like royalty upon his stately form. A snowy white turban was held in place on his head by a silken cloth of many colors. A long sword with a hint of gold hung from his shoulder. The old nomad chieftain's hooked nose, white beard and mustache gave him an air of stature and authority. Having all the majesty of a sultan, he advanced cordially with stately modesty. "Hail, strangers. Are you tribesmen from Talma?" he asked.

"Peace be upon you. No, we're not of Talma. My name is Jude, and this is Hadia, Phares, and Levi from Beth Nahar. This is Tobias from En Gedi. Who do you say you are and where are you from?"

"And upon you be peace. My name is Seria of the Nazir tribe. This is my family." He waved his arms toward the wayworn women. "We are Anakim nomads, always wandering, always seeking. We've heard Eden lies in a place called the Land of In-Between. We would like to find it. Do you know where it is?" he asked with a pleasant stare.

The Land of In-Between, I thought.

"We don't know where Eden is, and you had better wander back the way you came. Giants inhabit this land, and they don't like outsiders. They slay people. If you insist on going farther, vultures will gather and fly along to accompany you. They know they can expect food," Tobias warned.

"We know nothing of giants and are grateful for the warning. Please, reward yourself. Take one of my wives. They are well trained and will serve you well." The old chieftain smiled and waved his arm toward the women.

Levi and Tobias covered their mouths to muffle their laughter. I smiled openly for I was greatly amused. Phares winked at me.

"You are most generous, sir, but it won't be necessary to take one of your wives. It's only fitting to warn others of danger," Jude said.

The chief's smile vanished. An awkward silence followed. I felt we had offended the dear man, but we could do nothing about it. He touched his beard and shrugged his shoulders. With a melodramatic air he said, "Very well. Let me give you one of my headstalls for your magnificent horse."

Reaching behind his back, he pulled out a slender headstall with a worn but beautiful lead rope. The rope had silver bells and bands on it. Pressed into the headband was a gold crest embossed with the word 'peace.'

Jude reached for the headstall. "Thank you, Seria. I will adjust it to fit Israfel."

"Seria, have you passed others on your journey?" I asked.

"Yes, we passed two men and a little girl on horses a while back. We were amazed to see them on horses. They had a large red dog; a hawk sat on the shoulder of one man. Little girls should not wander the land. They belong at home where it's safe," he replied, glaring at Phares and me.

"It sounds like the same people the merchant caravan passed," I whispered to Phares. "I hope we see them."

"Now, what is your 'news'?" Seria asked.

Jude told them about the land we crossed and about the war in Bashon. He then concluded by announcing our departure. "Seria, we must leave."

Seria touched his hand to his head, and then waved us on. "God preserve you."

We bowed low and moved around the strange wayfarers.

"Well, I didn't know the tale of the Land of In-Between was known so far and wide," I said, surprised. "It seems everyone is searching for it."

"Rumors have circulated for decades about Eden's location. I hope you're not thinking of pursuing that folly," Jude said firmly.

Phares and I exchanged looks. I ignored the warning.

"Jude," Phares said, "I'm afraid we're getting near the Great Snake's cavern. I know it's well past his 'coming out' time, but I'm still frightened."

"Don't fear, Phares. We'll see him if he is out. Just look for his tracks."

"Oh dear, I'm not going to rest one bit until we get past his lair," she moaned, biting her lip.

"At least we're riding. The men have to walk," I replied.

"Small comfort—"

"Stop!" Levi shouted. "I see a track—snake track!"

Studying the graceful curve in the sand, Jude said, "The image is old. I don't believe we need worry about it."

"How do you know it's old?" Tobias asked.

"Look closely; there is a buildup of sand between the ridges of the track. If the track was fresh, there would be more of an indentation. We'll move on and put a good distance between us and the Great Snake. Hurry up!"

The Falcon Hills rose like heavenly eyebrows, enticing us closer. We were unaware of the presence of the Great Snake as it slithered down a tree, watching us.

CHAPTER TWENTY-FIVE

Destroyers

"Give us your goods or you'll meet your Maker today."

J ude, I heard you mention Dowlatabad. Where is it?" I asked.

"It's a village where the old upper road to En Gedi begins. You should take that road home. It may be out of your way, but it's safe. Most likely I won't be around to escort you when you return."

"May I ride Israfel by myself? I do love him so."

"Yes, Hadia, you may. However, you must ride without ropes and blankets. You need to feel his satiny, warm coat and feel his muscles swell as he carries you away. To be drinkers of the wind, you must unite as one. Trust him to carry you without harm. You will gain courage in doing so."

"I can't do that. I need the ropes to hold on to."

"Yes, you can. I wish to have Phares do the same; it will be an act of courage for her, too. We're not far from the Falcon Hills; ride now."

Jude reached up and helped Phares and me dismount. He then removed the ropes and blankets, turned to me and said, "Ready?"

I shook as I whispered, "Yes."

I put my foot in the cup of Jude's hands, grabbed the reins, and swung my leg over Israfel's back. He felt warm, smooth, and wonderful. I turned him from the Troop and urged him on. Gathering all my courage, I pressed my legs hard against his barrel. The powerful stallion leaped into a gentle run.

The wind billowed my hair, gathered it up, and scattered it in the air. My face tingled; my eyes teared from the stinging air and scorching sun.

"Oh, Israfel, I do love you so."

I stopped and turned Israfel around. Pressing him on, I felt his muscles ripple beneath my skin. His coat was warm and damp. I didn't want the ride to end. Stopping short in front of Jude, I slid off. "Jude, I can't believe I rode a horse by myself!"

"I knew you could. You were called to be a horse woman."

"Horse woman? I'm called to be a horse woman?" *No wonder my desire for a horse haunts me.*

"It's your turn, Phares," Jude said.

"Jude, I can't ride without ropes."

"Daughter of man, when you face your fear you'll find courage and strength you never knew you had. Here, let me help you up."

Before she could object further, Jude helped Phares mount. She turned Israfel away, quickening his pace across the desert. She swayed and bounced to the rhythm of his hoof beats.

I knew Phares was afraid she would fall off. I saw her grab his mane and lean forward as he sprinted into a slow run. Then she sat straight and rode smoothly. Shortly, she turned Israfel around and returned.

Phares giggled. "Jude, I did it. I rode by myself!" she said, sliding off Israfel.

Jude smiled as he reached for the blankets and ropes. "I'm proud of you, Phares. Now, we must move along."

We rode due east, up and down, up and down sand dunes across the desert. Soon, the lush hills were sighted in the fading light. A soft pink glow ruffled the hem of the sky. It wasn't dark, it wasn't light, it was twilight. A lone bird called its mate. Frogs croaked. Sweet grass and dampness wafted in the air.

"Jude, what's that?" I pointed to a flat, brown stone almost hidden in the gravel.

Jude dismounted and examined the unusual stone. "It's a grave marker. We are in the Vale of Remembrance—the vale of graves. This is the grave of Bin-Aliya, the most renowned woman around. Her father was the famous warrior, Istah. She was the mother of eight celebrated warrior sons."

It wasn't often a woman was given such recognition. *She must have been held in high esteem,* I thought. We bowed our heads in reverence.

Flames flickered high from the evening watch fire casting ghostly shadows on our faces. Mumbling distant thunder echoed as darkness erased the day.

"They're crying. The clouds are crying," Tobias said.

"What do you mean 'the clouds are crying'?" I asked.

"Thunder—that's the clouds crying."

"I do declare, Tobias. You have quite an imagination! Yes, you would make a good storyteller."

Phares made brew from the roasted mandu beans the merchants gave us, sprinkling in some of the spices. The quiet of night was broken with enchanting music. Tobias' fingers worked magic with his whistle stick.

"I must leave on the morrow," Jude said softly.

Surprised, I begged, "We don't want you to leave. Can't you stay longer?"

"You're safe now. My mission for you has been completed."

"We'll miss you," Tobias said.

"I don't want you to go. I have more questions for you. Besides, I haven't asked you a riddle," Levi said with a wan smile.

"I'll miss you too, but there'll be another time for questions and riddles. You'll see."

I studied Jude. *Another time—when will that be?*

"I believe there's more to your journey than exploring. Therefore, I leave you a riddle to solve: 'Look to the left and look to the right. Look for the hole that lets in the light. Follow the light that shines on the stones and there you will find the path to home.' "

I sat in awe. I wasn't brave enough to ask what way—what home? *What does he mean there's more to the journey than exploring? Does he know our secret? If so, how did he find out? Who is this person who seems to know all?*

"Well, it seems everyone's tongues are tied. Has no one anymore to say for the eve?" Jude asked cheerfully.

Tobias coughed, Phares shifted her sitting position, and then Levi started laughing. "My tongue's not tied. I can talk all night."

"I bet you could, but we're not about to let you. Besides, it's time for you to turn in," I said sternly. "Jude, do you think we are rid of the Destroyers and the giants?"

"The giants, perhaps; the Destroyers, no. The giants rarely leave their domain, even for revenge. The Destroyers will go to the ends of the earth to try and get what they want."

"Will we ever get to relax?" Phares asked.

"Maybe in our sleep," Tobias teased.

"Blessed dreams, Troop," I said, untying the body scroll. I tucked it under my blanket, relieved to have it off. The chafing scroll had left my skin irritated.

Eager to rest, I crawled into my blankets and pulled closed the shutters of my eyes. Fireside flames danced, casting moving shadows on the trees. Other shadows moved too; ones with voices. O-No's low growl stirred me as he got up and slowly padded away. I listened for sounds and looked for shadows.

"Uh-oh. Trouble," I muttered. "Phares, Jude, someone's out there."

Everyone sat straight up. Our eyes darted back and forth, looking for enemies.

We grabbed our weapons. I felt for the body scroll and shoved it deep under my blankets.

Suddenly O-No's barking pierced the night air. We jumped up, ready to defend ourselves.

"Get away, mutt! I'll slice off your mangy head," a loud voice bellowed.

"Slay the cur!" a raspy voice screamed.

"Shew yourselves," Jude demanded.

"We'll shew ourselves all right. Give us your goods, or tonight you'll meet your Maker," slurred a gruff voice. Dathan and Korah stepped into the moonlight swinging their daggers, kicking O-No.

"We have nothing of use to you. Leave us alone!" I shouted bravely.

"Dare we believe you? Never! Your map and goods now, or we'll slay your wretched dog!" Korah whirled around and grabbed O-No by his neck. He climbed on his back and held him fiercely, his butcher-face flushing.

"Jude, help us!" I cried.

"Stop! I have a treasure. It's of great value. It can bring you enormous riches. You will grow in knowledge and power," Jude said, with a set jaw.

The blackened-faced enemies glared at us with penetrating eyes that pierced our brains. "We like the thought of possessing power," Korah replied with a grim smile. "Tell us more."

"I'll give you the treasure at first light on the morrow by the fire-pit. Let the dog go. I won't let him attack you."

The Destroyers, cloaked and somber, huddled. After a barter of words, they let O-No loose and turned to us. Before they could say anything, Jude spoke.

"Sons of man, you are Dathan and Korah of the Caananite tribe."

Jaws gaping, the Destroyers looked amazed. Dathan eyed Jude and growled, "You possess magic. No stranger knows our names. What you say is true. We'll return in the morn and collect the treasure. But, sham threats and false promises stir revenge. We'll hunt you down and slay you if you have lied to us."

"I tell you the truth, I am the Son of Yesterday. My word is true. However, you must leave our camp tonight and move away until you no longer see our watch fire nor hear our voices. Is that clear?" Jude instructed.

Dathan and Korah hesitated a moment, and then nodded at each other. "Yes, we'll leave now." The Destroyers moved slowly into the darkness, looked back once, and then disappeared.

"Now what, Jude?" I questioned.

"Treachery is the habit of their mind. We must leave now. I'll take you to the bellowing cliffs. There are caves to hide in. You'll be safe and can see anyone approaching from a long distance."

"I don't think we'll ever get any sleep at this rate," Phares complained.

"All of you are strong and sturdy. Little slumber for one night won't hurt. You can catch up on your sleep another time."

Tobias grumbled. "Not another night journey—bellowing cliffs? What are bellowing cliffs?"

"Don't be alarmed, the cliffs are harmless. Sometimes the north wind blows against them, causing a sound like bellowing voices," Jude answered.

"I take it you're going to leave a Book of Wisdom for them also," I said with a thin smile.

Jude grinned. "Yes."

"Oh dear, now we have giants *and* Destroyers angry. If we return home safely, it will be a miracle. And how will we sleep in noisy, bellowing cliffs?" Phares complained.

"There you go Phares—always thinking the worst. Can't you ever be hopeful? After all, look to the past. You survived it and you will survive the future too," Tobias said.

Phares wrinkled her nose at Tobias, and then turned to me. "They asked for the map. How do they know about the map?"

I frowned and drew my shawl close. "I don't know."

CHAPTER TWENTY-SIX

The Thief

"It's not here—the map. I don't have it. I must have left it by the stream!"

It's as dark as a bottomless pit out here," I muttered. The feeble moon cast little light as I followed Jude, slowly picking my way through the pitchy darkness. Roosting owls swiveled their heads and eyed us with half-closed eyes. *Hoot…hoo…hoo…hoot.*

"Owls—bad luck," Tobias muttered.

"Why do you say that?" I asked.

"They send bad omens to people. Who knows what curse they will cast upon us?"

"Oh, Tobias, to you everything is a curse. How can you believe such nonsense? You need to rely on God instead of your silly superstitions. Why don't you give it a try?"

"I have grown up on traditions. They are not superstitions."

"They're superstitions. Give them up. Look at creatures as God's beautiful creations—not things to fear."

"I don't know, Hadia. It's hard to change."

"But you said you didn't want to lie anymore. You gave that up. Why can't you give up superstitions? If you don't feed your superstitions, they'll die."

"Maybe. I'll think 'bout it."

Conversations ceased as we groped our way through the thicket. The night seemed deceptively quiet, but the hills held no lack of life. Tree crowns billowed in the gentle breeze. Tree dwelling mice cried out a loud two-note whistle. Flying squirrels glided overhead. Crickets called to each other in low chorus, and then crescendoed to a high pitch. Bats soared for insects while other creatures moved soundlessly through the underbrush.

"We're almost there," Jude said in a hushed tone. "Let's find a cave above the ground, but not too high so your entry and escape can be quick. We'll hoist Raz up. He must not be seen."

"Eee! This is going to be quite a feat!" Tobias said, grinning.

Caverns scooped out by the winds of ages dotted the walls of the bellowing cliffs, giving an eerie appearance of eyes.

Levi pointed to a dark shadow in the cliff. "Look, that cave looks good."

"Yes, it will do. Hurry, get inside. The Destroyers may not wait till morning for their treasure. Tobias, you go first and tie the ropes to some boulders so we can lift Raz. Levi, remove Raz's supplies and hide them."

"How am I going to get up there? I can't scale a wall," Phares wailed.

"Mount Israfel and I'll hoist you up," Jude replied.

"What about you and Israfel?" I asked.

"I'm not staying. I'll lure the Destroyers into going another way, and then I'll be going on. You'll be on your own."

"Alone? Travel alone without you in this danger?" Phares moaned.

"Yahweh, the unseen but ever present God, will protect you. You'll find courage."

"I don't want to find courage. I want to go home!"

Paying no attention to Phares' laments, I said, "All right, let's climb. You too, Raven. We don't want you tipping off the Destroyers."

Unknown birds fluttered at our approach. We found our way into the cave, ready to wait out the night.

"Daughters of man listen carefully," Jude called softly. "She is not lost, but will be found. When you see three, there she will be."

I stared in awe. *How does he know? Who is he?* I wanted to ask him how he knew "she." Instead, I simply said, "Thank you, Jude. God preserve you."

"Farewell dear friends. We'll meet again someday."

Jude slipped silently away. We stood silent, staring at each other. Then we made a small watch fire, spread our blankets, and settled in for the night. Silence was soon broken by piercing laughter of wild hyenas.

"Hyenas," Tobias muttered. "They're magic. Witches ride them like camels. If you attack a hyena, the witch will take revenge upon you."

I was chagrined at his nonsense. It annoyed me that he believed his silly superstitions.

"I do declare, Tobias, witches don't ride hyenas. Is there anything you're not superstitious of?"

"You!"

Phares and Levi laughed. A grin tugged at the corners of my mouth. I had to admit he was entertaining, which was more than I could say about myself. And so I too laughed!

The moon sailed across the black sky. Curious notes of night sounds sang a capella. The night breeze rubbed twisted branches of the wild fig tree together, sounding like squeaky wheels. Rushing air betrayed darting black bats. Crickets hissed. The hyenas continued their macabre laughter.

Morning heralded without incident. We were ready to leave our home in the sky.

"Sister, would you wear the body scroll awhile? It's rubbing my skin." I held it out.

"Yes, of course."

"I'm going down to make sure it's safe to leave," Tobias said.

"Be careful, Tobias," I replied. "If you're not back soon, we'll come looking for you."

"Don't worry, I'll be fine." Tobias scrambled down the cliff and disappeared into the thicket.

"I won't feel safe until we're out of here and on our way," Phares muttered, pacing the floor.

"Phares, why do you always complain? I do declare, it gets a bit tiresome."

"My complaining isn't any worse than your bossiness. You're always telling us what to do."

"Well, someone has to be the leader."

Phares stared at me. She opened her mouth to speak, but then shut it. Finally, sinking to the ground, she leaned against the wall and spoke. "I'm not complaining; I'm simply saying we won't be safe until we are well on our way—far from the Destroyers. You shouldn't feel safe either. They're after the map. How they know about it is beyond me."

I sighed. *I am bossy.* "It's beyond me, too, how they know about it."

Our speculations hung in the air as Tobias returned. "Hello, I'm back. I didn't see anything suspicious."

"Oh good! Tobias, we'll need you to help lower Raz. It will take all of us," I said.

"I'll be there."

Tobias wrapped two ropes around a boulder and tied the ropes to Raz. Gathering our strength, we lowered the little donkey.

Tobias handed Phares a rope. "Here, Phares. Put the rope around your waist and we'll lower you."

"Oh dear, I don't think I can go down on a rope!"

"Well, then, you'll have to scale the cliff or be left behind."

Phares took the rope, dropped it over her head, and lowered it to her waist.

"All right, Tobias, but don't let me fall."

Tobias rolled his eyes. "Eee!"

Levi packed Raz and we continued on through the brush in aimless fashion. The dawn was awash in a sea of pink. A lone purple cloud drifted across the eastern sky. Stars paled and vanished. The snapping of undergrowth gave alarm to an owl as it clumsily took wing at our approach. I scanned the land around me, seeing in the light what I could not see in the dark. Red veins streaked across putty glazed cliffs.

The errant wind raked the tangled treetops, rousting legions of birds. Giant butterflies flashed wings of brilliant colors. Dragonflies soared and darted, preying on insects. Snakes with catlike eyes searched for frogs and lizards. Mosquitoes were legion. We followed a silver stream lined with trembling willows. My attention was suddenly arrested by the phenomenon of a curious wail.

"The cliffs are bellowing!" Tobias hollered. "It sounds like a mother calling her child."

"Where...are you...darling?" the wind bellowed.

"It does sound like a woman singing," I said. "Do you think she ever finds her child?"

"It's just the wind, Hadia. There is no child," Tobias chided.

I grinned. "I know it's the wind. The Falcon Hills are lovely, aren't they?" I sighed.

"Yes, but I haven't seen any falcons, have you?" Phares asked, craning her head.

"No, not yet. Let's stop. I think it's safe to eat and take rest here."

We spread blankets on the bank of the silver stream. Figs, rocky fragments of cheese and "sweet lumps of delight" were passed around. O-No stretched out lazily and waited for a tossed morsel.

"The trail seems well-worn. Wild animals probably frequent it," I said.

Tobias gave a sly grin and poked Levi. "Yes, like lions, bears and *dragons*."

"Tobias, there isn't any such thing as dragons," Levi said with a smirk.

"I wouldn't be so sure 'bout that. I've heard many a tale 'bout dragons."

"Tales, just tales. Dragons don't exist."

"Maybe, but you don't know what lurks in these hills, or what's on the other side of them."

I shook my head. "Phares, let me look at the map."

Phares reached under her mantle and untied the body scroll. "Here." She handed it to me.

I unrolled the body scroll and laid it on the grass. "It looks like the trail crosses another valley and ends at the base of the Purple Mountain. We'll look for the trail at the foot of the rock."

"What rock?" Phares asked.

"The rock Jude spoke of, the one with the hole in it. Well, enough talk. I know you would rather nap, but we must keep moving."

We took a final drink from the silver stream and marched on.

"Oh no!" Phares wailed, rubbing her hands around her middle.

"Now what's the matter?" I asked impatiently.

"It's not here—the map! I don't have it. I must have left the body scroll by the stream!"

"It can't be! We must return for it immediately."

"Let me get it. I can run fast. It won't take me long," Tobias pleaded.

"All right, but hurry. It must not be found by outsiders."

"I'll hurry." Tobias turned, dug his heels in the ground, and took off running as fast as he could. I felt a deep heaviness in the pit in my stomach as I watched him streak out of sight.

Tobias' run to the stream and back took much longer than I expected. I was about to go looking for him when I heard my name.

"Hadia, I'm back."

"Tobias, did you find the map?" I asked.

Tobias squirmed and rolled his tongue around in his mouth. "I couldn't find it. I'm sorry...."

"Tobias, this is terrible. We *must* find it. Phares and I will return and look for it. No, we'll all return and look," I demanded.

We returned to the silver stream and searched for the body scroll. We could not find it.

"Maybe it fell in the stream," Phares said despairingly.

"Well, if it did, it's gone now," I said sharply. "I never thought you would lose the map. What will Grandfather say? How can we face him? I only hope no stranger finds it."

"I'm sorry. I should have been more careful."

"You're sorry? Is that all you can say? How could you be so careless?"

Phares melted into tears. "I don't know what else to say. I knew I shouldn't have come on this journey. I told you I would only be in the way."

"Hadia, don't be so hard on her," Tobias said. "Any of us could have lost the map."

"Ha! Maybe you, but not me."

Tobias lowered his voice. "Nobody's perfect, you know."

The map is gone. Scolding Phares is useless. Tobias is right. I could just as easily have lost the map as Phares. I put my arm around my sister and patted her shoulder.

"I'm sorry I was so harsh with you, Phares." Phares wiped her nose; her eyes pleaded forgiveness.

Conversation was interrupted by the sound of a vulture perched overhead. The vulture sat rigid, its cold, green eyes penetrating mine. I stared back, feeling an evil presence. A putrid odor hung in the air.

"We must continue." I hammered Bidinko's walking stick on the ground. "When we started our journey I vowed not to let anything or anyone stop us. We can't turn back. We'll find Eden…without the map."

"We'll find Eden!" Levi shouted.

I gave a thin smile, relieved to have someone boost my waning confidence. Our way uncertain, I had not the slightest idea where to go next except to stay due east. There was no time for misgivings.

"All right, up we go!"

CHAPTER TWENTY-SEVEN

The Tinkers

"O-No, it's all your fault. Now look what you've done!"

We moved on. O-No ran ahead as always, looking for something to give chase to.

Raven hopped a ride on Raz. *"Faster—faster!"* he cawed.

I thought Raz looked as if he were saying, "Look—I'm only a donkey. If you want to go faster, fly."

"Tobias, Phares—stop! What's that noise?" I asked, tilting my head.

"What noise?" Phares asked.

"There it is. Hear it?"

"Yes. It sounds like music."

The sound of the mystical music drew close. Drums, cymbals, whistles, rams' horns, and other peculiar instruments clanged in the air. We stood still as the sound of the strange music drew near. Then, there they were, an odd-looking lot—three men dressed in curious attire.

Their heads swayed with enormous red turbans squatting on their skulls. They sported multi-colored leg wrappings, red and gold baggy trousers and funny looking brown sandals with turned-up toes. Jackets with flounced bodices of every color imaginable draped over their trousers. They were adorned with earrings, metal chains and bracelets.The bird-witted figures in holiday garb and clownish carriage were a silly sight!

"Peace be upon you. Who are you?" Tobias asked, stepping cautiously backwards.

"And upon you be peace. We are the Azeer brothers. I am Tollog. These are my brothers, Motlog and Hoklog. We are tinkers. We make fun, juggle and entertain for your amusement."

"Who's your tribe?" I asked.

"We have naught but our tunics, mantles, and instruments. We are orphans. We do not know what tribe we're from," a rotund man replied.

I scowled. Their homely faces were hard to read. *Without a tribe, a person is suspect. I hope there isn't more to their funny business than entertainment.*

"Where do you make your abode?" Tobias asked.

"We live in Aboo Goosh," a short, bald man answered. He had drums tied to his waist and cymbals in his hands.

"Yes," hollered another, juggling balls in the air. "We're here to entertain you—for a price, of course."

The harsh music gonged, a tumbler tumbled, and the rotund man continued juggling balls in the air. Their exaggerated, comical gestures were the funniest display of vigor I had ever seen.

"Shall we proceed?" the short tinker asked. "One bag of time will give you incredible entertainment." He reached down, grabbed a fist full of dirt and thrust it into a leather pouch punctured with holes. "What have you to trade?"

"We can't afford to barter for entertainment," I said.

"Please, we are just trying to earn our keep," another begged. "Let us entertain you."

Why are they in the hills to entertain? I thought. *Where are the spectators?*

"Why are you out here in the middle of nowhere? You hardly have an audience in the hills."

"Oh, not true m'lady. There are audiences in the hills. Why, just yesterday we played and danced for two lads and a little girl on horseback. They loved our merriment."

"Horseback? They rode horses?" I asked.

"Yes m'lady. We were surprised. We have never seen people on horses."

Horses! "*When you see three, there she will be.*"

"Hmm…we need to take leave," I said. "May God prosper you. Farewell."

Looking forlorn, the tinkers bowed and moved aside.

"Those are the strangest people I've ever seen," Phares said later, giggling.

"Sure cheered me up!" Everyone broke into laughter.

Jumbled thoughts tumbled through my mind. I thought of the dream I had at Granna's: tinkers danced, beetles jumped, and a man wearing an alabaster amulet kept reaching for a white raven. *The tinkers have danced and the beetles have jumped. Would the man with the alabaster amulet appear?* I thought of Jude's strange prophecy: "*She is not lost, but will be found. When you see three, there she will be.*" There were three tinkers, but…I let out a deep sigh. *I wish Jude were with us.*

The trail inclined steeply. The woods thickened. Suddenly, there rose a great commotion. An enormous spray of obsidian falcons soared overhead. The sky clowns rose and dove, turning and tumbling, sometimes playing tag, and then they descended into the trees. Some toppled off perches backward to swing upside down by one leg. With wits and wiles as sharp as their beaks, the uncanny birds' *cr-r-ruks*, *pr-r-uks*, and *toks* pierced the air. Their screeching could be heard many hills away.

"Ravens, ravens!" Tobias yelled.

O-No barked fitfully as we scanned the trees with penetrating eyes. I laughed and watched the silly birds. "Those raucous featherheads seem to be making it their mission to investigate us," I said.

"Hadia, do you see a white one?" Tobias asked, with a hopeful look.

"No, not a one. It doesn't matter; Jude said we shouldn't be looking for the white raven."

Tobias' eyes sparkled. "Yes, but I never said *I* wouldn't look."

I thought Raven looked like he had never seen so many of his kind in his life. He looked afraid, like he didn't want to get acquainted. He jumped on my shoulder and cawed, "*Help! Help!*"

I laughed. "Raven, I didn't think anything frightened you."

"I think we should rest and eat," Phares suggested.

We spread out a blanket and reclined on our elbows. Sweet dates, cheese, and nuts were passed around.

"Hadia, what did Jude mean when he said, 'Where there are three, there she will be'?" Tobias asked in a curious tone.

"We're looking for a little red-haired girl. That's all I can tell you. We need to leave now. Keep a lookout for the bridge."

I gathered supplies, and then stopped a moment to comtemplate the sublime hills. They were weather-beaten with age, leaving me feeling that they had seen many changes; not once, but thousands of times. They abounded with deer, jackals and other unseen wildlife. Glades appeared in the forest, hosting miniature prairies of painted flowers and bluish grasses. Dim light filtered down through the forest and settled in hollows, stunted trees, and streams. When night approached, animals would come to drink and make their abode on the fertile banks.

The ravens were still cawing, hopping from branch to branch, showing off their sky tumbling. I gazed at them once more, and then mending my pace, I continued up the hill and soon reached the summit.

The trail began its descent. It gave way to a deep, dark valley. A river snaked through the bottom of steep, frowning cliffs, some pocketed with caves. Descending the steep forested hill, we wound down into its dreary valleys, up one hollow and down another. Cedar trees soared into the sky like green giants. Old boulders piled like ancient ruins gathered in creek beds. The rugged, winding trail soon straightened, leading to a small, level clearing.

The landscape was dotted with sunlit patches of little glades and mountain meadows. Rabbits scampered. Chipmunks popped out of their underground burrows. A hawk sat sentinel on a rugged rock outcrop.

"Mushrooms!" Tobias yelled. "I'm going stop and get some."

"All right, but we're going on ahead," I said.

"I'll catch up with you in a bit."

"Help! Help!" Our chorus of voices pierced the air. I prayed Tobias would hear our cries. It wasn't long before he answered our distress call.

"By founds, now what kind of a mess are you in?" He peered down into the black pit.

"Tobias, get us out of here. I think this hole is a bear trap. Hurry!" I cried.

"I don't want any bear hugs today," Levi said with a grin.

Phares twisted her hair. "Oh dear, how will you get us out?"

"How do you *think* I'll get you out? With ropes, of course." Tobias grabbed ropes off Raz and proceeded to drop them into the pit. "Tie the ropes around your waist. I'll tie them to Raz."

Phares and I each tied a rope around our waists. Tobias tied the ropes to Raz and turned him around.

"All right, Raz, let's go," Tobias commanded. Raz barely moved. "What's wrong? Oh, the rope is caught. There, now we can go-oo-oo-oo…!" Tobias tumbled forward and fell into the pit as O-No brushed past him.

"Ow!" Tobias scrambled up. "O-No, now look what you've done! You're so clumsy!"

"O-No, it's your fault!" I wailed. "Can't you ever watch where you're going? You're always one step behind trouble. Now, how are we going to get out of this hole?"

Raz returned to the edge of the trench and gazed down. He looked at O-No as if to say, "It's all your fault!" He then brayed loudly.

O-No peered into the hole, wide-eyed. He hung his head, tucked his tail between his legs, and gazed at us. Then looking up, he sniffed in all directions. After a moment, he turned and ran back up the trail, barking feverishly.

CHAPTER TWENTY-EIGHT

The Three

"I know of only one bridge in these parts—the Bridge Beyond Time."

O-No, did you bring help?" I cried, looking up at the panting dog. A trio of strangers rode up on horses and peered into the hole.

"What have we here—food for bears? How did you manage to get into this predicament?" a young clean-shaven man asked. He looked astonished.

"The hole was covered and we fell in," I said. "Please get us out."

"Don't worry," replied the stranger. "We'll get you out."

The young man led Raz away from the hole while the other man pulled on the ropes. He hauled Phares and me up the filthy wall. Reaching the top, we stumbled to our knees. Our clothes were dirty, our hands and faces grimy, and our hair was in disarray. We were a mess! I pulled twigs from my hair and wiped dirt from my clothes. "Thank you. We are beholden."

"Eee! What 'bout me?" Tobias yelled.

One young man threw a rope to Tobias and said, "Tie it around your waist."

Tobias obeyed. Soon he was out of the smelly hole. For a moment, everyone stood and stared at each other.

"Peace! Who do you say you are?" one stranger asked.

"Peace! I'm Hadia, and this is my sister Phares and brother Levi. We are of the Karka Tribe from Beth Nahar. This is Tobias of the Bebe Tribe from En Gedi. Who do you say you are?"

"My name is Japheth," the young, clean-shaven man said. Turning his tall, lean body toward the others, he said, "This is my brother Shem and my sister Norah. We are from Naphtali, and are of the Lamech Tribe."

I gazed at the green-eyed man. Woven strands of yellow and light brown hair fell to his shoulders, tucking neatly behind his ears. His straight nose and square jaw gave him an air of authority. A large, hooded hawk perched on his shoulder.

Both men were well clad. They wore blue linen mantles over faded yellow tunics. Fine silver daggers were strapped to their waists; bows and arrows hung from their shoulders.

Dark brown eyes flashed below Shem's bushy eyebrows. His mustache wiggled when he spoke. He looked a few ages younger than his brother. Leaning against a burnished brown stallion with a long, luxurious mane, he smiled and stroked his reddish beard. "My horse's name is Yolly."

The bulky little horse snorted and pawed the ground. Eyes as dark as night peered between long strands of black hair. Yolly held no white markings on his legs or head, making him easily camouflaged at night.

"My horse is named Shine," Norah said shyly. She petted the satiny neck of the chunky white mare. "She's as gentle as can be."

I studied Norah in awe. She appeared about Levi's age. Fire-red hair framed her delicate face. Little dots like sprinkled nutmeg graced her snub nose. Her large brown eyes looked amazingly like Levi's.

Oh—could she be Levi's twin? Is it possible?

"Hadia, what are all of you doing out here?" Japheth asked.

"Well…uh…well…we are on a mission."

"What do you mean 'a mission'?"

"We are in search of a trail."

"A trail? What trail?"

"A trail near a bridge," I answered.

"We know of only one bridge in these parts—the Bridge Beyond Time. It's between the elephants not far from here."

I inhaled sharply. *The Bridge Beyond Time!* My pulse quickened.

"Elephants!" Phares wiped her forehead, "I'm not sure I want to cross a bridge between elephants."

"No, not real elephants—they're two elephant-looking boulders," Japheth said. He laughed.

"Oh, thank heaven. I thought they were real."

"We would be glad to shew you the way," Japheth said, "but if you cross the bridge, it will be dangerous."

"Why?" I asked.

"Many ages ago, Shem and I crossed the bridge and found the land to be like no other. There are dragons, scarlet beasts, and horrid creatures. Strange people guard pockets of gold throughout the hills. Yes…it is a perilous land. It would be foolish to cross the bridge."

"Oh dear," Phares said under her breath.

"I don't know what made me think this journey was going to be easy or free of danger," I said, "but I'm going on. I don't want the rest of you in danger. Phares, maybe you should stay behind with the children."

A chorus of "no's" filled the air. "What do we do, just wait around to see if you ever come back? Hadia, all of us made a vow; all of us are going. God will keep us safe, including the children," Phares answered.

God, why am I always finding myself backed into a corner? I thought. *If they go, I'll have to accept responsibility for what comes to pass—good or bad. I don't know if I'm strong enough.* Everyone stared at me.

"*God, give them a hedge of protection, and let no peril touch them.*" *Grandfather's prayer,* I thought. *If God is protecting us, I'm not responsible for the outcome—but can I trust Him?*

"All right, everyone…let's carry on."

"See, Levi? I told you there were dragons," Tobias quipped.

Levi scowled at Tobias. Norah turned her head and giggled.

"By the by, Phares, I believe you owe me an apology. The Nephilim giants were just like Granna described," I said with a smirk.

Phares rolled her eyes and shrugged her shoulders. "Eh, you're right. I apologize."

"Giants! You have seen the Nephilim giants?" Norah asked, wide-eyed.

"We have not only seen the giants, we have fought them. Who knows, they may be looking for us even now," Levi replied, looking all around.

"The giants have never been known to travel our way. You probably won't see them again unless you return home the way you came," Japheth said.

"Japheth, have you seen Destroyers in this area? They've been hunting us," I said.

"Yes, Destroyers do wander our land, but I haven't seen them of late."

"I guess we'll always have to look over our shoulders," Phares moaned.

"We can take you to the bridge now," Japheth announced with a wave of his arm. "We should arrive about sundown. It's a good place to make camp."

I waved everyone forward. "All right, let's go!"

"We would make better time if you rode our horses."

"Ride your horses? Are they safe?" I asked.

Japheth laughed. "I can't guarantee they're safe, but riding is better than walking."

"But, there are four of us. One would have to walk," Phares said.

"You could unpack your donkey and let Tobias ride him. We can all carry a bit."

"Eee! Raz is not the best mount in the world."

"I know, Tobias, but we'll make better time if you ride, all right?" I pleaded.

"Oh, all right. I don't seem to have a choice in the matter anyway."

"Tobias, you're a dear."

"Eh—sure."

Tobias and Levi quickly removed supplies from Raz and distributed them among us. We then mounted our steeds—Levi behind Norah, I behind Japheth, Phares behind Shem, and Tobias on Raz. Then we rode off—the seven of us.

Flocks of ravens flew overhead. I scanned the birds hoping to see a white one. The sun began its descent. The trail continued to spiral downward.

Japheth stopped his horse. "Horas, you need to go catch yourself a bite to eat."

"Your bird is named Horas?" I asked.

"Yes, and my horse's name is Bolly."

Bolly was as dark brown as Yolly and equally void of white markings. The sturdy, brown stallions made a fine pair.

"Yolly and Bolly—what funny names! Wherever did you come up with them?" I asked.

"Norah named them. It was just baby talk, but we kept the names anyway."

"Oh," I replied, trying not to bounce against Japheth. Bolly's choppy movements left a lot of space between his back and my bottom. *He isn't as smooth as Israfel. I shouldn't complain. Japheth said riding is better than walking.*

"Japheth," I said, "how did you come about your horses? No one in our land rides horses—they're wild. How did you gentle them?"

"I heard a tale of an old man who caught wild horses and tamed them. We didn't believe there was such a man, but we looked for him to see if the story was true. Many ages went by before we finally found him, and when we did, we believed."

"Did he teach you how to catch and gentle them too?" I asked.

"Yes, but we bartered for three of his tamed horses. That's how we came about the ones we're riding." Japheth reached down and stroked Bolly's neck.

"It must be wonderful to gentle horses. I hope to do that someday."

"If you do, you'll be the first woman to do such a thing. You won't find favor with the men in your village."

I tossed my head. "I don't need their favor."

Stunted pines with polished bark leaned on the windward side of prevailing winds, pointing the way toward the bridge. Fallen trees lay about in disarray along with jumbled rocks, making trekking difficult.

"There it is!" Japheth pointed to two gigantic boulders.

Only a smear of sunlight remained. Monstrous, black elephant silhouettes loomed against the sunset. A deep ravine plunged below the narrow bridge sandwiched between the boulders.

An odd bird perched on a sign at the entrance of the bridge. Its peacock-colored feathers were few; its head large, its man-face round and flat. Its beak turned up. It smiled—wickedly.

"Keep going, keep going," the strange bird said, swiveling its head toward an obscure trail beyond the bridge.

It spoke!

Startled, I jerked backward. "Did you hear the bird speak?" I asked, straightening myself up. We stared at the bird, and then my eyes rested upon scrawling words on the sign.

Beyond the Bridge of Time
Is a land of another time
To enter in and return again
Your land may be in another time

"Japheth, does that sign mean what I think it means?" I asked.

"Yes, but I think it's just to scare people. Our land didn't change when we returned."

"Eee! That bird looks evil. Let's get away from it," Tobias cried. "The bridge doesn't look safe either."

"It does look a bit rickety, but it's sturdy enough," Shem said.

"You didn't say if you were going to continue. Are you?" Japheth asked.

"Of course we'll go on. Our mission is more than finding the bridge," I replied.

"Just what *is* your mission?" Japheth asked, furrowing his forehead.

I gazed ahead to the Purple Mountain. *We're so close. What can I say? I don't wish to lie.* "We want to see what lies at the foot of the Purple Mountain."

"As I said before, you'll see more than you bargain for. You'll be in grave danger. If you insist on this madness, let us proceed a way with you. We have never slain dragons, but we've had plenty of practice slaying other evil creatures."

My mouth went dry. "Japheth, I need to speak to Phares. Please let me off."

I dismounted and asked Phares to meet me at the side of the trail. "Phares, you heard Japheth. What do you think? Should they come with us?"

"It would be easier to fend off evil creatures and people with seven of us than four. We can use all the help we can get."

"You're right. Let's ask them to join us." I took hold of Phares' arm and leaned close. "We must warn Tobias and Levi not to reveal our secret. You know how loose their tongues can be."

Drawing close to Japheth, I said, "we would be honored to have you journey with us. I just pray your lives won't be endangered."

"I'm not afraid. We'll be safe."

Satisfied, I hollered, "All right, Troop, let's set camp!"

Famished, we sat cross-legged on blankets around the watch fire. Diving into our food, no one hid their runaway appetites.

"Hadia," Phares said, "we should send Raven home in the morn with a message. Grandfather will be anxious to hear from us."

"Yes, he'll be glad to know we're almost there."

Japheth rubbed his chin. "Almost there. Where is 'there'?"

I bit my lip, turned my head, and ignored his question. I prayed he wouldn't ask again.

Norah, Levi and Tobias talked and laughed quietly. I studied them closely. Norah and Levi looked too much alike not to be related. Signaling Japheth, Shem, and Phares to move closer, I whispered, "Japheth, is Norah really your sister?"

"Well, yes and no. We have raised her, but her birth mother died in childbirth. She thinks our mother is her mother. Why do you ask?"

I took a deep breath and revealed my secret. "Levi had a twin sister when he was born. Before Mother died, she asked me not to mention the girl to anyone. She told me to wrap some gold wire around her wrist and put her by the wayside. We prayed she would be found by a kind stranger. I'm sure Norah is Levi's twin sister. They look the same age and both have red hair and tiny brown spots on their faces. I noticed something else—strands of gold wire on her little finger. There was a man who traded with my mother, gold wire for food. I believe that man was Jude. He must have found Norah and took her to your home."

Japheth's eyes widened; his jaw dropped. "Yes." He paused a moment, as though in deep thought. "Yes…my mother told me a man on a red horse brought her to us. She had a gold wire wrapped around her wrist. When she was older, we wove the wire into a ring. She could be Levi's sister. Imagine! We're related. Well, not quite. How are we going to tell them?"

"Not *how*, but *when*," I replied, my voice trailing off. "We should give them some time—time for them to discover the secret."

Phares glanced over her shoulder. "I agree."

"By the by, who's Jude?" Japheth asked, raising his brows.

"He's a man who helped us cross the Valley of Tremble, the land of the Nephilim giants. He has traveled it many times. He was the only one who could get us safely across," I answered.

"I see...I believe I have heard of such a man. I did not know his name."

Night settled in. The land fell into shimmering moonlight stillness. Stars shone with bright intensity. Silver objects streaked through the heavens. Nighttime was lapsing to a hush.

Norah, you're Levi's sister—I've found you....

Look to the left
Look to the right
Look for the hole
That lets in the light
Follow the light that
Shines on the stones
And there you'll find
The path to home

Jude

CHAPTER TWENTY-NINE

Beyond the Bridge of Time

"I heard the man-bird echoing, 'Keep going—keep going.'"

Hadia, are you ready to pray?" Japheth asked.
"Yes, I'm ready."

We bowed our heads. "Yahweh, incline Thine ear to us," Japheth prayed. "Forgive us our sins. Give us safety and guidance. So let it be."

Morning had arrived in all its brilliance. The valley was a patchwork of pink and violet. The bright sun sparkled. Trees spread their limbs, providing lovely shade. A small flock of ravens landed in a nearby pine. They shook out their feathers, preened, and cocked their heads at us. There was not a white one among them. My thoughts turned to home. *We need to advance quickly or we won't be home in time to protect the lambs from wolves after they're born.*

Levi and Norah sat cross-legged, the dogs at their sides. Hearing their laughter, I was curious and moved closer. I wondered if Levi was springing his silly riddles on Norah.

"Norah, what's your dog's name?"

"Her name is Anni." Norah scratched Anni's back.

"That's a nice name. Was Anni good when she was young?"

Norah's deep brown eyes sparkled. "She was. She never got into trouble."

Levi laughed. "O-No was always into mischief when he was young. We were always saying, 'Oh no!' That's why we named him O-No."

"Does he still get into trouble?"

"Yes, that's how Tobias landed in the bear hole—O-No knocked him right in."

Norah covered her mouth, smothering her giggle. "I hope he isn't naughty anymore."

"Me too. We can't afford any more of his clumsy goings-on."

I loved Norah's giggle. It was so pure and innocent. Her bright red hair glistened in the sun—just like Levi's. I smiled. "All right you two, it's time to leave."

The man-bird seemed not to have left its perch on the sign. We mounted our steeds and lined up to cross the bridge.

"I don't want to go first or last," Tobias grumbled. "I don't see a bottom under that bridge."

I teased him. "Tobias, when did you turn into a coward?"

"I'm not a coward. I'm cautious."

"If you're not a coward, then why do you want someone else to go first?"

"Well, I—"

"Never mind, Tobias. I'll go first and you follow me," Japheth said, waving him on.

Bolly eyed the bridge and hesitated. "It's all right, Bolly, let's go." Japheth kicked his ribs. Bolly put one hoof on the bridge—like testing uncharted water—and then sprinted across.

It was Raz's turn. He balked. I thought his look said, "It's too dangerous!"

"Now Raz, you'll have to cross the bridge, or we'll leave you behind," Tobias ordered. "You'll be fine—just fine."

Raz balked another moment and then carefully placed one hoof at a time on the boards. After much pleading from Tobias, he crossed the bridge.

"Good boy, Raz, I knew you could do it."

Raz looked like he was saying, "I'm not a boy. I'm a donkey, and don't forget it!"

The rest of the Troop followed without mishap. I heard the man-bird echoing, "Keep going. Keep going."

"Japheth, do you have other brothers or sisters?" I asked.

"Yes, I have another brother."

"What do you do when you're not hunting?"

"I help my father on his building project when I am not overseeing the Harvest of Plenty. I am Warden of the Harvest. It is my duty to see that all the harvests are brought into the storehouses."

"Warden of the Harvest—I've never heard of that position. It must carry a big responsibility."

"Yes, it does. What about you, Hadia? What are your duties?"

I hesitated and then said in a bland voice, "I tend our family's sheep and help Grandfather with chores. I do long to do something other than herd sheep."

"What would you like to do?"

"Well, for one thing, I would like to leave Beth Nahar—on a lovely horse. I love horses."

"I love horses too," he replied. "Hadia, women don't run off without an escort. Who would go with you?"

"No one."

I tried to continue my conversation with Japheth, but words faded as I looked from side to side for the rock with the hole in it—the one Jude said to look for. We picked our way around many boulders, making it difficult for me to search out *the* one rock. As I glanced at one boulder, I would miss another. I could easily pass *it* without noticing.

"Is something the matter?" Japheth questioned, turning around.

"No, why do you ask?"

"You keep turning your head back and forth like you're trying to avoid a pesky fly."

"I wish to see all there is to see." *Did I just lie?*

The quiet land crawled by as the stark, white sun continued to rise. Boulders flanked the narrow, sandy trail. The farther we went, the larger the boulders became. Clusters of incense cedars sprang up here and there. The sun played hide-and-seek with drifting rosettes of clouds. We rode steadily on, stopping only to refresh at a creek.

"Japheth, we should stop," I said, "it's almost middle-day. The animals need a rest and so do we."

"All right, this is a good time to stop."

We spread a blanket under a tree and shared our food. Japheth and Shem passed around figs, almonds, and olives. We added a few dates, nuggets of cheese, and wheat cakes. The soft warm dates were melting honey sweetness in my mouth.

Norah and Levi tossed olives and almonds at each other's mouths, trying to catch them. They caught few, leaving O-No and Anni scrambling to snatch them as they landed on the ground.

I watched as Raven hopped close to Horas, who was perched on Japheth's shoulder. I wondered if he thought, 'How can that dumb bird see if his eyes are covered?' Horas was silent. Raven hopped away with a look that seemed to say, 'He must be stuck-up too. How dull!'

"The air smells like hyssop and lilies," Phares said. She closed her eyes and drew a deep breath. "Can you smell it, Hadia?"

"Yes, it's heavenly."

"Well ladies, we best be on our way. Shem and I can't afford to linger," Japheth said.

"Of course," I replied. "All right, Troop, we need to leave."

A pale blue haze hung in the air. Crescent-shaped hills stood at attention in the distance. Fire-colored mounds lapped at the feet of the Purple Mountain rising above the valley. It roared and beckoned—a phantom sound heard only by those seeking the Garden of Eden. We had gone but a short way when I saw it.

"Oh!" I gasped. *There it is—the rock with the hole in it! It's just as Jude said it was. I must tell Phares.* I took joy at seeing the rock.

"Japheth, stop a moment."

"What is it?"

"I need to talk to Phares."

"All right."

I dismounted and hurried to Phares. "Phares, I need to speak with you." Phares dismounted and we huddled together.

"I saw the rock with the hole in it. It's over there on the right side of the trail. Come, I'll show you." We walked to an enormous boulder with a small hole in it toward the top. "Look, here it is."

Phares gazed at the hole, and then turned to follow the light shining through it. The light shone on two small boulders separated wide enough for one horse at a time to pass between.

"Here's where we turn. It's the ancient path Jude talked about," I said excitedly.

"I don't see much of a trail."

"It will have to do, Phares."

"Oh dear...."

"All right men, turn this way." I waved my arm toward the two boulders.

Japheth scowled. "That doesn't look like much of a trail to me."

"I know, but it's the way I want to go."

"All right, if you say so."

We lined up single file and plunged into the uncharted wilderness. Distant mountainsides and meadows lay before us in unspoiled majesty. Huge birds soared on air currents as the fierce, white sun hung directly above.

I heard Norah and Levi giggling and turned around to eavesdrop. I couldn't resist listening—I knew Levi was teasing her.

"Norah, did you know you don't breathe through your nose? You breathe through your belly button!" Levi said.

"Surely, you jest."

"No, I'm not. Really—the air coming from your nose is coming from your belly button."

"If that's true, how did Adam and Eve breathe? They didn't have belly buttons," Norah said smugly.

"You don't know that for sure. We take air in through our belly button and it comes out through our nose," Levi replied, with a twinkle in his eyes.

Norah tossed her head, bouncing masses of red, curly hair.

"Levi, you make mirth of me. I don't believe you."

"Wait until you hear some of Tobias' superstitions! You won't think my tales and riddles are so silly."

"Speaking of riddles, do you know what you can always count on?" Norah asked.

"Ay, I know that riddle. Your fingers. You can always count on your fingers. You like to tell riddles too?"

"I love to tell riddles. Would you like to hear another?"

"Maybe. Isn't it odd that we both like riddles and know some of the same ones."

"Perhaps."

"Don't you find it interesting that we both have red hair and seem to be the same age?" Levi asked.

My smile faded. *Does he suspect they're related? Maybe he's jesting.*

"What are you trying to say?" Norah asked.

Levi laughed. "Maybe we're related. Maybe we're twins."

"How could that be?"

"Maybe one of us was given away." He laughed again.

"Well, if one was given away, it would have been me. Baby girls are never wanted."

"Norah, I'm jesting. You know how I like to make mirth. No one gave you away."

Norah squeezed her eyes hard. "How can you be so sure? You just said we looked enough alike to be twins. What makes you think we're not?"

Levi stared intensely at Norah. "Well, I suppose we could be."

CHAPTER THIRTY

The Tomb

"I looked over my shoulder; the cat was gone. The odor lingered."

Oh, Levi, I found your twin sister. Will you forgive me for leaving her on a deserted wayside? Will I become a monster in your eyes? Norah, how will you feel when I tell you about your birth? Will you hate me for abandoning you? Will you want anything to do with me after our journey is over? Oh, God, be in all of this. My thoughts were jerked short by the sound of my name.

"Hadia, you haven't heard a word I've said," Japheth said curtly.

"I'm sorry. I…just…oh, nothing."

"I was trying to tell you I see something ahead. It looks like some kind of ruins. Hold on tight." Japheth dug his heels into Bolly's ribs.

I wrapped my arms around Japheth. By this time, I didn't care if I put my arms around a man. I didn't wish to fall off a running horse.

I peered around his shoulder to see what he was talking about. Yes, there was a large tower and ruins of some kind. The closer we drew, the larger the tower became. Fields and tottering walls lay abandoned. Ruinous sandstone abodes without inhabitants languished in the silent land. Stunned, I shielded the sun from my eyes. "It looks like a tomb!"

"By my father's mustache, would you look at that!" Tobias shouted.

Everyone stared. Carved into a hillside stood a tall, narrow sandstone tower. Massive marble pillars flanked the door. A cone-shaped dome crowned the top. It wept with decay, but was hauntingly beautiful, evoking a vanished world.

"What is it? I've never seen anything like it!" Levi asked with an astonished look on his face.

"That wasn't on the map," Tobias said.

"Map? What map?" Japheth asked.

"Uh…uh…never mind," Tobias muttered.

We dismounted and tethered the animals. Over the door of the tomb an old, scored inscription read: 𝔍𝔫 𝔱𝔥𝔢 𝔟𝔢𝔤𝔦𝔫𝔫𝔦𝔫𝔤 𝔴𝔢𝔯𝔢 𝔱𝔥𝔢𝔶….

"Oh, could *they* be Adam and Eve? Is this their resting place?" I gasped.

I was spellbound.

It whispered, "Come closer." It beckoned, "Touch me." It bid, "Savor my incense." It was from a realm of an ancient time long ago.

"We're even closer than I thought."

Japheth furrowed his brows. "Closer to what?" I ignored his question and ran my hands up and down the marble pillars, coating my palms with decades of dust.

"What's this?" I asked. A sleeping riddle of strangly scrawled words crawled across a dusty pillar: 𝔍 𝔞𝔪 𝔫𝔬 𝔪𝔬𝔯𝔢, 𝔟𝔲𝔱 𝔤𝔬𝔫𝔢 𝔟𝔢𝔣𝔬𝔯𝔢, 𝔍'𝔩𝔩 𝔪𝔢𝔢𝔱 𝔶𝔬𝔲 𝔱𝔥𝔢𝔯𝔢 𝔟𝔶 𝔱𝔥𝔢 𝔊𝔞𝔯𝔡𝔢𝔫 𝔊𝔞𝔱𝔢. 𝔍 𝔞𝔪 𝔫𝔬 𝔪𝔬𝔯𝔢, 𝔟𝔲𝔱 𝔤𝔬𝔫𝔢 𝔟𝔢𝔣𝔬𝔯𝔢, 𝔟𝔯𝔦𝔫𝔤 𝔱𝔥𝔢 𝔨𝔢𝔶 𝔞𝔫𝔡 𝔡𝔬𝔫'𝔱 𝔟𝔢 𝔩𝔞𝔱𝔢. Had a mysterious finger of providence written it? "Phares, look! Aren't these words from that little melody you sang earlier?" I asked.

Phares took notice. "Yes, they are," she replied in a hushed tone.

"Where did you learn that song?"

"I don't know. It just came to me."

"All of this must mean something, but what? I don't wish to go any farther. Let's stay the remainder of the day. We can leave at first light on the morrow."

"We can make a pen for Raz and the horses between the tomb and the hillside. It will take only a few poles and branches to fence one side," Shem said.

We made haste and put up the makeshift fence. A nearby stream provided water for everyone.

"Look here!" Tobias called. "A cave. Do you suppose it's a witches' cave?"

"There's one way to find out. We'll explore it," Japheth said.

Phares looked horror-stricken at the suggestion. "I want no part of caves."

"There you go again, Phares, afraid before you even try. If you don't come in, you'll be left outside by yourself—with dragons," Tobias mocked.

Phares looked around. Finally she shrugged her shoulders and said hesitantly, "Well, all right."

We ducked low and scrambled in. Standing up, we were awed by an enormous chamber. A thin stream of light splashed through a gap in the ceiling. It landed on a silent pool of water off to the side of a trickling stream. Boulders lay carelessly about in sandstone ash.

Small crawlways cluttered with rocks and mud covered the ground. Gray bats clung to the ceiling. Shards of pottery, oil lamps, grinding stones, reed mats, and animal furs lay sprawled about.

The walls held numerous drawings. I traced my hands across the images, reaching back through the ages: beautiful pastures, streams, trees, and flowers; a man, woman and child; stars, moon, and sun; wildlife and livestock; dogs and horses—and one white horse with a horn in the middle of its forehead. *What a strange horse*, I thought. *If only the walls could talk.*

The underground wilderness gave witness to the home of an unidentified family ages ago. The mysterious air was laden with incense. There were piles of tiny goat-skin bags containing a sweet elixir of oils, perfumes, and potions.

Two narrow passageways opened through a far wall. The passageways were dark and dank. Japheth, Shem and Tobias squeezed through one black passageway, feeling for projections.

"Eee!" Tobias shuddered. "I can't see my own hand."

"Nothing on earth is as dark as a cave. We'll need oil lamps to find our way," Japheth said, leaving the black tunnel.

Phares turned around. "This is as far as I go."

Levi chuckled. "Men are more suitable for exploring than women."

"Wait a minute," Norah interrupted with hands on hips, "I'm not afraid. I'll go."

Phares sighed. "If Norah is going, I'm going too."

Shem moved to the supplies. "Let's unpack and ready the lamps for the morrow."

We made a small watch fire beneath the shaft of ceiling light. Phares mixed wheat flour and water, and molded it into soft dough. She pinched off little pieces, patted them into flat circles, and put them into the hot coals. Covering the patties with ashes, they were ready to bake. We laid blankets around the fire-pit. The cave would make a fine home for the night.

"Why are the horses fussing?" I asked nervously.

"I don't know," Japheth answered, "let's take a look."

We ducked low and hastened outside. It was quiet—too quiet. Raz and the horses paced in circles. Bolly nickered. O-No and Anni stood on point, facing west.

I scanned the horizon. Suddenly, I caught sight of a small, brown cat crouching nearby. Its vivid green eyes bore in on me. It flicked its tail back and forth, arched its back, and hissed.

"Here kitty, kitty," I called. The cat rose on all four legs, arched its back higher and hissed louder.

"That's no kitty," Japheth said. He moved in front of me. "That's a cat, a dangerous cat. Stay away from it!"

I stared at the growling feline. It didn't act like a family pet. There was something strange about it. I smelled a putrid odor and felt an evil presence.

"You're right. It isn't friendly; it seems evil. And that odor! It's familiar. It will be a sleepless night tonight. We'll take turns standing guard. Now, let's have our bread while it's warm."

I glanced over my shoulder before entering the cave. The small, brown cat was gone. The odor lingered.

CHAPTER THIRTY-ONE

Chamber of Terror

*"This is your grave, this is your tomb. We've prepared
your final resting room."*

Hadia, are you ready to explore the passageway?" Japheth
asked.

"I guess so." *I'm not, but I don't want to look like a coward.*

"Cave! Cave!" Raven cawed, landing on my shoulder.

"Raven, stay outside," I ordered. "If you come in, you'll never
find your way out."

Raven flew outside. *"Not fair! Not fair!"*

"Light the oil lamps," Japheth said.

We lit the lamps and walked single file into the dark passageway. Downy white bats dashed madly past our faces like driven
apple blossoms. Their transparent wings and pink feet skimmed
the top of my head.

The light from the oil lamps revealed a high-ceilinged chamber.
Grand arches and majestic statuary burst into color—all in stone.
The utter darkness had become a glittering palace as in a fable
from long ago.

A trickling stream glinted. Mineral sculptures put on a dazzling display of curious formations. Soaring stone columns,

slender icicles, and knobby coral clustered like grapes, marched in the distance, luring us farther into the passageway. Gnats and beetles flew in our faces as we sidestepped webworms and blind salamanders.

"Ugh!" Phares flailed her arms through spider webs. "I feel like I'm in the belly of a beast. Maybe I should have stayed outside."

"Too late now, Phares," Tobias teased, "You won't find your way out alone. You'll just have to stay and have a good time."

Phares gave a brittle smile. "Tobias, you're not amusing."

Ancient animal bones lay scattered on the floor. Humid dampness floated in darkness as the shadowy walls revealed more tunnels. We followed the corridor as it wound and turned, opening into large chambers, and then into smaller ones. One small, irregular chamber held pits of human bones. A crude inscription scrawled across an epitaph tablet lying in the dirt. Loathsome mummy odors choked my nostrils, permeating my clothing.

"I've seen enough of this place. Let's get out."

Leaving the smelly chamber, the walkway narrowed, branching into a perilous path. A deep abyss on each side made walking treacherous. We continued on until my ears were alerted to a faint sound. I jolted to a stop.

"Quiet," I ordered in a cracked whisper. "I hear something."

Everyone stopped, rooted in place. Silence prevailed.

I took a shaky breath. "I thought I heard something. This cave makes me nervous."

A rotten smell like decaying maggots gagged me. Then a low growl echoed against the walls—a familiar growl. The hair on the back of my neck crawled. I raised my lamp and moved it across the wall until the light shone on two glowing, green eyes. Like lanterns suspended mid-air, the eyes glared, hypnotizing me. A stabbing fear of nausea came over me.

"Kitty?"

Without warning, the small, brown cat sprang into the air and lunged for my throat.

"Help!" Razor-sharp claws dug into my neck.

Japheth and Shem were quickly upon the wild feline, pulling its tail and striking it. The cat howled. It scratched arms, scraped faces, and tore scalps.

"There, that takes care of you!" Japheth threw the cat as hard and far as he could. It screamed and clawed the air. Then a loud thud resounded.

"Oooh, my neck," I moaned, wiping blood from my skin.

"We had better return to camp and take a look at your wounds," Japheth said.

"Wait." I wheeled around. "I hear footsteps."

I strained to catch the sound again. My breathing became irregular; my knees tottered. That *knowing* feeling rippled along my spine. *Someone else is in the cave. But who? Oh, for open light to face the enemy. These winding passages will make it difficult to escape. A wrong turn and we'll never reach our exit. The underworld will become our grave.*

"I hear it too," Japheth whispered.

"Shew yourself!" I shouted.

"We'll shew ourselves all right. We want your map! The map for your children or I'll kill them, just like I killed your father!" a sinister voice boomed.

Korah and Dathan bounded into the light. They swung their daggers and uttered foul curses. Korah grabbed Norah, Dathan grabbed Levi. My pounding heart echoed against the walls of the cave. Hate welled in my soul.

With a sudden rush of breath, I said, "You killed my father! I have waited for such a time as this. I vowed to drive a stake into your dark heart!" Shaking, I raised my dagger.

"Hadia, no! Let God have His way," Phares begged.

My eyes darted to Korah, and then to Phares.

"Please, Hadia," Pharis said, "your desire for vengeance will give cause for regret later."

I felt anguish deep within my being. *"I pray someday you'll let it go."* Slowly, I lowered my dagger. "What makes you think we have a map?"

"You are of the Yousif clan, the Karka Tribe. Our tribe has always suspected the Yousif clan possessed a map showing the way to Eden."

A sorry jumble of words tumbled from my mouth. "We don't have a map. You have followed us for nothing. Let the children go or God will take revenge."

"You foolish girl, your childish threat sounds deaf in my ears," Korah answered, twisting Norah's arm.

"Ow!" Norah wailed.

The Destroyers stood dangerously close to the edge of the path. A step backward would send them into the pit, taking Levi and Norah with them.

Phares picked up a splintered animal bone and glared at Korah. "Let them go or you'll be sorry!" she shouted, and stepped forward.

"Aaaaargh!" Korah roared. Fire kindled in his eyes. "You little wench, how dare you threaten me!"

Swinging the bone in fury, Phares burst ahead and thrust it into Korah's foot. It cut deep into the bone, spurting blood everywhere. He screamed and reached down, swaying back and forth. Losing his balance, he fell backward into the bottomless pit.

"Ayy…Ayy…Ayy!" The thin, piercing death screech echoed and echoed. Then there was silence.

"Curse your father," Tobias muttered. "God's sword be upon your tribe!"

The malevolent Dathan barked. "You miserable hag, now your fate is sealed! I shall slay all of you!" Dathan's eyelids narrowed to slits. A tight smile creased his face as he turned to push Norah over the edge. Fear twisted a knot in my gut.

O-No and Anni lunged at Dathan, fiercely gripping his legs. "Howwww…get away! Get away! I'll kill you!" Dathan released Norah and kicked furiously at the dogs.

"Norah, run!" I cried. Norah fell forward, jumped up and made a dash to safety.

The dogs continued their savage attack, causing Dathan to fall backwards, joining his brother in the yawning grave. His pitiful cry for help echoed until it faded away. Trembling, we sat down to gather our wits. "They are ended! They are dead!" Tobias said jubilantly.

"O-No, Anni, how did you know we needed help? How did you find us?" I asked.

"I know," Norah exclaimed proudly, "it's simple—they heard. Remember, dogs hear better than humans. And they don't need light to find their way. They put their noses to the ground, and there we were."

O-No dog-smiled and looked like he was saying, "It was simple." We hugged the dogs, and then agreed it was time to return to safety.

Viscous mud coated our sandals as we slowly moved ahead. Hushed conversation echoed softly. Our silhouettes cast ghostly shadows on the wet, craggy walls. I was anxious to escape the cave lest it become my coffin.

Disjointed tree trunks protruded from the walls, giving the appearance of monsters. A winged creature flew by, grazing the top of my head. Our lamps continued to bathe our faces in a strange red glow. Suddenly, our lamps flickered.

"Where's the wind coming from?" I asked, puzzled.

"I don't know," Japheth replied.

Misty shapes appeared and disappeared across our path—djinns—evil spirits.

"Eee! Let's get out of here—quick!" Tobias yelled, looking over his shoulder.

The breeze turned into wind as the contorted shapes danced around us. They chanted: "This is your grave, this is your tomb. We've prepared your final resting room." The wind blew hard; our light disappeared. The spirit voices had grown to deafening proportions. The misty shapes took on a phantasmal yellow glow.

"Help!" Phares screamed.

The djinns swirled around Phares, chanting and cackling in a high-pitched howl.

"This is the witches' tomb. Die, and then you can talk to the dead. We'll prepare for you a resting place, my precious." They laughed in macabre unison.

Shaking, I yelled, "Japheth, slice the djinns in half."

Japheth's sword swished, slicing the djinns in half. Levi sprang forward to further slice them. I jumped in front of him. "No! Stop!" I screamed frantically. "They'll double and live if you cut them again!" Levi lowered his sword.

We watched as the contorted shapes slowly withered; their glow faded. I couldn't stop shaking. I was cold. Would I ever be warm again?

"Japheth, we need to get out of here—now!" I said adamantly.

"All right, everyone, stand still. I don't want anyone straying off the path," Japheth said, taking command. "O-No and Anni will take us out of here safely."

Japheth kneeled down carefully and reached out his hand. A wet tongue kissed his face. "O-No! Thank heaven! I never thought I would welcome dog kisses. Everyone hold on to each other. Follow me when I tell O-No to take us out."

Japheth took hold of O-No's tail and yelled, "Out O-No. Out!"

O-No and Anni put their noses to the ground and plodded their way through the winding passages. Long minutes passed as we moved noiselessly along.

"This black pitch makes me dizzy. I can't tell if I'm coming or going. How do we know we're not going in circles?" Phares cried.

"We'll find out sooner or later," Japheth said, urging O-No on.

Pebbles dropped silently into the abyss, descending endlessly. Blood trickled down my throbbing neck. My mind played games, revealing creatures seen only by me. I staggered as the creatures danced in my head shouting, "Die! Die!" The djinns seemed to have had their final say.

"Hadia!" Japheth called, grabbing me as I stumbled. "Here, sit down."

What fight in me drained away, leaving me weak and wobbly. Japheth gently lowered me to the ground. "O-No, Anni, stay. Don't anyone move."

I sat down and leaned forward, my hands steadying me. I took deep breaths and tried to calm myself. I felt like I was in a black bag that had been shaken violently.

Mud stuck to my hands when I felt something, like a leather strap. I pulled on it, but it was caught. "Japheth, I've found something."

"What is it?"

"I don't know," I tugged on the strap. Suddenly, it came loose. A pouch bounced at my knees. "It's a little bag. I wonder if anything is in it."

"You can look when we get outside."

"Look. I think I see light!" Levi called.

"Where? I don't see any," Phares said.

"I know I saw light. Maybe it's not there now, but I know I saw it."

"Japheth, I feel better. Let's leave while we can," I said, trembling.

"If I never see another cave again, it'll be too soon," Phares grumbled, exiting the dark passageway.

"It wasn't so bad, Phares; just another challenge, which you met with success. Aren't you proud of yourself?" Tobias grinned. "Do you realize you saved our lives? If you hadn't attacked the Destroyer, we would all be dead."

"That's right," Japheth replied. He patted Phares on the back.

"Phares, I can't believe you attacked the Destroyer! Why were you not afraid?" I asked.

"I feared for our lives and remembered what Tobias said about courage. He said if I was to have courage I would have to do something courageous. I knew I was taking a risk, but it was one I had to take."

I gave my sister a hug. "Phares, you were very brave."

"Maybe, but please, don't ever invite me into another cave!"

CHAPTER THIRTY-TWO

Gift Horses and Found Treasure

"It doesn't seem right to take the horses of dead men."

Hadia, open the bag you found," Japheth said.

I reached for the grimy goat-hair bag. *I hope there isn't a spider in there.* I opened it carefully and peered in.

"What's this? A key! What could it possibly unlock—the tomb?"

"Let's find out," Japheth said, rushing ahead.

We hurried to the tomb and looked for a keyhole. Nothing could be found. My mind filled with jumbled thoughts. *Bring the key and don't be late. Bring it where?* I slipped it back into the bag and tucked it away.

"I don't know what the key goes to, but I do know you now have your own horse, Hadia." Japheth smiled.

"What do you mean, Japheth?"

"The Book of Wars says the booty goes to the victor. We are the victors. The horses belong to us. You and Phares take the horses. Which horse do you want, Hadia?"

Two stout ebony mares with white markings hung their heads over the makeshift fence, nudging Yolly, Bolly, and Shine. They didn't seem interested in Raz. They were covered with colorful trappings: blood red blankets, braided gold ropes with apple green and royal purple tassels, headstalls and breastplates of gleaming gold. Tinkling silver bells swung from slender reins of worn leather.

One horse had two white legs and a star on its forehead, and a curly mane. The other horse had three white legs and a faint crescent on its forehead. Their finely chiseled heads revealed liquid brown eyes.

I was astonished. "Japheth, do you mean to say I may have one of these horses?"

"Yes. Your dream has come true. Choose one."

"I don't know. It doesn't seem right to take the horses of dead men."

"The Book of Commandments says the wealth of the wicked is laid up for the righteous. They were Destroyers. They chose their destiny. It's all right."

"Oh, Hadia, pick one," Phares urged.

I strode between the two horses, rubbing my hand down their necks. I studied them closely. They were about the same size and color. One turned to push her head into my neck.

"You're a friendly one," I said, catching sight of the star on her forehead. "This one—I'll take this horse."

A noise of excitement went up as the Troop yelled and clapped their hands.

"That leaves the other one for you, Phares," Japheth said, grinning. Phares' smile was as broad as a river as she reached out to pet her new horse.

"They now have new masters. Now they need new names," Shem said.

"New names? Why new names? We don't even know the old names," I replied.

"It's tradition—a victor always names the claimed horses. It is a sign of authority, both to the horse and to the defeated," Japheth explained.

"Well...hmm...all right."

"I know. Name them Dawn and Dusk. Dawn for the one with a star—like the morning star, and Dusk for the one with a crescent—like the crescent moon," Norah said, clapping her hands.

"I like those names. Phares, what do you think?"

"Yes, those are fitting names—Dawn and Dusk."

"Well, Norah, you've done it again," Japheth said, laughing. "Naming horses seems to be your calling."

"Maybe someday I'll get a horse too," Tobias said. "No offense, Raz, but you aren't the easiest to ride and you aren't very pretty either."

"Where are those ugly black dogs?" Levi asked.

"I hope they went back to where they came from—Hell," Tobias retorted.

"Tobias, let's repack Raz when we leave. You can ride with me," Shem said.

"Oh good! Sorry, Raz, like I said before, you're not the easiest to ride."

Flat bread baked as our evening wound down. We gathered cross-legged on blankets around the fire-pit in the cave. Musky smoke spiraled up through the hole in the ceiling. A sense of awe came over me. I felt as though I were sitting on sacred ground, supping with the parents of humanity.

O-No and Anni were curled up together close to the fire. Raven and Horas perched on a nearby boulder, eyeing each other. I thought they looked ready to take flight at a moment's notice—from each other.

Food was passed around: cheese, bread, and dried figs. Appetites satisfied, we propped up blankets and reclined on our elbows.

"Who has a story to tell?" Shem asked. "Idle tales upon the tongue drive the empty hours."

"I do," Norah replied eagerly.

"Let's hear it," I said.

"It's not exactly a story. It's about a dream I often have."

"A dream? Maybe I can interpret it. I love to interpret dreams," Phares said.

"I keep having a dream that someone is knocking on my door. Someone I know, or should know. When I open the door, no one is there. I look around and go back inside, feeling sad. What could it mean?" Norah's eyes looked distant and questioning.

My mouth went dry, my heart picked up speed. *Does she know? Is her spirit trying to tell her she wasn't alone at her birth? I must tell her the truth.* Strangled by fear, words stuck in my throat. I forced myself to speak. "Norah, have you had the dream lately?" Norah furrowed her brows and stared into space. There was a sad watchfulness in her eyes. After a long pause, she said, "No, I don't believe so."

No one spoke. I dreaded this moment. I took a deep breath. "I think you have always missed someone, and you wanted that someone to knock on the door and find you."

Norah looked at Levi. "Yes, I feel as though I have always missed someone, like a brother or sister." Norah dissolved into tears.

Levi reached over and gave her hand a reassuring squeeze. "I'll be your brother."

"Levi, you *are* her brother," I said softly. "Mother gave birth to twins. She was dying and was afraid Father wouldn't be able to care for two babies. She told me to leave the baby girl by the wayside, trusting God would find a good home for her—and He did. Mother loved the baby girl. Norah, I have longed to be with you."

Levi and Norah looked stunned. Norah squeezed her eyes hard and clutched Levi's hand. "How could you long to be with me? You threw me away!"

My voice cracked. "Norah, that's not true. You must believe that Mother did what she thought was best for all of us. She died giving life to you."

Levi's face tightened. "I had a sister and you didn't even tell me about her? Why, Hadia, why? I have always trusted you. Will I ever be able to trust you again?"

"A day hasn't gone by that I didn't want to tell you. But I couldn't. Mother made me promise not to tell anyone. I was scared to break my promise, and afraid you would hate me. I'm breaking the promise now." *God, forgive me! Mother, forgive me!*

Levi's eyes narrowed. His voice hardened. "You have cheated me of my sister. We could have looked for her."

Am I losing my little brother too? Levi, don't widen the empty space in my heart. Please, God, help them understand.

No one seemed to have anything else to say. Japheth fixed his gaze on me. There was tenderness in his eyes. "This calls for a celebration! We have found each other!" He was the only one smiling.

I gave a quick dismissive smile. "Yes," I said tonelessly, "we must celebrate."

The evening fire burned brightly, casting shadows on the wall paintings. Images of wild animals, barely visible, strode between trees along streams. Snakes coiled up tree trunks and the Tree of Life stood with a man and woman on each side. The paintings were captivating. Again, I thought, *if only the walls could talk.*

Tobias pushed himself up. "Hello, what's that?"

"What is what?" I replied, looking all around.

"Eee! Treasure!" He pointed up.

Tobias pulled a gold chain from a bird's nest cradled between two massive boulders. Jeweled necklaces and more gold chains followed, all interlocked.

"Leuce's treasure!" Tobias cried.

"Bring the nest down," I said, trying to restrain my excitement.

Tobias carefully lifted the nest, brought it down, and laid it on a blanket.

"Oh my!" Phares cried.

We were wide-eyed. A few white feathers lay carelessly over the pile of jeweled necklaces, rings, earrings, and bracelets. The jewels sparkled—icy white, sun yellow, grass green, blood red, and sky blue.

"Empty the nest. We'll divide it evenly," I suggested.

Tobias turned the nest upside down, releasing the bobbles to strew about, and then returned it to its resting place.

"I want Norah and Levi to pick out rings first," I said.

Tobias scattered the jewels in a wide circle until all the rings were found.

"I want that one," Norah said. She pointed to a delicate gold ring with a large red jewel sitting in a cluster of snow-white pearls.

"It's lovely," Phares murmured, slipping it on Norah's small finger.

"Oh, Phares, I shall love this ring forever. It will always remind me of finding my brother."

Levi pointed to a wide gold band with a single large turquoise set in the center.

"I like that one!"

Japheth nodded. "Good choice, Levi."

"Well ladies, pick your favorite," Shem said, smiling.

Phares and I ran our fingers through the jewels and we each drew out a ring.

Phares reached for a gold ring with a large pearl mounted in the center. A line of amber jewels marched down the sides of the ring.

"I'll take this one. I love it!" she said, slipping it onto a right-hand finger.

"It's beautiful, Phares," I cooed. "I know which one I want—the square yellow jewel with the small blue jewels. It's exquisite."

The men each found a ring of their choice. The rest of the jewels were divided among us. We carefully bundled our riches in sacks and agreed that Raz would carry our newfound fortune.

"I do declare, I don't think I can take much more excitement," I said. "Finding Norah, fighting Destroyers, and receiving a horse and jewels is almost more than I can handle." I laughed. "However, I am not above buying a couple of camels on the way home with part of my newfound wealth."

"I wonder if Leuce will return before we leave," Phares said, looking solemnly at the empty nest. "I don't wish to see her disappointment."

"Maybe in time, we'll find out," Norah replied quietly. She gazed at me, and then turned her face away.

Hearts break silently.

How can I help Norah feel wanted? How can I restore Levi's trust in me?

CHAPTER THIRTY-THREE

The Scarlet Beast

"A voice like the clap of thunder and the roar of a lion screamed, 'Woe!'"

I wonder if Shem has a lady waiting for him at home," Phares whispered to me.

"Why don't you ask him?"

"Oh, I couldn't possibly do that!"

"You'll never know unless you ask," I said. "He may be wondering the same about you."

"Hadia," Japheth interrupted, "We can only travel with you one more day. We must return home soon. Our father needs us to help on his building project."

No, Japheth. Don't leave yet—please stay a little longer. "Oh Japheth, I'll miss you; however, I understand. We need to know the way to each other's homes. I can't lose Norah now that I have found her, and I must know how to find you, too."

Japheth's eyes beamed, and he said softly, "I don't want to lose you either, Hadia."

"Time to eat!" Tobias hollered.

Breakfast was gulped down. We gave one last look inside the cave, making sure all supplies were removed. Raven flew home with a message for Grandfather. We gathered to pray and made ready the animals for departure.

The horses snorted and pawed the ground. O-No and Anni ran around sniffing everything. A few birds flapped high in the early morning sky.

"Dawn, I do hope we'll get along," I said. "I'll try to understand your ways." The beautiful bay mare pushed her head into my neck and nickered. We mounted and continued east—at least I believed we were headed east.

"Look!" Norah said, "the ground sparkles!" We pulled rein and looked down. Traces of gold dust glittered at our feet.

"Oh my," Phares said, "this is the land of gold. I wonder where we can find some to take home."

"I don't know, but we have company," I said grimly.

Ogres holding rocks closed in on us. Stringy hair hung to their waist. Their hands and feet were enormous. Their heinous faces were like monkeys. Razor sharp fangs protruded over their bottom lips. Grotesque dog-like creatures stood at their sides. The monstrous people circled us and screeched in high piercing voices.

"This is our land, this is our gold. It's not for you to hold. Leave or die. Leave or die." Then they chanted in an unknown lauguage: "Tou, Tou—Ay Clo—Tou, Tou."

"I don't know what that means," I said, "but I think it means trouble. Run everyone! Run!"

We spurred our steeds as rocks flew all around us. The dog creatures followed, growling and snapping. The men fired arrows at them, striking many. We continued running the horses until no ogres were seen.

"All right," I hollered, waving my arm, "we can walk the animals now."

"Hadia," Tobias said, wide-eyed, "we can't go back, but I don't think I can go ahead. There are too many scary things happening."

I laughed. "You're right, Tobias. We're not going back, at least not this way. Be not afraid. Surely we won't face anything as bad as what we've already faced," I assured him.

"Promise?"

"Well…no…but we can't become cowardly now."

"Eee!"

"Tobias, I haven't seen any dragons," Levi said.

"Your journey isn't over. You might be surprised."

"Tobias, tell Norah one of your silly superstitions."

"They are traditions—*not* superstitions," Tobias retorted.

"What do you see today you're leery of?" Levi asked, his brow rising.

"I don't see anything—yet."

"Trust me, you will. You always do."

Norah smiled. "Tobias, I have never met anyone superstitious. You need to trust God. He will guide and protect you."

"I only understand superstition—er—traditions."

Norah rolled her eyes, and then said, "Let's run the horses!"

The Purple Mountain rose in the distance, beckoning us to the Garden of Eden. The land was green and beautiful. It was as though nothing was ever meant to change in this valley of old. The ancient land endured. It was the same today as from the beginning.

It was middle-day. The white sun bore down upon us as we passed hills and dells and crossed creeks. "Time to rest," I called. We spread blankets under a large shade tree and devoured lunch in no time.

"Ohhh—delicious," Japheth said, wiping his mouth with his sleeve.

I turned to Japheth as he raised his sleeve to his mouth. Then I saw it—an alabaster amulet on his wrist! "Japheth, where did you get your amulet?"

"I purchased it from a man at market in En Gedi a few ages ago. I believe his name was Zamir. Yes, that was it—Zamir. Why do you ask?"

"Zamir was my father's name! I don't ever remember seeing an amulet on my father. I once had a dream. There were dancing beetles, which we have seen; tinkers, which we have seen; and a man with the amulet reaching for a white raven. You must be the man in the dream."

"If the dream comes true, the white raven will appear. Did the man catch her?"

"I don't know—I woke up."

Tobias removed his head cloth and ran his fingers through his hair. "That's some dream, Hadia."

Flapping wings interrupted our conversation. "Raven, that was quick." I reached for the message tied to Raven's leg, anxious to read Grandfather's 'news'. "What? This is the same message we sent earlier. Why didn't Grandfather receive it?"

"There's probably a good explanation, Hadia. Send it again," Phares said.

"Raven—home—home! I hope nothing has happened to Grandfather. He's all by himself."

"Now Hadia, there *you* go worrying. It won't do you one bit of good."

"I know."

Everyone was quiet for a moment, and then Tobias pulled out his whistle stick and began to play. He always knew when soothing music was needed. Leaves rustled, lulling us to slumber, but not for long. A soft commotion startled us.

"Hello, there she is!" Tobias shouted. "There she is—the white raven!"

"Quiet. You'll scare her away," I said in a hushed tone.

No one moved. The white raven perched on a low branch. Skittering down the tree, she hopped close to us. A gold chain dangled from her mouth. Ever so carefully, Japheth reached for her. She flew away.

"Well, there's your answer," Japheth said. "The man in your dream never caught her, but the dream came to pass."

"I guess we were never meant to catch her. She was not destined to be caged, and we were never meant to have unlimited wealth. It would probably be our demise and her death," I said soberly.

"But we know where she takes her jewels," Levi replied.

"Yes, but she'll never return to that nest again. It has been defiled by humans. To her, humans can't be trusted. They steal. Didn't we?"

"She's a lovely raven. She should be free, like us," Norah said wistfully.

"Yes," I said, "she should be free. Well, Troop, time to leave. Up we go."

We rode without slacking our pace across rolling downs for long stretches of time. The narrow trail drew us into single file. "Dawn, you are as wonderful to ride as Israfel—so smooth," I said. She tossed her head and swished her tail. I petted her neck. "You're welcome."

Suddenly, a strange sensation stirred the air. Rabbits scampered; wild beasts bolted, and birds quit singing. Dawn stopped and pawed the ground. A shrill whinny blew from the depth of her belly. Soon all the horses were snorting and neighing.

My body trembled and my heart raced. Something was dreadfully wrong. Dawn reared and pawed the air. It was difficult to stay mounted. Raz brayed in terror. The dogs barked furiously.

"What is it, Japheth?" I asked.

"I don't know."

A horned, scarlet five-headed beast rose above the crest, swinging its heads back and forth. Teeth as long and sharp as swords gleamed as it opened its mouths. A voice like the clap of thunder, and the roar of a lion screamed, "Woe! Woe! Woe!"

The words fell on our ears like hammer blows. Smoke as yellow as sulfur blew out of its many nostrils. A horrid stench filled the air. Its tail of many huge-headed snakes whipped back and forth. Its eyes were cold and gray as marble. It was five camels tall and three hippopotamuses wide!

"Surely, we won't face anything worse than what we have already faced." My prophecy rang false—I was wrong!

I turned Dawn around and spurred her hard. The Troop followed. O-No and Anni ran full speed ahead of the horses. Raz struggled to keep up with us.

"Japheth, Raz is falling behind. He'll be killed!" I screamed.

"We can't stop. We must keep going or we're all going to die!"

"Raz, hurry—hurry—Oh, hurry Raz!" I called desperately.

The Scarlet Beast was getting dangerously close to Raz when Raz took a sharp turn running hard. The beast followed him. They plunged into a drop-off and disappeared. We drew rein and looked back.

No, God. Not Raz! I thought. *Why? Why? He didn't deserve this. What have I done? What have I done?*

"Raz! Raz!" Levi cried.

Everyone dismounted. We were stunned into silence for a moment, and then tears burst forth. "Don't look into the abyss! The memory of seeing Raz dead will be too heavy for our minds to carry. We can't help him," I said mournfully. No one spoke. The land was quiet once again.

"Raz saved our lives," Shem said softly. "Let's give him honor. Let's make an altar in remembrance of his sacrifice."

We placed a small pile of stones near the edge of the cliff and gave thanks to God for our safety, but I didn't understand why Raz wasn't spared. My body shook with sobs.

"I'm sorry about Raz, Hadia," Japheth said. He leaned down and wrapped me in his arms. Then, his brows furrowed. "Hadia, what's your journey all about?"

I wiped my eyes. "Japheth, I can't tell you. Maybe someday, I will."

My languishing quest felt like a flickering lamp-wick. I felt I had arrived at the end of the world, with Eden nowhere in sight. All my hopes fell swoop. *Reaching Eden seems as remote as reaching the moon. The door seems shut and bolted. Why else would these disasters keep happening? And why didn't Grandfather warn us of dragons? God, if we're to keep going, why do bad things keep happening?*

"Why?" I wailed. "Why?" I whimpered. "Why?"

I wanted a divine answer from God. *Why should I expect one when He knows I'll probably question it anyway?* I wept.

Japheth said nothing, but his quiet strength comforted me. "Do you wish to go on?" he asked tenderly.

My words became faltering and undecided. "I don't know. I hadn't counted on people and animals dying for my quest."

"Hadia, did you push Bidinko down on the King's Highway?" Japheth asked.

"No."

"Then you did not cause his death. The soldiers caused it. Did you chase Raz over the cliff?"

"No."

"Then you didn't cause his demise. The beast caused it. You can't blame yourself for something you had no control over."

"Hadia, you made a vow," Tobias cried. "You've come too far to quit. You must carry on!"

I did make a vow, I thought. *Are vows made to be broken? Is it a sin to break a vow to yourself? Will God be disappointed if I don't keep it? Does He even care? Do I care?*

"What about our supplies? They're gone."

"We have enough food to share. There's plenty of water available and we can hunt for wild leeks, sorrel and tubers," Shem replied.

"Hadia, if you don't complete your journey, you'll regret it. Give it a few more days. We'll go a little farther with you. What do you say?" Japheth asked.

"I thought you needed to depart soon."

"I do, but I can't leave you like this. I'll manage."

Should we continue? I wondered. *Up to now, our wretched attempt to reach Eden has failed woefully.* I took a deep breath and closed my eyes. Swishing horses' tails, singing birds and croaking frogs resounded. Then I heard something land at my feet. My eyes flew open.

"A dove!"

The gentle bird circled me, cooing sweetly. Then, it took flight...*toward* the Purple Mountain.

I waved my arm at the Troop. "All right, let's go."

CHAPTER THIRTY-FOUR

Racing to Eden

"Greetings. This is my goat, Dinah. We've been waiting for you."

The heart of the world passed beneath the hooves of our horses. The blue silk sky and endless wave of green gave no hint of the horror that lay behind us. Birds sang, trees sighed.

Time passed sweetly, time passed sadly. The final stretch of the journey was shrinking. I longed to see Eden, the cradle of civilization, the home of our first parents, but my soul was troubled.

Grandfather is not alive, I thought. I just know it! Perhaps this journey has been a folly after all. Maybe I am selfish and self-centered. Jude said it is the motive of the heart that determines our choices. What is my motive?

We stopped to rest and eat in a sheltered glen abundant with flora and water. Phares and I looked for wild berries and mushrooms. Soon, we were ready to eat.

"We found a few berries, but no mushrooms," I said. "We can wash up and refill our water skins in the stream over there." I pointed to a cluster of fir trees.

"Hadia," Phares whispered, "I know something that will cheer you up."

Curious, I turned and looked at her. "What is it?"

"I overheard Japheth and Shem talking about you. Japheth told Shem he had grown quite fond of us, especially you. He said you moved with grace and spoke with wisdom—qualities not found in most women your age. Shem told him he should tell you how he feels. Japheth said he would if he could find the courage. Now, doesn't that make you happy?"

"Well, that was an earful! Yes, it does make me happy. I am fond of him, but I can't let him know. He would think me a harlot."

"Eee! Look there!" Tobias said, pointing up to the sky.

I looked up. Two winged creatures glided above my head. Their bodies reflected crimson, gold and silver. Their torsos were like cows, their heads like dogs. Short stubby legs dangled; tails like logs of cedar navigated them. Circling us, their red eyes blinked rapidly. *I hope they're winking,* I thought. Seeming harmless, we ignored them.

"I wonder where that sweet essence is coming from?" Norah asked.

"Eden, of course," Phares said, with a twinkle in her eye.

"Really? Could the Garden of Eden be around here?"

"I suppose it could. What do you think?"

Norah giggled. "I think it could and I think I should like to see it."

"Perhaps you'll get your wish. One never knows."

I scowled at Phares and shook my head.

Whoosh Whoosh.

"Raven! Come here, silly bird," I said.

Raven landed on my shoulder. *"Hello! Hello!"*

I removed the message and read it aloud. "Dear Hadia, Phares and Levi: I'm sorry to tell you your grandfather has died. He collapsed while fetching water at the east gate well and never regained life. We buried him beside your father at Potter's Field. Villagers are tending your flock. May God comfort you. Love, Granna."

"No! No! Not Grandfather!" Levi shrieked.

I grabbed Levi and cradled him in my arms. *No! Not Grandfather. God, why? Why now? He wasn't supposed to die alone.*

"Levi," I said, "Grandfather is in a better place. Death happens, but it's not the end of life. It's the beginning of eternity with God, without sin, pain, or sorrow."

"I don't want him in a better place. I want him alive, with us. With *me!*"

"I know. I want him here too. Now, we must be brave and press on."

"But Grandfather is dead!"

"I know, Levi, but we are alive. Grandfather would want us to continue," I said gently.

Levi wailed. No amount of comforting could console him. Nothing I said removed his pain. Nothing I said removed *my* pain.

"Hadia, we'll clean up. We best be on our way if you want to reach the Purple Mountain before sundown," Japheth said gently.

"Thank you, Japheth."

I let go of Levi, stood, and gazed upward. Raising my eyes to the sky, I cried silently to God. *Will death's sting ever exhaust its rage against us? Shall we be bound to it forever? What new miseries will doom us? Is this punishment for my folly?*

I buried my face in my hands and wept. The empty space in my heart grew.

We made ready the animals and continued eastward. Tobias retrieved his whistle stick, turned around and sat backwards on Yolly's fat rump. Swaying to the clip-clop rhythm of his gait and swishing tail, he pushed lovely music into the air. I knew he was trying to soothe my troubled heart.

"Let me sing you a new song; made it up myself!" he said proudly.

"Even closer, almost there, it could be almost anywhere.
Even closer, almost there, when you see it you will stare."

It was a lively little melody, easy to catch. I opened my mouth to sing, but the words wouldn't come. *Will I ever sing again?*

Grandfather, Grandfather, I'm sorry I wasn't with you when you died. I'm so sorry. Grandfather, I love you so much. Life will never be the same without you. Why did you have to go and die while we were gone? Couldn't you have waited until we came home? I don't know why I'm talking to you like this. You can't hear me, but God, You can. Dare I ask You why? Dare I question You?

Silence.

Trust Me—

"Trust You?" I murmured.

Riding through streams and dells, meadows of sweet grass and wild flowers passed by. The hard white sun was well behind us. Yolly jerked to a stop and threw his head high, throwing Tobias to the ground.

"Howwww! Why'd you do that, Shem?" Tobias wailed.

"I'm sorry Tobias, I didn't stop Yolly. He stopped himself."

A band of horrid little creatures gathered around us, frightening our steeds. The hideous beasts were the size and shape of a coyote. Long, talon-like claws extended from their feet. Their scaly bodies shone like pearl-white sea shells. They swished their horse-like tails. They were frightful. Sinister smiles traced their womanly faces. I expected them to speak.

They did.

"Go no farther. Go no farther," they growled.

"Eee!" cried Tobias, quickly scrambling back up onto Yolly.

"I'm confused. First the man-bird says to keep going and now these *things* tell us to go no farther," Levi said.

"If we don't obey, they might kill us," Tobias answered.

"Why are we even debating this? They're animals. We're in control. Run the horses—quick!" I commanded.

We spurred our steeds into a fierce run. The woman-animals followed, nipping at the horses' heels. O-No and Annie led the race. I prayed they wouldn't try to fight them for I was sure they would lose the battle.

The fat bodies of the creatures were to their disadvantage; they simply couldn't keep up and were soon left in a cloud of dust.

Not far away stood a tall hedge of cedars. We set our faces toward the cedars and urged our horses on. Taking great strides, their hooves barely touched the earth. I wondered if the others knew why they were caught up in the race, or what the fuss was about. We arrived near the hedgerow at the same time.

Numerous birds of different descriptions flew in all directions; bright blue birds, red birds, yellow birds, and green birds. They were singing and chattering like busy market vendors. Enthralling fragrances permeated the air. Lilies, roses, and hyssop left me breathless. I needed to talk with Phares—alone. I quickly dismounted and called her to join me.

"Phares," I whispered, leaning close, "I'm sure the Garden of Eden is behind the hedgerow. We'll have to tell the others if we wish to go farther, otherwise we must send them away. What should we do?"

"They are honorable people and have been helpful. We can ask them to take a vow of silence. Besides, Norah is part of our family. She's entitled to know. As far as I'm concerned, they may go with us."

"How do we know they'll keep their vow?"

"How do we know Tobias will keep his?"

"Very well, we shall tell them." I turned toward Japheth.

"Well, ladies, why the race? Something mysterious behind the cedars?" Japheth asked, grinning.

"Yes, I believe there is. It's the Garden of Eden," I answered.

"Verily, you're making fun!" Shem said wide-eyed.

"No, I'm not making fun. The Purple Mountain is on the map."

"What map?" Japheth asked, wrinkling his forehead.

"The map that has been in our family for generations. The map showing the way to Eden," Levi blurted.

"Japheth, remember when you asked what *almost there* and *even closer* meant? We were talking about Eden—almost there—even closer—to Eden."

Japheth, Shem and Norah looked astonished. "Here—the Garden of Eden?" they murmured.

"Yes!"

Norah clapped her hands. "Hurray! I get to see Eden!"

Japheth slapped his forehead. "Now I understand why you've traveled so far. Demons haven't possessed you after all."

My voice lowered. "All of you—Japheth, Shem, and Norah—must take a vow never to divulge what you see, or reveal this location. Do I have your word?"

"Yes, it will be our secret. May Yahweh strike us dead if we break our pledge," Japheth said.

"Look, there's a bit of a path over there." Phares pointed to a small grove of birches. "Let's follow it!"

O-No and Anni romped ahead, curious with newfound smells. Raven cawed, *"Watch! Watch!"*

It was a narrow path of bent emerald green grass, wild with a riot of weeds. A breeze scattered leaves over moss-covered stones. We stopped to let a flock of sheep cross in front of us. *They're no larger than cats!* I thought. A chorus of "Ah's" resounded as everyone stared in awe at the diminutive sheep.

I turned my head and saw a wall. "Look—a gate!"

Ivy and pink roses hung on a white gate in the middle of a sandstone wall. The gate swung shut, as though someone had just passed through. A faint song rang in the air, a sweet melody it was. I pushed against the gate.

"It won't open. Help me, Phares."

Phares and I pushed hard. The gate wouldn't budge. "It's locked! Maybe the key you found in the cave will unlock it. Give it a try, Hadia," Phares said.

"All right." I fumbled for the little bag. "I can't find it—it's not here! Now we shall never get inside. We've come all this way for nothing!"

"Get ahold of yourself, Hadia. What is written must come to pass. Hide not your faith. Let God show you where the bag is. He is all knowing," Japheth said sternly.

Why is my faith always being tested? I continued feeling my body for anything foreign. Then I grasped something caught in back of my sash—the bag! "Oh, here it is. I found it. I found it!"

Pulling the key from my bag, I slid it effortlessly into the keyhole and turned it. The gate gave way, creaking and rasping on ancient hinges. We quickened our pace, eager to see who was singing.

"Oh my! Who's that?" Phares asked.

A lovely lady sat on the grass under a weeping tree, dining on sweet peas and buttercups of dew. Her feet dangled in a laughing creek; drifts of flowers wound through a mass of long, golden hair. A wreath of tangled vines crowned her head. Her gown floated with delicate lacy white flowers making soft whispering sounds when she moved. A carved wooden staff lay at her feet.

Her air was noble, her beauty celestial. Sky blue were her eyes, exceedingly fair was her skin. Her countenance was sweet and goodness prevailed. She sang light and lyrical like a child: "Meet me there by the garden gate, meet me there and don't be late. Meet me there by the garden gate, bring the key and don't be late." Scratching the head of a small white goat wearing a blue collar, she smiled.

"Greetings! This is my goat, Dinah. We've been waiting for you. Won't you please join us?"

I was captivated. Who was this woman? Why was she expecting us?

CHAPTER THIRTY-FIVE

Isha

"This may be the last time mortals see it."

My name is Isha—I am Isha-woman," the lady said in a velvet voice.

"Greetings m'lady. Thank you for your invitation," Japheth said, bending low.

Everyone else gave little curtsies. I gazed in awe upon the fair lady and wondered what 'Isha woman' meant. *Why is she so far from civilization? She seems mystical. And her goat—what an odd companion.*

"Welcome to my garden outside the Garden." Isha nodded and waved her staff.

It was a lovely garden filled with an array of flowers and herbs. Roses and lilies scrambled among wild mint and hyssop. Grapes, blackberries, and flowering vines clamored up the sandstone wall.

"What do you mean *outside* the Garden?" I replied.

"My dear, The Garden of Eden, of course. It's on the other side of the cedar hedge. My garden is outside of Eden."

"Oh my!" I gasped. A noisy mirth of "oh's" and "ah's" arose.

Isha laughed. "Of course my garden is well away from the hedgerow. One can't get too close you know; you'll get singed."

Levi looked bewildered. "Singed? What do you mean?"

Isha stood, brushed leaves from her gown. "The flaming swords of the cherubim. They are Yahweh's angels armed with dreadful and irresistible powers to keep intruders out of Eden. They whirl swords of fire. It'll singe the hair right off your head if you get too close. Want to see?"

"Eee! I don't think so! We're probably too close as it is," Tobias retorted.

"I want to see!" Phares cried.

I jerked my head around. "I can't believe you said that, Phares. You're usually afraid of everything."

"I found courage when striking the Destroyer. I'm no longer bound by fear."

Isha walked toward the hedgerow. "Stand back!"

The world burst into light. Rumblings and peals of thunder clapped. Two cherubim sped back and forth at Eden's entrance like flashing coals of fire. They had the forms of men with four faces: one of a man, one of a tiger, one of a ram, and one of a hawk. Their feet were like those of a calf, gleaming like burnished bronze. Lightning flashed between them as they raised and lowered flaming swords, swirling and twirling, fanning scorching heat. When the creatures moved, I heard the sound of their wings, like the roar of rushing waters.

I trembled in awe, realizing that everything I had ever heard about Eden was true. We had found Paradise—we were standing on sacred ground! I removed my sandals and fell face down. Everyone fell face down.

The flames died as Isha walked back to us. "See, quite a warning, isn't it? You can get up now. You're safe."

Shaken, I stood and trembled like a dog shaking water from its back. It amazed me that Isha would tempt the creatures.

"My name is Hadia. This is my sister Phares and my brother Levi," I said. "We are of the Yousif clan of the Karka Tribe in Beth Nahar."

"My name is Japheth, and this is my brother Shem and sister Norah. We are of the Lamech Tribe from Naphtali."

"I'm Tobias," Tobias said proudly. "I'm of the Bebe Tribe in En Gedi."

"Guests, I'm thankful for your company. It's been over forty ages since I've seen a living soul. Let's see…it was…a man…yes, it was a man named Josef—Josef Yousif from Beth Nahar. Quite a nice gentleman."

"That was my grandfather's name! You saw my grandfather?" I asked, anxious to hear more.

"Yes. I believe he said he had a son named Zamir. Zamir was to visit me in his time. Why did he not come with you?"

"Father was murdered by Destroyers when we were coming home from market. That's why we're here. We're fulfilling his commission."

"I'm so sorry, my dears." A moment of silence passed. "I can see you are weary with travel. Come, let's make a fire and I shall serve you food. We can exchange stories and then you must take rest in my home." She pointed to a cave in the hillside.

"We are beholden. Thank you," I said.

The day's end was drawing near. I was all too willing to take rest and eat. My stomach had been rumbling for some time.

Flames glowed from the watch fire. Stars mounted up. The moon curved on a flawless sky. A night owl called its mate. *Hoot! Hoot! Hoot!*

"Eee! Owls. They bring—"

"What do they bring, Tobias?" Levi asked mockingly.

Tobias removed his head cloth and squirmed. He furrowed his brows and ran his fingers through his hair. "Nothing…nothing," he mumbled. He put his head cloth back in place.

"Levi, Tobias, come with me," Isha said. "I can use a little help with food preparation." Obeying, Levi and Tobias followed Isha and disappeared into the dark.

It didn't seem but a short time when they returned. Isha's arms were loaded with silver bowls of food. Levi and Tobias held eating vessels of silver and gold; they handed each of us a platter. Isha spread a linen cloth on the ground and set the food in the middle. A bowl of water sat to the side for hand washing.

"Let's give thanks to Yahweh. The meal can become holy when reverence is given," Isha said, lowering her head. We bowed our heads and invited God to bless the food.

We sat down on goat-hair mats around the linen circle. "Levi, pass the vetches. There are peas and beans, lettuce, radishes, and leeks. Save room for corn cakes and lentil soup."

Levi passed the food. The musky aroma of thick lentil soup tantalized my appetite. I tossed my peas, beans, lettuce, and radishes together and ate, leaving just enough room in my stomach for the corn cakes and lentil soup.

Steam rose from a blackened kettle over the fire pit. "Have some mint tea," Isha said cheerfully, handing me a steaming cup. "It's good for your body and refreshes your spirit."

I polished off my meal with a bright red pomegranate. Levi unabashedly asked for seconds. The others savored plump apples and figs for dessert. I felt I had feasted at a banquet for royalty. With the repast over, we were beginning to show signs of life.

"Your garden must be related to the Garden of Eden. The food was heavenly!" I said, wiping my mouth.

Isha's eyes twinkled. "Yes, you might say it is," she replied with a thin smile. "It's time to share our tales. Storytelling keeps our past alive. It helps preserve our history so we won't forget what we once knew." Everyone reclined on their elbows, ready for the stories to begin. "Who wants to go first?"

"I will." I raised my hand.

"Tell me about it, Hadia," Isha said softly.

"It's a dreadful story, one I shan't forget. Yesterday we were attacked by Destroyers deep in a cave. They were going to kill us. We managed to escape when they fell into a pit. It was ghastly!

"Today, we were attacked by a dragon. The Scarlet Beast drove Raz, our precious donkey, over the rim of a cliff. Dear Raz, we'll miss him always. Our supplies and new-found treasures were packed on him. They too are gone.

"If that wasn't enough, Raven brought a message from our friend Granna, telling us Grandfather died. Misfortune and grief follow all my days!"

Isha gave me a look of kindness. "Hmm…" she said when I had finished. "You have suffered a tragic loss. Yours is a sad story, my dear, and one you will want to pass on to your children. They will want to hear how you overcame your adversities."

I scowled and gave her a sullen answer. "I don't know if I can overcome these adversities. I'm not feeling very brave right now."

"No one escapes sorrow. Thorns find their way into many gloves. Do you wish to live life without trials?"

I paused. Isha stared intently at me. "Sometimes I do," I replied wearily.

"If you do my dear, then you wish to live a life half-full. You cannot guess your own strength without trials. They show us who we are, what we are made of. Your soul is downcast now, but He who made the soul is able to make it anew. You'll see."

I was vexed. *What does she know about sorrow?*

"Ah, that must have been the Edge-of-the-World Cliff. I had a harrowing encounter there once." Isha furrowed her brows. "I was walking along the edge when my apple fell out of my hand. I lost my footing trying to grab it. I almost went over the rim!"

"Oh dear!" Norah cried.

Isha drew close to Norah. "Did you see the ledges leading to the Endless River?"

"Ledges?" she answered, surprised. "We didn't look. We didn't wish to see poor Raz all in a heap."

"For all you know, poor Raz could be stranded on a ledge waiting to be rescued."

"Eee!" Tobias cried. He untied his sandals and kicked them in the air. "Is it possible he could be alive?"

Isha poured herself another cup of hot, steaming tea and reached for a lumpy, brown fig. She didn't seem in a hurry to answer. "It's possible," she finally said, popping the fig into her mouth.

Looking perplexed, we glanced at each other. "Oh, Hadia," Levi said, "we must rescue Raz if he's alive. We must."

My little brother looked so full of hope. Dare I disappoint him? "If Raz is alive, we'll rescue him—I promise."

Norah stroked Dinah's scruffy coat. "Isha, are there more scarlet beasts?"

"No, it was the last of its kind, unless of course, the beast is still alive—with Raz."

"Oh no! Could it be alive too?"

Isha drew the tea to her mouth and took a sip. Dinah bumped into her, causing her to choke. After she contained herself, she answered Norah. "If Raz is alive, why not the beast?"

We groaned. I wrinkled my brows. I hadn't expected the possibility of facing another living beast. It could complicate Raz's rescue. My thoughts turned to the reason for our mission. *Eden, I want to see Eden.* "Is it possible to see Eden before we leave? I do so want to see it."

"There's a lane that climbs high above my cave. We'll hike the lane to a magnificent lookout. From there, you can see Eden, Hadia." Isha threw her head back and laughed. "All of you shall see it!" Her voice lowered. "This may be the last time mortals see it."

What does she mean it may be the last time? I wondered.

"The night is late and the morrow's sun will rise soon enough. I bid you bedless no longer. Sleep in my home tonight. We'll arise before the sun comes up. Follow me."

Isha reached for her staff, stood, and waved us to follow. Like dutiful lambs, we followed the shepherdess. The little white goat ran ahead, bleating in harmony to the tinkling brass bell on her collar.

Isha had a goodly chamber. Camel-hair rugs covered the dirt floor. A low table and a few stools stood against the wall. Deep silver bowls and stacks of fine, white linen cloths sat on the table. A pile of cooking utensils lay in a heap near a small fire pit. Two tall lampstands stood at each end of the cavern. The cave smelled of smoke, dried herbs, and flowers. It was adequate. There would be room for all.

Japheth brought glowing coals from the fire outside and placed them in the cave's fire pit. He dropped a few tree branches over the embers and soon small puffs of smoke snaked upward. The fire was soon ablaze.

Isha waved her arm. "Levi, Tobias, help me bring in water. We'll need to wash before taking sleep." Levi, Tobias, and Isha each tucked a silver bowl under their arm, left the cave and soon returned with them full of water.

"Now, dear one," Isha said, setting a bowl of water before me, "you can wash the remainder of the day from your feet."

I washed my face and hands, and then washed the grime from my feet. With my stomach full and my feet clean I felt thoroughly refreshed.

Isha stared into the dancing fire flames. Her voice lowered. "Did you know that when you pray, your prayers become incense? The incense drifts up to heaven into golden bowls. All the golden bowls sit before Yahweh, fragrant prayers offered up to Him."

Silence hung in the air. We gazed into the flickering fire. I thought each was probably imagining his prayers rising in the smoke.

"Isha, have you ever seen a red camel?" I asked.

"You know about the Red Camel? Who told you?"

"A traveler told us about it, and then Jude, the man who guided us safely across the Valley of Tremble, spoke of it."

"Yes. I saw the Red Camel once, many ages ago. I know not where it is, or if it still exists." Isha sat mute a moment, staring into the fire. "It belongs to no one," she murmured. Her face brightened. "I suppose you want a Red Camel?"

I grinned. "Well, who wouldn't?"

"I have a riddle," Levi cut in. "What does everyone have in common?"

We all smiled at each other. I wondered who would outsmart my little brother. "We don't know, Levi," I said. "What do all of us have in common?"

"God! God made all of us. That's what we have in common."

"Oh, Levi, is that the best riddle you can come up with tonight?" Norah said, rolling her eyes.

"Isha, your staff looks interesting. May I see it?" I asked.

"This staff is from ancient days. I've had it so many ages I don't remember not having it." She handed it to me.

I grasped the slender staff and examined it. A Tree of Life, a man and woman, and a snake were carved at the top. The snake's tail coiled to the bottom. Curious, I asked, "Could it have belonged to Adam and Eve?"

"Who knows?" she answered dreamily, handing out woolen blankets. Dinah bleated and poked her nose into everyone's supplies. "Dinah, leave our guests alone!" She laughed. "She can be a bit of a nuisance, but even a goat will do when one has no other company."

Dinah skittered to the side of the cave, dragging one of our blankets. Tobias jumped up and yelled, "Hey, bring that back, you little thief!" Everyone broke into laughter.

Isha smoothed her mantle and paced back and forth. "I sense danger. You must cross the Bridge Beyond Time before the sun sets on the morrow," she said grimly.

"Why? What will happen if we don't?" I asked.

An uneasy look clouded her face. "I'm not sure." She paused, and her face tightened. "Ah…it's the bridge. The bridge won't be there after the sun sets."

I looked at Isha in dismay. "It won't be there? Where will it be?"

"I don't know. It will just disappear." She turned around, reached under a table, and pulled out a strange looking horn.

"Here, take this with you. You may need it."

"What is this?" I asked, bewildered.

"It's a horn of marvelous power, to be sounded only in life-threatening situations. Blow the wide end, and the sun will stand still for a hand's-breadth of time. Blow the narrow end and the moon will stand still for a hand's-breadth of time. Should you need to buy time—blow the horn."

I reached for it. "Do you think I'll need to use it?"

"That remains to be seen. The horn has never been blown that I know of. If you blow it, the course of time will be changed forever. Once it is blown, it must be destroyed. In the wrong hands, they could tilt the world up-side-down."

I took the horn carefully. A camel-haired rope was strung through the wide end. "I don't think I want the responsibility of this horn. I'll be carrying the weight of the whole world on my shoulders. No, I can't take it." I handed it back.

"Hadia, you are a woman of great courage. You must finish the commission Yahweh has entrusted to you. Lean not unto yourself. Let Him lead you."

"I'm not worthy of such responsibility."

"That's true—you're not worthy. None of us are. But some are chosen to complete tasks Yahweh wants fulfilled. You, my dear, are one of them." Isha smiled sweetly.

I stared at the smooth, white bone, pushing my hand through my hair and pondered what I heard.

"All right, Isha, I'll take it. I hope I don't have to use it. It's frightening to think I have the power to stop the sun or moon."

"You'll do just fine, my dear." With a pensive look on her face, she said, "The horn is from a horse of another time—a powerful white horse with a horn in the middle of its forehead."

"A horned horse?" *Like the horned horses on the walls of the cave.*

Isha leaned forward and fixed her eyes upon mine. "There's another matter I must warn you of." She paused and steepled her hands; her fingers were long and slender, graceful. Her eyes narrowed.

"It's an Evil Presence. It tries to attach itself to those seeking Eden. It will appear innocent, like a kind person or friendly animal. Be careful whom you befriend and don't pick up any stray animals."

An Evil Presence...like that cat.

The fire's flames drew down. Soft light shimmered, casting deep shadows on the walls. "Tonight, dear ones," Isha cooed, "trade your nettles and thorns for peace lilies. Lie down and sleep sound. The morrow brings new life."

I studied the mysterious woman. *She hadn't had visitors in over forty ages? How can it be? She doesn't look a day over forty ages herself! I wonder....*

At the forest edge is a path of stone with
Scattered leaves, and moss o'ergrown
Hidden away at the end of the path, a gate
Silently swings. The gardener of ancient
Times just passed near, listen to her sing.
Her hair drifts with lilacs, tangled vines crown
Her head. Her white lace gown floats, making
Soft whispering sounds. She glides across
Emerald green grass wild with a riot of weeds.
She dines on sweet peas, sips buttercups of
Dew and splashes her feet in a laughing creek.
She's come to tend her Paradise lost with bags
Of wildflower seed. Then sighing, she turns and
Bids farewell. She'll return again, haunting the
Garden she lost long ago because of the
thorns of sin.

Hadia

CHAPTER THIRTY-SIX

The Walk to Paradise Garden

"It was the land that existed between Creation and Disobedience."

O h, no!" I cried.

"What is it?" Phares asked.

"The garden gate key—I can't find the bag."

Phares wrinkled her nose and laughed. "You and that bag are having a hard time staying together, Hadia."

"Don't make mirth of me, Phares. The key means a lot to me."

"Why is the key so important? Isha said the bridge will disappear. There'll be no way to go back and unlock the gate."

"The key unlocks more than the gate. It unlocks—"

"Maybe it unlocks your heart."

Is my heart locked? "My heart isn't locked."

"Oh? Maybe not, but sometimes it's sure hard. Have you looked everywhere?"

"Yes, I've looked everywhere. Who knows where it can be?"

Phares' face brightened. "Hadia, ask God for the key. Maybe someday a miracle will happen. Maybe the key will find *you*!"

"Phares, keys don't just get up and walk."

"I know. That will be the miracle—how the key finds you."

The key will find me? I closed my eyes. *All right, God, I need a miracle. Please, let the key find me.*

Our walk to Paradise Garden had arrived. We trod the sacred lane in great strides, setting our faces toward the peak. Time was not to be measured this morning, but rather to flow with. It was still dark. Eden was to be viewed at the first ray of the rising sun. The woods reached up to blot out what was left of the morning stars. O-No and Anni raced ahead of everyone. Dinah followed, bleating noisily.

"We're almost there," Isha said.

"I think I have heard those words before," Japheth replied with a thin smile.

Isha pushed wispy strands of hair from her forehead and smiled. "Maybe, but not from me."

Like the pink glow of a wick set in a lantern at its lowest setting, light began to grow. Flower-perfumed air breathed fresh exuberance into my spirit. We had but a short distance to go before reaching the plateau.

O-No, Anni, and Dinah beat everyone to the summit. O-No dog-smiled and looked back as if to say, "What's taking you so long?" Anni looked like she was trying to dog-smile.

"Levi—Levi—wait for us," Isha called.

Levi trudged slowly up the lane. He did not pause. The set of his shoulders told us he was not in a happy mood. We caught up with him.

"Why are you downcast?" Isha asked.

Levi stopped and turned around. "I was thinking about Grandfather. Had I been there with him, he might not have died alone."

"Maybe. Maybe not. We know not the hour Yahweh chooses to take us to Him. You could have been in the village, or who-knows-where. It's not for us to know the mysteries of Yahweh."

"I was disobedient. I left without permission. God punishes those who are disobedient."

Isha's face clouded as though lost in a sad memory. "Yes, how well I know—"

"Maybe that's why my beloved Raz fell over the cliff; it's my punishment!"

Isha shook her head. "Yahweh isn't mean. He does, however, want us to see the errors of our ways. Hopefully, we learn from them. Don't be too hard on yourself. Let's spend the remainder of the day in gladness and happy memories." Grabbing Levi's hand, Isha laughed gaily. "Come, let's beat the others." They took off running and didn't stop until reaching the summit.

The sun rose above the peak of the lane. Slanting rays turned the land scarlet. An exaltation of larks scattered across the path, startling everyone. Squirrels scampered up trees as tidings of magpies scolded us.

"Well my dears, here we are; the Garden of Eden—the Land of In-Between."

"The Land of In-Between," I murmured. *"You will reunite on your journey to the Land of In-Between." Mother's promise! But how did she know?*

We crowded around Isha, sighing and gasping. Everyone removed their shoes. I had never seen anything so incredibly beautiful in my entire life. To describe the indescribable in words is useless. Words cannot interpret color. It was as though time moved in the past—it stood still. It was indeed Paradise found.

The Garden was furnished and adorned by nature. The sky was its roof and the earth its floor. Leaves, grasses, trees, and shrubs of every kind and shape were hundreds of shades of green. Flowers of every size and design flourished, all in bold colors, all intensely fragrant. The trees sang cradle songs: "Come, rest in my shadow." Crystal streams meandered through the land with so many animals and fowl they could not be numbered in a day. The animals held lively conversations.

Hundreds of birds sang; sweet, delicate notes poured from their tiny throats. Prides of lions lay with flocks of sheep; gaggles of geese pranced with bouquets of pheasants; herds of horses roamed with packs of wolves—all in harmony—all in order, peaceful and lovely.

No wonder Father wanted us to see Eden. To see it is to experience it. I was afraid to turn my face away for fear the scene would vanish, never to be seen again.

"Oh," I gasped. "Isha, look! The horned horses you spoke of. They're magnificent!" The large white horses grazed contentedly. Their long white, wavy tails hung to the ground, their white curly manes draped to their knees. Their horns shimmered like silver spears.

"Isha," I said, "why do we not see these lovely horses in our land today?"

"They are the noble horses of Paradise. They could not exist in a world full of sin; it would stain their purity. They are to remain in the Garden."

"Isha, why do you call Eden, the *Land of In-Between?*" Norah asked timidly.

"Well my dear, the Land of In-Between was the land that existed during the time between Creation and Disobedience. Yahweh placed the Tree of Life and the Tree of Knowledge of Good and Evil in the Garden. Adam and Eve were not to eat from the Tree of Knowledge, which would make them knowing of good and evil. But they disobeyed, thus becoming mortals. They lost their privilege to eat from the Tree of Life.

"Oh," Norah replied wistfully.

"You'll understand someday, my dear."

Eden, my real home. "Eve, Eve, why did you do it? Why did you trade Paradise for forbidden fruit? And Adam—why did you just stand there and let her do it? Why didn't you stop her?" I murmured.

"What did you say, Hadia?" Isha asked.

"I…uh…I was talking to myself, or I should say, to Adam and Eve. I don't know why they weren't satisfied with what they had. Paradise—it's perfect! Why did they disobey?"

"For the same reason *we* disobey. We don't believe we'll suffer the consequences of our disobedience. Are any of us ever satisfied?"

Hadia, why are you never satisfied?

Paradise left me spellbound. "It must be wonderful to be able to see Eden anytime you wish, Isha."

Isha's eyes held a far-away look. "Yes, but viewing it from the *inside* was nicer. Seeing it from the outside is not the same."

Viewing it from the inside?

Japheth reached out, took my hand and whispered, "You are as beautiful as the Garden."

My cheeks burned. My heart leaped. *Oh, Japheth, I do care for you. I hope you long to have me with you—forever.* I looked deep into his eyes and squeezed his hand. Sighing, I said, "Isha, we must take leave if we're to rescue Raz and cross the bridge before sundown."

"Yes, dear, but first you must take food. You need nourishment so you won't become faint on your journey. Come everyone, we shall go and eat."

I was glad to take food: soft bread, figs, goat cheese and grapes. The meal was finished off with creamy goat's milk, a refreshing reminder of what we'd missed for weeks. Dinah butted in, looking for a handout, and knocked over the milk.

"Dinah, you naughty girl. Leave," Isha scolded.

I stood and brushed crumbs from my mantle. "Isha, we can never thank you enough for your hospitality and for showing us the Garden of Eden. May God shower you with as many blessings as there are stars in the sky."

"You're welcome. It was my pleasure." Isha moved close and put her hand on my shoulder. "Hadia, your cause has given you a courageous heart; you overcame barriers, which will give you the ability to overcome others. Be not faint-hearted, always stay your course and doubt not yourself. You are made of sterner stuff than you think. May you return home safely, blessed with happy memories. We'll meet again one day—beyond Eden." She gave my shoulder a gentle pat.

I swallowed hard, brushed my eyes, and wished this moment could last forever. I had a strange feeling that Isha's prophecy about Eden never to be seen again by mortals, would come to pass, and that she would remain only a fragment of memory deep in the chambers of my mind. The future would have me wondering if the mystery woman ever existed at all. *"We'll meet again one day—beyond Eden."* *We will? Where?*

Isha turned to Norah. "Norah, you were not thrown away. Your mother treasured you. Yahweh told her you would, one day, be reunited with your brother and sisters. From this day forth, you are not to be sad or bitter about being separated at birth. Rejoice now that you have found your family."

My heart pounded. *How does she know?*

"Hadia, is that true? Did Mother tell you we would one day be reunited?"

"Yes, Norah, it's true. Mother promised we would meet again."

"Oh, Hadia," Norah said, reaching out to me, "I'm sorry I didn't believe you. I shall never again feel unwanted."

I cradled Norah in my arms. *My empty space was filling.*

"Levi," Isha said, "your sisters are your mother's gifts to you. She would not want you to be bitter toward anyone. Rejoice and be glad you're together."

Norah and Levi looked incredulously at each other. "How do you know about us? Who told you?" Levi asked, bewildered.

"It doesn't matter how I know. What matters now is what you're going to do now that I have told you."

Levi took my hand. "Sister, I didn't know you carried such a heavy secret. I'm sorry I got mad when you told us about being separated. I hope you won't be sad anymore. I love you."

"Oh, Levi, I love you too. I'm so happy we finally found Norah." *Thank you, God.*

Japheth cleared his throat and said, "Well, we best be leaving if we want to cross the bridge before sundown."

"Yes, you must take leave. I have prepared food and supplies for your journey." Isha pointed to a pile of bundles on the ground.

"Thank you, Isha. Thank you," we chorused.

The horses snorted and pranced as we readied them for the journey. O-No and Anni ran hither and thither, sniffing and barking. Raven cawed, *"Home! Home!"*

"Hadia, I have something for you," Isha said. She handed me a small wrapped parcel.

I reached for the package. "What is it?"

"You'll see, but wait until later to open it."

Why does she want me to wait? What could it be? I tucked the package under my sash and blew her a kiss. "Thank you, Isha."

I gave one last look at Isha's garden, the entrance to her home, her staff, and her goat.

I don't want to leave.

"This is not your earthly home. You must return to Beth Nahar," an unheard voice whispered.

"I know—I'll go home," I murmured. I reached out and broke some branches from The Weeping Tree.

"It's time to go home everyone—up we go!"

I searched for steeds of old, but for
Naught I looked. 'Tis a tale I suppose,
They never were. Then time stood still
As they appeared, prancing melodiously.
Trumpets neighed, phantoms played,
Hooves stomped, manes tossed high,
Shimmering horns pointing way.
With gathered muscles they leaped in
Air swallowing fields beneath. I ran to
Join them in their play, but 'twas not to be.
Like vapor dreams they vanished those
Fabled horses of old, leaving glitter dust at
My feet was all that I could see.

Hadia

CHAPTER THIRTY-SEVEN

Homeward Bound

"He stole the map? How could he commit such deceit?"

Gray light slowly unveiled the morning. The air was without movement and as fragrant as ambrosia breath. As the day wore on, the white sun cut through the air like a warm knife slicing through butter. We crossed hollows and crests. Birds of all sorts fluttered; songs tumbled from their throats. Tree frogs croaked from willow thickets. Quail called peevishly, trying to keep their brood together. The sun was high as we neared the Edge-of-the-World Cliff.

"Japheth, do you hear someone?" I asked. "Listen!"

Japheth pulled Bolly to a stop and listened. A faint cry for help moaned.

"Help! Help! Hadia, Phares, where are you?"

"It's Raz! It's Raz! I know it's him!" I cried sharply. "We must go to him!"

"Hadia, donkeys don't talk."

"I know, but that's Raz calling. I know it's him. Hurry!" I spurred Dawn into a fierce run and headed toward the rim of the cliff.

"Help! Help! Someone save me!" the voice cried miserably.

We jerked our horses to a halt and dismounted. Running to the edge, we cautiously peered over.

"Woe! Woe! Woe!" rolled a deep voice from the depth of the belly of the Scarlet Beast. It screamed, swinging its heads and whipping its tail of snakes furiously, trying to reach Raz. A fluorescent glow shone around the dragon. Dull, bluish slime spewed from his mouths. Raz's eyes bulged wide as he leaned into the sheer vibrating wall.

Jumbled rocks lay scattered about the ledges. Many more protruded from the wall. Barely visible, a thin, white ribbon of water churned at the bottom of the canyon; the Endless River.

Isha was right, I thought. *The Scarlet Beast is alive! If I hadn't been such a coward and looked to see what happened to poor Raz when he went over the cliff we could have rescued him. Now, he's scared out of his wits! How are we going to save him?* "Japheth, how will we get Raz out safely?"

"Everyone line up. Each of you put an arrow into one head of the beast left-to-right. Hadia and I will shoot at all of the heads!" Japheth answered.

"Eee! We're no match for this beast!" Tobias yelled.

"There's no time for fear. Concentrate on your skill to navigate your warfare. Every arrow will have to strike its target—not one can be wasted. Our supply is diminishing."

We stood rooted in place, bows bent waiting for Japheth's command.

"Ready! Send your arrows!" Japheth ordered.

The twang of the arrows sang in the air as they found their targets, burying deep into the beast's scaly heads. One-by-one, each head snapped back as it felt the sting of death.

"Woe! Woe! Woe!"

"Send more arrows!" Japheth called out.

Following his command, we continued sending arrows until the beast heads dropped forward, and it fell backward.

It crashed and bounced to the bottom of the canyon with the force of an earthquake taking ledges and boulders with it. Soon, only its tail of snakes was seen whipping in the air as it disappeared into the swirling water of the Endless River.

For a moment, we were stunned into silence. Then, we broke into jubilance, rioting into a chorus of cheers. "Yeh! Yeh!!"

"Raz! You're all right now. You're safe!" Tobias called.

"Raz, don't worry, we'll get you out," I promised.

"Shem, it looks like there's a path leading to the ledge. Let's follow it," Japheth said.

Japheth, Shem and Tobias crept along the narrow path, balancing precariously. Raz was a sad spectacle. He was as weak as the day he was born. Tobias assured the shaken little donkey of his safety.

"Raz, you'll be all right, old boy. We'll get you out. Looks like you lost your halter and pack. Treasure's gone too. Well, at least you didn't lose your life. Come, follow us. We won't let you fall." He tugged on Raz's neck, urging him to follow. Soon, they were on top of the plateau.

I threw my arms around Raz's fuzzy neck. "Raz," I frowned, "why didn't you just follow the path to the top? Well, thank heaven you're all right. We heard you calling. Speak to us now."

I thought Raz looked befuddled, as if to say, "Silly girl, donkeys don't talk—they bray."

"I know he called us. I heard him," I retorted.

Phares laughed and said, "We're sure you've been in the sun too long."

"I'm glad we have the sandal latches Trevez gave us. We'll make a headstall for Raz," Tobias said.

"Oh, the horn," I cried, feeling for the rope. "I must have left it in the cave. I have to return and get it."

"Hadia, you can't return. We have to cross the bridge before sundown," Japheth said sternly.

I mounted Dawn. "You go ahead. Dawn is swift. I'll catch up with you later."

"It isn't worth risking your life. Please don't go."

"Isha said we might need it. Besides, I'm responsible for its safekeeping. I'll be back in time to cross the bridge."

Tobias threw his head cloth to the ground. "Eee! You're as stubborn as Raz!"

"Hadia, please don't go," Phares pleaded. "We'll get along without it."

"No, I must go." I whirled Dawn around and dug my heels into her ribs, leaving the Troop in a cloud of dust.

"It's madness! You're not going by yourself. I'm going with you!" Japheth mounted Bolly and spurred him ahead.

"Well, I guess the rest of us best be for going. Some of us have to remain sane," Shem retorted.

Running Dawn so long was wearing on me. My sides ached; my face burned; my eyes watered. Dawn had heart, but her pace was slowing. She too was becoming weary.

"At last—the hedgerow," I muttered, urging Dawn forward. Soon, the garden path appeared. I quickly dismounted and ran down it. I slowed to a walk, and then stopped. My eyes caught sight of ivy and pink roses in disarray on the ground. I reached down, picked them up, and held them close to my bosom. My brows knit in bewilderment. *The flowers are here. Where's the wall? Where's the gate?*

"Japheth, the wall—the gate—they're not here. Where could they be?"

"I have no idea, but we can't stand here all day wondering. Hurry." He grabbed my hand, "We must go to the cave—now!"

We started running and reached the mouth of the cave in no time. Ducking low, we entered. I was astonished! The cave was empty!

"Japheth! Where's everything? Where's Isha?"

"It's a mystery to me."

I gazed around the cave and caught sight of Isha's staff leaning against the wall. I walked over and grasped it. "Isha, Isha." I slumped to the ground with a thud and let out a deep sigh. "Japheth, where is Isha? Why did she leave her staff?"

"I don't know where she is, or why she left her staff. I'll look for the horn." He glanced around. "Oh, there it is, and something else."

"What is it?"

"Dinah's collar."

"Dinah's collar? Why is it here?"

"Hadia, we'll probably never know what all this means. I do know, however, that we need to leave. We've only a short time to get to the bridge. Come on. Let's go!"

Japheth reached his hand down to pull me to my feet. I fell into his arms and cried. He held me close, stroking my hair. "You're just tired, Hadia. It won't be long; you'll be home soon."

Japheth hung the horn around my neck along with Dinah's collar. Shaking the little bell, he laughed. "Dinah would be pleased to see you wearing her collar."

I returned a pitiful laugh. He leaned down and brushed his lips across my cheek.

"Now stubborn lady, let's leave."

"Wait, I want to see Eden one more time."

"We don't have time!" Japheth looked up, threw his hands in the air, and shook his head in disbelief. "Now I know you *are* mad!"

I turned and ran to the side of the cave, but the lane was not to be found. I looked around. Bramble vines and wild blackberry bushes grew where the lane once was. "Oh—it's gone!"

"This may be the last time mortals see it."

Japheth drew in a deep breath. "You need not see Eden again. Your memory will bring it to mind anytime you wish to see it."

I sighed deeply. "Yes, I suppose you're right. Seeing Eden once is enough. Well, what are you standing around for? I'll race you to the horses!" I keenly felt the wolf of urgency stalking, urgency to hasten to the Bridge Beyond Time.

The band of women creatures sprang out from a hedge of thorn bushes. They rushed to the heels of the horses, snapping, tearing their flesh. They chanted: "You're still here! You're still here! Leave! Leave!" Their voices pierced our brains.

"We're leaving! We're leaving!" I screamed. Leaning forward, urging Dawn on, I felt the horn's rope break loose from around my neck. "No!"

Japheth turned to see me grab The Horn as it slid downward. I struggled to stay upright. "God, help me!" I felt invisible arms lift me to the center of balance on Dawn.

We ran the horses a good distance, and then seeing no sign of the woman creatures, we brought them to a halt for a short rest.

"Japheth, I don't think my heart can stand anymore near-death experiences. It almost stopped when I nearly dropped the horn and struggled to stay on Dawn!"

"Hadia, your heart is stronger than you think. It won't stop before Yahweh is ready to promote you to heaven."

"Japheth, I think it was an angel that kept me from falling off Dawn."

Japheth rubbed his chin. "Perhaps it was an angel—perhaps."
Now, do you trust Me?
"Is that you, God?" I murmured.

The descending sun glared, hampering our vision. The wilderness sang a song of silence, a song only heard with one's entire being. One had to free the mind of the day's clutter. Then and only then, could we hear the song and feel the breeze whispering in our ears, view flirting wildflowers and soaring eagles. My spirits lifted to a new high as we flew across the land.

Soon, I saw the Troop moving a short distance ahead. "Japheth, there they are!" I waved the horn high above my head; the Troop returned a wave. Soon, we reunited.

We took time to apply fig mashes to the wounds on the horses' legs. Tobias removed his head cloth and ran his fingers through his hair. "Hadia, I need to speak with you—alone."

I sensed a note of concern in Tobias' voice. "Of course, Tobias. Is anything wrong?"

"Well, not exactly. I just need to talk with you a moment." He dismounted and motioned me to follow him into the thicket.

"All right, what is it?"

"Hadia, a rising tide of regret has come over me. My great sin is too heavy to carry. I can't carry it any longer. I lied to you. I told you I didn't find the map, but I found it and kept it for myself. Greed overtook my soul. An evil spirit blew cold across my heart, begging me to steal it. Now I fear someone else might steal it. It could fall into hands worse than mine. I feel awful! I can't live with myself for what I've done. I'm in deep distress."

Tobias fell prostrate before me. "May you not hold me guilty forever. My sin is great. I beg your forgiveness."

Did I hear him right? I thought. *He stole the map? How could he commit such deceit after all we have been through? Oh, Tobias, why? Why?* "Tobias, stand up. Do not bow before me. Only God is worthy of that."

Tobias slowly stood and hung his head.

"Tobias, how could you steal from us? You're a traitor and a deceiver."

"I'm sorry, Hadia. I did a very foolish thing. I'm sorry. I won't ever do anything like that again. I promise."

"Undoubtedly you considered your villainy beforehand. How can I believe you? How do I know you won't break this promise? Promises are easy to make, but hard to keep. Apparently, you haven't learned how to keep yours. The women at the bathhouse were right. You still scheme. You haven't changed one bit. I don't know, Tobias. I'm not sure I can forgive you. You've disgraced yourself—and us."

"Hadia, I'll prove you can trust me again. You'll see."

"What were you going to do if we didn't find Eden? Just let us wander around forever like lost sheep?"

"Well...uh...I—"

"Never mind, nothing you say now will be believable. Say no more." I glared at him. "I'm not sure you'll ever see your mother's ring again, either."

Tobias hung his head. "Hadia, turn around so I can remove the body scroll and give it to you."

I turned around with heavy shoulders. I closed my eyes and shook my head. *I was so sure I could trust him. His deceit is more than I can handle right now. I won't tell Phares just yet. Well, at least I have the body scroll back—that's comforting.*

"All right, here it is," Tobias said. He handed the body scroll to me. "I don't want my great sin on me anymore, and I don't want God striking me dead. I was sure when Raz went over the cliff I was being punished for stealing the map."

I shook my head and smiled wanly. "Don't take credit for that. I'm sure Raz didn't go over the cliff because of your disobedience. I'm glad you felt guilty enough to confess your Great Sin. Maybe in time I can forgive you. I'm not going to mention this to the Troop just now. I don't want to see their disappointment." We returned to the others.

"What was that all about?" Japheth asked, raising his brows.

"Oh, just a much needed talk. The day is fleeing and so should we. Up we go!"

CHAPTER THIRTY-EIGHT

Ambush!

"All witches know about caves of the dead. Would you like an omen?"

I don't know if I should tell Phares about Tobias' deception, I thought. What good would it do? If I tell her, she might lose heart—just as I have. He already broke one promise. How can I expect him to keep others? If I share his confession, it would weaken my burden. I hate carrying secrets. It wears on the soul. Maybe I should wait and see what he does to make restitution.

A great length of time passed, leaving Eden far behind. The winged creatures of crimson and gold appeared from out of nowhere. They glided above, winking their red eyes. *I guess they like our company.*

Golden haze veiled the thin line of the Falcon Hills in the far distance. Clouds gathered on the horizon, shadowing bits and pieces of the valley. A brisk breeze rose up to meet us. We rode in wordless silence along a ragged hillside. Occasional snorts from the horses were heard. We passed through glens and meadows, and crossed gentle creeks. Soon, we were at the tomb. It stood stately as ever.

"Let's look inside the cave. Maybe Leuce forgot 'bout us and brought more jewels," Tobias said.

"Wishful thinking, Tobias. Leuce is a lot smarter than you," Levi replied.

"What's that supposed to mean?"

Levi shook his head. "It means she knew we would return. She isn't dumb enough to hide her jewels here anymore."

"Well, maybe it was wishful thinking. Doesn't hurt, does it?"

"Ha! Only if your head is cracked."

We filed into the cave. It was strangely quiet. A thin stream of sunlight shone through the ceiling hole, spotlighting floating dust. Leuce's nest was as empty as the cave. The fire pit held coals—warm coals!

"Uh-oh. Trouble," Japheth whispered, looking over his shoulders.

"What is it?" I asked.

"Someone has been here. The coals in the fire pit are warm."

I shuddered. "Smells like moldy blankets—Destroyers!"

"But I thought there were only two following us!" Phares cried.

"There probably *were* only two until they came up missing from their tribe. Their clan could be looking for them—and us. It's almost sundown. We must make haste and cross the bridge," Japheth said.

A limping footfall sounded nearby.

A witch came forth with blazing red eyes. Her dark visage was ominous and foreboding. She cast her eyes upon us like a falcon stalking prey. Long black hair cascaded down her back. Her tunic was white, her mantle crimson. Odd gold trinkets dangled from copper chains that hung around her neck. Her hand clasped a wand of human bone.

"What's this? Birds in my net, and I didn't even have to set a snare?" The witch cackled gleefully, waving her wand.

"Witch Rasha!" Tobias said coldly.

"Blessed be, Tobias. So nice to see you again."

"Eh! I'm not glad to see *you*! What are you doing here, anyway?"

Rasha shrilled, "Why, I'm here for the same reason you're here—to speak to the dead." She fingered the trinkets on her necklace.

"We're not here to speak to the dead. We're here to—"

"To what, Tobias?"

Tobias ran his fingers through his hair and said coldy, "It's not for you to know."

"Is that a nice way to talk to an old friend?" she asked with an air of an offended goddess.

"You're not an old friend. How did you know about this cave?"

"All witches know about caves of the dead. Would you like to speak with one of your ancestors? I can bring up their spirits." Cold laughter echoed in the cave.

"Tobias, stop this nonsensical talk. We're losing precious time. We must get across the bridge," I said sternly.

Rasha shrieked. "The bridge! Why hurry to the bridge? Is it going to disappear?" She laughed with evil glee.

I stared a moment at Rasha, and then said, "Let's go, Troop."

"Just a minute, my precious. You leave not before giving me one of your lovely rings. Of course I don't expect it for nothing. I will stir up a magic brew or omen for you in exchange." Rasha tucked her wand under her arm. A thin smile curled her purple lips.

"Yes, that would be fair." She stepped forward, rubbing her hands together.

"We are not giving you one thing, and we certainly don't need your magic brew or omen. Now, move aside," I demanded. "We're leaving!"

Rasha stood firm and raised her wand. Her eyes narrowed and her lips pursed into a tight line. "Give me a ring now or I'll see that you never cross the bridge."

"Japheth, Shem, we must stop her!" I cried. "Time is fleeting!"

A sinister look cloaked Rasha's face. "Now men," she crooned, "don't come any closer. I have the power to freeze you in your steps. You will die in this cave. Give me a ring now, and you may leave—alive."

"We'll be giving you something, but it won't be rings!" Japheth yelled.

Japheth, Shem, Tobias, and Levi lunged at the witch, knocking the wand out of her hand. There was a great scuffle. Rasha screamed as the men twisted her arms behind her back. They pushed her into a narrow dark passageway and started piling rocks in the opening.

"Everyone help. Bring more rocks," Japheth ordered. After what seemed forever, there were finally enough rocks to keep her inside, at least long enough to escape.

"Hurry, Troop," I yelled. We ran out of the cave as fast as we could. I saw the day ready to change places with the night.

"Our speed will be fierce. The dogs are still weak from their battles. They won't be able to keep up. We'll have to carry them part of the way," I said.

"Shem, you carry O-No; Japheth, you carry Anni."

We mounted our steeds and stormed away down the long westward slope of the land, into the setting sun. Wind and pounding horse hooves resounded in my ears as the land seemed to stretch endlessly. A change in the weather was coming. Innocent clouds seen earlier in the day now loomed above us, blotting out the remaining sun. The troubled sky thundered. Lightening streaked across the land.

Dark shadows crept down the Falcon Hills. Sundown was dangerously near.

Hello, who's that? "Japheth, I see a horse and rider. Who can it be?" I asked.

Japheth saw the stranger, and drew rein. "Stop, Troop, someone comes yonder. Be careful. Remember Isha's warning."

The stranger dismounted and faced us. It looked like a woman. Drawing close, I stared at her. *Why is she out in the middle of nowhere by herself?*

The woman bowed. "Hail—blessed be. My name is Natas. Where be you bound?"

I gazed upon the woman with suspicion. She looked familiar. Long dark hair cascaded to her delicate shoulders. Pale milky eyes matched her smooth, creamy skin. Her voice was delightful. She wore a purple tunic and scarlet cape with gold embroidery. A thin gold rope held back her hair. A faint odor permeated the air—a familiar odor.

Half smiling and half frowning, Levi called out, "We're on our way to the Bridge Beyond Time." Covering his mouth, he muttered, "Uh-oh."

I glared at Levi and gave him a 'don't-say-anymore' look.

Natas smiled. "I'm going there too. Perhaps you would like to follow me. I know a short cut."

"Short cut! We could use a short cut. Time's running out," Tobias said, turning to me.

I scowled and shook my head. *Foolish lad, doesn't he know when to keep silent?*

"What do you say?" Natas said, waving her arm. Her eyes changed color—pale blue.

"Follow me and you'll make it in time."

Make it in time? What did she mean by that? I wondered. *What does she know about our time? Maybe she doesn't know anything. But if she's telling the truth, we could use the short cut. She looks innocent.* "I'm Hadia. We would be glad to follow you, but we must hurry."

Phares drew close and whispered, "Hadia, her words are gracious, but they're filled with ill will. Remember Isha's warning. That woman could be an Evil Presence."

"Yes, she could be, but she looks harmless. Besides, she's only a woman. How dangerous can a woman be? The sun is almost down. We'll go with her." I turned to Natas. "Let's go!"

Tobias and Shem shook their heads. Japheth leaned over his horse and reached for my arm. "Hadia, I believe you're making a mistake. She's full of empty promises."

"Japheth, I'm in command here. I'll take that chance. There seems to be no other way if we're to cross the bridge before sundown. We're going."

"It isn't just *you* taking a chance. All of us will be a part of your decision and your demise...."

Natas continued to smile as she mounted her horse. "Come, follow me. We'll be across the bridge before the sun sets."

I felt strangely drawn by an invisible force, pulling me toward her. She waved at me again. "Come on! Come on!"

I hesitated. *"You may be smart, but you're not always wise!"*

Maybe she is an Evil Presence. Maybe I'm leading the Troop to their demise. What if Phares and Japheth are right and I'm wrong? The stakes are high, but God is on our side. How can we lose? Besides, I know what I'm doing.

"All right, Troop, let's go!" I called.

Natas turned her horse toward a flat meadow and spurred it away from whence we came. Her scarlet mantle billowed wildly. Her hair flew like a flag. We followed, urging our mounts to reach their fastest speed. She guided us across a gentle creek cradling careless boulders. The craggy black hills soared against a melon skyline. Only a hint of sun remained.

"Look! The Elephant Boulders!" I cried, "Make haste!"

Dim ghosts of elephant-looking boulders stood sentinel, straddling the bridge silhouetted against the disappearing skyline. I dug my heels into Dawn, kicking without pity. We sped across the grassland, past hills and creeks. Without warning, a small band of Destroyers charged from behind the shoulder of a hill in the middle distance. They waved daggers and battle-axes, yelling war cries.

"No!" The chill of mortal terror filled my soul.

"The bridge. Cross the bridge!" Japheth yelled. "Cross the bridge!"

"Run, Dawn! Run!" I screamed, kicking her ribs violently.

With a final burst of speed, Dawn sprinted forward. The race was long and hard. I was afraid Dawn would crash before we reached our destination, but her heart was bigger than I thought. She picked up even more speed as we drew near the bridge. It rattled and swayed as we thundered across. The sound of hooves against wood clattered as Raz, Norah, Levi and Natas followed.

Japheth, Shem, and Tobias were close behind when they stopped and faced the enemy. The infidels ran full speed toward them, determined to perish the men.

"Your bodies will soon be the prey of wolves and falcons," one Destroyer yelled.

Japheth swung his sword at the lower hind leg of one Destroyer's camel—hamstringing him. The camel crumpled to the ground, landing on top of its rider. The rider lay prostrate with broken head and limbs. Shem and Tobias, riding double, swung swords and daggers, fending off the remaining band. Unable to avoid colliding with the enemies' camels, they slammed hard into them, throwing Shem and Tobias to the ground. Japheth raced his horse to aid in their rescue.

"Aaarrgh! Yaaww!" bellowed a Destroyer, spurring his camel toward Shem. "Meet your Maker!" He advanced to attack like a tiger against a dog.

Shem dashed to the side, slashing the hind leg of another Destroyer's camel. The camel fell, tossing the Destroyer into the air. He then stretched lifeless onto the ground.

Japheth, Shem, and Tobias turned their attention to the two remaining Destroyers who had leaped from their camels, rushing to attack them. With vigorous blows, the men left deadly wounds on the Destroyers.

O-No and Anni charged and clamped their jaws onto the enemies' legs. With the Destroyers' attention diverted to the dogs, Japheth, Shem and Tobias mounted their horses, whirled them around, and raced across the bridge.

I looked back beyond the bridge. "O-No, Anni, come! Come now! Japheth, they won't come. They'll be killed!"

Tobias leaped off Yolly and ran back across the bridge. "O-No, Anni, come! Come now!"

The dogs released their enemies and sprinted across the bridge. Tobias didn't follow the dogs. Instead, he faced the Destroyers, taunting them.

"Why don't you try to catch me, cowards!"

"Tobias, no. Don't be foolish. Hurry. The sun is almost gone. Come back while you can!" I yelled.

"Hadia, Tobias is not going to make it across the bridge before the sun sets," Phares cried. "Quick—blow the horn!"

I raised the wide end of the horn to my mouth and blew. The sound was low and long. It echoed mournfully across the land. The earth lurched. Time stood still.

Tobias continued to antagonize the Destroyers as they ran to seize him.

"Tobias, run—run! Please! I forgive you. I forgive you!"

The Destroyers were almost upon Tobias when he turned, ran across the bridge, and then stopped at the entrance. Holding onto the bridge railing with his left hand, he slashed the rope railings on the right side. The bridge dangled and swayed violently, throwing the Destroyers into the abyss.

Tobias hung on precariously by a thread.

"Japheth, Shem, Levi, grab him!" I cried.

"Tobias, take my hand!" Japheth said.

Tobias' right hand clasped onto Japheth's hand.

"Let go of the railing. Take my other hand."

Tobias looked down into the abyss. His eyes rolled back, his head bobbed.

"Tobias, don't look down. Let go. Take my hand."

Tobias opened his eyes wide and reached for Japheth's hand.

"Pull me, pull me!" Japheth shouted to Shem and Levi.

Pulling with all their strength, the men dragged Japheth and Tobias to safety.

Exhausted with fatigue and terror, they lay on the ground, catching their breath. The remains of the bridge evaporated as the sun vanished beneath the world. A thick and heavy darkness fell upon us. We huddled together, at a loss for words. I wondered if the dreadful eve held more terror.

"We shall go no farther. We'll set camp here tonight," I said.

Moonlight burst forth, aiding our bedtime preparation. We unpacked the animals. Japheth, Shem and Tobias prepared a watch fire and then we spread our bedding around it. Water was retrieved from a nearby stream. We set out food and settled in, ready for a well-deserved rest. Our talk turned to the events of the day.

Tobias was willing to give his life for us, I thought. "Tobias, that was a foolish thing you did—endangering your life for ours. You were very brave. We are beholden. Thank you."

"I wasn't trying to be foolish," Tobias said, running his fingers through his hair; he had long ago lost his head cloth. "I just love all of you and didn't want anyone to die."

"We love you too, Tobias," I replied.

Everyone patted Tobias on the back, each assuring allegiance to him. The dogs whimpered, cutting our conversation short. "What is it, dear ones?" I asked. O-No and Anni crawled close to me. Phares and I ran our hands over their bodies. Wet, sticky goo clung to our hands—blood.

"They've been injured," I said. "Phares, help me mix a fig mash for their wounds."

We bound up the dogs' wounds, exercising as much tenderness as possible.

"Now, you should feel better," I whispered, giving each dog a hug. "Sleep safe and sound, my little ones, morn will sweetly come." *Please God, heal them.* I turned my attention to Natas. "Natas, where do you abide?"

"You might say I live everywhere. I have no home to call my own. I wander from town to town, village to village, and comb the mountains and plains."

I studied her. *Without a home, one is always suspect. I have never met a wandering woman. What kind of a woman would want to wander?*

CHAPTER THIRTY-NINE

An Evil Presence

"Blessed be, ignorant one. I wouldn't drop it if I were you."

Hadia, what did you mean when you told Tobias you forgave him?" Phares asked.

"What are you talking about?" *I can't tell her about his great sin just yet.*

"I heard you tell Tobias you forgave him. What did he do that needed forgiving?"

"Why, I do declare, Phares, I believe this journey has muddled your head."

"Not so. I heard you speak those very words."

"Like I heard Raz speak?" I replied grinning. "Maybe you've had too much sun too."

Twisting her hair, she looked quizzically at me. "I heard you say those words. If you don't wish to explain them, then I won't concern myself anymore."

I breathed a sigh of relief. I wasn't going to tell about Tobias' great sin, not now. He was probably grateful he didn't have to confess. He had already made his atonement. I turned back to Natas.

"Natas, don't you find it difficult and dangerous roaming the country, being a woman?"

"Perhaps, but I'm not afraid. I can take care of myself. Say, it's too bad your donkey had such a dreadful fright with the Scarlet Beast. I hope he won't suffer any ill effects from it."

How does she know about the beast? My stomach started to feel queasy.

"Yes, it was a terrible thing—" *What's that at her feet?* "Watch out! There's a snake!"

"Get back everyone! I'll kill it," Japheth ordered, reaching for his sword.

Everyone moved except Natas. She looked vexed. "It's just a snake, a harmless snake."

"Only a *dead* snake is a harmless snake. Move away, Natas. I'm going to kill it," Japheth said with a set jaw.

Natas' eyes turned cold. She glared at Japheth. "So be it." Her voice was hard. She scooted herself back just as Japheth swung his sword and decapitated the snake.

"Ugh! Get it out of here," Phares said, jumping backward.

Japheth kicked the head and sent it flying. The body jerked and wiggled as he lifted it with a stick and carried it away.

Levi laughed. "Snakes don't scare me; I don't know why they scare you, Phares."

"Look, Levi, common sense is what I have. Fear can be a good thing when it comes to safety. You could use a little of both," Phares answered.

"All right, Troop, we've had enough excitement for the night. The morrow will come soon enough. Let sleep come and dream with pleasure," I said.

Glad at the fall of the empty daylight, I crawled under the covers in my boundless bed chamber and gazed at the heavens above. A great object with a luminous tail and broad blue gleam streaked across the sky. Sleep didn't soon come. My mind raced with jumbled thoughts.

Do I need to keep the map? Levi has seen Eden. The Bridge Beyond Time is gone. Isha said, "This may be the last time mortals see it." Japheth said, "You need not see Eden again. Your memory will bring it to mind anytime you wish to see it." I see no reason to keep the map. I shall destroy it.

I reached under my mantle, untied the body scroll and removed it. I rolled it up tightly and wrapped my blanket around my shoulders. Grabbing my dagger, I slipped silently into the dark.

Jackals howled in the distance. Tree frogs croaked and a lone owl swiveled its head toward me, scolding me with a *hoot hoo hoo hoot.* Approaching the abyss, the boulders loomed like elephants ready to charge. I held the body scroll tightly in my fist, and then let it unroll. It snapped and dangled. I grabbed the dangling end and stretched the map out with both hands. It no longer held a spell over me.

"Blessed be, ignorant one. I wouldn't drop it if I were you," Natas said in a chilling voice. She stepped forward.

I jerked around and clutched the map to my bosom. "Natas! Why would you say such a thing? What do you know of the map?"

Natas' eyes narrowed. She raised high a rod of glowing red coals. "I know the map leads to Eden," she hissed. "I'll take it now!" A putrid order permeated the air.

"It was *you* following us! I know what you are. You're the Evil Presence, the Devil in a woman's body."

A sinister smile drew across Natas' face. "Yes, but you won't be around to tell anyone."

I felt captive. I hoped that by asking questions, I could stall my appointment with death long enough for someone to hear us. "Why do you wish to go to Eden?"

"Eden was *my* first home, too. It was created for meeeee! I long for it!" A vain look traced her face. Her lips tightened. Her eyes grew wide and black, piercing my brain with such intensity I thought it would explode.

"It was created for you until you wanted to be God. If you followed us, why do you need the map?" I said as loudly as I could.

"I never reached Eden. When you attacked me in the passageway, you severely injured me. I couldn't continue, so I decided to wait for your return."

"What do you mean we attacked you? You weren't—"

Kitty! "The cat. You were the cat. And the pig, the lizard, and the vulture."

Moving closer, Natas raised her rod. Her eyes turned white. "Yeeessssss! Now give me the map, or I'll blow your precious horn!" She spat out each word as she raised the horn high above her head.

"No! Give it back! The horn must never be blown again. The world could turn upside down."

"What do I care? I'm immortal."

"Yes, but you'll spend eternity in Hell."

"Give me the map now or I'll blow the horn." Her voice was chilling.

God, help me. I can't let her have the map or keep the horn. Help me—Help me.

"God, help me!"

Natas lunged, swinging the glowing red rod. I ducked. She swung again, grazing my shoulder. The heat seared my flesh. She continued wielding the rod, forcing me to the very edge of the abyss.

"Hand me the map, or you, your family and friends won't live to see another sunrise."

"Japheth! Help me! Help me!" I raised my dagger and rushed to my enemy.

"Oww!" Natas shrieked.

O-No and Annie's jaws clamped deep onto Natas' legs, tearing skin and cracking bones. She tripped and fell, releasing the horn. I grabbed it and jumped to the side. Natas pushed herself up. The dogs continued to attack. She stumbled again and fell forward, slipping slowly into the abyss. She clung to the edge screaming, "Help me! Don't let me fall!"

"Why are you afraid? You said you were immortal." I turned my head and covered my ears. When I looked back, she was gone. I crumpled to the ground, shaking.

Japheth rushed to my side. "Hadia, are you all right?"

"Oh, Japheth, what a fool I was. Why didn't I listen to you? You were right. Natas was the Evil Presence. My stubbornness could have cost the lives of everyone." Trembling, I buried my head into Japheth's chest and sobbed. He put his arms around me.

"Hadia, we all do things we regret. Don't hold this against yourself. Everything's all right now. Let's thank Yahweh that no harm came to any of us."

"What happened?" Phares ran up, with the Troop close behind.

"Natas...she was the Evil Presence. She stole the horn and tried to take the map from me. She was going to kill me! O-No and Annie attacked her and she fell into the abyss. Oh, Phares, she was terrifying!"

Phares drew her arms around me. "I'm so sorry. Thank heaven you're safe." She let go of me and frowned. "The map? You have the map? I thought it was lost."

"Tobias...Tobias found the map when he returned to the silver stream. He said an evil spirit blew across his heart and begged him to steal it. He was going to sell it for a tidy sum."

Phares turned and glared at Tobias. "Is this true?"

Tobias hung his head. "Yes, it's true. I'm sorry. Will you ever forgive me? I told Hadia I would never do anything like that again."

"Hadia, why didn't you tell me about his confession?"

"I...I...I didn't want you to lose faith in him. I was going to wait until I saw something that told me he was truly repentant. Now I've seen it. He saved all of us from the Destroyers. He was willing to die for us. I have forgiven him and I hope you will too. I trust him."

Taking a deep breath, Phares' face softened. "That was a terrible thing you did—stealing the map—but I'm glad you came to your senses. Yes, Tobias, I forgive you. Now, we can enjoy the remainder of our journey in gladness."

"Thank you, Phares. Thank you, everyone."

"Hadia, what's this?" Phares said. "Your shoulder! You've been hurt."

"I know, but I'll be all right."

"You best come back to the camp and let me tend your wound," Japheth said firmly.

"I will, but I need some time by myself. I won't be long. Please, leave me alone for a while."

Japheth stared at me with a puzzled look on his face. "All right, we'll leave, but don't be long." He leaned over and kissed my forehead. "Be quick!"

The others returned to camp, leaving me alone in the dark. I bowed my head and gave thanks to God for protecting me and the Troop. I held out the body scroll and stared at it. I then took my dagger, slashed it into shreds, and threw the pieces into the abyss. They floated silently out of sight. *I forgive you Tobias. I forgive everyone.*

I returned to camp. Phares anointed my wounds with fig mash. Exhausted, I crawled into bed and pulled the blanket to my shoulders. The moon and a few twinkling stars floated through scattered clouds, casting feeble light on the land. O-No and Anni curled under the blankets with Norah and Levi.

"Under starry skies my sheep bed down; I whisper words of love. Sleep safe and sound my little ones; morn will sweetly come," I whispered.

All was calm. All was all right.

CHAPTER FORTY

Exodus

"There's more to the journey than the destination."

The stars grew pale and the shades of night disappeared as the clear dawn awakened us. Yesterday's clouds had drifted away. I lifted my covers and peeked out. I saw Raven staring at Horus. He probably wondered why the dumb bird never had anything to say. O-No and Anni were up, limping stiffly, and looking for something to eat.

Unaccustomed to wearing a ring, my finger had swelled during the night, leaving it numb. I twisted the ring around and around to ease the swelling. The large, deep yellow jewel was intoxicating. The blue jewels were brilliant. *I wouldn't trade this for a herd of camels...well, maybe for the Red Camel.*

The others stirred. Japheth and Tobias prepared the morning meal. Shem tethered Raz and the horses in lush grazing grass, while Levi and Norah refilled the water skins. I performed a refreshing chore—I watched.

"Breakfast is ready!" Japheth shouted, banging a pan.

We scrambled around the watch fire, eager to eat. Wheat cakes with honey, nuts, cheese, dates, and hot mandu were passed around. Isha had provided generously.

I noticed Shem looking at Phares. I wondered if he was trying to figure out if she was betrothed to a man back home. Phares caught his glance and blushed.

I pushed my empty plate aside. "We need to talk about returning home," I said. "We'll need to part ways soon."

"Hadia, follow us home to Naphtali. Our parents will welcome you. Besides, I'm sure they would like to meet Norah's family. What do you say?" Japheth asked.

"I don't know. What do you think, Phares?"

"I suppose it would be all right. There's still time to get home before lambing. A good rest would be nice. I'm sure the animals would like it too."

"Hmm...all right, Japheth, we'll go with you. Your offer is most generous."

Levi slapped his knee. "By my father's beard! Norah and I will get to tell more riddles!"

Tobias jumped up to fetch a handful of nuts and stumbled over Levi. "Tobias, will you ever quit wrestling with your feet?" Levi scolded.

"Tobias, you're clumsy, but loveable. I have something I think you would like to have," I said, slipping a gold ring off my finger; "your mother's ring."

"Eee! I didn't expect to see the ring again after what I did."

"Yes, I didn't think you would have it back either. I'm glad we were both wrong."

"Thank you, Hadia. Do you still want to leave Beth Nahar?" Tobias asked.

"Well, I did. But for now I'm content to stay."

Tobias laughed. "By founds, I'm glad to see you've come to your senses and will stay at the place of your nativity."

I smiled, grateful he cared. He ran his fingers through his hair. "Hadia, may I have a word with you—alone?"

Oh, now what's he going to confess? Not another great sin, I hope. We walked away from the others. "Well, what is it?"

"Uh...I wondered...uh...I wondered if I could tell Phenias Frairhair, the storyteller in Beth Nahar, 'bout our journey. People would pay plenty to hear the story of our quest. I'm going to ask him if I can be his heir to pass on his stories. What do you say?"

I paused a moment to consider his request. "Yes, our journey would make a lovely fable." I smiled and wanted to tousle his hair as I do Levi's. "I suppose it would be safe to tell. Who would believe such a story anyway?"

"Does that mean I can tell him?"

"Yes, you can tell him. Besides, the body scroll is gone. I shredded it to pieces and threw them into the abyss. No one will ever have the map again."

"You threw it away? Why?"

"There's no need to return to Eden. There is a time for every purpose on earth. The map was to be used for this time, and now it has passed. The Bridge Beyond Time is gone. There's no other way to cross the abyss."

"How will future generations remember Eden if they don't go back?"

"Tobias, we don't need to see it to remember. We just need to pass the story on to our children. Remember what Isha said? 'Storytelling keeps our past alive; it helps preserve our history so we won't forget what we once knew.' Maybe someday, someone will write the story in a book, along with the Books of Wars, Prayers, Commandments, Wisdom and all the other important books of God—one great book."

"Eee! That would be a grand book!" We were silent a moment. "Thank you for trusting me again," Tobias said warmly.

I flashed him a smile and returned to the Troop. "It's time to pray." We bowed our heads. "Heavenly Father, hear our prayer. Incline Your ear to our praise. Thank You for leading us to Eden and saving Raz. Thank You for protecting us. See us home safely. So let it be."

We cleaned up the camp and readied the animals. "Well, Troop," I said, "there's one more item to take care of—we must destroy the horn. Help me gather some large stones so we can grind it to pieces."

We pounded the horn with the heavy stones. It was hard work and it took a long time before it resulted in a mountain of powder. "At last, it's done," I said.

We gathered at the edge of the abyss and threw the powder into the air. It swirled and twirled, drifting like fine sand. For one brief moment, I thought I felt the earth jerk.

"All right, Troop," I said, "let's go home!"

The horses danced and pranced, snorted, and swished their tails. We turned west.

Tobias kicked Raz's ribs. "Come on Raz, old boy, let's go." Raz didn't budge. He turned his head back toward Tobias. "All right, all right, you win. You're not old and you're not a boy—you're a donkey!" He laughed.

Raz spread his lips, revealing slimy, yellow teeth. Tobias chuckled. "Is that supposed to be a donkey-smile?"

I giggled. "He does look like he's donkey-smiling."

Raven cawed, *"My name is Raven. Fly with me up high. There's joy in the sky. Home, home."*

O-No and Anni lagged behind, walking stiff from their battles. O-No gave Anni a dog-smile. To my surprise, Anni dog-smiled back!

I caught sight of Levi handing his sword to Norah. *Why in the world is he giving her his sword?* Then I remembered his vow: *"The day I give my sword away will be the day I forgive the Destroyers."*

Norah hung the sword on her back. Tobias pulled out his whistle stick and began to play the "Forest Trail Song." I heard Levi say to Norah, "Here are the words: 'I strode the Forest Trail on a bright and sunny day. I laughed and played and sang and danced…Hey, hey, hey.'" And so they sang, "Hey, hey, hey…."

I thought about the men who journeyed with us. *Bidinko sacrificed his life for us. Shem, Japheth, and Jude were so helpful. And, Tobias—dear Tobias; he was willing to die for us. Phares was right. Not all men are unkind or evil.*

"Hadia," Japheth interrupted, "may I call on you after you return home?"

I pushed back my hair and smiled. "Why yes, it would please me to see you again. Bring Norah too. She must see her birthplace."

"Of course."

"Japheth, I'll be forever grateful to you and Shem for journeying with us. I don't believe we would have completed our mission had it not been for you two."

"You find little favor in your accomplishments," Japheth replied. "Congratulate yourself for keeping your vow, which was, I remind you, 'no one or nothing would stop me.' " He reached out his hand to mine, leaned over, and brushed his lips across mine. "I hope you'll find favor with my mother and father."

"I hope so too," I whispered. At that moment the wonder of the journey crystallized—forward faith had triumphed. The empty space in my heart filled to overflowing.

At noon, we took pause to rest. I dismounted and found a shady place to sit by myself. I wanted to open my package from Isha, alone. The solitude was perfect. I felt a magical stillness in the air. I looked around and listened. A sparrow twittered in a nest in a nearby tree. My eye caught something in the far distance. I squinted hard, trying to discern the moving form. *A camel—it's a camel—a red camel!* The Red Camel stopped and turned toward me. It gave a playful toss of its head as if to say, "Catch me if you can." I laughed. *You can tempt me all you want, silly beast. You know I can't catch you.*

The Red Camel turned around and bucking like a horse, it sprinted away.

The time to bid the land farewell had arrived. I promised to remember it in the ages to come; the golden desert, the nodding palms, the solemn hills, the gigantic mountains, and the deep quiet spaces of the forest. *I shall behold Eden and the land I traveled no more. I pray in the days to come when I close my eyes, they will appear before me once again. I can never forget you, Eden. I will never forget you.*

I caressed Isha's staff. I had given Bidinko's walking stick to Levi. Reaching under my mantle, I retrieved the parcel Isha gave me and opened it. A soft gray dove flew out, startling me. I looked up and watched the gentle dove glide gracefully to the ground. It cooed tenderly, and then took flight. I turned my eyes back to the package and beheld a folded piece of papyrus paper, a large pink pearl strung on a gold silk cord, and a dusty, time-worn book with gilded edges. The lustrous pink pearl was smooth in my hand, glowing like a lovely sunset.

I unfolded the stiff paper. It read: You are a pearl beyond price and forgive her.

"Forgive her? Who is 'her'?" I whispered. I needn't have asked the question. I knew who 'her' was. I buried my face in my hands and released the tears that had choked me for so long—Mother!

I finally admitted what I had always denied—I was angry with my mother. I was angry because she died when I was just a child; angry because she made me leave Norah at the wayside; angry because she made me keep it a secret; angry because I had to take her place in the household; angry because she ended my childhood—

"*What about God?*" a voice asked.

"God? I'm angry with God?" I murmured.

"*Oh, yes. You've pushed your anger down deep, telling yourself you would never blame God for your misfortunes, but you have.*"

Tears streamed from my eyes. I began to realize the sadness I had felt throughout my life was not due to my series of unfortunate events, but due to my self-pity and hardened heart.

"*You will not change until you surrender.*"

I raised my hands to the sky. "God, incline Your ear to my plea. I surrender. Forgive me for my anger toward You and Mother. Forgive me for my anger toward those who sinned against my family. Unlock my heart of stone and carve away all that is not pure. Make it a heart of flesh. So let it be."

I heard sweet laughter. "Ara-Belle, is that you? Where are you?" The laughter continued like that of a small child playing hide-and-seek. I joined in. Laughter burst forth from the depth of my lungs. *Hearts mend softly.*

Soon, the land became quiet. "Ara-Belle! Ara...Belle! Ara-Belle?"

Silence.

Flapping wings startled me as a white raven settled upon my shoulder.

"Leuce! What are you doing here?" The garden gate key dangled from her mouth.

"The key—you found it!" I cupped my hand as she dropped it.

Leuce tilted her head and stared at me a moment, and then took flight toward the Purple Mountain. I watched her fly away until I could see her no more.

Maybe someday a miracle will happen. Maybe the key will find you.

I held the little key high above my head. "Yes, God, I have made You too small in my eyes. Forgive me. Thank you for unlocking my heart. Thank You for Your miracles."

I strung the little gate key on the gold cord with the pink pearl and tied it around my neck.

I looked at the tattered book in my lap. I could tell it had been opened many times. The inscribed words on the mellow sepia cover captured my imagination. Barely legible, it read: 𝕮𝖍𝖊 𝕭𝖔𝖔𝖐 𝖔𝖋 𝕾𝖊𝖈𝖗𝖊𝖙𝖘.

The Book of Secrets? Now, I'll find out what secrets the book holds! Carefully, I opened the cover. I saw no writing. I turned a few pages, but I found no words. *Where is the writing?* I turned the book over; nothing was on the back. I looked around, expecting someone to arrive with an answer to the mystery. Quickly, I turned page after page. They were white, blank pages—empty of words. *This is the Book of Secrets? This is the book everyone hopes to find? What kind of mirth is this?* "God, what does the Book of Secrets mean?"

"Open the book again," a voice whispered.

I fingered through the book and stopped on the last page. Finally—words. They read: 𝕮𝖍𝖊 𝕰𝖓𝖉.

"The end? How can it be the end? There's not even a beginning!"

Cradling the book, I studied it. I stared so hard, I fell into a trance. My mind raced. Thoughts jumbled and tumbled in my head.

"Yours is a sad story, my dear, one you will want to pass on to your children...They will want to know how you overcame your adversities...This may be the last time mortals see it...We'll reunite again, someday...You are a pearl beyond price...You'll come home a different person...There's more to the journey than the destination."

"Hadia? Hadia, did you hear me?" Japheth asked, tapping my shoulder.

"I...guess...I didn't hear you. What did you say?" I shook my head to make sure I wasn't dreaming.

"I was thinking your journey has the makings of a lovely story. I think you should write about it."

"Oh, Japheth, don't be silly. Who would want to hear about my journey? Besides, Tobias wants to tell the storyteller, Phenias Frairhair, about it."

"It's not Tobias' story. It's yours. No, if it's told at all, *you* should tell it."

"That's kind of you, Japheth, but I...I don't know."

Japheth's voice lowered. "Maybe Eden won't always be here. A great flood of water might come and wash it away. Hadia, you must tell your story so we won't forget what we once knew."

I stood, dropping the Book of Secrets to the ground. I stared at the empty white open pages. A little smile tugged at my mouth. "Well, maybe someday I'll write about it."

Japheth slapped his leg and nodded. "Good! Now that that's settled, we can be on our way. My father is probably wondering what has happened to me."

"Yes, you have been gone a bit longer than you anticipated. By the by, you never told me your father's name. What is it?"

"Oh, it's Noah."

"Seek, and when you find, you will be astonished!"
—The Book of Thomas

Contact the Author

Email:
leilarae@verizon.net

Web site:
www.leilaraesommerfeld.com

ART:
Front cover by Michael Chesnakov
Back cover and horse drawing of Israfel by Leila Rae Sommerfeld

Another book by Leila Rae Sommerfeld:
Beyond Our Control - Rape

Pleasant Word

To order additional copies of this title call:
1-877-421-READ (7323)
or please visit our Web site at
www.pleasantwordbooks.com

If you enjoyed this quality custom-published book,
drop by our Web site for more books and information.

www.winepressgroup.com
"Your partner in custom publishing."

Printed in the United States
92320LV00008B/175-189/A